LOCKE AND KEY

Cristin Harber

LOCKE AND KEY

This is a work of fiction. All of the characters, organizations, and events portrayed in this novel are either the products of the author's imagination or are used fictionally.

ISBN-10: 1942236778
ISBN-13: 978-1942236771

www.cristinharber.com

PROLOGUE

Suburbs of Baltimore, Maryland

ALEXANDER GAEV HATED when classes ended each day almost as much as he hated the weekend. It wasn't that any subject piqued his interest or anyone in his eighth-grade class liked him, but at least at school he had the comforts of heat and lunch. With the voices of classmates at his back, he headed to the comfort of the loud shopping mall to take in all its distractions.

The place was a money-spending monstrosity—he should have hated it for torturing him with things he couldn't have, couldn't want. Clothes that fit and were new. Food that was hot and homemade. His mother only cooked *kvass* and *pelmeni* when Dad had men from the neighborhood come over. They called themselves the Bratva, and more and more, the Bratva would drink and smoke the night away at their home as they made their plans to carry out orders from the Mikhailov bosses.

Those Russian bosses scared Alexander, and maybe all the Bratva men also, which would explain why they stole cars and stripped them, and then farmed out the pickpocketing and shoplifting to neighborhood women and teenagers. Some of the kids on the corner said the Mikhailov bosses did bad things to those who didn't listen. Alexander didn't know what those bad things were, but he knew his parents believed in the power and loyalty of the Bratva. They probably loved those guys more than him and his sister, Tanya.

He pushed through the heavy glass doors into the mall, into his sanctuary, where he could live as an American and pretend the throwaways of the Soviets, living like their neighborhood was Little Russia, didn't dictate his life.

But they did. The Bratva would party at his little, rundown house until the vodka bottles ran dry. Then the men would pass out with the cigarette smoke so thick that it still hung in the air when Alexander's alarm went off. Tanya would cluck about the passed-out bodies they'd have to step over as they left for the school bus each morning.

He wandered along the crowded mall walkways then checked his watch. One hour until the time he promised his father he'd help work on a car, stripping it for parts. He never asked where the cars came from and didn't want to know. That way, he could pretend they weren't stolen.

Alexander ducked into Sherman's. Expensive trinkets sparkled as far as the eye could see. He liked to brush his hands over the clothes, touch the leather, and inhale the colognes. The extravagance was very American—*he* was an American, but he didn't feel like one. Not as a first-generation American with Russian as his native tongue and accented English. Then there was his haircut that never seemed to look right, his clothes that never seemed to fit right.

"Sir, can I help you?"

The voice made him jump. Alexander ran his hand along a glass case. "No."

"If you need anything…" She eyed his too-short pants and worn jacket.

But Alexander moved around the corner and headed to another rack before he'd let her questioning look humiliate him.

A prick of awareness caught his attention, and his eyes tracked to the side. What was his mother doing here?

Alexander ducked behind a jewelry stand and studied her. Mama had wrinkles that had arrived too early, courtesy of cigarettes, alcohol, and Dad. She wore her best slacks in an attempt to fit in at Sherman's, but it was her long coat with the oversized pockets that Alexander focused on.

He'd never seen her shoplift, but there was no other reason she wore that coat. He moved to stay out of Mama's line of sight. She inspected a row of necklaces—the long kind that dangled—occasionally holding them to her neck.

Now earrings, too. Mama pulled her hair back, tilting her head to the side. She looked up at the light and then around, moving to another mirror. Same modeling moves, switching the handful of earrings and necklaces.

"Sir, can I help you?"

He jumped back as the Sherman's clerk did a harsh up-and-down inspection of his ill-fitting clothes. It was a miracle she didn't ask if he were homeless. "No, I'm fine."

"Are you interested in a scarf—"

"*No.*" Had she seen what he was watching? He'd be in trouble if he brought attention to his mom. His stomach turned. The clerk's eyes narrowed, but she wandered away with a promise to check back.

Paranoia crept up his spine as he sensed that the clerk had followed him. He moved around, eyeing his mom as he did. Her methodical ways intrigued him.

"Son." The store clerk tapped his shoulder. "We have a no-loitering policy. Do you need anything?"

"I'm not loitering. I'm *thinking*." Again, he walked away from her, wishing he could watch his mother work. How funny was it that the clerk questioned him about loitering when his mom was nearby shoplifting, all so they could have more alcohol and cigarettes.

He rolled his eyes. Why couldn't he have parents who paid more attention to him than they did to the Mikhailovs—a mom and dad who asked how school was, not whether Alexander or Tanya could help with Bratva business? As if it were ever a question. It was more like an expectation. But he wanted his dad's attention, and during Bratva business was the only time the man talked to him.

"If what you're thinking"—the clerk trailed him—"isn't about a scarf, I'm going to have to ask you to leave."

Alexander rolled his eyes. "I'm trying to imagine my sister in one of these. Okay? She deserves it."

Pity flashed in the clerk's eyes. Alexander didn't know how to handle the combination of familial loyalty and disgust.

"All right, then," she cooed and gave him a sympathetic shrug. "I'm sure she would look lovely in any of these."

"Mm-hmm." His gaze shifted to his mom, surprised that she was still in Sherman's. "She would."

"Are you okay?" the clerk asked.

"Fine. *Dah.* Yes." He focused quickly on the woman in front of him. Damn, he didn't like speaking to others, particularly in Russian. Maybe Mom shoplifting made him nervous. Alexander stepped away and stumbled back into the pathway of people. They blocked the view of his mom. Or maybe she was finally gone. She'd been in the store for a while. He checked his watch—oh, he needed to leave soon too. If he didn't help tear that car apart, Dad would be pissed.

Wait, there was his mom. She was still there? Two store clerks hovered next to her, haphazardly checking tags. Were they on to her?

Alexander's stomach dropped. If Mom had clerks tailing her, she needed to leave. Now.

The two clerks came closer, triangulating. There was no doubt. She'd been made. And then there was a security guard, hanging back and ready to assist. *Damn it.*

His mind rushed. What was he supposed to do? Maybe help. If she were caught, Dad would be a nightmare, but that wasn't his concern. The Mikhailov bosses were dangerous.

Adrenaline fueled his anxious thoughts, and Alexander rushed ahead. Almost without a plan, he grabbed anything he could. Racks of purses caught in his arms. They toppled and crashed. He punched a tower of boxes. Rings scattered, and the river of people shouted and skidded.

"What are you doing? Stop!" The sales clerk who had pitied him chased the expensive boxes.

Alexander bolted away, having no idea what to do but lead the Sherman's security away from his mother. He was part of the Gaev family team. Wasn't the point of the Bratva that they protected their own? The Mikhailovs might even hear about how brave he was!

His arm was yanked behind him, and he swung around to face a security guard.

"Son, you need to stop," the security ordered. "Do *not* resist."

He pulled back, gritting his teeth, and suddenly, his mother was next to the security guard. "What are you doing?"

What was *he* doing? What was *she* doing! She was supposed to go! He created a diversion for her to escape.

"Ma'am," a clerk said behind them, placing a hand on her shoulder. "Can you come with us?"

Rage exploded deep within Alexander. "Do not touch her!"

The man tugged his mom back as the security guard urged him away.

Mom kept her eyes on him. All he could see were her hazel eyes. Her experience. Her calm. Whatever came next would be okay.

"It will be okay," she whispered like a lullaby.

He realized he was pulling on the guard's arm. "Why are you still here?"

"*Khoroshiy mal'chik,*" she said with a maternal voice he'd never heard before.

Good boy? That didn't make sense. Unless… He squinted. "Are you proud of me?"

"Your father will be too," she promised.

He'd made them proud. Had that ever happened before? But everything had gone so wrong. He could imagine the fighting that would happen when Dad found out she didn't complete her job, and if it were up to the Mikhailovs, she could be in danger. They'd owe money or worse, though he didn't know what that meant.

A crowd of store employees and shoppers gathered around. Hot embarrassment burned in his cheeks and set his ears on fire—but his dad would be proud. Never once in his twelve years—not for football or wrestling, not for good grades or report cards—had they been proud of him.

Alexander's chest expanded. He felt taller than before—broader, stronger, smarter than he'd ever been. "*Ya tebya yublyu, Mama.*"

"I love you too." She beamed as the creases around her eyes deepened.

Now he understood what made a man: family and loyalty.

CHAPTER ONE

Twenty Years Later

THIS HELICOPTER'S UPWARD maneuver to a rescue mission was goddamn hell—if hell was a frozen Russian tundra during a snowstorm. Locke Oliver dug his thumbs behind the dark straps that belted him into his seat. The five-point harness stood out like a tic-tac-toe board across his arctic camo. He leaned into his headset, ready to razz his team leader, Rocco. "I thought someone said we were headed to a resort."

The center of gravity tipped, and the helicopter pitched back and forth, stabilizing.

"I did," Parker said in their earpieces from the safe confines of Titan Group's war room. "Sochi is an hour away."

"This is a frozen hurricane," Locke grumbled.

"He speaks." Jax laughed. "Our boy Locke must be mega-worried."

Bishop muttered in their earpieces, echoing Locke's thoughts about Jax's need to be the team's constant dickhead.

"Quit your bitching," Brock mumbled as he piloted the helicopter. "If Rapunzel doesn't like the snow, he doesn't like the snow. Who the hell likes ice pellets the size of bullets?"

"If it's not buzzed, it's long?" Locke grumbled again. Brock's humor was one thing. Easygoing. Jax… was Jax. A prick.

"You could use a haircut," Rocco said, looking unfazed by the goddamn blizzard they were flying into for an extraction mission. "And maybe listen better in the briefing. A frozen hurricane might've been mentioned."

"It was not," Parker interjected from Titan's warm, dry war room. "Don't sully my reporting with your BS."

"Jax and Locke were hoping for downtime by the pool." Cash leaned back from his position next to Brock at the control panel.

"Looking for ladies," Roman added. It seemed like he wanted to be on this helo as much as Locke did.

"Easy, baby," Brock crooned as they lurched.

The wind howled against the belly of the helicopter as they gained altitude in the Krasnaya Polyana Mountains. Locke ground his molars. He didn't doubt Brock, but conditions changed fast. He'd call this damn near a whiteout, and this bird was moving back and forth like popcorn on a windy day.

Brock's voice crackled with interference in the headsets. "ETA, two minutes."

"Simple job." Rocco readied them up for the subfreezing op. "We have one task: to find this dude and haul his ass home."

The team responded with ooh-rahs and hoorahs. Locke grunted too, closing his eyes and focusing on what they knew. A DC-based teacher with an elite exchange program had found himself the target of the FSB. Russian Intelligence was no joke, and if they wanted him dead… The guy was lucky he'd found a safe place to hide at the ski resort.

The request for extraction had come in under duress, and when Titan received the information from St. Andrew's High School that the FSB was hunting one of their own, Locke had written the guy off. They had little information. Something about disrespecting *the Mikhailov family.*

Disrespecting the Mikhailov family? No telling what that meant. The Mikhailovs ruled the Russian government and ran organized crime. An American could play cards wrong and insult a generation of Mikhailovs. Either way, that corrupt and powerful family wanted a piece of his American ass, and it didn't bode well for the teacher surviving before Titan arrived.

Locke listened to the *ping-ping-ping* of the sleet against the metal. This wouldn't be a silent in-and-out job. That was the only way to do it—get in and get the fuck out—and they were choppering in because the roads were closed. Even the ski resort had shut down. Due. To. Snow. *In Russia.*

The helo lurched, and Brock cursed a storm in his headset. "Thirty seconds." They spun sideways. "Or less. Goddamn. Getting this bird down."

Locke's ears popped, and the air was thin. They swayed hard side to side. *Mother Nature needs to chill the fuck out.* Roman's ironclad face again matched what Locke was thinking.

"Piece of cake." Jax kicked back, and Locke half wanted to punch him.

"Someone shut him up," Brock growled.

Conditions weren't as predicted—they were so much worse. They would never have gone up in this crazy weather.

"Ten seconds." The toll of piloting this shitstorm covered Brock's words. "Five. Fuck it. Out. Out. Let's get that hatch open and punch out!"

The helicopter jarred to a hovering standstill. Locke slammed his teeth together.

"Smooth as silk," Rocco muttered, yanking off his headset and grabbing his facemask and pulling it down.

"Stay safe," Parker said. He even sounded warm all the way from HQ in the States.

Locke pulled his headset off and donned the facemask and comm piece. The hatch opened, and hell howled with its white wind.

"We're a go," their team leader said.

The frozen mountains mocked them. The howling wind blew cold and cruel, and Locke's toes curled. It would be a miracle if the teacher weren't a solid piece of icy human meat. Even if the civilian were sheltered in a ski-patrol shack, Locke didn't see how survival was possible in this icebox.

Locke jumped into the whirlwind and sank into the fresh snow. "Whoa, baby!"

With a snarl, he unsheathed the shovel and dug his pathway forward as the *tink-tink-tink* of icy snow hit his goggles. Crunch, cut, crunch, cut. He dug and moved, sweat and heat building under his thermal layers, until the Titan team hit the trees.

"Eyes up," Rocco ordered. "Get down. Keep your head on the swivel."

The wind howled as he dropped, and damn, the snow made every move a thousand times harder.

"What are you seeing?" Parker asked from the other side of the globe.

"Sideways snow," Locke reported. "White as far as the eye can see."

Others echoed the same.

"Pulling out," Brock's voice crackled from the helicopter. "Be back when you radio." The helicopter lifted away and dropped into the snowy valley.

"Titan Two, keep moving," Rocco ordered.

Locke, Jax, and Bishop—dubbed Titan Two for this job—pushed up but stayed at surface level.

"Eyes and ears," Rocco said, referring to his sniper and spotter, Cash and Roman. "Head out. Keep us clean and clear in case those FSB fucks are hanging close."

Cash and Roman melted into the white abyss.

Titan Two moved boots too. Every step took the strength of ten. Thin air and snow-weighted steps depleted oxygen from their bodies. What condition would the teacher be in?

"There we go." Jax signaled their rendezvous location. "Twenty yards ahead."

"Good eyes," Rocco said.

Locke caught sight of the ski-patrol shack. *Shack* was a questionable term. If it had electricity, that would be a miracle. The thing had been made for the ski-resort conditions but maybe not for long-term housing. The SOS cell phone call had been placed to the US almost thirty hours earlier, and even that call, their intelligence report said, was broken and marred by interference then cut short. There wasn't a follow-up phone call, and all return calls and attempts to find the signal had failed.

Titan Two closed in on the drift-covered shack. The snow had all but blocked one side. Too much longer, and it would be buried in totality with no new air supply. Locke glanced at the white, pillowed snow. Hell, if the building was covered, forget ever finding it. Even though Parker had triangulated where the call had come from, it almost looked like a snowdrift. Too much longer, and they wouldn't be able to help.

"No known targets," Roman announced.

"Stay on guard." Rocco signaled for them to move.

Warily, they stepped from the tree line into the open snow and moved to the front of the ski-patrol shack and dug to make an entrance. A minute later, the door was visible.

"Knock, knock," Jax joked, and Rocco pushed him aside.

Shovels sheathed, they grabbed their weapons, ready to breach the door and enter. Hopefully, the civilian would be alive. No one wanted a dead teacher. Rocco pushed the door in and cracked the light. They filed in, taking positions, and Locke saw a hump under a layer of blankets. Nothing moved.

Damn it... dead teacher.

They stood at the ready, waiting. Bishop and Rocco were on either side of Locke.

Jax stomped a boot. "Wake up."

The blanket moved. A small twinge of relief surged in Locke's blood—wait. The blanket moved *twice*. Locke's finger caressed the trigger for whoever else might unexpectedly join them.

"We have *two* people here," Rocco reported to HQ as they all lifted their weapons, targeting the moving lumps under the blankets. "Parker, you read me?"

Unexpected situations didn't fly well in Parker Black's war room. Maybe the teacher's disrespect of a Russian family had nothing to do with a simple card game but rather with a person—a much bigger problem for Titan and the extraction.

A couple slowly sat up. They could have been cold or sick. Who knew? But they were alive. That was what mattered—assuming they were friendly—and they huddled under blankets and coats. Locke didn't see a risk or weapons pointed their way.

Rocco gave the stand-down-and-help gesture, and Titan moved into action. Jax helped them onto their feet, gave the couple instant heat packs, and quickly changed out their layers for thermo-care resuscitation blankets. Locke readied for hunger and hydration, and waited for first aid requests.

"Ma'am." Bishop moved to the teacher's companion, assessing. "How are you?"

Locke stepped in to follow up on the teacher, but the flash of the unknown person—a woman, *a redhead*—caught his eye. A cold shiver of recognition tugged at his subconscious. He couldn't shake the eerie feeling, but he needed to focus. The sense of déjà vu tickled his spine, and he rolled his shoulders, handing the teacher an energy bar. "Thirsty?"

"Yes." The teacher—Alex Gaev—nodded.

Bishop had separated the couple. Locke tried to look out the corner of his eye, but the mask blocked his view.

"Thanks." Alex guzzled the liquid in the bottle and glanced at the woman.

"Your girlfriend?" Locke questioned.

"No, someone the school sent." His teeth chattered as he pulled the parka's hood farther over his head.

"We didn't know there were two of you." He took the guy's trash, shoving it into a zippered compartment.

"Phone died."

Locke nodded and pulled off his facemask completely, needing a better glance at the redhead. Bishop stepped out of Locke's line of sight, and he met the gaze of the woman's blue-green eyes. He couldn't see the few freckles he already knew she had, just like he couldn't ignore how deeply her presence cut him, like a knife into his soul. All the memories came rushing back as the only woman he hated stared back at him.

Mere feet separated them, and Locke stumbled back. God, his chest compressed like an avalanche slide had buried him alive. "*No.*"

Cassidy Noble was a living memory of loss. Of memories and heartache. Of death and destruction. She reminded him of explosions and the worst that war had to offer.

Cassidy's blue-tinged lips fell open. "Locke?"

The room came to a standstill.

"You again?" Locke's fists bunched in his gloves—until the wind howled, and he swore he could hear bombs exploding in Iraq when the black sky glowed as bright as day. Those detonations had ruined his life. Ruined so many lives. Except he blinked back to the Krasnaya Polyana reality and stared at the woman who held all the blame caused by her flagrant—

Jax grasped his bicep. "You good, man?"

In no way was Locke good. He recoiled, his ice-cold blood matching the temperature outside. Had they risked their lives for her? No way. He shook his head. No way could the universe screw him like this.

"What's going on?" Bishop approached him cautiously, as if Locke were a rabid animal, and Rocco moved closer to Cassidy.

Locke never misspoke. He never took a misstep. He sure as hell wouldn't spit venom at civilians they were there to rescue. But the words that fought to roll off his tongue at that moment were inhumane. His forehead pinched. His neck felt tight. He couldn't breathe—

"Locke." Cassidy stretched her arm out.

"Don't you dare," he snapped.

Whiplash and shock hit Titan at once. The wind died to a whisper. Even Mother Nature wanted to hear what was happening.

Underneath the layers of Polartec and winter camo, his chest punched to escape the snow-soaked suit. "Of all the people and places, in a situation that could kill *another team*..." He raged, unable to look at his enemy. His shaky breath sputtered. "You're here?"

Her bluish lips trembled. "I—"

"Stand down, Locke." Rocco stepped in front of her, a gloved hand extended like a gate that Locke should not pass. "No more."

That woman was everything that was wrong with his world and with how the military operated. Case in point: Rocco was protecting her!

Her eyelashes fluttered. "If I could explain—"

"*No.*" Again, Locke's hands bunched into fists.

"Stand down," Rocco ordered. "Get your ass back."

Back? He'd moved? Locke blinked. *Fuck.* He had. "I'm having a conversation."

Jax and Bishop flanked him, eyeing one another like they readied for a takedown.

"An aggressive one," Rocco said, stepping closer to him in the already small shack. "With one of our extraction targets."

Rocco, Bishop, and Jax had boxed him in. Alex Gaev stood in the background, and fucking Cassidy Noble was to the side. Some days, the paycheck was harder to earn than others.

"Take a breather," Rocco said, an edge of *no bullshit* lining his words.

"I'm good." Locke lifted a shoulder burdened by years of things he should have said and couldn't say now.

"We'll finish up," Bishop quietly said.

What the hell? He was done with their patronizing bullshit. "I said I'm good."

Locke brushed by Rocco—whose fist came slamming down as a barrier.

"Do. Not. Move. *Comprende?*"

Did he comprehend? Stress pulsed in his forehead, above the bridge of his nose. No. At the moment, Locke couldn't comprehend shit, which was why he needed to work. He was so fucked-up by Cassidy that he couldn't point out the color white while surrounded by tumbleweeds of snowdrifts. That was how wracked his brain was by the redhead hidden in a parka.

"Got it." Locke knocked Rocco's wrist away—

"Wrong move." Rocco hauled his ass back and released him. "Try again. Do you got it, Locke?"

His skin crawled to get off this mountain. "Christ. Yeah. I got it."

"Good. By the door," Rocco ordered. "Stay your ass still."

Locke ground his hatred for Cassidy into his molars, flexing his fists in his gloves, and tried not to implode. He couldn't—no, he fucking wouldn't—be another Cassidy Noble casualty, just another of her talking points. How fast would she try to profit from this rescue? Maybe she'd staged the FSB guys to further her career.

Or she could make a meme out of it. Throw it on social media. Perhaps Washington insiders needed to hear what she had to say? *Or not!* Locke tried to remind himself she'd had her ass kicked straight off the high-and-mighty all the way down to fallen-and-disgraced.

Cassidy wasn't shit!

But it still didn't help him right now. He couldn't see straight, couldn't breathe right, couldn't tear off the layers that kept him warm and safe but had a stranglehold on him, squeezing the life out of him. Locke spun, needing to get the hell out of the ski-patrol shack even if that meant straight into Russia's Arctic freeze—and he slammed into Jax.

"Brother," Jax said.

What the fuck? They were not brothers. They were barely buds. Working beside Jax was like walking next to a wall—if that wall was an asshole with an attitude problem. That *he* thought to stand up for Cassidy…

"I'm cool," he lied.

"Bro, you're not." Jax's dark eyes held no emotion. "I'm doing this for you. But you can't get around me. Fuck her, whoever she is. She isn't worth it."

Jax didn't know how worth it those men's lives had been. Locke wouldn't touch her, but damn, he wanted to tell her… something. Anything. Everything. Whatever it would take to regain the footing he'd lost the day she destroyed his life. But what words were even adequate?

There were none. For so long, he'd said only the right words, and only when necessary. Locke snarled. That woman talked and talked and talked some more.

Jax knocked him in the chest. "I'll haul your ass out of here if that's what you need."

Bishop stepped behind Jax in at show of support *against Locke*. Fucking hell.

Locke rolled his shoulders and tried to find the truth of it somewhere inside. "For real. I'm fine. I'm good."

Slowly, everyone ignored the awkward reunion and returned to their tasks. Except for Locke. The nightmares of his past paralyzed him as Titan doted on the woman who'd ruined his life. Hoorah.

CHAPTER TWO

BETWEEN LOCKE AND Alex, Cassidy didn't know which way to direct her eyes or what to pay attention to as her teeth chattered. Both men had her attention and ire. That anger went both ways. Man, did she have a way with the male species or what? She certainly knew how to create misunderstandings of epic proportions. She stared at her winter snow boots and tried not to think about the last time she had seen Locke.

His blond hair had been clipped—and was coated with dripping blood, speckled with sand and dirt. Trickles of it seeped down his cheeks, painting rivers through the dust that collected on his cheeks.

He didn't cry. Others did, but not him. His whisker-covered chin never trembled. His eyes never wavered. Such a staunch beacon of strength when the chaos of the attack settled around them.

Even years later, frozen instead of sweating, Cassidy couldn't shake how vividly horrific the Sadr City attack had been. She ducked into her well-worn parka as though she could seal herself away from the memories, from the acrid smoke and scent of death in the Iraqi air.

How many years had it been? Didn't matter. Nothing would erase the devastation that came from the attack the media had dubbed the Night of Fire.

Alex came up behind her as the rescue team regrouped. "How do you know that guy?"

She shrugged. "Long story."

"He seems like your type of friend." Alex was fishing for information. Maybe he should be an investigative reporter. Except his questioning was questionable, falling flat.

"I don't have a type of friend." She twisted her mouth and then pressed her cold, chapped lips together. "And we couldn't have seemed that friendly."

"Is that all I'm going to get?"

"Yeah, why?"

He laughed. "I finally have a chance to turn the tables. Maybe I should be more direct. Did your ex just show up?"

"Ha, no." But she dropped her head back and stared at the sketchy shack room. "You're right, though. I *have* been asking you a lot of questions. We almost died."

One second, Cassidy was on a teach-abroad program, earning extra cash in Russia, and keeping up her international street cred, and the next, she and Alex were running for their lives under gunfire.

So far, Alex's nonanswers had been unacceptable, which she'd reminded him about since the moment she caught her breath and they realized no one had tracked them into this dinky hut. Alex's saving grace was that he had a way off this mountain that didn't involve them hitchhiking on snowmobiles. Good thing too, because neither one of them was prepared for the weather to turn.

"If not an ex-boyfriend," Alex said. "How do you know him?"

"Will you explain the woman I saw and—"

"*No.* You didn't see that. Someone else must've looked like me."

"Right." Bullshit. "And how did you know someone was going to shoot us? Did the woman tip you off?"

The only thing he had told her was that men were coming with guns and they had to leave their belongings and run.

Alex's hazel eyes narrowed. "Explain that guy, and maybe I might remember more about the woman."

That guy... She turned toward Locke. He obviously blamed her for *everything.* Who reacted like that merely from seeing her? That hurt, but he was still hurting too. Enough that two men he worked with acted as human shields, blocking him from her.

Maybe if Locke had a chance to say what he needed to, he wouldn't look like a homicidal bully one second from self-destruction. She turned to the man who appeared in charge of the group. "Locke should come over here if that's what he needs."

"Oh, come on." Alex stepped to her side. "Don't goad him."

Locke pivoted, glaring with enough anger that Cassidy stepped back.

"Stand down." The man in charge shook his head. "Locke and—" He turned to her as if asking her name.

"Cassidy," she said.

"Cassidy," he repeated. "To your corners, and stay quiet. Like fucking two-year-olds."

Her eyes peeled back. Well, hell. She was trying to help.

"That's okay with you, Cass?" Alex stepped to the side with a wave.

She ignored Alex and stood in the corner as ordered, sneaking glances at Locke. Her head pounded, and she wanted to get away from his anger. Even if it was semi-justifiable. If he only knew the truth. If he would only listen. The stubborn jackass.

"It's time," their team leader barked. "Let's go."

Saved from her own thoughts by the Special Forces. How ironic. But they still had to travel back to the United States. Many more hours left with Locke.

That was fine by her. She had a goal for this trip, and even having to be rescued and having Locke show up wouldn't ruin it.

When she was at home and staring in the bathroom mirror, Cassidy had promised herself that she wouldn't see herself as the politicians and the media saw her. She didn't have the poor judgment Locke probably thought she had, just like she wasn't unpatriotic for refusing to give up her sources like he probably believed as well. This redhead was feisty, friendly, and fiercely committed to what she did well: the truth. The opposite of Locke Oliver.

CHAPTER THREE

CASSIDY SHIVERED, AND their rescue team hadn't even opened the door yet. The howling wind ridiculed them mercilessly as the group drew closer to leaving. *Soon...* She wriggled her toes in her boots. Soon, she would have warm clothes and hot coffee.

"Into hell we go," someone muttered.

The door creaked open, and no matter how many layers Cassidy had on, she recoiled at the all-white sight awaiting them. An arctic abyss.

The rescue team had weapons out and surrounded her and Alex. They surged and trudged into the snow. The wind knocked her sideways, and she kept her focus on the tree line. They'd said that was their goal, promising the journey would be easier in the trees, where they'd wait for a helicopter to arrive. *In this wind...*

Each step took every muscle to work overtime. "Alex, wait."

He didn't hear her or didn't care, pushing farther ahead of her than she could keep pace with. Someone pushed her from behind, urging her to keep up and lifting her over drifting snow humps. "Thanks," she huffed as heavy snowflakes landed on her cheeks.

She was sweating and freezing at the same time, breathing made her lungs ache, and she needed more help than she wanted to admit to as they crouched at the base of tall, snow-covered pines.

A helicopter ascended from the closed snow trails, rising as snow swirled faster than the wind could even blow it. The man in charge of their group motioned with his arms, and the team moved en masse. Struggling in the drifts, she faltered, tripping, and strong hands grabbed her, lifted her back on her feet, and kept her moving.

"Thanks," she mumbled again, exhausted and running low on energy.

She hadn't had decent sleep in days, nor food or drink except what they'd just given her. Fading fast, Cassidy's muscles seemed too heavy, her head too light.

The helicopter appeared from the valley. If there wasn't the worry about angry gunmen, she might have stood in awe of it, but there was no time for that as it hovered. As it was now, adrenaline was her only motivator.

Her tired legs throbbed. She only had to stay upright long enough to use the landing skids as a step up, then in. It sounded straightforward, but her muscles were exhausted. Her mind faded. Each breath didn't feel strong enough, like it wasn't getting as much as oxygen from her gasps.

They came to a stop, and she leaned forward, gloved hands on her knees, panting as she waited for each of the men to push into the helicopter.

"Cassidy! Eyes up!"

She tilted her head up. God, she was dizzy. Their hands reached down, and the white world began to spin. "Oh… no." Her eyes closed, and she tried to find her bearings, reaching for help. She blinked open as the wind changed direction and stung her cheeks. The helicopter bobbed and floated, moving side to side in the harsh wind, and a masked man hung out, reaching for her. If she could focus on getting in… if she weren't so drained, fatigued… "I can't—"

Confident hands grabbed her waist and tossed her up to another set of hands that pulled her upright. Cassidy blinked, getting her bearings, not having the energy to thank anyone yet rejoicing because that was exactly what she'd needed.

Unsteady on her feet, she let a white-camo-clad man assist her into a seat as the man who'd helped her along hoisted himself in, pulling his mask to his forehead. *Locke.* He'd been the one behind her. He'd picked her up. Put her in. She tried to wrap her mind around his hatred and his help—a hand came close and pressed a plastic oxygen mask on her face and—oh, that was nice. Easier to breathe.

"Breathing better?" he asked as the helicopter lifted away.

She took a deeper breath. And another. "Yes."

He sat next to her, removing his mask and hat to reveal dark hair and eyes, and pulled on a headset. "Good. I'm Jax."

She tilted her head, not wanting to move too much. That was far more work than she was prepared for. She eyed him belting himself in, looked around, and did the same.

She pulled the oxygen mask away. "I'm good now, I think."

A moment later, after Cassidy had caught her breath and Jax cut off the oxygen flow to the mask, she closed her eyes to the rock and roll of the helicopter and prayed as they descended the mountain. All she wanted to do was go home. There was so much work to do, and it all had to do with the question of why Alex couldn't help but lie.

LOCKE HAD KEPT his eyes on Cassidy the entire time Brock piloted their chopper through the storm. The woman was fearless. Maybe *tired*, but fearless.

They landed in a place where Titan had a jet fueled and waiting to take them home. In all that time, he hadn't lost sight of Cassidy. Until now.

The team hit the bathrooms at the private airport to change from the arctic camo to normal clothes that they'd fly in. One by one, they headed to the waiting jet.

Locke was the last one on, taking a phone call with Parker about an old job in Chicago. Soon as Locke wrapped, he hustled to the private jet and bounded up the stairs. It wasn't often he had flown in a Learjet, and he was ready to relax.

The lights were dim, and everyone was conking out already. He'd be asleep as soon as he searched out a seat. Roman and Cash were already sleeping on two sets of couches, and Rocco had clearly set up shop at the table and chair, though he was nowhere to be seen. Bishop had his feet up on the seat across while talking to Alex, and Jax was passed out and had his shit all over the seat next to him. *Fucking hell.*

Locke rounded a partition as Rocco came around. "Sit down and make nice."

His team leader's usually even brown eyes were bloodshot and exhausted.

Hell, they were all tired. "Roger that."

"Make no trouble for her."

Her? Locke's eyes tracked over Rocco's shoulder. Damn it. Last seat available was next to Cassidy. "Boss? There's bullshit history there, and I don't think it's—"

"Are you going to cause a problem?" Rocco growled, exhaustion adding grit to the question.

Damn it. "No."

With a nod that might as well have been *you wouldn't dare*, Rocco walked past the partition and settled into the desk and chair far away from Cassidy that Locke would've sold his truck to trade for.

This was going to be awkward. But with his every muscle aching, and half the team snoring already, he planned to be lights out before Cassidy Noble said two words to him.

Locke grabbed an army sweatshirt and stowed his go-bag in a bin nearby. The sweatshirt could be anything. A pillow. A blindfold. Another partition if he needed to block the view of his red-haired enemy.

Without the protection of the death storm and the dark belly of the chopper, Locke couldn't avoid the vibrant—though exhausted—sparkle of the woman he'd last seen in Iraq. Cassidy was curled in her seat with a book in her lap, toying with the pile of dark-red hair knotted on top of her head. The plane's interior lights showed an almost hidden smattering of freckles and her blue-green eyes. There were valid reasons why she had done well as a television correspondent in the desert. Even in hellacious conditions, she could still look camera ready.

"Joining you," he mumbled and lumbered into the luxury seat. Aircraft confines and comfort weren't made for men like him, and already the space seemed too intimate. Add supple leather, and this felt… too close for comfort. He'd kill Rocco for the forced seat assignment. Hell, he'd kill the whole team.

Her slight chin upturned and long eyelashes blinked in recognition of him standing there. "I'm sorry I upset you," she whispered.

"Not upset."

"Gee." She smirked away the whisper. "Fooled me."

"I would have thought your buddy Alex would sit with you."

"Too much time together." She rubbed her thumb over the corner of a paperback book. "Maybe I just have that effect on men I work with overseas."

He frowned. "Maybe."

"Don't be a jerk, Locke. I don't see you winning awards for attitude and compassion."

Great. A lecture. Somehow, words of wisdom about how to behave didn't seem appropriate coming from this woman. "Don't care anyway."

"We should hash out—"

"I'm asleep, Cassidy."

"I'm willing to have a conversation about it."

Nope. Not going to happen. Especially surrounded by his team. Stuck in a tin tube with his nightmare for hours on end? No. Locke grumbled, balled the sweatshirt into a pillow, and closed his eyes.

"Right. I'm asleep too, Captain Avoidance. So much for talking it out. *Again.*"

Talking it out. Did Cassidy want a fight on an airplane? Really? They could *talk out* the loss of life, maybe hold hands and chant their way to inner peace.

The loudspeaker crackled once, and a *real* captain came on. "It's a short runway and a long trip. Buckle in, and go to sleep. We'll be wheels up before you know it."

How the hell was he going to sleep sitting next to…? Locke stole a glance out of the corner of his eye, and Cassidy was dead out. Her pink lips parted, and she leaned against the wall, oblivious to the world.

Dreaming, she didn't look like the devil or seem like someone who had enough venom in her to destroy an army unit. With her thick red hair knotted high—some pieces had fallen free, covering part of her face—he could see her allure.

Her book slid off her lap and landed cover side up. It was not what he'd have guessed she'd pick for a leisure read. Then again, he didn't know a thing about Cassidy Noble.

Shadows of Truth. His eyebrow rose as he focused on the subheading: *Reality's Fight for Freedom.* Scowling to himself, he mulled over her choice of reading material and the fact that she'd fought to tell him something in the snow shack from hell and even just before she fell asleep.

Their aircraft launched into the air. She didn't stir, only shifted, sliding her weight from one side of the seat to the other—toward him. And she slouched, piled against him, asleep and unaware, and damn his manners and the soft purr of her dreamy relaxation as she nuzzled against his shoulder, and he went ramrod straight. Paralysis had taken over, and it seemed his biceps had coaxed her into falling further into sleep. Cassidy was the cause of his tormented, sleepless nights, and he wanted to shake her awake, but he couldn't rip his shoulder away.

He had a reputation as a man of few words with a shoulder to lean on—interesting that the one person he hated was literally taking advantage of that shoulder, and after he had given her *too many* words and not listened at all.

Locke tucked the army sweatshirt under her neck—as a barrier—and she looped her arm up and snaked around the new pillow, latching onto his forearm in the process.

"No, no, Cassidy," he whispered, failing to extract himself. "Don't do… that."

She sighed and pouted in a deep sleep. Whoa—that was quite the face. But he wouldn't fall for it. She'd be lethal with that pout, those lips, and that hair if she had half an idea the effect they had. "Not cool, woman."

This time, he'd get out of her grip even if he woke her up. Locke held his breath and tugged his arm. His face scrunched, but finally, he was free.

Quickly, he looked around. No one had been watching. *Jesus.* He shook his arm, smoothing out his shirt, and the warmth of her touch dissipated. The idea that Cassidy had been wrapped around him was absurd.

"She's a snake." He'd never forget the Night of Fire and the deaths of men who were like his brothers. Locke rubbed his arm then scrubbed his face with both hands, trying to fight the confusion and the memories and maybe have a normal flight's worth of sleep.

She stirred, but she didn't look evil. No horns hiding, no whiptail curled beside her. He needed to remember all women looked pleasant when they slept. The sweet, sighing lady next to him was nothing but a trap.

CHAPTER FOUR

TWO DAYS. TWO whole days had passed since Titan had returned from the Krasnaya Polyana Mountains, and all Locke had thought about was Sadr City. The entire team sat around the war room table under the intense scrutiny of Jared Westin. The heavy aroma of coffee hung in the air as Boss Man cracked his knuckles.

With each bone popping, Locke imagined that Jared was ready to punch his face in. Even Thelma, Jared's bulldog, gave Locke the stink eye when he walked into the meeting. Everyone knew he'd been out of line in that damn snow-covered ski-patrol shack. Even the damn dog.

On screen, the thermal images remained paused. Overall, the post-op situational assessment was positive. But after this meeting was over, Jared was going to shred him.

If he could have changed his initial reaction to Cassidy, yeah, he would've played it differently. But bonus points for sitting next to her on the plane, right? Maybe Rocco had even set that up so Locke wouldn't get fired.

Locke chewed the inside of his cheek. What was done was done. Dole out the punishment. Commence with the ass ripping. No one wanted a boot from Boss Man, but if it was coming, get it over with and move on. All the post-op analysis was slow torture. Locke's attention turned back to Boss Man's lecture on attitude problems in the field.

"Yeah, jackass," Jax mumbled next to him and stuck a pen in his mouth.

Locke twisted in the chair. "Say something?"

He smirked, shaking his head. "Nah, bro."

Rocco slammed his hand on the table. "Shut your faces. Both of you."

Jax grinned like an asshole, pen still between his teeth, as Rocco leaned back in his chair. The temperature dropped a hundred degrees in the room as Jared turned steel eyes toward Locke's corner of the table. Even Jax buttoned down the asshole routine as Jared balled his fists and planted them on the table like two tree trunks holding up a massive attitude problem.

Yeah. The day sucked, and it wasn't past nine in the morning.

"Jax," Jared boomed, and the walls shook.

For all Jax's bravado, Locke could feel unease curl in the pit of his teammate's stomach.

"Yes, sir."

"You're on notice. I'm done with the bullshit and the attitude. I will personally remove it from your stinking face if I see it again. Do you read me?"

"Loud and clear."

"And you." Black laser eyes moved away from Jax and drilled into Locke. "*Stand up.*"

Locke hit his feet. *Motherfucker. This sucks.*

Across the room, Jared righted himself. They were two big guys with a table full of tough men and women between them. Venom fueled Jared's eyes. Ripcord-tight tension flexed in his cheeks. Even the tendons in his neck acted as though they wanted to crawl out of the man's body and strangle the life out of Locke.

He took a deep breath. Public flogging—all right, he'd survive. Humiliation—got it, bring on the embarrassment. Cassidy had dealt with that too, in the public eye, no less. Not that he wanted to find her as an ally in this, since she was the cause of his problems.

"Make peace with it." Boss Man's ass-kicking words bitch-slapped Locke across the room. "Whatever *it* is, find it and do it."

He blinked, dumbfounded. He wanted to glance around to see if he was missing the ass kicking that about to commence, but he didn't dare move a muscle.

"All right." Jared turned to Rocco. "That's it. Got anything?"

That was it…? Locke, still standing, tried to understand if Rocco and

Jared had moved on to regular business or what.

"Nothing else." Rocco pushed back in the rolling chair. "Oh yeah. Don't forget dinner at Winters's tonight. Bravo Zulu, guys and gals. Bravo Zulu."

Everyone stood up with job-well-done camaraderie as Locke dropped down. *Make peace with it?* Make peace with the Night of Fire and with Cassidy Noble? Jared didn't have a clue.

Jax peered down at him as the room emptied. "Dude, that motherfucker straight shaved fifteen years off my life," he grumbled, eyeing Locke. "Apparently, yours too."

Locke ducked his head in his hands and leaned forward on his elbows. Shit, this morning sucked. A hand slapped his back, and he turned to see Cash walk by.

"No one's slapping *me* on the back." Jax elbowed Cash, who threw a middle finger into the air.

"Learn not to be a dick," Locke muttered.

"Really?" Jax stretched with a Cheshire cat smile on his face. "The man of few words with gravitas and bullshit all but clobbers a woman on an op, and you're telling *me* not to be a dick."

"Shove it," Locke muttered.

"What?" Jax leaned back in the chair and laughed. "She give you the clap? Stole your pretty-boy heart?"

Locke lunged and wrapped his hand around Jax's throat, knocking over their chairs, and he pinned him to the wall. Nose to nose, both men stared, Locke's hand still gripping his teammate's throat. "Fuck you."

"Whoa, assholes." Bishop wrapped an arm around Locke's chest, handily separating them.

Locke didn't want a fight. He wasn't there to get into it with a man who needed to be his brother. He just needed Jax to shut the fuck up.

"You cool?" Bishop had him wedged against his chest.

"Couldn't be better." Locke shouldered away, not entirely losing Bishop's hold on him.

"Yeah, we're just fucking around," Jax said, still smiling as if he needed his face punched in.

Bishop maintained his hold up to Locke's neck as he stepped forward, giving him a hard yank before pushing him free. "You? You good?"

"As it gets," Locke said flatly.

A deep throat cleared dramatically. Locke turned. Cash was standing by the doorjamb, watching Titan's newest teammates fall the fuck apart. He stared like a babysitter unsure about what to do with his charges. The three of them fell silent.

"They're fine," Bishop said.

"Looks like." Cash smirked and shook his head. "Locke… look." Titan's sniper let seconds drift. "If you need to find some peace, you should talk to Brock. And Jax? The asshole routine is old, man." Then he shook his shaggy blond hair and let the door slam.

"Hell." Bishop dropped into a chair. "I should knock your ass to the ground for that."

"Then do it, bro. I don't care." Jax tossed his middle finger again.

Locke was ready to volunteer. That asshole was about as mature as Locke was in high school.

"Seriously." Bishop ignored Jax and tossed a pen at Locke. "She's the catalyst. But"—Bishop widened his eyes—"what gives?"

"I lost my team in Sadr City."

"*The* Sadr City attack?" Jax sobered.

Locke lifted his eyebrows, daring him to throw a middle finger or say something fucked up when the Night of Fire was mentioned.

"Damn, bro…" Jax mumbled, finally acting like a decent human being—and Locke saw the light dawn. "The lady, the redhead. Fuck. That's"—he gestured—"what's her name?"

"She's the reporter?" Bishop asked. "Man, people either believed her or hated her guts."

"Cassidy Noble. *The reporter.*" Locke's molars ground before he could work his jaw loose. "Men died. She's to blame. Can we leave it at that?"

They were smart enough not to say anything for a minute.

"You know, a lot has come out since then," Bishop said.

"A lot hasn't," Locke snapped. "And too much came out to begin with. Everyone fucking died because of it."

Bishop hummed in thought.

Locke rubbed his knuckles into his eyes, letting tension tighten in his tendons. "It's her fault they died. She killed them."

"Insurgent attacks, man. They fucking killed them," Jax said. "If she killed anyone, she'd be in prison."

"She's a traitor." Locke threw his fists down as blood pounded in his ears.

"Didn't she go to prison?" Bishop asked.

"Not for killing anyone," Jax said.

"She's a traitor," Locke repeated, growing furious that they were discussing her.

"She's not there anymore." Jax's dark eyes narrowed. "Traitors head to prison for a lifetime. You can't call her a traitor just because some headlines screamed—"

"The headlines fucking screamed the truth," Locke said, remembering the news as it filtered back to Iraq. "The woman is a cold-hearted, traitorous murderer."

"Then why is she walking around, free to live her life and get stuck in Russia?" Jax raised his eyebrows.

"Man, I was overseas too, and I still remember watching the reports and news." Bishop leaned against the wall. "But it's been a while, and I know other information trickled out—"

Locke saw red. "You're questioning me? On Sadr City?" Hell, he was so angry he *heard* red. "Are you out of your goddamn mind?"

"Just sayin'—"

"I was there! I held their bodies. Watched them die! *I saw her.* Heard her. Knew who she was with and what she was saying! I knew!"

"Not enough to get your facts straight, bro," Jax said.

"Enough," Bishop snapped. "Both of you, give it a break already."

Jax threw both hands in the air. "Just saying. If this is what has you all moody-blues-brothers, silent-goddamn-night all the time, and it's been *this long*? Educate yourself. Don't live in fear and the past."

Locke blinked, stupid and dumbfounded for the second time that morning. "What the fuck ever." He needed to clear his head and get far away from Jax.

Jax chuckled, antagonizing the hell out of him. "Then Google her sweet ass if you're so interested in disagreeing."

"When did you become the voice of reason?" Bishop dropped into a chair and eyed Jax, who had his phone out.

Jax lifted his middle finger, not looking in Bishop's direction. "What's her name again?"

"Cassidy Noble," Locke spat out, disgusted that he had to repeat it.

"That's right. Noble." Jax thumbed her name into his phone, and Locke waited for his teammate to agree. After a couple of seconds, Jax tapped the screen and read. He scrolled, tapped, read, and repeated the whole damn process over again.

"Did we save a traitor or not, Jax?" Bishop asked, stretching, seemingly not in the least bit concerned that they'd braved an arctic hurricane for a traitorous, murderous bitch.

"Not," Jax announced.

"What the fuck, man?" Locke rolled his shoulders, needing to get out of the conversation. "You didn't look up the right lady, or you didn't read her shit right."

"I'm reading about an embedded journalist who almost died right alongside you."

"Yeah." His lips drew in disgust. "And?"

"And she wouldn't release her sources."

"Of course she fucking wouldn't. What else?"

Jax shrugged and scrolled. "Some bullshit here, a little bullshit there—"

"Out of every fucking thing that has been written on her, *those* are the two things you choose to define her as? Jesus Christ. I'm out of here." Locke didn't want to end up in jail for knocking off a teammate.

"Stand your ground, Lone Ranger," Cash said from where he stood by the door.

Fucking hell. Locke hadn't realized Cash had reappeared. Damn snipers and their ability to sneak into places. "I didn't realize we had a babysitter. Or that you were a spy."

"Locke, my man, you are on thin ice. You read me?" Cash strolled into the room and clapped and held out his hands.

Jax tossed the phone. Cash caught it one-handed. After an eternity of the same tap-and-scroll bullshit Jax had danced through, Cash nodded his shaggy blond head. Locke thought he and Cash must have some camaraderie, maybe because neither kept his hair clipped, but Cash wasn't on Locke's side any more than these jerks were.

Cash tossed the phone back to Jax. "All this says is—"

"*She's to blame.*" Locke would stand by that to the end of his days.

Two lines formed on the bridge of Cash's nose. "Damn, you're a headache. It says that she listened and stood by her man. Which is more than I can say about you at the moment."

"You think I didn't stand by the men who died?" Locke growled, stepping toward Cash.

Cash eyeballed him, ready for any challenge that would quickly go to blows. "You need to get yourself in check before Rocco or Boss Man benches your ass."

Locke recalibrated. "I've never wavered in my support for anyone in Sadr City. None of the men in that unit. No one that she claimed she was protecting."

"Well," Cash snapped, "you're wavering in support for this team now, asshat. Try that thought on for size. When Jax is Mr. Calm and Courtesy, *you have a problem.*"

"Dick," Jax mumbled.

"Denying it?" Cash turned his head slightly.

Jax shook his head. "Nope."

"Didn't think so." His eyes narrowed in assessment. "All right, then. We're in agreement?"

"But I don't get it." Bishop pushed out of his chair. "Why did anyone say she was to blame when enemy combatants killed Americans?"

Locke pivoted, seething. Maybe *they* needed to Google. "She was a distraction. A leaker. A writer of bullshit. And a reporter of crap."

"Who leaked to her?" Jax asked. "Was it true? Why aren't you giving her any credit when there are pages of hits calling her a damn hero for what she exposed?"

Locke's stomach churned. "Would you shut the fuck up? Even if she was, even if she did, they knew our weakest link. It was a precision hit."

"It was an awful day. Has anyone ever denied that?" Cash asked quietly. He shook his head. "No one."

"Goddamn it!" Locke seethed. "She reported where we needed more men. That the front lines weren't covered. That the combatants we were training weren't up to snuff and the resources were lacking."

"It was true," Bishop mumbled.

"So fucking what? You don't say it! You don't! You don't talk to civilians; you don't tell reporters."

"Someone did." Bishop took a deep breath, knowing firsthand what they were lacking overseas.

A vein pulsed in Locke's temple. "My unit became a political lesson learned, which is a clean way to say *mass casualties and loss of life*. Because of politicians and their deals, and reporters and their guesses and leaks." His tight chest ached. "She's the reason we were hit. She killed them."

They fell silent.

"I get it," Bishop said, shaking his head. "She did her thing. People died."

"They would've died anyway." Jax rubbed a hand over his face as if even *he* didn't want to say that. "Insurgents saw what you saw. Why are you fighting this so hard?"

Locke dropped his head. "Fucking hell… I don't want to make *peace with it.*"

"Cassidy Noble probably feels a lot of pain too," Jax said. "She got nothing for what she did."

"Nothing but a fall from grace and a target on her back for people that needed a scapegoat." Cash gestured toward Jax's phone. "Brother, make peace."

No. Locke took a page out of Jax's book and lifted a middle finger. "Sit and spin."

ALEXANDER GAEV LEANED back in his faux-leather chair that creaked when it moved. It looked nicer than it was and fit in with the rich décor at St. Andrew's High School. His classroom was just as he'd left it, and the substitute teacher had followed his exact instructions for the weeks he'd been abroad.

The program had been a success, not including the dramatics at the end that he would have to explain to the governing board. But academically, the Russian students learned American English, and he "learned" Russian. They traded stories and talked about culture. It was good, after all, for each culture to learn about the other. The school had its choice of reporters tagging along, which would make St. Andrew's more prestigious, bringing in more donations.

Alexander checked the clock as the bell rang. The familiar sound of high school students flooded the halls. The booming roar of laughter and gossip rolled down the expensive, exclusive floors until his polished-wood door flew open.

"Welcome back, Mr. G!" Justine beamed. She was always the first one in the classroom for homeroom. The routine hadn't changed. Students would be predictable, and that was what he counted on.

Alexander pushed back from his wood desk, and the next kid behind Justine slapped him five. One by one, the children of Washington's most elite and influential took their seats in his class. Their phones were out, their fingers going as fast as their mouths. So many conversations were happening at once.

He gave a quick head count, submitted the information to the office, and took their questions for the next four minutes.

Ring. Ring. Ring.

"All right, guys. If you're not in my AP English, out of here!" He threw his thumb over his shoulder and then caught a football tossed from the side. "Oh, you think I lost my touch?"

Half the class laughed.

"Sorry, Mr. G."

He tossed the football back to the second-string quarterback. "Not as sorry as you'll be if Coach hears you lost your ball today. In the locker before first period. Now."

New students filed in. Everyone hit their seats, and the same questions about Russia came out all over again.

Was it cold?

Was there really a rescue?

Were there mail-order brides?

Only high school kids would ask that.

Alexander walked in front of the classroom, uncapped a marker, and scrawled out the homework assignment for that evening. "Five-hundred-word essay on this." He punctuated the topic then drew a line under it.

Low word count, but their homework would require research. No one was typing this out on a tablet. "And changing things up, instead of emailing everything, I'll send you a link to download an app."

That drew some eyes to him. Good, because he had just worked out a deal with Ivan Mikhailov. *After the bastard tried to kill me.* Information in exchange for access.

"What's the app do, Mr. G?"

"You can just upload your homework to that baby." Alexander paced the front row of desks, knowing that at least one of his students was on some app at the moment. "No more emails if you want to redo, resend, re-whatever. Just re-upload as many times as you want until I pull the assignment in the morning. At which time, it will say 'assignment: closed'."

A few faces nodded. A couple of students didn't seem to realize he'd spoken. All in all, that had been a success. "Questions?" Like any of them would ask him about installing or using an app. "All right, then. Books open. Page 202."

A hand shot up.

"Yeah, Laney?" He should've seen that coming.

"When will you send out the link?"

"After I've talked to each class. Sometime after lunch." Alexander glanced across the sea of faces. Not a single kid was fazed.

How many of them downloaded links without question? Every one of them. They grabbed pictures online without question, downloaded apps, and sent their personal information to anonymous sources on the Internet. Of course they would do it for him. He never worried that this wouldn't work. But he hadn't thought that it would work with a one hundred percent completion rate until… that moment.

LOCKE REFUSED TO get a headache, but this never-ending day could suck it. It wasn't very often that anyone was ordered to report to Parker's IT room—not that Locke had worked at Titan Group more than a few months. But Rocco made that more than clear.

The techy-gadget part of Titan wasn't Locke's comfort zone. If someone would hand him an assault rifle, a grenade, or even a tablet full of schematics, he'd do just fine, and by the end of his day, the job would be done. Whatever that job was. There'd be no questions, just mission accomplished.

But walking into Parker's ice-cold office, the quiet hum of electronics buzzing with a wall of flat screens straight ahead that served as the nerve center for all operations? No thank you. Locke was miles out of his comfort zone.

Parker Black, IT rock star and the eyes and ears of their operations, remained in the corner at his desk, seated on the edge of a black leather chair, inspecting several screens at once. To Locke's untrained eye, it looked like multiple points of view on two separate operations. Probably not something he should disturb. But he'd been summoned. So… he tapped on a table and hoped to hell that he didn't distract Parker from a life-and-death situation.

"One second." Parker lifted his hand up, his finger pointing, without turning Locke's way. Locke remained mum in the silence that was his comfort zone. Plus, Parker was interesting to watch, a genius in his natural habitat.

Finally, Parker pushed away from the screens and stood. "Hey."

Locke nodded but didn't show any bullshit enthusiasm for a directive he wasn't entirely sure he understood.

"Know why you're here?"

"Rocco said get to your lair." Locke tilted his head toward the wall of wonders, accouterment, and gadgets. "And here I am."

Parker gave his office a once-over, checking the screens that had gone dark when he stood, the many keyboards, and other things that Locke wouldn't have been able to name with a gun put to his temple.

"Here's the deal," Parker said. "You're not focused, and it's throwing the team off."

"*I'm* throwing the team off?" Locke furrowed his brow and bit his tongue, thinking of the countless ways that he, and probably Bishop, wanted to punch Jax in the face.

"And apparently, you have half a story about Sadr City—and maybe the reporter."

"I don't," Locke said.

"You do. Boss Man wants you to make peace with whatever's throwing you off."

There was that phrase again. *Make peace.* "It isn't her."

"The fact that you said *her* and not Sadr City…" Parker's eyebrows lifted. "The shitshow in the war room says otherwise."

"Misunderstanding is all," he grumbled.

"Here's the deal."

Locke steeled himself.

"When the guy who's most likely to hold open a door for a woman nearly jumps her shit rescuing her, it's going to raise a few eyebrows."

Locke bit his tongue.

"And when the same guy who doesn't have much to say unless it's the right thing suddenly starts spewing a metric ton of bull crap? Problematic again."

"I'm that guy, huh?" He ground his molars.

Parker gave a placating smirk. "I don't know what you know about Cassidy Noble, and what you think about the Night of Fire, but you're going to learn what's real and what's fake."

His stomach bottomed out. "Excuse me?"

"You're going to deal with it and function as a healthy extension of this team."

Locke's mouth parted, but nothing came out. "Why?"

Parker shrugged. "This is Titan's version of therapy. We deal in intel."

Well, no shit. But he didn't need more intel than what he'd lived through.

"You think you know. I get it, man. I do." Parker crossed his arms. "But maybe you're just too damn close. Listen. Watch. Process, and move the hell on. Do you understand me?"

The words were like a sucker punch, and the intent was downright evil. "I'm not moving on from that night."

Near pity surfaced on Parker's face. "Then you'll never cut it here."

Locke gnashed his molars. If he lost his job at Titan over Cassidy Noble, he would never forgive her destructive abilities.

Parked nudged a chair to him. "Sit your ass down and watch tapes I pulled together. Get your intel-therapy done and processed before Jared decides your weak link isn't worth rehabbing."

Locke gave a flat smile. Not a lot of a choice, was there? "Right. I'm here, ready to listen and watch." He'd watch whatever and then never bring up Sadr City, the Night of Fire, or Cassidy Noble again. Easy.

"Good. If you didn't do this today, Rocco probably would've benched you. And if you're benched and still can't get it together? Then you're out of a job. Who the fuck wants to get fired from Titan? *Nobody.*"

Fucking hell. "No one understands—"

"Everyone understands. We've lost people in combat. At home. People we've been married to, related to, and loved. You're not the only one."

Locke scowled. "Right…"

"Dude, you are too levelheaded, too good, and too right for Titan to mess this up. Grab some water. Some beef jerky. Some coffee. Settle in, and get some perspective."

THREE HOURS LATER, Locke had finished watching every C-Span-recorded congressional hearing, each subcommittee discussion that never made its way onto the twenty-four-hour news-cycle highlights that were boiled down even further by the time they'd reached him in Iraq.

Locke had reviewed—skimmed, to be honest—every article, report, and questionably classified document that Parker had forced down his throat. The stack of papers had been thick but intense.

Nothing on his opinion of Cassidy Noble had changed. She still shouldn't have been an embedded reporter. She shouldn't have been assigned to interview his commanding officer, Michael Draven, as if their elite Special Forces unit were some spectacle for the viewing public at home. Locke distrusted her from the get-go, and Cassidy still had reported on things that should never have been reported in public.

But… that crazy redhead was feisty as all hell. He'd forgotten about that. There were downtimes on base when they had nothing to do and she dicked around with them. The first couple of weeks she was there, he saw her walking around with a red spray paint can. He never asked her why. The place sucked, and maybe she was getting high off the fumes. He didn't know, didn't care. But he started to notice the occasional red paint marks in the shitters. The bright-red marks stood out against the wood walls of the permanent dividers and in the green ones of the port-o-potties.

He wasn't the only one who had noticed the attractive redhead show up—but some decided to broadcast their thoughts in vulgarities on the bathroom wall. She calmly covered them up in true Cassidy fashion, in bright-red spray paint, in a style that said, *Fuck you; I see you, but I am taking you down.* She made her point without saying a word.

Though, damn—she had a way with words, and watching her battle politicians during hearings was fierce, just like the way she took on other reporters when she appeared on news panels. Those times reminded him of when she had gone head-to-head with soldiers. Locke rubbed his face and leaned back in his chair. That was probably why she was sent to Iraq—to bust people's balls.

His phone buzzed with a text message.

BISHOP: *Where you at? Gym, range, or beers later? Your pick.*

Locke could use some stress relief. Maybe they could they find a combination of all three options.

LOCKE: *In Parker's office. "Finding my peace" by force.*

BISHOP: *LOL. Beer is probably best then.*

LOCKE: *Probably... I'm watching politicians fight over who's to blame for 26 men dying.*

BISHOP: *Shit*

BISHOP: *Upgrading beer to liquor?*

LOCKE: *Yeah. Maybe.*

Cassidy was to blame for the loss of twenty-six men in his unit. But what he hadn't known—or maybe hadn't read or heard because he had been in mourning, had still been serving, or hell, because it had been years ago—was that she spent days in prison for reasons *other* than loss of life.

Cassidy had gone to prison because of a congressional deposition... or because she was protecting something... or someone. He didn't get the technicalities of it, but she'd been locked up because she wouldn't talk.

LOCKE: *Hey. Did you know that reporter went to prison?*

BISHOP: *Yeah??? Jax was showing links earlier.*

LOCKE: *But *when* this was in the news.*

LOCKE: *Before. Back in the day. Did you know then?*

BISHOP: *I was overseas on the back of a donkey with a sat phone and a bag of bullets. Wasn't getting breaking news.*

LOCKE: *Roger that.*

He wasn't as far off the grid as Bishop had been. Why hadn't Locke heard *the reason* she'd gone to prison? Amidst the memes and the spin, no one had explained that it wasn't for the deaths of soldiers.

Granted, he didn't get news on the regular in Iraq. But fucking hell... that was a big mislead. He was an actual victim of the attack, and even he hadn't known she refused to name her source and had protected someone in his unit.

That realization was a paradigm shift. "Shit," he mumbled.

Except, just because she didn't go to prison for the deaths of soldiers, that didn't mean she wasn't guilty of it.

But... Cassidy had stood up for someone in his unit—who hadn't come forward—or who'd died—and served time to save his name. What did that say about her? Not terrible things. Locke buried his face in his hands and leaned over. "Screw it."

She was still to blame. This was only a new layer of the story. He hadn't known because… why?

"Because that wasn't the point," he informed the redhead reporter who was paused on the flat screen. Locke could recite the names, ages, and ranks of those who'd died because of what she reported. That *was the point.*

He pressed Rewind on the remote and watched Cassidy sit before a US senator who was red in the face, huffing in anger.

With dark-red hair hanging straight to her shoulders, she looked back at the angry man, her expression unflappable. "You're asking me to betray a soldier's confidence—"

"They died!" The senator nearly came out of his seat.

"Sir, you're asking me to reveal a confidential source. Confidentiality is, at the very basis, a foundation of freedom of the press. If Americans can't provide information to the press, then I can't report it."

"You *can't* report it!"

"That's incorrect, sir." Her head tilted as defiant blue-green eyes flared. "I *did* because I should; it was the right thing to do."

His cheeks darkened another frustrated shade of red. "If you don't reveal your source, you are defying this Congress!"

"Then I'm defying Congress, because the entire sanctity of our press and the journalistic system falls. The American way of life falls."

He flapped a printed newspaper photocopy for onlookers to see. "And I will quote your report *one more time* for the record—"

"Editorial," she corrected.

"Excuse me?"

"You read the report before." She nodded to his stack of papers. "What you just held up looks like a copy of an editorial piece I wrote. That would be my opinion."

He snapped the paper back and pulled his glasses to focus. "'The mission objective is impossible. The forward operating base has pulled army soldiers out when it's most needed. The frustrating reason is simple and political, and only because of an agreement signed by the administration. They campaigned on a future hardline date, ignoring that people would die, and did die, including women and children, all because a politician wanted to win an election. We needed more boots on the ground, and Army Command has repeatedly asked the Pentagon for such resources. All requests were approved until they reached the highest levels, only to be denied because of an international political agreement, which has been well documented according to my unnamed source, who is knowledgeable about the request process.'" The senator tossed the paper aside. "Miss Noble, who is your—"

Cassidy crossed one hand over another. "I *will not* reveal my source. *Sir.*"

"Then you're in contempt of Congress. It's that simple."

Locke pressed Pause. She had a spine of steel in the face of that bastard who breathed fire and asked for the name—in theory—of the man, who was in his unit. If she gave in and revealed the name, her source would lose his career and probably go to the brig for many years. Locke worked his jaw at the thought of her protecting his unit.

A bright light broke into the room, and Parker walked in. "Hey, man."

Locke cleared his throat. "Hey."

"Thought you'd be done. How goes intel-therapy? Major life revelations?"

Intel-therapy might've had a few enlightening moments, but Locke wasn't in a sharing mood. He nodded, rubbing a hand over his chin. "It goes. It's done now. Free to leave, I assume."

"Guess so." Parker swept his arm out as Thelma, Jared's bulldog, trotted in. She groaned as she hit the floor, sprawling legs and wrinkles in every direction.

Locke bent down to give the dog a rub on her wrinkly head. "You find a cool place to take a nap?"

Thelma snorted her answer.

Dim lights and ice-cold air conditioning had to make this one of the wrinkly pup's favorite places. Thelma pushed up and gave Locke a lick on his neck.

"Ha-ha, easy." When was the last time he'd laughed?

Thelma didn't care. She slobber-licked him again, and he rolled his shoulders back, squatting next to Thelma as Parker went to his chair. Locke needed to clear his mind and shake the hours of Cassidy and Sadr City away. The intensity was too much to hold onto.

Maybe that was why Jared let the dog wander the halls. Dogs were good stress relievers. He playfully tugged on Thelma's ear. "Coincidence she's in here?"

"Is anything in this building an accident?" Parker didn't look away from a screen.

"They're using you, Thelma, but you're a good girl. Even if you're used for your kisses..." Locke pushed off the floor after Thelma gave him another slobbery kiss. "All right. I've gotta run." He stretched an arm across his chest, needing to stop the dull ache that had started in Russia and hadn't left yet.

Parker grabbed the remote to see where Locke had it paused. He pressed Fast Forward and then Play when it got to another senator's turn to grill Cassidy. "Oh, this part was the best."

"What Ms. Noble's reports point to, which I think all of my colleagues can agree to, is that our troops need more boots on the ground. More assistance. And a legally binding political agreement with a head of state is what killed them—not Ms. Noble bringing to light the fact that there were holes in manpower. Insurgents knew that. ISIS knew that. We were the last ones to know that, and thanks to Ms. Noble, we knew that sooner rather than later. Too bad it wasn't soon enough, and too bad no one in these respectable halls did anything about it."

Parker paused the video. "You know what I noticed when I pulled the hearing footage?"

"Hmm?" Locke didn't need a replay of any senator's grandstanding oration or the contentious gaveling and the shouting match that occurred between the elected officials; he wasn't sure that he wanted to hear Parker's take either.

"The senators that railed her for reporting what happened in Sadr City? None were re-elected."

Thelma groaned.

Parker flipped the remote in his hand. "Don't know if that's at all related. It's just interesting."

"Huh." Or maybe Locke did want to hear Parker's thoughts—though not today. Someone needed to hold those at the center of power and money accountable for their actions, and people like Cassidy did that. Locke didn't hate reporters. His problem was with her. Wasn't it? Though he saw her side from somewhat of another perspective now… Anyway, it didn't matter. "I'm out."

Locke grabbed his phone and checked to make sure that Boss Man and Rocco had not assigned any weirder assignments.

Again, Parker flipped the remote into the air. "If you ever want to talk, people are around."

Locke lifted his chin, ready to catch up with Bishop. "Thanks. Hey, I have a question."

"Yeah?"

"What was the deal with the Krasnaya Polyana job? Who contracted that?" How would he have run into her outside of the US twice in one lifetime?

Parker reached into a jar on his desk labeled BACON BYTES and tossed Thelma a treat. "Gaev teaches at St. Andrew's, an elite high school in DC that has Titan on their emergency call list."

Right—he knew that from the pre-op meeting. Locke watched Thelma chew her snack. "But what kind of high school calls in for an extraction team or even knows who we are?"

"The kind where senators and billionaires send their kids."

"Ah." He hadn't thought about the fact that the uber-wealthy and powerful would be able to contract for his services one day.

"Let's just say that school has parents important enough that we're on their insurance rider." Parker tossed another treat to Thelma. "If anything happens to those kids, we'll go get them. Apparently, if anything ever happens to one of their teachers, same thing."

Locke hummed. "That's a nice benefit."

"It's an excellent school," Parker said. "It's the sort of thing that makes you wish we could go around the world fixing all the wrongs for all the kids out there. But we're not the cops, and if we can help, Jared tries to make it work out. Even if a school isn't filled with the rich and famous."

Locke chuckled at the ol' good-natured grizzly. "He's good people."

"Yup. But don't let him hear you say that. You'd be out of a job for sure."

CHAPTER FIVE

HOCKEY WAS ON the TV, and there was a longneck bottle of beer sweating on a beat-up coffee table. Alexander's substitute had left him a pile of sophomore English papers to grade. He kicked up his heels and got comfortable. His laptop was open, and surely one of his students would turn in their homework right after school. "Tick, tock, kids. Teacher's watching."

All he had to do was wait, though patience wasn't really in his repertoire. He had weeks to do this. After all, he'd just worked out the deal with Ivan. He didn't think it would be so easy and had come up with it on the fly. But when the angry Russian who'd once tried to kill him showed up on his doorstep, he had expected to die.

Ivan said he'd been impressed that Alexander had enough "clout" to pull in a rescue team. Though it was sad that the man Alexander had once thought might be his father-in-law only decided to make nice when, after almost a decade, he thought Alexander had something to offer to the FSB.

There were not many options when it came to the Mikhailov family. Alexander had learned that long ago. Their empire was a much scarier version of the Bratva he'd grown up around. Saying no rarely worked out well.

But this was the first time Ivan had paid positive attention to him in years, and Alexander had something the other man wanted. A first. Now they *both* wanted something from one another, and that was his way to gain access to Alyona he'd never had before.

He checked the laptop's screen. Still no action from his students.

Maybe the app wasn't working—he'd hastily pulled it together. He pushed the laptop into a better position and let his fingers fly over the keyboard, double-checking his work. It was fine.

"Patience." He vibrated with energy and cracked the top off the beer, not because he wanted to drink but because it might help him concentrate.

Mining information on his students' parents didn't have to start that night. But it could, and that would be his first step toward proving his worth to Ivan, the FSB, and Taisia, and all of that meant they'd believe he deserved to see Alyona again soon.

He grabbed the bottle and tipped it back, taking a swig. When would the students submit their homework? Alexander had calculated the essay assignment so that students would use a home laptop. It would require research but had a speedy turnaround. Where were the overachievers?

Alexander tapped his foot and—his computer chimed. *Hello, go-getters.*

"Who do we have first?" He put the bottle down.

On screen, Olivia Falconer, the daughter of Senator Falconer, was the first to the finish line. Perfect. Good little Olivia had followed directions flawlessly. She'd downloaded the app as instructed. He kept his fingers crossed that she was at her house, not a friend's or a library. *Be at home, Olivia. Be at home.*

His computer chimed with another notification. Olivia uploaded her assignment, and Alex's fingers went to work on the keyboard as he slipped in through her upload link. They were two passing electronic blips on a portal, and she had no idea he was now sitting on Olivia's laptop.

"What's here?" he mumbled. Good God. What wasn't? Even for a responsible student, she had too much trash on her computer.

Yes, there was homework. Yes, Olivia was *very* organized. Folders of memes. Folders of pictures. Gossipy crap. All the garbage kids could pull off the Internet.

None of that was why he crawled through her files. What Alexander needed was to access Olivia's Wi-Fi connection and see what other connections were live in her household. He wanted into her father's files. That would be where it got tricky. The chances of them using the same computer were slim to none. These rich kids all had their own computers. Some of them probably had a couple of computers, and they likely couldn't imagine the conditions he'd grown up in.

What did Senator Falconer have on his phone? Email, schedules, text messages… his life. The only way that Alexander could hop from computer to computer was if they were on at the same time or if there was a cell phone using the Wi-Fi connection simultaneously.

But it didn't look like anyone else was home or online. Not a problem. The connection was established. He could always come back now that he had a link to Olivia's house. "Goodbye, Falconer residence. I will see you later."

Once there, he could come and go as often as he pleased if someone was using that Wi-Fi connection and the password wasn't updated. No one ever updated their home passwords.

The guesswork wasn't ideal, though. Waiting until Senator Falconer was home, using his cell or computer? Hmm… that was why Alexander was smart to start on day one—and why he would prove to Mikhailov he could have access to Alyona.

But what he needed was a trigger. Maybe if Alexander did phone calls with parents and sent them a link where they would have to open something in an email while on the phone call. Parents didn't want to come to the school for parent-teacher conferences anyway. This could be win-win. If he just had thirty seconds when he knew the senator was using his email, Alexander could get in there.

Two more chimes came from his laptop, and two more students had submitted their homework via the links, establishing permanent portals onto their devices, likely at home.

"Who do we have now…? Nope. Don't care." The first name wasn't on his list of targets. Dad was a trust-fund baby and likely played video games all day, and the mother was a celebrity chef. What use was that? Alexander established that connection just in case.

The other student had a parent who worked for the IMF. "You'll come in handy."

There were weeks left before he needed to turn the information over to the Russians, and this would all go very quickly and be very useful. The Mikhailovs wanted to see what he was worth, and they'd find out he was worth a lot.

"Ivan wants to sell his granddaughter? *Bam!*" Alexander linked to the IMF family's house. "Whatever it takes."

Not that he hadn't proven himself time and time again over the years, whether it was to the Bratva or to Taisia.

"I was always a good soldier." Wasn't that what Dad said mattered? Alexander slammed Enter. He had even put his time in working directly for Ivan, and to what end? So that years later, he was doing this. Alexander's keystrokes were more aggressive than needed, but that matched his souring mood. "Family. Soldier. It's all the same."

Soft footsteps crept down the creaking stairs. "Alexander, did you call?"

His eyes sank shut, heavy with exhaustion from just the words calling to him, and he reeled in his aggression before facing her. "No, Mama."

Her shaky hand clung to the rail she leaned on. "Oh…"

Maybe he should turn some lights on. The living room was lit only by the television set and the fluorescent light spilling from the kitchen. The sun barely shone through the draped windows. His mom took another unsteady step and stopped to hold on to the rail. "Is your dad home yet?"

Where did she think his dad was? Outside stripping cars? Drunk somewhere? Or out hustling, working for the family, like Alexander was doing but on a much bigger scale? "He's out."

"Oh." She tied and retied her frayed housecoat, swaying. She really shouldn't have let go of the railing while she concentrated on the sash. "He'll be home soon."

What more was there to explain about Dad? It didn't matter, and Alexander wasn't going to get into it. "Are you hungry, Mama? Want an early dinner?"

"No." Taking longer than she used to, even compared to the previous week, Mama turned. The stairs squeaked under her slight weight. She crept with one foot, then two feet onto each stair, making her way back to her room, where Alexander had set her up with a small television and satellite. All day long, she could watch game shows and 1980s prime-time TV to her heart's content. She could live in her moment, whatever moment that might have been.

"Christ." He rubbed his forehead and snagged the bottle to swig a few more sips of beer. He replayed the last few minutes of the hockey game while he waited for his laptop to chime again.

Upstairs creaked. Mama was moving around. Why wouldn't she sit and watch her shows? Maybe he should check out the celebrity chef's files. Perhaps there was a recipe or something that he could nab, something nice for his mom—easy to make and tasty. He rubbed his sternum, uncomfortable, as a twinge of guilt needled him. Everything was for family, even when it was hard, and it was always hard.

This—his mother—was just a different kind of hard. He didn't know what to do. Tanya was never around to help. Shit, he could call her, but he would just get her voice mail.

While he was on his trip, Mama had had a much harder time. Tanya didn't help as she should, and now Mama was worse. He should hack the celebrity chef's files. Make his mom a nice meal.

But what was the point?

The stairs squeaked again, and he pursed his lips and sighed, deciding to down the rest of his beer instead of looking up and seeing what she wanted this time. Tossing the empty bottle on the coffee table, he stared at the TV screen until Mama cleared her throat. "Alexander?

"Yeah, Mama?"

"Alexander, do you know where your father is?" she asked as if she hadn't asked the same thing five minutes ago.

"Yeah, Mom. He's dead." Harsh but true. It didn't matter how often they had this conversation. She wouldn't believe him—unless she did, in which case Alexander's night would be ruined. He made the mistake of looking up, and her face twisted as if she half-remembered and half-thought he was a twelve-year-old boy. "Playing, Mom. He's out hustling pool. He'll be back later. Are you hungry?"

"Don't say that about your father." She pointed a finger and shook it at the kid she probably saw. "And no."

There had to be some comfort in not remembering tragedies. When Mama's mind first started to go, one of the first things that she lost was Dad's death. It was almost as if this disease had a silver lining. She forgot how badly she missed him when she didn't realize that he was gone.

Alexander looked at the stairs. If she hadn't gone back, and she wasn't hungry, maybe tonight was one of the nights when she realized her husband wasn't coming home. "Do you want to see a cute kid?"

"Sure, whose kid?" she asked in a sad voice.

"It's my daughter, Alyona. I call her Aly."

"You're too young to have a kid." His mom laughed. "Kids are expensive. You have no idea what Dad and I do to support you."

Alexander was absolutely a twelve-year-old that night—young enough to be corrupted, yet so young that she might try to parent him. "I know you do a lot."

In her dementia, Mama had rewritten herself as a doting parent. It irked the shit out of him most times, but that night, when he wanted to see his daughter, when he was doing whatever was asked of him to do so, he could forgive his mother. "She's cute. Someone once said she looked like me."

Mama relented, maybe clinging to the distraction too. "Sure, let's see this Aly who looks like you."

Slowly, one step at a time, his mom crept down the stairs, giving Alexander enough time to pull up one of the only pictures of his daughter. It was selfish, but he liked having this conversation with his mom every time it happened.

"Ah..." His mom took the phone from him and held it far away. "Look at that little girl."

Alexander waited, hoping to hear what made the FSB deal worth it.

"That hair and those hazel eyes. That chin. I can see why you kids play pretend. She looks just like you. When you grow up, maybe you'll be lucky enough to have a little girl this pretty."

CHAPTER SIX

EVEN WITH THE window rolled down and the radio volume low, Locke's headache drilled at the back of his head as the highway mile-marker signs flew by. He called Bishop, but there was no answer, and Locke decided to head toward Bishop's wife's office. If he turned out to be wrong about where Bishop was, then he'd kick it in DC. No big deal. He just couldn't go home alone.

He twisted the top of the water bottle, pitched it back, and guzzled. Locke didn't want to call any of his military buddies up because Cassidy would come up in the conversation. Not that they would bring her up. But it was as if her name was on the tip of his tongue—he couldn't help talking about her since they'd returned from Russia.

She was all he could think about. That, and Sadr City. After Parker's day of video and reports, Locke couldn't see straight without thinking about the men who'd died. His old wounds were raw, and the burden he clung to was heavy. Maybe he should've asked if Thelma could come home with him.

Bishop had a dog too. Maybe he'd ask to borrow him.

Hell, half of Titan seemed to have a pet. Maybe that was a secret to life outside of the military. Get a goddamn dog.

A horn blared—and Locke yanked back into his lane. Shit.

He needed to get his head screwed on straight. Tossing a hand in the air to say he was the jackass, he rolled his shoulders and cracked his neck.

The trill of his phone stole his attention. Bishop's name was on the screen. Locke swiped the phone. "Hey, man."

"Ella and I are getting dinner downtown in a while. You hungry?"

"Vegan froufrou? Yeah, I don't know about that."

"It won't be a steak house." Bishop laughed. "But probably not frou-frou."

"Early, isn't it?" He wasn't in the mood to do an early dinner. "Nah, I'm more in the mood for a beer."

"Good, so am I," Bishop said. "I'll blame you, and we'll go do that instead."

"Great. That's what I need today—Ella chewing my ass."

Bishop chuckled. "She'll be okay if it's just us. I mentioned Jared was on the war path, and she can appreciate you might need to blow off some steam."

"Mentioned, huh?"

"She sees things for what they are."

That meant Bishop had talked about what happened in Russia and at Titan HQ, and his wife was worried. "Whatever you say." Everyone was worried. It wasn't like he was just having *a moment*. He was obviously unraveling at work, and the whole team, plus significant others, were on red alert. Awesome. "Where are you?"

"Her publicist's office."

That had been his first guess. At least Locke wasn't losing his mind. "All right. I'll see you in fifteen."

He ended the call and changed lanes to exit 395, ducking off the bridge right in time to cross over into Southeast DC. Locke rolled past the Capitol. Everything about Cassidy he had just watched had happened right near there. Congressional hearings. Depositions.

He slowed to find that protesters blocked his turn onto First Street, and Locke tried to map another way to Ella's publicist's office. Two blocks that way…?

They'd had a job over here a few months earlier, and he semi-knew the area, but he didn't have the DC streets committed to memory, and Capitol Hill police waved him in the opposite direction he needed to go. Fucking hell. His headache didn't need this.

Rerouted, Locke turned and tried to backtrack to where he needed to go. There was that park he recognized, and a school—the school. He slowed and peered out the window, taking in the high school he had seen a thousand times and never thought twice about. *St. Andrew's.* How about that? Where Alex Gaev taught and—Locke's neck snapped to the side, and he slammed on his brakes. There was Cassidy Noble.

Of all the people, on all the days, there sat the red-haired ghost from his past. She wasn't close enough to seem like a visitor to the school, but what else was over here? Not much on that block. With her glaring, investigative-reporter stare, Cassidy looked as if she were casing the joint.

"What the hell are you doing?" He let his foot off the brake, craning his neck as he passed. She stared at a back door facing what had to be the faculty parking lot. Was she watching for the teacher? Hard to tell in his mirrors.

Locke came to a stop sign and waited longer than he should have before proceeding. Hell, he was curious, so he turned right to retrace his path and come back.

At the corner, across from where Cassidy sat, he waited. She didn't notice.

"She's nuts." He threw his truck into reverse, backed up a good thirty feet to the nearest parallel parking spot, maneuvered into it, and threw his truck into park.

Never once did it appear that she noticed him watching her stare at the school. Yeah, that was weird. The whole thing was odd, and he was going to talk to her.

Locke opened his door and jumped out. Seconds later, he was by the side of her Jeep. Still, she didn't notice that a man stood by her passenger window. Man, when Cassidy was focused, the rest of the world was an afterthought.

"Hey." He rapped on the window.

Cassidy jumped, and he chuckled as she let loose every curse word he'd heard in the last two months.

"Are you going to unlock the door?" he asked, mildly amused.

She rolled her eyes and slammed her hand onto the console, opening the door.

At the click, Locke opened the front passenger door. "Cassidy."

"Why would you scare me like that?" Her wild blue-green eyes narrowed, and her cheeks had tinged red, making her faint freckles invisible. "Do you know how insane it is to sneak up on a person?"

He leaned down. "What are you doing here?"

Her brows knit when she squinted, but she managed to fold her hands in her lap. "Nothing."

"Nothing. Looks like it." Locke pulled back and put an elbow on top of her car. Deciding it was best to join her, he folded into the seat, shut the door, and turned to see her taut face all kinds of pissed off. *Welcome to my world, Cassidy. I had intel-therapy today...*

"What are you doing?" She dragged out each word as if offering him the phonetics.

"I'm joining you. Thought that was obvious."

"I can see that," she snapped.

"Good, seeing as you're a reporter. The observe-and-analyze part of the job would be in danger if you couldn't pull off—"

"Why are you invading my personal space?"

"This is where that prick works, huh?" Locke turned toward the oh-so-prestigious St. Andrew's. It looked like any other school, except with nice brickwork and landscaping that *Better Homes and Gardens* could do a photo shoot at.

Her blue-green eyes deepened inquisitively. "Why do you think he's a prick?"

"I asked you a question first."

"I'm not here to play games," she said.

"But you are here to do something, and I wonder what that is."

She muttered under her breath and faced forward. What the hell was he doing in her Jeep, anyway? There were two small notebooks with scattered notes written across the pages going all different directions, and he bent over slightly to read one, turning the booklet.

"Do you mind?" She slapped her hand over his.

He laughed at the sting and pulled away. "I'm curious."

"Don't be."

"You look like you're spying on an ex. Like there's another girl—"

"God, you're an asshole!" Both of Cassidy's hands slammed into his shoulder.

Of all the things that Locke was prepared for, a two-handed Cassidy sledgehammer was not one of them. Then she did it again!

"Hey, hold on."

"Oh, shove it." She leaned across his chest—she smelled like honey and sugar—and opened his door. "Out!"

The door closed immediately.

"God," Cassidy growled. She pushed over him again, cursing, and pulled the handle, throwing the door open a few more inches. "Out!"

"Jeez, Cassidy."

"No, sir. No way." Back on her side, still smelling like a heaven-sent saint, she laid into him again. "Get out of my car."

"Cassidy, I was just playing."

"Get. Out."

He got out of her Jeep but stayed on the sidewalk. "Okay."

Maybe what he'd said was insensitive—on a dick-move scale of one to ten, a solid eight. But she didn't need to throw down like she was challenging him to an arm-punch war. "Calm down."

"Are you joking me?" Her beautiful, wild eyes bugged as she leaned over the console to yell at him. "You got in my car *unannounced*. I should call the cops. You had the *audacity* to assume that it was a relationship problem. You're a sexist pig, Locke. Shut the door."

Sexist pig…? Numbly, he closed the door, mumbling, "Remind me never to make a crack about redheads."

She'd probably deck him, thus confirming that she had that fiery temper redheads were known for. Was he a sexist pig? If his mother heard those words attached to his name, she'd probably fall over dead, only to rise again and lecture his ass. Shit.

The Jeep's engine revved, and he couldn't tear his eyes away as she pulled off the curb like she couldn't wait to get away. Another car skipped the stop sign, and Cassidy laid on her horn, zooming to avoid getting hit.

"Careful, Flamethrower," he grumbled as she sped away.

What the hell had just happened? Fuck. He wasn't a sexist pig. But hell, he'd just said things that were borderline sexist. Or maybe not so borderline. *Damn it.*

A woman approached him on the sidewalk, and the frustration building inside his gut, clouding in his chest, won when he couldn't contain the urge to explain, "I'm not a sexist pig."

She stepped off the curb to avoid him.

"I'm not!"

She looked both ways and crossed the street.

Since when did women run and speed away from him? He stormed back to his truck, slamming his hand into a lamppost as he passed it. Sharp spikes of pain ran up his knuckles into his forearm. It hurt like a mother bear, and he gritted into the well-deserved pain. The shit Cassidy had just called him on was true. What was his damn problem with her?

His phone rang, and Locke pulled it out. *Mom.* He laughed. Fucking A—the woman had eyes everywhere. Locke towered over his mother and outweighed her by at least a hundred pounds, but she was fierce, opinionated, and had unbelievable timing. Back in the day, his buddies' moms let them off the hook for cutting school. Not Locke's mom. In his mind, the lecture still sounded as clear as the ringing phone: "*People say boys will be boys. But not in my house. I'm raising a man.*"

He swiped the phone. "Hey, Mom."

"Oh no. I can tell by the sound of your voice. What'd you do?"

He laughed and dropped his head back. "Screwed up at work." He took a deep breath and straightened up. "Just knocked my fist into a lamppost."

His mom hummed in the phone. "Not very smart."

"Not very. You doing okay?"

"Just checking in on my favorite son."

"Your only son."

"Semantics." She laughed.

"That only son of yours might have screwed up."

"How so?"

Locke turned toward where Cassidy's Jeep had peeled off. "I said something to a woman who was involved with Sadr City, and you can guess how that went."

His mom hummed again. "You can't bring back those boys, sweetie."

His chest ached, and in one swoop, his mom knew how to boil a problem down to basics. "I know. It wasn't really about that." He drew in a long breath and let it out. "I don't know."

"Well, you can always jump on a flight and come home whenever you need a break. Okay?"

He nodded. "Okay."

"Do good things, Locke. That's why you're remarkable at what you do—you step in when there's not an easy way out. Love you."

"You too, Mom."

The call ended, and he pocketed the phone and dropped his head back to stare at the now clouding sky.

A bell rang at St. Andrew's, and high school students burst out the door seconds later. They fled to a small lot of expensive cars and grouped on the sidewalks.

But he still wondered why Cassidy had been waiting. Why take that reporting job to begin with? The pay had to be pennies compared to what she could earn for the time spent in Russia. Was she building up her international résumé again? The job was done, though. Maybe she was just moving on.

Whatever. It didn't matter.

Locke needed to get his head out of his ass and stop making assumptions about things that he thought he already knew. Things like Cassidy Noble. Who apparently smelled like honey and sugar. He shook his head, shocked at everything he'd found out about her that day.

CHAPTER SEVEN

CASSIDY VIBRATED WITH annoyance and replayed what just happened. How dare Locke get in her car? How dare he suggest her interest in Alex was based on a personal relationship? Cassidy yanked the steering wheel hard and slammed on the gas, turning—shit. The tire clipped the corner of the curb.

"Whoops." Her cheeks went hot. "Not my smoothest move."

But that was what Jeeps were for. Had Locke seen that, or was she far enough away? Not that he'd keep his eyes on her. But if he did, he'd judge her driving skills.

Let him. Cassidy didn't care.

"Ugh." What was he doing over there, anyway? Following her. He hated her, even when she tried to talk to him. Except he'd just jumped in her Jeep. What *was* that?

Flop.

Her ears pricked.

Flop.

Did she run over something? She would've seen it, would've heard it.

Flop.

Oh, crap. She had hit the curb. *Dear sweet God, please tell me there wasn't damage to my tire.* She checked her side-view mirror as if it had some miraculous view of her tire.

No such luck.

Ding. As her warning light chimed, the bright-red indicator flashed on her dashboard. There was no question at all. Cassidy had a quickly emptying, nearly flat tire.

"No! Not right now." She slapped both hands against the steering wheel, pulled the car over, and parked. With a deep breath, she jumped out to inspect the damage, mentally chanting that the noise had been something stuck on her tire.

Nope. The indicator light had not lied. Her tire was on its way to pathetically flat.

And… she no longer had a donut because of that little run-in with a pothole last week. Ugh! She hated DC's godforsaken potholes.

Triple A was useless, even if she called them. Cassidy threw her arms in the air and kicked the flat tire. "Why now?"

A truck slowly pulled next to her, and she flat-out refused to look over. She could sense Locke Oliver's smirky presence. There were some combinations she couldn't handle. Him plus a flat tire? No. Not that afternoon. She waved her hand, motioning for the truck to pass. "I'm good. Go away."

The window rolled down, and the truck didn't budge. He honked, and she relented, glancing over.

Locke's chiseled face waited patiently, not smugly. Damn, did he live to play hero? "Do you need some help? Or do you just like kicking your car?"

Saw that, did he? She hated him. Why did he have to be the knight in shining armor? "Don't worry. Triple A is on its way. You can go."

"I just saw your flat tire." He laughed. "Saw the whole thing. The kick was a nice touch."

Awkward…

"You haven't called Triple A yet."

"Okay, truth warrior." She waved goodbye. "I'm calling now."

"I'll wait," he said, shifting into park in the middle of the road.

She physically braced herself to keep from rolling her eyes. "I don't need a babysitter. You're not going to wait."

"Do you not have Triple A? Is that what this is? Because I can change your tire." He put his truck in gear. "Don't call. I'm faster."

Locke pulled over before she could think of some story to stop him. Her mind blanked. How to get out of this? She didn't have a tire for him to change, and the situation was just getting more complicated by the second because she didn't want to get caught in another stupid lie.

As he walked over, she noted that he was not unattractive. Had it been any other day, any other man, any other situation, having a guy like that rescue her would've been pretty amazing.

Her heart was pounding. Oh boy. Okay, he made her nervous in a way that she hated. Did he amble? Saunter? It wasn't a walk. Maybe she was still on a high from throwing him out of her Jeep.

"I'm fine. Really—"

"Open the hatch, Cass."

Cass? Like a good deed equaled a nickname? She hated that as much as she hated the way his blond hair hung over his eye just enough that her fingers itched to brush it away. All of it drove her batty. And that made her stabby.

"Cassidy?" He tucked the stray hair away without her help, thank God.

Well, hell. "I don't exactly have a spare tire."

Her words visibly played through his head. "So no Triple A?"

"Yeah, basically." She tossed her hands. "They can tow me somewhere, I guess."

Locke burst out laughing.

"Would you stop it?" she said.

"Okay, all right." He crossed his thick arms, his chest still rumbling. "Kind of funny. But okay."

"None of this is funny." Did laughing make men more attractive? Because she was *trying* to ignore how he'd laughed. His chuckles died down, but then she noticed the Henley that worked over his muscles like magic. Ugh, his biceps rounded obnoxiously as he folded his arms. It was truly stupid how the cotton hugged the curves of his physique—damn near illegal, honestly.

"I have a one-time offer." He smirked, unaware that she'd eyeballed his arms like they were chocolate dangled in front of a girl on a diet. "You're coming with me."

"I am?"

"Aren't you?"

She balked. "No, I'm not. Why would I do that?"

"To get a new tire, Flamethrower."

CHAPTER EIGHT

CLEARLY, LOCKE HAD lost his mind. It had to be a lethal combo of Titan's intel-therapy, Cassidy calling him a sexist pig, and his mother reminding him to step in when he didn't want to, because Cassidy could have called Triple A for a tow. She likely hated him, but still, he wasn't going to leave her on the side of the road without offering to help.

"I'll take you to get a tire and throw the sucker on." It was almost entertaining to watch her squirm. "Unless you have some other grand plan."

"I don't have a grand plan."

"Clearly." He couldn't help but grin. "I don't have anything else to do right now." Except that he did: Bishop and Ella. Of all the places that Locke thought he might go that afternoon, he never thought he'd be taking Cassidy to a tire store. "Give me a second to see where we should go."

"I'll just have it towed," she said decisively. "Then metro home."

"Okay, then. You want a ride to the station?"

"It's only a couple blocks away. Now that I have my grand plan, I'm going to call Triple A." She grabbed her phone and walked away.

"Right." Locke shrugged a shoulder and pulled his phone out to find text messages from Bishop.

BISHOP: *Where you at?*

BISHOP: *You alive?*

Locke was an hour late. Not his usual way of doing things.

LOCKE: *Hey. Sorry, something came up. Catch up with you later.*

BISHOP: *You doing ok??*

LOCKE: *Ran into someone I used to know.*

That was true enough. He put his phone away and returned to find Cassidy far more upset than when she'd left him. "So…"

Her fingers tapped the edge of her cell. *Upset* wasn't the right word. It was more like annoyed. Aggravated. The woman did not hide her emotions well at all. Maybe that was a good thing when it came to deciphering her.

"*So,*" she said, drawing out the word. "Three hours for a tow. If I had a freaking spare tire, it would be forty-five minutes. But since I'm just relocating from point A to point B? Apparently"—she wiggled her fingers in a dramatic fashion—"I'm not that important. *Ugh.* I should never have said I was in a safe spot."

Her rant was justifiable. Three hours was a long-ass time. He wondered if she would take him up on the ride. "If my tire would fit, I'd give it to you. Sucks."

"Yeah." She bit her lip, drawing one eyebrow down, then made twisted faces as if the words were stuck on her tongue and she wanted to ask for the help but had drawn a line and was stubbornly figuring out how to cross it.

"The hell with it," he mumbled. He wasn't an asshole. "Let's go."

Locke tipped his head toward his truck and started walking. She'd either join him or not, and he'd change her tire. All Cassidy had to do was cross her stubborn line.

He opened his door and pulled himself inside, refusing to look in the rearview mirror. "Come on, Cass…"

He caught her in his peripheral vision, and his chest relaxed. She opened the passenger door and crawled in. He cracked the top of his water bottle and tipped it back to take a sip.

"Do you know how long this might take?" she asked. "It's about to be rush hour in DC. You hate me, and we'll be stuck together forever."

"I don't hate you." But didn't he? Locke capped the bottle and put it in the console. "Does anyone do anything nice for you? Or do you let them? I mean, your walls are skyscrapers."

"Asks the guy that jumped into my car and yelled at me. After he yelled at me when he was part of the rescue team saving me from a berzerko situation in freaking Russia!"

Point, Cassidy.

"Then..." He rubbed a hand over his chin. "It's an olive branch. I'm offering to get you a damn tire in almost rush-hour traffic. I just came off as an asshole—"

"A *sexist* asshole."

He groaned and rolled his eyes but forced a smile. "In that very small, one-time situation, I came off as a *sexist*"—he added the same emphasis she did—"asshole, and I'd like to make that up to you."

"Let's go to the tire store. Thank you."

Locke grabbed his phone. "Hey, Siri. Where is the closest place to get a tire?"

On his phone screen, a list of locations came up, and he handed her the phone. "I have no preference. If you don't, then pick the closest one."

Her fingers touched his on the handoff. They were softer than Locke expected. He snapped his hand away as though she'd shocked him.

Cassidy gave him a crazed side-eye. "Just back out of the offer to help if you think I'm some leper."

"I don't."

"Because we can write off earlier. I'll take this as a crazy-ass, alpha-male Titan Group apology. We're all good. No need to go tire shopping with me, all right?" She reached for the door.

Locke grabbed her shoulder. "Wait. No. Chill out. You read that all wrong."

"I get that you still hate me." She held up a finger, bouncing it between the two of them. "Though this makes me think maybe hate isn't a strong enough word. Your skin won't dissolve if you touch me."

"Ignore that." Because he planned to ignore his reaction to her—seriously, noticing how soft her skin was? Nope. He didn't like it.

"You being nice—this whole tire thing—is throwing me off."

"God, would you quit already?" She made him feel awful when his motives were honest. "I don't hate you." Maybe he didn't anymore. "Look, I'm working through some shit. I don't know. Yes, seeing you brought that up. But I'm trying to make peace with it."

She didn't move, didn't respond. Cassidy almost wilted. It cut him. He needed to draw the attention away from what he'd just said.

"What are you working through?" she asked.

"Nothing." He stifled the impulse to share his discomfort with her. "Something. I'm not sure. I have to accept something that I don't even want to deal with."

"I had to accept what happened in Sadr City," she whispered. "Because of how quickly they yanked me back, put me on TV, the hearings—"

"That's not what I meant." His skin prickled with a cold chill. "I don't want to talk about it."

"I don't think either one of us will ever be *at peace with it*."

No shit. 'At peace with it.' What was up with that phrase?

Cassidy gave a heavy, sad sigh and seemed to sink deep into her seat under the weight of the tragedy. He had to change the subject for both of them. Never in a million years did he think that the woman he'd watched for hours in Parker's office would wither under the weight of this kind of conversation. But maybe a private talk was harder than a public hearing.

"Tell me what you were doing at St. Andrew's," Locke said, shifting into drive as the GPS directions began.

Locke eased off the brake and decided to let the silence hang in the air until she started talking about St. Andrew's. Minutes ticked by. They were coasting down Route 295, and still, she hadn't said a word. Maybe this plan of action wasn't the right one.

"How'd you end up reporting with the teacher in Russia?"

He easily handled the heavy flow of traffic. At least it wasn't bumper-to-bumper.

A tension that he couldn't explain filled the cab of his truck. He couldn't place it, didn't understand it, didn't like it, and at the same time, welcomed it. All of it was new and uncomfortable.

"Locke!"

"Yeah?"

Her eyes were wide, as though she had been explaining everything and he had not been listening.

"Our exit—you're going to miss it." Cassidy pointed. "Right there."

Shit. He hadn't heard one thing from his GPS. Quickly, he threw on his turn signal and checked his mirrors, gunning his engine to slip into a small space between two cars. Locke maneuvered tightly to the right and moved down the exit ramp.

He slowed down before muttering, "Thanks."

Cassidy covered her mouth and laughed. "Least we know you can drive."

He gave her a side-eye, and then she laughed harder, which was worth a small laugh of his own.

"Yeah, yeah." He shook his head. "All right, you made me think far too hard about things that are far too easy."

"Obviously," she said, still giggling.

"If you'd say what you were doing at St. Andrew's, we wouldn't miss the tire store."

"But then what fun would that be?" Grinning, she tugged a piece of red hair from behind her ear and twisted it.

Damn, her smile. He had to do a double take. It might've been one of the first times she'd given him any honesty.

"What's that look?" she asked.

He shrugged. Locke preferred to keep his mouth shut. Words were a commodity. They were to be used when necessary. But at the moment… her smile made him painfully aware of her lips. Hell.

Locke cleared his throat and concentrated on driving. The tension in the truck pressed on his chest. He cracked the window as though a stream of fresh air might alleviate the uncomfortable ache he didn't know how to explain.

"I don't remember you being this quiet in Iraq." She rubbed her hands on her thighs, pushing them to her knees and back slowly as if she were uncomfortable also. "Did that change after I left?"

"Something like that." Though his team would probably say he talked much more since they'd returned from the Krasnaya Polyana Mountains.

She settled back against her seat as the phone chirped an upcoming turn. "I wanted international experience on my résumé again."

He glanced over.

"You asked earlier about St. Andrew's. And I have lovers and haters in this town. I keep thinking if I can beef up the international experience, I'll end up back on air." She shrugged. "Investigative reporting if primetime never comes back my way."

"Why Russia?" he asked.

"Why not Russia? Or any other hotspot? There's a list of probably thirty or forty places that I'd go, given our international relations. But Russia is in the top five, particularly considering what's been happening in the last few years."

Locke couldn't argue with that assessment. It made sense, but other parts didn't.

"The school reached out to you randomly and asked if you wanted to go along?" That was where his details were fuzzy, and her behavior made him question the relationship with Alex and the integrity of any reporting she might do.

"It's an interesting school," Cassidy said.

"I keep hearing."

"It's very elite. It's private, expensive, and serves an exclusive clientele. I still connect with former colleagues who fall into that category. They support my effort to rebuild my career, and they're strong advocates for their school."

"They send their kids there?"

She nodded. "When a teacher approached the board of trustees about a teacher exchange, they agreed to it, but there was no way that St. Andrew's would let a great press opportunity go by without having top-notch reporting."

He hummed as he mulled over what she said.

"And," Cassidy continued, "whether you choose to admit it or not, I'm a hell of a reporter and a bit controversial. Controversy equals more clicks and reads."

"A bit?"

She didn't respond to his jab. "They wanted op-eds placed in mainstream media outlets. My name could all but ensure that."

"It wasn't about bringing a Russian teacher to St. Andrew's for a few weeks?"

She shook her head. "They didn't *just* want to expand educational opportunities for their kids. They wanted to broaden the school's visibility. At home and abroad."

"Why?" He glanced at her, and judging by the annoyed look on her face, he was missing the point.

"It's a golden opportunity for fundraising and name recognition. Continue to establish the school's reputation as the best of the best, across the globe."

"Sounds a bit much."

"Have you been in there? It's *all* a bit much."

Locke grumbled. It seemed like a stretch even as schools went, and he couldn't wrap his mind around the concept that they would sponsor a media person to travel abroad on what was essentially a fundraising and marketing campaign. But what did he know?

"I think," she said, "you're drastically underestimating the inferiority complex that DC has when they compare themselves to New York City. Some DC schools are internationally known—maybe one or two—and the one where Alex Gaev teaches? They jumped at a chance to have me travel with him faster than you can say, 'Get an op-ed in the *New York Times*.'"

It all came down to perception. Looks could be deceiving, and the school had almost killed Cassidy just to change the inflated opinions of a few snobs about a place that likely already had an excellent reputation.

"Your destination is on the right," the phone announced.

They couldn't miss the giant tire in front of them. They pulled into the lot, and Locke turned to Cassidy, realizing—not for the first time that day—that maybe he needed to pay attention to the obvious.

CHAPTER NINE

CASSIDY'S HAND RESTED on the door handle, but she turned back to Locke. "Hey, wait."

He looked confused—or seasick. She couldn't get a good read on him, but either way, his paling face wasn't what she expected. "You okay?"

"Yes." Locke cleared his throat as he shifted his truck into park.

Again, she tried to understand what his facial expression was, but she came up empty. "If you're sure."

"Positive." He grabbed his water and chugged a few sips.

All righty, then. Cassidy didn't care to owe people favors. It never worked out for her. "If I tell you what I was doing at the school, can we call this even?"

"Info for the tire change?" His blue eyes lit up, and his loose hair fell forward as he faux contemplated. "I don't know, Red. It seems like you're getting the better offer."

"*Red?* The offer might be off the table, *Blondie*."

He dared her with a try-again smile and managed to do something sinful with his eyes. What was that? And for all that was holy, why did she notice? Cassidy steeled herself against the hair-eye combo that did silly things to her insides.

"People don't call you Red?" Locke asked.

Her blood pressure went up, as did her eyebrows. "My name isn't Red."

"That's a shame."

She rolled her eyes. "It's a good offer."

"The name Red?"

"No!" Not thinking, she batted his arm. Damn. *Damn.* Daaayummn.

Just another reminder that the magical, muscle-building Henley wasn't making things up. He had bulges of muscle piggybacking their own muscles under that shirt. "I'll tell you what I was doing. And you won't hold this over my head, and never mention it again."

"You lied about having a spare tire and calling Triple A. I might bring that up again." He winked.

And. She. Died.

Cassidy had no choice. She jumped out of the truck. The hell with having him hold it over her head. The hell with knowing someone who could wink and make her melt.

"Hey, Cassidy." His voice trailed her into the tire store.

She marched in like she knew exactly what she was doing. In reality, Cassidy couldn't rub two fucks together and get a clue in the tire department. She went stomping around the store, mad, for whatever reason, and in search of a salesperson.

Two minutes later, she'd lapped the entire store and met Locke on the side, where he was intently watching her strut the rims section.

"See anything you need?" One eyebrow was up and teasing her.

What she wanted to do was give him the middle finger, but instead, Cassidy shook her head. "Other than a salesman, nope."

"This is what you need." He pointed to a piece of paper. "They're going to throw it in the back of my truck."

"Wait. What?" She spun around incredulously, waiting to pounce on any salesperson. Seriously, where were the people who worked here? It didn't matter. She was having very inappropriate reactions to Locke and wanting to maim a member of the sales staff. Maybe it was better just to leave. "Let's go pay."

"Already done. You ready?"

Cassidy balked. "Wait. You bought my tire?"

He pushed his shoulders up. "You were… exercising."

Ahhh, she was going to kill him. "*No.*"

"Nope. Don't 'no' me."

"I just said I don't want to owe you anything."

He lifted his shoulders as though it was not a big deal. "But in no way was it meant to be an asshole move."

"Though it *was* a bit presumptuous."

"That you need a damn tire?" He scoffed. "Yeah. Totally."

"That I couldn't pay for it."

"I didn't say that, Cassidy. Jesus. Chill."

They glared at each other. A salesperson meandered out, a cheesy smile on his face that waffled as she turned the full force of her irritation his direction. "I was everywhere in this store."

"I saw you," he said.

"I didn't see you!"

"You looked like you needed a minute." The man gestured to Locke. "He said what you needed. There's one option in stock."

"Ugh—" She took a quick breath, forcing a polite smile on in place. "Thank you for my tire."

"Um, you're welcome."

"Come on, Cassidy. We both want to miss traffic, and that's it. No hidden agendas." Locke turned for the door and left her with the salesman.

"It's a great tire," the salesman said.

"Thanks again." She shuffled after Locke, mad because he'd bought her a tire—which was kind of, sort of, a nice thing to do.

Now she definitely had to explain what she was doing outside of St. Andrew's and tell him her thoughts on Alex Gaev. How would a man as protective as Locke Oliver react to Cassidy's decision to question Alexander *again* on what had happened in Russia?

LOCKE DRUMMED ON the steering wheel, going nowhere. Rush-hour traffic blew big, hairy donkey balls. They were stuck bumper-to-bumper, and Cassidy hadn't said a word since they pulled out of the parking lot. He was content to let her fester and stew in whatever was in her head.

"He's not who he says he is," she mumbled, facing the window.

Locke stared at the red brake lights in front of them. "The teacher?"

"He's a teacher. He works there..."

Locke was positive Cassidy had a secret that she didn't want to tell. If he looked at her, she hid in her shell.

What kind of bad things did teachers do—oh shit. "Like… you have concerns that he did something illegal?"

"Maybe," she mumbled.

Locke drummed his thumbs again on the steering wheel. He didn't know much about it, but there were some sick fucks out there, and they went out of the country to do their sick-fuck things with underage kids. He broke from his straight-ahead attention. "Cassidy—if you have concerns about him with minors—"

"What?" She snapped her head around to face him. "No. Not like that."

"Oh, okay." He pursed his lips. "Then what?"

"I saw a woman sneaking around our hotel while we there. More than once."

Locke relaxed, giving her a sideways glance. That was what she was worked up over? "I think those things happen, Cass."

"No, I'm serious. He made this big deal for us to go to Sochi—"

"The resort town near the ski slopes?"

"Yes." Cassidy nodded. "When, I mean, why would we do that? We had no reason to. None of the parents were putting us up there. No students. That's when everything went wrong. Except *I saw* that same woman from before. I *think* it was her. Then there was the warning phone call. Someone gave us a heads-up that a hitman was coming. That's the only reason we had time to put on parkas and boots before we ran. Why was she in two different places we visited? The second one, where they were trying to kill us? That's crazy."

"Huh," he mumbled.

"There's something there." She shook her head, looking lost in thought.

"If you've never been shot at before, I can appreciate how it must feel."

Her eyes went wide. "Hello, Iraq! I wasn't in battle, but I was around enough, and this was different. His reaction when I asked about the lady? It was off. Every time."

"No guy wants to talk about their hooker. He probably didn't pay up."

Cassidy clucked quietly and shook her head again. "There's more to it."

"You're back in the States now," he said. "What else could be the matter?"

"The thing is, he denies ever seeing a woman."

"Still not an issue."

"Her people tried to kill us. It's an issue."

"He should've paid for his hooker." But if that was why St. Andrew's had to call in their sweet insurance policy, their rates would probably jump higher than they already had if word ever leaked. "Tread carefully on hooker-gate."

"You're making light of something that has more to it."

"Explain to me how you know," Locke said.

"I just do. I have a sixth sense. That, and he picked up Russian way too fast. His familiarity with culture and language was downright concerning."

"You think an ambush conversation would yield new intel?" Though unexpected intel-therapy did wonders for him, it didn't change his perspective *that* much.

"Yes," she said without missing a beat. "You think I didn't ask him while we were there? That I didn't push him for the truth?" She repositioned in her seat. "I wanted to see his face, read the expressions, and adapt my opinions based on what I saw."

"You can do that?" Locke asked, more curious about her ability to understand people than her guessing game in Russia.

"Yes."

He gave her a quick glance but couldn't catch her eye. "Are you good at it?"

She nodded. "Very."

"Look at me. What do you see?" He turned and held her gaze for far too long. His heartbeat pounded in his chest before he broke away and checked to see if traffic had moved. Not much, thank God. Otherwise, it would be the second time he'd spaced out about her while driving with her.

"I see…" She let the words linger, not finishing the thought.

Casually as he could, he glanced her way.

"I see our exit right there." Cassidy pointed. "Don't want to almost miss it again."

She changed the subject and avoided giving her answer, all while giving him a friendly jab. He grinned. *Well played, Cassidy Noble. Well played.*

CHAPTER TEN

THE SOCKET WRENCH clattered on the sidewalk as Locke wiped his brow with his forearm, and Cassidy teetered in her high heels on the edge of the sidewalk, trying in vain not to act like a perv. Really. She was in her thirties. She'd survived college, embedding in war zones—when there was no action, military men were walking around without their shirts on more often than she'd admit—and a bevy of boyfriends doing tasks that should've raised her blood pressure.

But Locke hauling a tire out of the bed of his truck, changing her flat like it was nothing, and tossing the wrench down—it was a freaking miracle Cassidy hadn't found herself magically, spontaneously pregnant. Because… whoa.

"Think you're good now." He turned to appraise his work, and *against her damn will*, her eyes appraised his butt. Solid ten. Give the man a trophy.

Mother of God. She was turning crass, and she almost hated him for how perfectly sculpted he was.

Cassidy gritted her teeth together. If she could lay blame on him for her behavior, she would have dropped that package of guilt at his shoes. But dang if she didn't have that whole take-responsibility part of her persona. She'd cling to that even if it meant she now had to label herself an ogler.

He pivoted back. "I'll get going now."

"Thanks." Oh, boy. He had no idea she'd been leering and just handed him an award for his backend. Cassidy tried to figure out what a normal, innocent smile should look like as she stepped off the curb. "I owe you. Big. I get it."

His chest lifted when he shrugged. "I needed a change of scenery. It's all good."

"Right. So… thanks. Again."

They stood awkwardly. She wanted to hug Locke. Or something. Not that she was a hugger. But they had this weird acquaintance-connection thing going on, and this was definitely a personal act of kindness, even if she'd tried to repay him with information on what she'd been up to.

"Call Titan if you need me," he said.

She nodded. "Sure. You could always come stake out Alex with me. I bet I could convince you he's up to something. Sometimes you have to be around to catch the gut feeling."

"Give me your phone." Locke held his hand out.

"Why?" Stomach in her throat, she dug it from her purse and kept it just out of reach.

"Because." He took it from her and stepped closer and took her hand, twisting the phone and holding her thumb to the fingerprint unlock. Gently, he let go of his hold and swiped the screen then typed. "This is my number." A moment later, his phone buzzed. "And now I have yours. In case I get an urge to smoke out teachers involved in your conspiracies."

Her heart's flutter double-timed as he took her hand again and replaced the phone. His fingers lingered, and—her phone buzzed.

"Not me," he said.

She checked the screen. "Oh—it's Alex." Surprised, Cassidy pointed to it, holding it for Locke to see. "Tell me that's not something. Timing is everything. Hello?" she answered, still trying to draw Locke's attention to the serendipity of Alex's calling just then.

"Cassidy, sorry," Alex said in her ear. "Catching up at school was busier than expected."

"Not a problem," she said, still trying to keep Locke's attention. "Soon as we can meet up, I can finish off this draft for the board of trustees."

"My schedule is packed lately, and—"

"I'll come to you. Shouldn't take more than thirty minutes. Not a second over. I'll put out a timer and everything."

Alex chuckled. "You don't have to do that. But this week, I… don't know."

"Friday night?"

"I have to be out near the University Club."

"Perfect," she lied. "I have a reception at the University Club. I'll meet you whenever works for you." She could picture Alex's hazel eyes clouding and went in for the kill. "I'll print verbatim whatever you tell me, so long as the trustees don't nix it. Deal?"

It was something he couldn't say no to. She'd figured that out in Russia. He had some farfetched opinions, and if he could tie it to their trip and the exchange program, he would. Anything too nuts, the board would cut.

"Well…"

"Please, come on," she pleaded.

"I can do thirty minutes, Cass. I'm not trying to be a dick. Just… I have a lot on my plate. Sometimes my situation seems impossible."

"Alex, you're an English schoolteacher. I appreciate educating the youth of tomorrow and all, but don't be too hard on yourself." He couldn't know that she didn't trust a word coming out of his mouth.

"True. I'll text you when I can pull away on Friday."

She bobbed her eyebrows at Locke. "Don't stand me up, hon. I'd be heartbroken."

"Wouldn't dream of it."

Cassidy ended the call and bounced on her heels, trying to read Locke, whose complicated expression she couldn't figure out. Again. "He's up to something."

"You're meeting him near the University Club?" Locke's jaw flexed.

"Yes."

"And if he has nothing interesting to say, you'll drop it?"

"Probably not." She put on her best on-air smile. "It depends on what he says in between his words."

He snickered quietly. "You think you can read people?"

"I can. Mostly." But not Locke. He'd asked before if she could read him, and she couldn't, which bugged the heck out of her.

Could he read her? Heat crawled up the back of her neck, and more self-awareness than she was comfortable with flooded her body.

Suddenly, Cassidy wanted to look down and see if her black capri pants and spiky heels worked as well as she'd thought they did when she walked out of her house that morning. The clunky necklace accentuated her fitted shirt, curving over her breasts. She'd long ago ditched her sweater. She switched her purse to the other shoulder, shoving her cell into it. "Thanks for the tire change, Locke. I owe you."

As she left, with every single step, she felt his gaze. From the back of her head, sliding down her spine, over the curve of her butt, to her thighs. Cassidy pulled herself into her Jeep, turned over the engine, and repositioned the AC vents to blast on her face. In no uncertain terms, she was all kinds of excited.

Not only was she mildly aroused, but her panties were wet, and her heart beat faster than it should. Her nipples were hard, and she was grateful that she had a vibrator waiting for her at home.

CHAPTER ELEVEN

FRIDAY NIGHT FINALLY arrived, and Cassidy's follow-up interview with Alex wasn't that interesting. She asked questions that were meant to pin him down about the trip to the ski resort, and he demurred like a pro, but she also padded the conversation with enough St. Andrew's-focused inquiries to gather quotes for her articles. True to her word, she had her cell phone on the café table between them and the timer on display. He was short on time, and she was prepared to respect that as the timer clicked down to the one-minute mark. Too bad every question that Alex answered sounded rehearsed. All she wanted to do was trip him up. But no, he didn't so much as blink funny. Her investigative-reporter's senses were on fire.

"I'll let you ask questions longer, Cassidy. Really." Alex nodded good-humoredly to her phone. "You didn't have to set up a timer."

"The only thing I have is my word."

He lifted his chin, aware from their get-to-know-you conversations in Russia about her thoughts on how DC had crucified her for being a liar—or worse, a traitor—when she didn't name her press source. Silence was very *different* from not telling the truth, but there was no telling that to the people with pitchforks on the Internet. They just made stuff up as they went, justifying it however they wanted to fit their cause.

"What did you have tonight?" he asked.

"Oh, you know..." She wouldn't lie, but maybe she'd dance around the truth at times. She *did* meet some girlfriends from college near the University Club earlier. "An alumni event." But she'd planned that after arranging to talk with Alex.

"You look nice," he said.

"Have to break out the cocktail dresses now and then. Otherwise, they take away my LBD card."

"LBD?"

"Little black dress," she said.

"Oh." Chuckling, he held out the lapels of this suit. "We have no card for the suits."

"Must be nice to put away the teacher's clothes for a bit."

He still hadn't gone into detail about his plans for the night. Not that he needed to. But she couldn't help but feel that his evasiveness had something to do with the prickles she got when a story was on the cusp of revealing itself. "Hot date?"

"More work-related." He shifted uncomfortably, and his demeanor changed from unflappable to skittish.

"St. Andrew's is all about the fundraising. Want to comment on that for the story?" Perhaps she was seeing this all wrong. Maybe the Russian woman was a financier.

"No. Different job. I should get going." He stood abruptly, his demeanor shifting entirely.

Skittish and ready to run! Cassidy pretended to be caught off guard, but her inner journalist was madly taking notes. "I'm sorry. I didn't mean to upset you."

"I'm not upset. I just have to go. Can we drop this?"

She stood and smoothed the little black dress. "Sure, sorry. I'll call you later. Thanks for my thirty minutes. If the board has any follow-up, I'll let you know?"

Alex nodded, but it was as if he were a different person. One mention of his different job, and *trigger*—he became the person she'd had to deal with occasionally in Russia—angry, abrupt, and awkward.

"Of course. Have a good night, Cassidy." As fast as he rushed through the words, he left his chair, pushed from the table, and fled out the door without so much as a look over his shoulder.

She waited long enough to finish her cup of coffee then grabbed her phone, tucking it into the clutch, and rushed out the door, her high heels click-clacking on the tile floor before the café door let her out onto DC's somewhat busy street.

Alex was tall enough that he stood out, and it was easy to keep him within her sight. He stood at a crosswalk then headed toward her Jeep, turning down Sixteenth Street, and jogged across to the other side. She ran into the street at the last second and made it before she became roadkill.

Alex passed her Jeep, and—he stopped. So did her heart. Oh, okay. He was jaywalking to the cross street.

Her eyes followed him, and *that* was the Russian ambassador's residence. Coincidence, surely—both her unwittingly parking next to it and him crossing there.

But Alex didn't go right or left. He waited at the gate—then pressed the buzzer.

She felt the adrenaline surge that came from watching a key piece of evidence surface, and her pulse rushed. She tried to get a better look, stepping behind a tree and dipping her head out. The gate opened, and there went Alex Gaev. Into the Russian ambassador's residence. "Holy shit..."

Every hair on her body stood on end as she slinked into her Jeep and decided to wait him out from her driver's seat. What was he doing in there? Who was in there? Her mind spiraled with questions.

Thirty minutes clocked by. No sign of him exiting.

Forty-five minutes. Adrenaline morphed in antsy unease. Cassidy had now Googled the hell out of the building and learned nothing except for the historical factoids about how it came to be in existence. Not that she expected the Russians or Alex to have posted their business online and clue her in.

If she could get a better angle and simply see through a window or something... *Damn it.* Cassidy tore off the too-high heel that had been digging into her backside and leaned over her steering wheel. Ugh, she couldn't breathe with this cocktail dress cinched around her waist like it had been vacuum-sealed.

She tore at the zipper—and oh, oxygen was a good thing, a nearly orgasmic thing, though she lately only knew about orgasms with the help of a vibrator fueled by highly inappropriate thoughts of a muscly man changing her tire.

She pulled herself off the driver's seat and shoved her face as close to the windshield as humanly possible. Its cold glass separated her from what she was investigating, yet she couldn't see through walls, so it didn't matter.

The quiet click of the back door sent her tumbling before a deep voice softly echoed over every nerve ending in her body. "What are you doing, Shortcake?"

Cassidy could have screamed in shock, but she managed to stop the awkward topple in her driver's seat, swinging around. "Locke!"

Smug, he leaned his full length back in her backseat while she lay on all fours across the front seat of her Jeep, her ass practically in the air. "What are you doing in here?"

His ruggedly handsome face had a serious expression. "What are you doing outside the ambassador's house?"

"Why are you in my car?" She wanted to shake him, strangle him, throw him out as much as—*wait*. "What did you just call me?"

"Shortcake," he answered from the shadowy protection of her backseat.

"Why?" As she found her seat again, she tried not to give away how much he got under her skin.

Locke gestured to her loose hair falling over her shoulder. "Strawberry."

"Strawberry. Shortcake," Cassidy spurted. "I'm not even that color redhead."

"Is there a Strawberry Shortcake color?"

"What are you, four years old? God!" Her fingers went to her temples, rubbing in tiny circles. "Get out of my car."

"Yeah, I don't think so, babe."

"What? Are you working Russian security or something?" She reached to the passenger seat to grab her shoe—a cold breath of air ran up her side and stomach as her dress dipped loose. Oh God—her dress was unzipped. Was it dark enough that Locke could see if she flashed him her lacy lingerie?

Judging by his hate-the-world expression, the guy hadn't seen her breasts. Or maybe he had noticed, but he'd reverted to loathing her so much that he wouldn't have dropped his eyes to steal a glance at her boobs. Who cared about this guy, anyway? "Get out of my car, Locke."

He tilted his head and gave a slow shake. "Get out of here, and I won't have to do things like this."

She made pointed and dramatic glances at her car windows. "We are in the middle of Northwest. I can do whatever I want. Go wherever in DC. You knew I was coming to meet Alex, and I asked you to join me—*not* hop into my car unannounced."

"Two weeks ago, you were rescued from Russians shooting at you, and now you're outside the Russian ambassador's residence." He raised his eyebrows. "I'm going to be real honest with you, Cassidy. All nicknames aside, I don't think that's a good idea."

She tried to zip the dress gracefully without drawing attention to herself. Which was impossible. The zipper made way too much noise. Who knew that little thing was like a chainsaw and the Jeep was so quiet? Any further attempt would only bring to light the fact that she'd undressed to get the job done. Classy. "I don't want to be here either. I'd much rather be at home in my PJs, with a bowl of cookie dough."

"Good. Then go." He waved his hand like a wand.

"After you." She waved back.

"Where is Alex?"

Cassidy nodded toward web images of the mansion. It was very historic and beautiful on the inside. Everything was gold and red. Maybe there was a reason Alex was there—maybe something to do with the exchange program—but then, why not bring it up when she was interviewing him? The board of trustees would love it.

His eyebrows arched. "That's some shit…" Then he glowered. "I'd like you to keep your sweet ass alive, and that means stopping you from poking around the Russians."

"And why's that?"

"Why would I like to keep you alive, or why might the Russians not keep you that way?"

She shrugged, pinning her arms to her sides to hold the dress in place. "Either."

"Those are people who don't need the headache of a rogue reporter. They hate the press. They kill the press—on a regular basis. You know that, right? Putin kills journalists. Putin is the ambassador's boss. You're outside their house."

"You might have a point. I get it," she grumbled.

"*Cassidy,*" he growled.

"If you want to keep slipping into my car, you get to listen to my spiel about Alex Gaev, who is a good-for-nothing wannabe spy or something—"

"Whoa. Wait." Locke recoiled, and finally, she could read one of his facial expressions. It screamed, *What the fuck?* "What did you say?"

"I said that—"

"Wait, no." He threw his hands in the small space of her backseat, crossing them back and forth like calling a time-out. "Seriously, Cassidy. Stop."

She stopped talking, only then realizing that her pounding heart had climbed into her throat. She'd finally verbalized what had been bothering her, and Locke still wasn't taking her seriously. He was either part of the problem or oblivious to it.

Semi-aware that she'd careened out of control but also not really giving two shits, she folded her hands together. "I'll pause."

"Look around, Shortcake. If what you just said is an actual thing…"

"It's an actual thing," she snapped. "What I'm trying to explain is—"

Locke moved like the hurricane-force blast that had brought them together in the Krasnaya Polyana Mountains. Harsh and efficient, he catapulted from one side of her Jeep to the other and had his hands around her in a split second. His warm palm pressed against her lips, and his breath tickled her ear. "If that's the truth, stay quiet, Riding Hood. You don't know who's listening."

Cassidy shivered. She couldn't help it. She curled into his hold. The bastard. His lips drew pinpricks that cascaded down her neck, and her pussy convulsed as he held her in his powerful arms.

Oh… Locke was potent. Solid as the mountain he had rescued her from, he was rugged and harsh, beautiful and deadly. Despite the layer of clothes, she could make out his expansive chest as he caged her to him with his hard arms.

The whiskers on his cheek brushed her skin as he eased back. He lowered his hand. "Read me?"

Cassidy blinked, trying to find words that could mask her natural aroused reaction. Silence had been his goal, but not for the first time, so much more blossomed, and she wanted to lean into his hand as it fell away.

Instead, she licked her lips and questioned his choice of nickname. "Riding Hood?"

Locke touched her hair. "Red…"

"Red Riding Hood." She should have hated it. Really. Their faces were inches away. The two of them were holding onto one another, the seats acting as a barrier, the ambassador's house acting as an excuse. She stared at his lips. His hand moved away from her hair and dragged down the slope of her neck, skimming over the strap of the loose cocktail dress.

"Locke." She breathed his name—then movement outside the Jeep window broke her trance, and she shook herself away. He resettled in the backseat.

"I don't know what you're talking about with Alex, but saying those things in a location like this?" Locke shook his head. "That's a no-go."

"I'm right."

"Even if you are, it's the wrong place to air those thoughts. You should wrap it up." He grabbed the door handle, shaking his head, letting the longish blond hair loose. "Have a good night."

"Bye." But she said it to the slam of the back door.

Maybe she had made leaps. But he was discrediting her nose for journalism. She had the ability to see the story form before she even knew it was there. All she had to do was follow the crumbs. The little scraps might not make sense, and they were scattered, but she could see how there were too many things that made her stop and wonder. Who the heck went to hang with the Russians after they ran from Russia?

Cassidy's phone rang, startling her. The call came from a blocked number. She answered, "Hello?"

"Go home," Locke said, not bothering to hide his displeasure.

Her eyes darted the length of the sidewalk even as her pulse picked up at the game of hide-and-seek, though her mark was another man entirely. "Are you babysitting me?"

"Doesn't matter. You haven't moved."

Her eyes slipped shut. Why did he aggravate her? She wondered why she was trying to prove to him that she was good at her job when, up till that point, she'd only wanted to earn back her career.

The answer wasn't easy. A slice of light caught her attention. The ambassador's front door opened. Alex, from behind the protection of the black iron gates, ambled out of the Russian residence.

"Gotta go." She slouched in her seat as he scanned the outdoors before he eased down the stairs, as confident as a man taking on the world, or maybe the United States, and strolled to a waiting car. He tossed an apple in the air and caught it again. As though Alex could feel her hard gaze drilling holes into the back of his head, he paused before getting into the car and scanned the perimeter again.

He didn't see her, no thanks to her not-so-stealthy parking job on the street. Alex took a bite of his apple and chucked it over his shoulder then ducked into the waiting sedan.

"What kind of ESL teacher has a chauffeured ride?" she mumbled.

A high-flying second later, a tinted Mercedes surged forward, and the gate swung open. Cassidy ducked into her seat, and appreciative that she had unzipped her dress—otherwise, that baby would have torn—and off went Alex.

To follow or not to follow... Her phone buzzed and showed a message from Locke. His words screamed at her on the screen.

GO HOME.

"Is all caps really necessary?" She swiped the text message away.

Things that should have bothered her: Alex was on the move, and she wanted to follow him, but Locke would know if she did. And Locke had slipped into her car while she was semi-undressed, and she'd barely heard him.

Her mind rushed as she tried to formulate a plan. The Mercedes was too away far to catch up with, and Locke was likely still watching her.

Giving a side-eye to herself, she made a big show of pressing the lock button and then held her middle finger up to her rearview mirror. "You're locked out, Locke."

Not like that would stop him anyway. Her text message buzzed, and she glanced down.

LOCKE: *Jesus, are you a two-year-old?*

She should really block his text messages. Ha. Like that would ever happen. Because hadn't she nearly hyperventilated when he wrapped his hand over her mouth? Oh yes, she had. Maybe her journalistic skills were right to be called into question. Or maybe she needed to get over Locke or stop running into him. Either way, he was the distraction that had caused her to lose Alex, and with Alex now in the back of a Mercedes, she was certain there was a real story to follow.

CHAPTER TWELVE

LOCKE AND SEVERAL of the guys from Titan had accepted the invitation to test a new weapons prototype at GUNS. The place was a legendary, internationally known as a specialty weapons maker, and the facility was off the hook. The outdoor course was like a carnival with targets that exploded with colored smoke and fireworks, and the indoor range was classic yet automated. They'd spent all day there, and even though it was closing in on late afternoon, Locke could've done the entire day again.

Sugar owned GUNS, and from the first time Locke set foot on the grounds and saw the raging bull sign out front and the polished wood floor inside, he knew she loved the place. But none of his teammates were paying attention to the fantastic firepower housed on these hallowed grounds. Their prying eyes had followed Locke around the range starting Saturday morning, and even now, standing in his firing lane, he could feel their questioning eyes behind him as he finished with the test weapon.

Taking a deep breath, he flipped the safety, placed the 10mm down, removed his protective gear, and slammed his hand on the target button. The shot-up paper came whooshing forward. Not too bad. Direct hits to the chest and head.

Locke turned, ready to talk about how Sugar had recently changed the 10mm's aluminum frame to steel. That was the point of their outing—she wanted to test the difference in recoil. But with Rocco, Cash, Bishop, and Jax showing so much interest in him, it appeared that he was on the discussion block as well. Fucking spectacular.

Sugar's pointy-toed boots echoed down the hall before anyone saw her walk down the range. When she appeared, Thelma trotted beside her. "What's the verdict? How's my recoil?"

"Better," Rocco said. "I want one of these babies."

"I want, I want." Sugar spoke as though she were annoyed, but having known Sugar for a few months, Locke knew she loved it. The aluminum-to-steel conversion on the 10mm was one of the first big projects she'd taken on since giving birth. Locke thought it was interesting to see Boss Man and Sugar's dynamic in the business and then see them outside of work at company barbecues and get-togethers. They were both hard as stone in both settings, but outside of work, there was another dimension to their relationship that Locke had to respect.

"Let's go into the workshop and tear apart one of the prototypes," Sugar said. "I have another idea I want some feedback on."

They gathered their bags, stuffed in glasses, protective ear covers, weapons, and other junk, and some in the group began to make their way there. Cash hung back, waiting for Locke. He was intentionally avoiding Jax and Bishop, though maybe it was Cash he should stay away from.

"Doing better?" Cash asked.

Locke grunted. "Peachy."

"You haven't knocked anyone out, so it seems that way. Just checking," Cash added. "You see her lately?"

"Yeah."

"Assume you haven't knocked her out?"

"Jesus, dude. I'm not a jackass. I wouldn't hit a woman." He shook his head. "I don't know if I should be disappointed in everyone else or worried that you all think I've fucking lost my mind."

Cash smirked and stood there, waiting. He had his bag slung over his shoulder and a worn cowboy hat in hand.

Locke looked up. "Don't test me. Ask me. All right?"

"You making peace with everything?"

"Yeah, I am. As a matter of fact, I'm going to see the reporter later this afternoon." He wanted to make sure Cassidy wasn't going to get herself killed… and he wanted to see if she was anywhere near the truth on her conspiracy-theory expedition.

"Huh." Cash tugged his hat down low. "Has this always been about her and not Sadr City?"

"It was always about Sadr City. Two different things, jackass."

The sniper chuckled, his eyes hidden from behind the worn brim of the hat. "Roger that."

Two different things. They might have started as one thing but had become distinctly separate. Speaking of which, as Cash led the way to where Sugar was about to put them to work, Locke pulled out his phone. The last message he had sent to Cassidy was about as mature as the two-year-old he had called her. But she had sent him a message.

> ***FLAMETHROWER:*** *Not that I'm following him. But if I were, he's at another event with Russians. *sideways stink-eye* Don't tell me that doesn't make your Titan sensibilities say what the...?*

Locke glanced back at *Flamethrower* and smiled. Maybe he should save Cassidy under a different name in his contact list. She had a serious problem with his red-hair-inspired nicknames. But Flamethrower was less about her hair and more because the woman liked to drop bombs. She made people think, caused fires, and gave no fucks. Locke dug that about her.

CHAPTER THIRTEEN

THE PARTY AT the restaurant was in full swing, and Cassidy was hanging nonchalantly near the bar and coat check. The two staff members had been called to help with the valet as no one in their right mind had coats that night. She was all alone with the occasional shawl and sweater, essentially standing in a dark and empty closet with a full view of who came and left, depending on which way she turned. There were pillars she could post against and—

A hand tugged Cassidy back, and in a red-hot, Russian-chasing instant, she knew that it was Locke and that she shouldn't bite—even if she wanted to. His very presence awakened a hunger that she was trying to ignore. The bastard wore a peppery cologne that seemed to be an automatic arousal trigger.

Wait—was that cologne and gunpowder? Cassidy inhaled deeply, clenching her inner muscles at the reaction to his arrival.

"Shhh," he whispered against her neck.

Oh, God. That grab-and-shush move might've been more dangerous than his wink. Coupled with how he smelled—damn, it was just the whole Locke Oliver package. Still, she mumbled. He ground against her, tugging her closer, and pressed his hand over her mouth *again*.

Truth—she had fantasized about this. Maybe it was fucked-up. Maybe it was hot. But hell, it was happening. He was dominant and forceful and covering almost every inch of her. The fact that she let him cover her mouth meant she trusted him, and damn it, that turned her on. Even her nipples were painfully erect.

Cassidy inhaled deeply through her nose, easing back against him. "What is it with you?" she mumbled against his palm.

His long fingers clamped loosely, but his harsh grip around her waist did nothing but swell her lack of self-control and excitement.

"Just checking in on our conspiracy theory." Locke's stomach pressed to her back, and he towered over her—another embrace she had imagined when her vibrator was between her legs. Her vivid imagination had him unfasten his pants, lift her skirt, and slide her panties to the side. He could take her against the wall. In her mind, she had no willpower…

Back to real life. Locke abruptly jerked them into the shadows of the restaurant. The sudden, forceful move should've made her screaming mad, but it only heightened her awareness of his strength. He handled her as though she weighed nothing. His power was intoxicating—she stopped her thoughts short.

Work. They were there for work. She tried to concentrate, even though her clitoris was throbbing at the thought of him pulling her skirt up and sliding his cock inside her. A hot flash ran down her neck.

"Do we know anything new?" His lips brushed against her earlobe.

A fire started where he'd touched her skin and set every nerve ending ablaze. It wasn't right, but it was what she wanted. She was craving interactions where they danced around… *this*.

He was holding her. Still.

Possessively. Dominantly. Determinedly.

Her breathing burned loudly—so loudly she could hear it. He had to also—Locke's lips brushed her skin again. Shameless. Was he testing her? Teasing her? Didn't matter. She couldn't fight it even if it was flirting—though lips on skin was a step beyond flirting.

"What's going on here?" she whispered breathlessly. Her lips tickled as they grazed over his palm.

"What's that, Cass?" His words might well have been a ruthless stroke to her most tender areas for how deftly he delivered the gravelly vibrations against her neck.

They had a game of cat and mouse. Cassidy raised her voice. "You have to take your hand off my mouth to find out."

He squeezed it over her mouth—firmly—before releasing, and her eyes nearly rolled back into her head. Still, he kept the other arm wrapped around her stomach. A wave of arousal threatened to make her weak in the knees.

Locke ducked close to her ear, purposefully rasping a five o'clock shadow against her neck, and again asked, "*Do we know anything new?*"

She whimpered. He had to have heard the quiet groan, and he swayed them together and—damn, she *felt* him. Cassidy's eyes went wide as he held her backside against his crotch.

Was Locke turned on? *Locke was turned on.* And he wanted her to know. The realization was as potent as a narcotic. It hit her blood, and she was high.

But he'd asked about work—and he moved his arm away. What was she supposed to do? She tried to recover. Shaking and stupidly pretending this wasn't a thing, she turned. Face to face, she couldn't read him!

He didn't move. Didn't touch her. Was the ball in her court? He'd asked about Alex, *twice.* But he had a hard-on!

Cassidy was so confused and turned on that she couldn't trust her instincts. She needed to do what she did best—work. Focus on the job.

"He's in there." Cassidy, failing to regain her composure, was still breathless.

Locke smiled. "Good to know."

She'd made the right choice in focusing on work. She was there for Alex. If Locke wanted to… pursue something, he could do it when she wasn't busy. He had her number.

"Cass…" His eyebrows challenged her to admit to their tension escalating.

There was *Cass* again. She hated nicknames—until they flowed from his mouth. They needed space, but she didn't trust her legs. They were as weak as her mind was wild. She tried to swallow, shifting away—

"Don't go." He moved close, and again, he was holding her, hugging her. Locke cupped her cheek and let his fingers slide along her jaw.

She was drowning in him as Locke's hand moved down her neck, letting the thump of her pulse jump against his fingertips. "I—"

"*Excuse* me," a woman snapped as she bustled in, grabbing her shawl, and she sneered on the way out.

"Oh, God." Cassidy jumped, her cheeks hot and her embarrassment swallowing her alive. She choked on the knot in her throat and covered her face, backing away from him. "I'm so sorry."

"Cassidy." Locke reached for her.

"So, so sorry." She tilted to face him, and they stood in the dark shadows. She was the reporter; he was the protector.

His voice rumbled, not judgmental or embarrassed. "You have nothing to say sorry about. To anyone."

"We might disagree on that." She'd staked the rebound of her career on Alex, but when Locke came around, she always seemed to forget.

"I don't *try* to upset you." The pregnant pause hung heavily. "Not on purpose anyway—maybe for fun, playing around, but I won't do that again."

"Okay…"

He was playing down their moment of intimacy. Maybe for him it had been nothing but an erection and a tease, while for her it was the stuff of nightly fantasies. How foolish was she? Embarrassment made her stomach drop.

But still.

Again, they were almost stomach to stomach. Too close. Too intimate. Too… much. "I'm not upset." But that wasn't true.

"You're something," he said.

"Something," she agreed. "True." Something she'd never, ever admit to. Tugging her bottom lip between her teeth, she couldn't map out his intentions—

"Don't do that."

"Do what?" Cassidy froze, wondering what she'd done wrong.

His gaze lasered in on her lips. "*That.*"

Finally, she saw the same desperate hunger on his face. The authority in his command made her shiver. Unquenched lust boiled in his eyes, and Cassidy didn't know how to handle *this* Locke—the uncontrolled and unscripted one. "Oh… um. I…"

In a tailspin, she couldn't decide whether to fight for what she could finally read on his face or pull her act together and act like they were working together. She did neither, standing there, still unsure.

"You keep biting that lip, Cass." Locke lifted an eyebrow and scorched her panties. "Don't do that."

"Okay." The devil on her shoulder whispered, *Bite your lip again. Or bite his.* Maybe they could kiss *and* work.

Locke lifted his chin, his gaze falling past her. "Alex is leaving."

Wait—*what?* Damn it. Surprised, her arousal went cold in a microsecond. She pulled away, and he grasped her arm.

"Hold on," Locke murmured, all business, as though he were faking an embrace, unlike before.

"I need to follow him." She batted his arm away. "Whether you agree with what I'm doing or not—"

"*Not.*"

Goddamn it. She'd screwed up. Frustration and aggravation were building at record levels. "Did you do that on purpose?"

He inched closer, as though they didn't already have a microscopic minefield brewing between their lips. "Do *what* on purpose?"

She wouldn't verbalize their flirtation. She couldn't. Besides, Locke *hated* her!

Or did he? There was a finger's length of distance between them. "When did you stop hating me?"

Locke spun her around. Before she could blink, the oak-paneled wall was at her back, and his muscled chest and waist were leveled against her front. Everything about Locke was harsh and hard and hungry once again.

"What the hell are you doing?" Cassidy hissed.

He pinned her wrists overhead. "Nothing."

Her body vibrated in dark corner of the abandoned coat closet. "*Locke Oliver.*"

"Nothing," he whispered. "At all."

He'd growled and rolled a hundred misconceptions into three words.

"Good. Me either," she said in a husky rebuttal, her wrists held high above her head. "You just screwed me. I needed to watch him. Follow him. And all I did was… spend time *watching* you."

"I don't know what you're talking about."

Cassidy met Locke's harsh blue stare and bit her lip.

"Fucking hell, Cass." Locke gave her no time to understand the range of emotions that played on his face in the zero point five seconds it took for him to lean forward and tug her lip between his teeth.

His bite sent a bolt of lightning straight to her pussy, overwhelming her with how fast he could take her from wanting to kill him to wanting to come. A strong hand cupped her cheek, and he leaned forward, biting her bottom lip—and he tugged, making it hurt just enough that she groaned for more.

She pulled back, shocked and surprised, her fingers spiking out only to ball again as she relished his teeth on her lip. Locke eased the pull and let her hands loose. They fell and knotted into his shirt—tight cotton spread across a rippled abdomen. Once more, he bit her bottom lip hard enough to make her yip—and make her wet and helpless to the pleasure from the bite—and his tongue ran over it, soothing away the sting.

Fresh air tickled her lip as he pulled away. He thumbed over where his teeth had been. "Go home, Cassidy."

She blinked as if she couldn't believe it. "You just kissed me."

"No, Red. I bit you." His hand smoothed over her cheek and threaded into her hair. "If I kissed you, you would know."

Her eyes went wide. Reality splashed over her like a cold wave. This was all a diversionary tactic to put distance between her and Alex. "You had to reach deep for that one."

His eyes narrowed, questioning. "You're going home now?"

Damn him. Hell. Alex was gone. Locke had played her for a fool. She was the laughingstock of journalists everywhere. Nothing would change about her situation that night. "I was just leaving."

CHAPTER FOURTEEN

Eighteen Years Earlier

"YOUNG MAN, COME here." The man's Russian-accented words curled through the air along with the smoke from his cigarette.

When the Cadillac parked at the mouth of the alleyway, Alexander's blood had run cold. Now his eyes tracked side to side, as though maybe he'd missed anyone else the boss could be speaking to.

No. There was nobody else sitting in the frozen alley beside Alexander, and the man stood out like a pariah. He wore a thick black jacket and fur hat, while Alexander shivered with his legs tucked underneath him for warmth. Curled on the dirty, pocked asphalt, he nursed a bottle of cheap vodka he'd stolen for both warmth and escape.

"Come here." His black leather gloves gestured, fingers beckoning.

Still, Alexander looked again on either side in case there was a reason why this Mikhailov boss had decided to speak to him.

Not wanting to show disrespect, he said, "Me?"

"Dah." Even with a simple word, the man sounded better educated than the Bratva and the caliber that hung out with his Dad.

"Can I help you?" Alexander offered all the manners and formality as he could muster with numb lips. That was the work of the alcohol. It wasn't that cold outside. Or maybe it was—he didn't know.

"I have a proposition for you. Would you like to go to lunch?"

His stomach growled as if answering for him. Somewhere in the back of his mind, he should question who this person was and what he wanted of him, but Alexander hadn't had lunch for some time now that school was on winter break. He'd eaten on and off several times, but nothing that would constitute a meal. "Sure."

The Mikhailov man pulled out a cell phone, and then the car in which he'd arrived revved its engine. "The heat is on. Let us go. My name is Ivan."

Ivan Mikhailov? That couldn't have been correct. He was like a king! Why would Ivan Mikhailov talk to him? In an alley? Maybe Alexander had had more to drink than he realized.

The man walked away with the clear understanding that Alexander would follow. Lunch involved getting in that car. While he should have been concerned, alcohol and hunger made him stupid. But *stupid* was relative—he was hungrier than he was stupid. He pushed himself up and followed the man into the waiting car.

CHAPTER FIFTEEN

Present Day

THE RESTAURANT'S PATIO was packed with the happy-hour crowd from Embassy Row and neighboring think tanks. Cassidy never liked nightlife that had a DC feel, where everyone had security clearances and the more they drank, the louder they talked about how they knew things they couldn't share. Power begot power begot privilege begot attention. And wasn't that what this town was all about?

"Excuse me." Cassidy quietly caught the attention of her server as her sparkling water was refilled. "The man over there." She tilted her head, gesturing nonchalantly. "Is he a regular? Do you know his name?"

"No, sorry," the waitress said.

"Could you find out his name?"

The waitress blankly stared and waited. Most folks had a price, and the young woman, maybe a college student, would probably stand there until Cassidy made an offer. Wait staff had helped Cassidy sniff out the start of more stories than she could count. For them, she'd forever be grateful. She opened her clutch and pulled out a fifty. "Last name too. It's that important."

Cassidy had turned in her *Times* op-ed on St. Andrew's to the board of trustees, and they, as expected, needed clarification on Alex's remarks. Again, like pulling teeth, it took days to get him to commit to meeting her. Finally, he'd made plans to meet her here to work on the comments—which would take no more than fifteen minutes of back-and-forth—but, so far, he was a no show.

He'd also ignored her texts. Marvelous… and suspicious, because he'd mentioned that later that night he was meeting people from his non-St.

Andrew's job at the same restaurant. Which was why Cassidy had stuck around.

An hour after her arranged meeting time with Alex, who she guessed were the non-St. Andrew's crew showed up.

Thirty minutes later, they too were pissed, but they were pissed in Russian, so she didn't know *how* annoyed they were, but she could read body language. That and facial expressions were a universal language—except when it came to Locke.

Her server came back as the other table began to stand and leave. *Shit.* Cassidy's heart jumped. She wanted to know more about them. Quickly, she snapped a picture as her server looked on with disinterest.

"His credit card said Ivan Jacobs."

Cassidy made a face. "*Ivan,* I might believe." But how many native Russians had the surname Jacobs?

"That's what I said too." The waitress preened. "Not my first rodeo. Last name Mikhailov."

Ivan Mikhailov. "You're amazing," Cassidy said.

"I'll still need a tip on the food and drink."

"Absolutely. Not my first DC rodeo."

As the waitress was stepping away, a hand touched Cassidy's shoulder. In an instant, she knew it was that lip-biting bastard she hated to fall for and had thought about nonstop since the days she stormed away.

"What are you doing here?" Cassidy waited until he took a seat so he could take full advantage of the professional-league eye roll awaiting him. "Because I am all kinds of not interested in talking to you."

He scooted his chair in as if he didn't notice the sarcasm and eye rolling. "Hey, Shortcake."

"And the nicknames do you no favors with me."

He gave her a closed-lip smile as if to say he didn't care if she liked the nicknames or not. "I like them."

"Why?"

"Because I think you do."

He was right, and she disliked him even more because of that.

"What are we doing here tonight?" he asked.

Cassidy folded her hands primly. "*We* aren't doing anything."

"I passed the Russians on my way in."

"Good." She clenched her jaw. "I hope you told Mr. Mikhailov hello."

Locke's eyes immediately jumped to the exit, but he didn't respond. Damn it; she couldn't read him, other than seeing that he recognized the last name.

"How'd you learn that?" he asked.

"I have my ways."

Locke repositioned his chair, scraping it on the patio tiles. "Interesting crowd."

"Depending on where your interests lie."

"And where do yours?"

"With Russians."

"Hmm." He pushed his chair back on two legs. "Then a happy hour of foreign-policy movers and shakers is where you want to be."

"Yup." The real question was why an English teacher would hang out here or go to the Russian ambassador's house.

Locke dropped his chair down, and she jumped as he touched her wrist. "You're mad about the other night."

Not a question—more like Locke decided to announce the truth. Too self-confident for his own good even when he must have seen her react to his simple touch. She hated how one little touch could do so much. Still, she put up a good front. "Gee. You think?"

"Don't be." His fingers ran along the curve of her wrist bone.

She shivered. Her nipples hardened—or had they been tight since he arrived? Cassidy pulled her hand away. "Go away, Locke. The whole bite-me-to-distract-me thing? You suck." As a matter of fact… She cleared her head and ignored that he turned her on with just a touch and a look. "What are you doing here, anyway?"

"I'm keeping tabs on Alex."

Her eyes went wide. That was enough to douse her arousal. "You're *what*?"

Locke shrugged broad shoulders. "You lobbed a pretty sizable accusation about him."

"Then where is he?" Cassidy threw her arms out.

"He was about to walk in an hour ago when he received a phone call. Stopped midstride. Took it. Had a pretty heated conversation, turned around, and left."

"What the hell?"

"Weird, right?" He shrugged. "The guy just went home."

"He…" What the hell? "But *you* came back here?"

"I saw your car," Locke said. "And I was curious."

"About…?"

"I don't know. I drove by. Your car was still here. I parked and came in."

Oh… what did that mean? "You still shouldn't have…bit me the other night."

Locke's blue eyes intensified. "Why are you so hell-bent on believing that it's because I wanted to distract you from Alex?" He leaned his chair back on two legs again.

Cassidy opened her mouth, unable to answer that, or maybe unwilling to. The waitress came over and held out the bill. "Are you leaving or adding an order?"

She looked at Locke and wasn't sure how to handle him. "I'm going." And then she immediately tried *not* to recalculate the tip as her waitress blatantly checked him out. "And I have no idea what he's doing."

"I'm leaving with you," he said.

"Separately, simultaneously," Cassidy clarified for his benefit, *not* the server's.

Locke rocked in his seat. "Whatever you say, beautiful."

Damn.

Damn, damn, damn him. The word skipped its way along every nerve until even her fingertips buzzed.

With the bill dropped on the table, Cassidy paid in cash and looked over to find him scrutinizing the conversation-worthy crowd—dignitaries and politicians, the likes of whom she might want to report on. But he was the most interesting one here.

"I didn't plan on coming in." He leaned back again. "Not my crowd. I don't think I fit in."

"Not mine either."

He dropped his chair and pulled it close to her. "They're all lost in their agendas. So damn important. All of them."

They were only inches separating them. "Importance is relative."

His full lips broke into a half smile, but it hitched higher on one cheek—and paused. "Hey, Red."

Red? She wanted to snap at him, but his voice went gravelly, and his eyes studied every inch of her, from her face to her feet, and even though her chin snapped up indignantly at the nickname, she loved his attention.

"You look good in a dress."

"Oh." Wow, he'd caught her off guard with that one, and the warmth of a blush hit her cheeks, flipping her stomach. "Thanks."

"I keep meaning to tell you that."

"You're too busy thinking about ridiculous names to think of a compliment. I get it."

"One will stick. It'll be a you-and-me thing." He leaned closer, an elbow on his knee. "But Shortcake is off the list, right?"

"It should never have been on it." Forcing a chuckle, she nodded and concentrated on the *you-and-me thing*, trying not to overthink the situation.

"True enough." He pushed back, and she hated that he moved away. "What's your favorite? It's not Riding Hood."

"*No.*" And she'd never admit to liking "beautiful," though she'd die a thousand times to hear that again. She'd replay that alone tonight, thinking about him, how she shivered when his fingers slid against her wrist, and what kind of things would be considered *you and me.* "You're not supposed to pick out your nickname, Locke—and stop focusing on my hair."

"Why? It's gorgeous."

"I..." Oh, fuck it. She wanted him so much it hurt—his mouth on hers, her fingers in his hair. But really, she wanted to see what she could say that might make him feel like she just did. What could she whisper, what could she do? Touch him, taste him, take him. She inhaled deeply at the thought of climbing on top of him—and he had *no idea* she had these thoughts. Oh boy. Cassidy pulled it together, regaining her composure, which meant maybe pushing his buttons.

He pursed his lips. "I'll find one that works for the both of us."

"I don't know. You've been doing so well so far."

He rolled his eyes. A first! Who knew he had it in him. It made her like him all the more.

"Come on, Cassidy. Let's go."

He pulled her out of her chair, sliding next to her as though he were meant to be there. The immediate connection at the hip made her mouth go dry and her insides wake up—more than they already had.

He smelled sexy and spicy—like something she couldn't name but might spend the rest of the evening trying to remember. Locke's fingers flexed into her side as they moved from the patio. The small covered walkway was nothing more than a brick alley leading them to a quiet night away—he abruptly stopped, disengaging from her side.

"You okay?" she asked.

His forehead pinched, and he glanced away.

Locke didn't say a word but refocused on her. He simply stood there, staring at her as if she had seventeen heads and all of them were purple—not red. No redhead nicknames were coming out of his mouth. He didn't look amused. He didn't look irritated or ready to lecture her.

"What's the matter? That's not a Locke Oliver face I know." He was impossible to figure out, and that was maddening.

"Cassidy." His voice had dropped very low.

Between his tone and her real name, anticipation curled uneasily in her stomach. "What?"

His eyes narrowed as though he was wary of her. "What happened that night?"

"What night?" With Alex or in Russia or—

"Sadr City."

That was where his mind went? "Why did you think about that?"

"Why not?"

Because it was years later, they weren't talking about Iraq, and maybe a dozen other reasons. But that was what pain looked like on Locke's face. Pain, plus confusion and destruction.

"What about Mike Draven?" Now Locke wouldn't even look at her—until he did. The judgment in his stare made her take a step back as he asked, "How close were you?"

"*What?*"

"You two date? Sleep together?" Locke lifted a shoulder.

Her eyes peeled back so far she must have looked rabid—but then her heart sank. Was he asking if she'd slept her way to a source and wondering if she'd do it again with him? Was he thinking about sleeping with her, and that was where his mind went? Was she forever stained with Sadr City?

Her eyes welled with tears, and she blinked them away, surprised they'd even sprung. It wasn't the first time someone had asked if she'd slept with Mike, but it had been in the context of hearings or even the politics of why female reporters shouldn't embed with male troops. Never had it been from someone she imagined sleeping with. "Tell me you didn't just say that." And thank God he didn't know what she'd just been thinking.

"Just a question," he muttered.

It wasn't Locke's business how close she was to his commanding officer. What Locke didn't know—hell, what most didn't know—was Mike Draven had been in a long-term committed relationship. With a man.

That wasn't newsworthy. Cassidy didn't care. Draven had been desperate for more resources, though, and sick and tired of getting approvals, all the way up the chain of command, just to be denied by his commander-in-chief based on a campaign promise that had nothing to do with keeping his men safe or leaving Iraq in a sustainable condition. The US had agreed to pull out, whether or not it was safe and sane.

Draven had been one of Cassidy's many on-the-record sources. But he was, more importantly, her anonymous source. And then the worst happened, just as he predicted: they were attacked.

She survived. Locke survived. Twenty-six men did not.

Sadr City touched on so many issues. She fell on the sword to protect Michael Draven's name, his sexuality, his leadership, and his memory. Because of it, she was disowned by so many in her field while so many others lifted her up as a hero. Cassidy never wanted to be a conversation piece. She wanted to do what was right.

Dissent and the truth—those were patriotic. The Night of Fire had made Cassidy a controversial figure.

But Locke didn't see any of that, and worse, he'd just questioned what she did sexually.

"No. I wasn't sleeping with him." Brushing him away, she picked her way across the uneven brick sidewalk and passed under an archway covered in barren wisteria branches.

"Cassidy, wait." He grasped her shoulder.

She shook him away and kept going to her Jeep. "If that's all, good night."

"No, that's not all." Locke hurried next to her. "You don't get to storm away."

"I don't get to?" Abruptly, she turned. Her war-torn, broken heart went cold. Inwardly, she raged, but outwardly, she became as calm as she did during a congressional hearing. "I've asked you before if you want to talk. You *repeatedly* said no."

He stepped closer. "Now I do."

"No." She jabbed him in the chest with her finger. "That's *not* how you open the discussion."

He dropped his chin and studied the finger jammed into his sternum. Obviously, she'd let go of her congressional-hearing chillness. Realizing that, she dropped her hand.

"Everything boils down to sex," he said. "It always does."

"I pity you if you really believe that." There were gag orders, there was the professional integrity, and there was the respect for her friend's personal life. It had kept her quiet, sent her to prison, and destroyed her career. Yet she wanted to share everything with Locke even though he hadn't earned a shred of it and had made an awful assumption.

Locke swatted away her limp hand. "How close were you two?"

"What does it matter?" A tear threatened to fall, and she swore that if she cried in front of him, she would never forgive herself.

His head dropped, and he let it hang before shaking it again as though he pitied her. Finally, he lifted his chin. The expression in his eyes wasn't pity. It wasn't anger or even the acidic vitriol that they'd just volleyed back and forth. What was it…?

"I don't want to see you be number twenty-seven."

"Nothing you just said had to do with looking out for me," she whispered.

Locke scrubbed his face. "Fucking hell. I don't know."

Uncertainty plowed through her like a locomotive train, heavy and unable to stop. "You don't have to look out for me, Locke."

"I know."

"Then stop."

"I…" He caught himself, and they both stared. "It was years ago, and it's not my business if you did."

Cassidy rolled her lips into her mouth, not sure if this was the start of an agreement or if he was angry that they had chemistry, and because of that, she allowed him to get away with his line of questioning. She didn't want to feel any spark and sizzle for someone who lobbed accusations like that. "You know that's sexist as shit?"

"It is? No, it's not."

"Assuming that I'd sleep with someone for information? That I couldn't get it without sex?" She scowled. "Sexist. As. Fuck."

"I didn't say that." His head dropped. "Damn it. That's not what I meant. But…" He rubbed his temple. "I didn't assume. I asked. I was curious."

"The thought shouldn't cross your mind, Locke."

He looked up and dropped his head back. "You know…" He laughed. "It's not funny. I get that. But fucking hell, you sound like my mom, and she's never wrong."

Cassidy unexpectedly broke into a small smile. "Well then…"

"He wouldn't either, would he?" Locke asked quietly.

Cassidy cringed. That was a loaded question she wasn't going to touch because it could mean so many different things. Did Locke think that Mike wouldn't sleep with her because of his leadership role in the army, or because he was her friend? Maybe Locke even suspected that Mike was in a relationship already or perhaps guessed his commanding officer wasn't attracted to women.

Cassidy shrugged and tried to ignore the fact that her shoulders were as heavy as the weight of the memories. "I'm taking off. Good night."

She pivoted on her heel and concentrated on the uneven brick sidewalk.

"Hey," Locke called.

Cassidy turned.

"Does the last name Mikhailov mean anything to you?" he asked.

She shook her head, though Locke's reaction earlier and the way he said it now meant that she should know that name. She made a mental note to Google it.

He nodded, looking away as if lost in thought. "Don't be number twenty-seven, Cassidy. It hurt too much to lose all of them, and losing you… be careful around anything to do with the Mikhailovs."

The twenty-six they'd lost, and how his voice ached for her—his pain radiated enough that she felt it, and her eyes sank shut. Cassidy inhaled deeply, wondering how long she could hold her breath before it hurt.

Holding. Still holding. Her lungs burned, and it hurt… Letting go of the breath, she opened her eyes, and he was waiting for her. Breathless and lightheaded, she said, "People told me life goes on."

His head dropped.

"But," she whispered, her throat hurting, "that's the worst part."

Locke had pinched the bridge of his nose before he ran his hand through his hair. "The Mikhailovs are dangerous."

"I'll be cognizant of that. Thank you." She stepped closer. "You constantly seem aware they're gone, and even if I was sleeping with Mike, don't ruin your memory of him because you don't want to get close to me."

He held her gaze.

"Night, Locke." That was as much as she could voice about what had been happening between them.

CHAPTER SIXTEEN

BRIGHT AND EARLY on Saturday morning, Cassidy nervously pressed the call icon on her phone. She twirled a pen at her desk and stared at the pile of balled-up notes she'd tossed at her trash can and missed.

Why calling Alex was suddenly nerve-racking made no sense, except for the fact that she was indeed investigating him, whereas before she'd just been suspicious of him. It was an entirely different game. The phone rang twice.

"Hello?" Alex answered.

She had expected his voice mail after he'd stood her up. Maybe it was because of her time spent reporting on politicians and people surrounded by scandal. Those types never answered their phones.

"Hey, it's Cassidy."

"Sorry about the other night." He groaned, genuinely sounding distraught.

"What happened?"

"I got sick. Food poisoning or something."

Liar, liar! Locke had seen him almost come in and then leave. "Yuck. Are you feeling better?"

"Much."

"Good, because I'm getting a ton of pressure to finish up."

"I know. The school board emailed asking about it too."

She bet those trustees didn't mess around. "Can I come over? Meet you somewhere?"

Alex hummed. "I'm slammed today."

"This will be quick. I'll work with you, meet you anywhere. It's just a couple follow-up questions. Tonight?"

He laughed. "You wouldn't be able to hear me where I have to go."

"Oh yeah?" She laughed too, trying to commiserate. Would he tell her again where he was going? She could work with that. "Where to?"

"Some place called Red Star."

"I'm familiar! A club?"

"Yeah, awful," he grumbled.

She groaned, sympathizing. "That doesn't seem like your scene."

"Nope."

"Certainly not mine."

"Nope," he agreed.

"Probably by about ten years." Cassidy was happy to find common ground and could hear him relaxing. "What exactly is St. Andrew's doing business there for?"

"Well, it's not exactly school-related—that side job I mentioned before. Anyway, I still have to be there, but next week? Honestly, Cassidy. I'm very flexible normally, just this weekend is tough."

"Okay, no problem." She bit her lip. "I'll make it work. Text you soon."

They ended the call, and Cassidy sat there with the phone in her hand. Why would Alex go to Red Star? That club wasn't too far from the Russian embassy, the coat check where Locke bit her lip, and the patio where Alex stood her up. Coincidence?

He was hanging with the wrong folks and spending time in their neighborhoods. Doing what, and with whom, she had no idea. The how and why evaded her.

"God!" Cassidy tossed her phone. "What is he up to?"

CASSIDY'S FRUSTRATION WITH Alex hadn't taken long to get over because her mind was stuck on Locke, and she'd immediately messaged her friend Jennifer with an SOS text for girl chat and a cookie-dough meet-up. Jennifer's response had been a string of emoji happy faces.

A couple of hours later, with a spoonful of cookie dough in hand, Cassidy leaned against the wall catty-corner to the Cannon office building with Jennifer as they watched the people wander out of the metro.

"I can't believe this." Cassidy ate her cookie dough and scowled at the score of their game. "You're winning by ten points."

"I am. So are we going to get into the nitty-gritty of why we're doing this?" A spoon dangled from Jennifer's hand. "Not that I'm complaining. I just—oh, there's one. Three points."

The intern-aged kid with a bowtie popped out of Capitol South's metro station. "Damn. How did I miss that?"

Congress was in recess, and it was the weekend. Jennifer didn't have much to cover, as most members had gone home. The ones who were hiding in DC weren't making news.

Jennifer had been a die-hard supporter of Cassidy's since the day they'd met, when Cassidy was released from prison for refusing to give up her source. Neither one took DC too seriously, to the extent that they had assigned point values for various Capitol Hill clichés and faux pas.

Five points for staffers who stood on the left side of the escalator—they should know better. Three points for bow ties. Three points for protesters with unintentionally misspelled signs. The rest were one-pointers: bicyclists on the sidewalk, strollers on metro escalators, taxi cabs that ignored stop signs…

But that wasn't the point of the cookie-dough meet-up, and Jennifer knew it. Cassidy shoved another spoonful of cookie dough into her mouth, mumbling a purposefully incoherent answer as to why they were having an emergency calorie-laden get-together.

"I didn't know you were seeing anyone." Jennifer pointed her spoon. "Not cool for leaving me in the dark."

Cassidy choked. "I'm not."

"Right. We're eating cookie dough and fashion-shaming preppy intern's regrettable casual wear choices at"—she grabbed her phone—"twenty past ten on a Saturday morning. Speaking of which, we need to upgrade the bow-tie thing. Weekend bow-tie wearers need an exponential value. But nonetheless, we're here. With cookie dough. And you're evasive as fuck. There's a man. Or there was."

Cassidy gobbled up another spoonful. "No comment."

"Mm-hmm."

"Mm-hmm," Cassidy agreed.

They ate in silence, and Cassidy thought over everything Locke had said and alluded to.

Jennifer tapped. "You liked him, huh?"

"Yeah, I think so."

"Why?"

"No idea." Cassidy dug into the cookie dough and made sure to get extra chocolate chips.

"Ha! Bull, honey. Bull with a capital B. You don't do anything without a reason."

True. "He's nice on the eyes."

"They always are."

"And…" This time Cassidy pointed her spoon at Jennifer. "I want to work with him."

Her friend's ebony eyes widened. "He's a reporter?"

"No."

"So, he's what? Cameraman? Private investigator? Sound tech? Who are you working with these days?"

"No, he's more like… I don't know. He's a buddy."

"A buddy, huh? I can think of different types of buddies you can have."

Cassidy rolled her eyes. Locke as a fuck buddy—in her dreams. Literally. But in real life, Cassidy was sure that a casual, no-strings fling with Locke would be a disaster. "I just like how his mind works."

"All the ones who are nice on the eyes have dirty minds, but don't confuse the words and promises for love when they make your panties drop."

"They haven't dropped." Cassidy blushed.

"Wait, really?" Jennifer tilted her head. "Tell me more."

"It's not like that. He hated me." She still wasn't clear when that had transitioned. "Except we almost kissed. But it wasn't a kiss; he just sort of bit my lip, and maybe it was a diversion. I think the best classification is buddies. Locke and I are buddies. I think."

Jennifer's hands flew up, backing the conversation down. "Wait. *What?* A diversion? He's biting you? What is going on?"

"See? It's confusing."

"What's the diversion?" Jennifer asked, looking as confused as Cassidy felt.

"I'm investigating a person of interest, and he didn't want to me to see something. So… he picked me up. Twirled me around."

"You're lying."

"It was one of those moments where you feel your heart, as if it's talking to you. Seesawing in your chest. When your arms feel like putty, and your legs are weightless."

"Oh, Cassidy…" Jennifer let her words drift.

"He said don't, and I did. So yeah."

"Don't what?"

She blushed again. "Bite my lip."

"I'm having a hot flash—he just bit yours?"

Cassidy nodded, failing to hide a Locke-fueled smile. "There may've been a little lip-tug."

Jennifer's spoon-holding hand limply fell. "Huh."

"Yeah, huh." What else was there to say?

"If we gave points for kisses, I'd call a bite a kiss, even if there wasn't tongue and smooch action." Jennifer dug for more cookie dough. "The intent was there."

"Remember, it may have been diversionary."

Jennifer sat with that for a moment then continued to scrape more cookie dough. "You had a moment. That's all that matters."

"Yes. I did…" Even now, the memory of his manhandling her into the corner, his arms wrapped around her, turned her on.

"Kisses that catch fire aren't fake." She punctuated the sentiment with a pointed heap of cookie dough. "They might be a million things. Scared. Too soon. Never enough. But you can't pretend a spark doesn't shine." Then she turned the spoon over and swallowed the cookie dough. "Damn. There's nothing as good as cookie dough and Cassidy Noble falling for a guy."

"I'm not falling. I'm eating cookie dough and ignoring that maybe my feelings were trounced by that guy."

"If he trounced them, then you had them, and that's something, considering it's you."

Her phone buzzed, and that moment where she hoped the text message would be from him absolutely killed her. When had Locke invaded her thoughts to the point where she hoped to hear from him when her phone buzzed?

Ugh. She shook her head, annoyed at herself. That feeling of hope should've been disgust, starting the moment when he accused her of sleeping with someone to get the job done. That was when he went from respecting her to questioning who she was, and that hurt, even if they did wrap the evening up with a heartfelt moment about staying safe.

Still, Cassidy held out a slice of hope that he'd texted her. She pulled the phone from her bag, and—it was him.

"Now, there's a happy face," Jennifer said, eyeing her phone. "Well, what's the boy say?"

Cassidy gave her a side-eye. "Not a boy."

"Ermehgawd. The *man*. Give me a break."

She swiped the message and read it then glanced back up, biting her cookie-dough-flavored lip. She showed the phone to Jennifer.

LOCKE: *So...*

"That's it?" Jennifer's dark brows lifted incredulously, and then her mouth made an *O* shape as wide as her eyes as the phone buzzed again, and Cassidy pulled it back to read the message.

LOCKE: *I'm a jackass.*

"That's like killer 'I'm sorry' in Dude," Jennifer reported in her most professional voice.

Cassidy squinted at her. "Do you string those words together on air?"

"Shut it, and do not downplay the significance of an apology from the *man*."

She typed back and let Jennifer in on her response.

CASSIDY: *I know.*

"Seems appropriate."

Her phone buzzed again, and Jennifer asked, "What'd he say?"

LOCKE: *Did you look up Mikhailov?"*

She had looked Mikhailov up, and she'd found more than she expected about the former KGB and FSB family with ties to Russian crime clans in the US, particularly a group that the Internet called the Baltimore Bratva.

CASSIDY: *Maybe…*

LOCKE: *There's an interesting meeting tonight at a local hot spot.*

CASSIDY: *Interesting. There's a teacher we know with plans to hit up a club tonight.*

LOCKE: *Interesting…*

CASSIDY: *Yup…*

"Let me see," Jennifer said and snatched the phone. "Oh, this is work. Well, maybe. Look at you two and your overuse of ellipses."

Cassidy rolled her eyes. "Thank you, grammar princess."

"Ask *the man* to the club."

She balked. "No way."

"It's not a date. You want to work with him. *Ellipsis.* He's done some legwork. *Ellipsis.* You two go work together. *Ellipsis.*"

"Why did I share with you again?" Cassidy hesitated then reached for the cookie dough—and Jennifer grabbed her phone.

"Jennifer! What are we, twelve?"

"Apparently," she said, quickly typing as she fended Cassidy off.

The phone buzzed as Locke responded to whatever Jennifer had typed.

"*Jennifer!*"

She read it and grinned, handing over the phone. "Nope, but you are a reporter with a partner."

CASSIDY: *Let's go.*

LOCKE: *Sounds good.*

"Don't even pretend you mind." Jennifer dug her spoon into the cookie dough. "Everything just happened like it was supposed to."

THE THUMPING BASS of Red Star vibrated outside the Russian club's doors. This wasn't where Alexander wanted to be. Clubs weren't his scene. Neither were most of the Mikhailovs' businesses. But he'd always been their errand boy. That was how he'd met Taisia in college.

The long line wrapped past the length of the velvet rope. Two bouncers Alexander knew from over the years stood by the door. If Ivan didn't require an update on Alexander's work, then he would rather be at home working on it, and getting closer to Taisia and Alyona, rather than talking about it. But Ivan liked to hear himself talk.

A woman in a skirt that was no longer than a tissue continued to walk by, back and forth, hoping for his attention—which she would never get. He ignored her and the heartburn that sloshed in his chest. It wasn't so much what he was doing, it was that Taisia didn't approve—but she never approved of his relationship with her father.

She'd had a fit the night before, promising this wasn't the way, dancing in circles that her father was getting worse and worse as he aged, not relaxing into retirement as they had one time mused he might.

Taisia didn't know how far up the Mikhailov organization Alexander had climbed. She couldn't have known the type of work he'd progressed to and how Ivan needed Alexander. Growing up with a high-ranking KGB agent as a father colored her vision of how influential and manipulative the Mikhailovs were. She constantly fretted over how the KGB worked over assets: *They work you. They wait until it's right.*

Maybe. But the time was right for both him and Ivan.

Taisia didn't see that the KGB no longer existed, and she acted as though the FSB and the KGB were one and the same.

Until it's right…

Alexander rubbed his chest, and Taisia's angry words echoed in his ears. "*You're working with my father, aren't you?*"

He was giving Ivan Mikhailov what he wanted: information gained illegally. Stolen from influential people.

Alexander squeezed his eyes shut. Anything was for sale if it meant access to his daughter. That was why Ivan had pulled off Alexander's kill order and opened the lines of communication. His daughter and granddaughter were for sale after years of Ivan's fury.

One of the bouncers flagged him over, and Alexander drew near. "Yeah?"

"He's running late. Would you like to wait on the inside?"

With the music, the alcohol, and the lust? "The fresh air works for me tonight. Thanks."

The bouncer nodded. "He's bringing someone for you."

Alexander tried not to cringe at how Ivan operated. He was a *bábnik*. Americans would call it a pimp. Women were commodities, and of course, Taisia would know this but also that Alexander wouldn't touch another woman.

What she didn't understand was that Alexander would do anything for their daughter. He'd worked with both their fathers and the Bratva his entire life. There was no question that he'd take it to the next level to see his daughter and become a family.

Across the street, a man held a pregnant woman's hand as they threaded through the late-night crowd. Alexander's mind flew back to years before, when Taisia had said the scariest, most fantastic words he'd ever heard. "The doctor said I'm not sick. I'm pregnant with a *baby. Rebenok.*"

A baby. Still, the word *rebenok* brought him to his knees.

Taisia had been his girlfriend. The baby was nothing that they had planned but everything that they could handle. There was no question it'd be hard in college, but their love made them stupid and blind and able to dream the impossible. A family that wouldn't be like the one he was born into. It would be a real family. A warm one. People who loved each other and did nice things. Who had nice things. Where kids were tucked in bed at night and food was served at meals.

He couldn't wait to have a family. One second, Alexander was walking around, waiting for the day that he could shout that he would be a daddy as Taisia smiled and giggled, patiently waiting until they passed a random day circled on their calendar. Because it would be "safer." Because things "happened."

What seemed like the next second, his dreams died. Things happened—*no*. Her father happened. Ivan couldn't stomach a grandchild born on American soil.

Alexander had never said goodbye. He came back from class, and the apartment was empty. Her clothes were gone. Their patchwork home of mismatched furniture, pictures in frames, and decorations pulled together by broke college students on a budget left no sign of her.

Ivan sent a low-level Bratva lieutenant to deliver a simple message. "Don't chase her."

Their apartment didn't even smell like her anymore. Everything had been bleached and wiped down from top to bottom. All traces of the woman he loved were gone, and Alexander was destroyed. He'd collapsed on the floor, weeping for his woman pregnant with his child. There had been nothing he could do over the years other than attempted and shared Internet messages.

Eight years later, he still hadn't held Alyona. Alexander respected Taisia's concerns, but to hell with her worry. They had an offer she was unaware of. Ivan had put his daughter and grandchild up for sale.

A Suburban with tinted windows pulled to the front of the club. Without a doubt, Alexander knew it would be the Russians. A moment later, the front passenger door opened, and Ivan appeared with a woman in his lap. She fell off, giggling and sloshed. Scantily dressed and ready to party, the model lookalike matched the stereotypical cliché of Russian FSB arm candy.

The back doors opened to reveal Mikhailov associates he knew. They followed the same routine as they exited the Suburban with women on their arms who were wearing what he would consider loincloths and sequin pasties. They had long legs and high heels, beautiful hair and bright eyes, and were marred by the mask of alcohol.

Maybe it had something to do with how Alexander had grown up, but he hated drunkenness to the point of oblivion. He didn't mind a good vodka and appreciated a good liquor. But getting drunk to forget, as these women were doing? He had no respect for that. They were the entertainment for the evening. And one of those beauties had been assigned to Alexander. Ivan was disgusting.

Speaking of disgusting, Ivan greeted him as they walked toward the entrance. The bouncers said nothing. Only a short nod, and the door was theirs to go through. One or two people who waited in line were stupid enough to complain, and the bouncers moved to throw them out. Alexander knew what would happen without even seeing the next steps as they disappeared into the dark cloak of the club.

CHAPTER SEVENTEEN

CASSIDY WAS TOO old to be in a club. The dress was too small. Too tight. Too everything that made it perfect for where she was going. The point was to blend in, and this dress did that. But that didn't mean Cassidy liked the ensemble. She wore a jet-black wig—not one that made her look like a Halloween freak, but a sexy one with a stylish bob—and it totally worked. She had a couple of them just for such occasions—undercover work. And she loved the shoes. Honestly, she loved the dress. Why lie to herself? But it was a date-ish dress that showed a lot of skin, and she worried it was too much as she waited for Locke.

Cassidy turned, and—the awe hit. There he was, ambling down the sidewalk like it was just another night where the sea of people parted for him. His clothes stood out but weren't flashy, his blond hair was brushed back but still had a bad-boy wildness that matched the sharp cut of his chin and jaw bones. She'd never noticed how gentle his eyes were and how his lips could turn up in an almost lazy smile.

"You're early," he said, closing the distance, his gaze tracking from her heels to her hair.

Cassidy enjoyed every second he took to appreciate her. It didn't feel as if he was ogling but rather as if he was memorizing her. "I am?"

"Well, I was, which means you are."

"Oh, well, maybe a minute."

"You're not a redhead tonight." Locke seemed as if he couldn't hide his smile—and was that a little color on his cheeks?

"You like?"

"There isn't a man alive who wouldn't appreciate how you look."

Now it was her turn with the smile she couldn't help. "Was I too easy to spot?"

"No." He gave an easy headshake. "I think I'm just damn good at knowing what you look like, Cassidy."

She shivered, his words traversing up her spine and pricking down her arms, leaving the hairs on her arm standing on end. "Oh…"

"It's hot. I'll give you that."

She blushed. "I was just going for different. And club appropriate."

Locke's smoldering blue eyes melted away every other person on the street. "Whatever you were going for, it worked."

Her heart jumped past a few beats before it exploded into fireworks. "Thanks."

He let that sit for a second before nodding. "Are you ready?"

"Off to work we go." She hoped she could pull it together and breathe like a normal, sane person. Time would only tell.

Locke put his hand on her back, escorting her down the sidewalk, and at that point she wagered that no, she wasn't going to be able to breathe easy around him. They passed the long line, and his fingertips pressed against the base of her spine, sliding to her hip. He had a casual, chill demeanor, and he approached the bouncer, quietly conversing before the man stepped aside. Whatever or whoever Titan knew, it came in handy.

"After you." Locke's hands trailed along her waist, falling away from her butt just as she ascended the stairs and walked in.

Yes, it was work, and they both knew how to dig into a cover, but his hands on her body were the things dreams were made of. "Thanks."

Once Locke and Cassidy were in the door, those hands possessively found her waist again, and the familiar position of her back to his stomach came into play. For two people who didn't know one another in a very personal way, they had clocked a lot of body-against-body time.

"Do you see Alex?" Locke asked as they made their rounds.

"No. You?"

"I see *nichto*."

She turned in his arms. "Is that zero?"

"Maybe? Good guess? I don't know." Locke kept his arms around her, walking them to the edge of an intimate dance floor with electronic beats.

The lights were low, and blue lasers jumped across the crowd as they swayed with the downbeat.

She couldn't help but dance to the music. She didn't know whether to blame the fact that he towered over her, that he had to dip closer to be heard, or even that they were simply pretending to hit the club, but her hips had a mind of their own as she rolled with the music. As she grooved, he moved with her, and when she caught his face, she liked that he wasn't unreadable. The man of stone was no more, starting with his smile but not ending with him moving on the dance floor.

Beckoning him closer, she whispered, "I was wrong about you."

His hair tickled her cheek as he brushed her ear. "Say that again?"

"Maybe I was wrong."

Locke pulled back and squinted, shaking his head.

He still couldn't hear her? It wasn't *that* loud. Cassidy grabbed Locke's cheeks and pulled him close, her lips pressed next to the shell of his ear. "I was wrong about you too."

"I know." He laughed as her hands drifted from his cheeks, but he gripped them there, sliding down her forearm.

Her eyes went wide. "You could hear me!"

"Every word." He wrapped his arms around her. "Do I have to apologize for that too?"

God, it felt good to let go in his arms. Cassidy laughed like she hadn't in… forever. It had to be the dress and the club—or the wig—or *the man* forcing her to relax, because she hadn't had a drop to drink. "Okay."

"Okay? That wasn't an answer to my question."

Cassidy sobered as they stood stomach to stomach. They still hovered on the periphery of the gyrating dance floor, and the darkness swirled around them. Her arms folded in between them, almost as though she could rest her chin on her knuckles, and Locke let go of her and moved his grip to hold her wrists, his thumb gently smoothing over her skin.

"You're not the one who's been hardheaded." She wondered if he knew the gentle touch made her want to kiss him. Funny, he was only touching her hands and her knuckles, but everything about the caress was soft and careful. It made her insides flutter knowing how he could do opposites:

hard and harsh, gentle and soft. He was Special Forces, an elite warrior, one of the strongest, bravest men she'd ever seen work. But here he was, and she loved it.

Locke's thumbs stopped, and he winked. "What's your angle here, Roxy? Reporters always have an angle."

Oh, the wink she was powerless to. His timing was flawless, but she wouldn't let him know—though all she could think about retorting with was the nickname. "Roxy?"

"Sounds like a redhead's name."

She wrinkled her nose and gave a little headshake. "Not really."

His hands glided over her forearms to her biceps then slid up and down her sides. The DJ brought down the song and transitioned to another. "Rusty."

"No."

"Big Red."

"Really?" She pulled back, not actually going anywhere, needing her hands on him like the club needed the music to flow.

Locke's grip lingered, reeling her back. "Back, babe."

Close again, they were swaying as though slow dancing in the mess of an electronic beat. "Why does there have to be a nickname?"

Locke stopped as the bass went staccato and the crowd grew wilder. "Everyone calls you Cassidy, Cass…"

"Yeah?"

"I want something different."

Her stomach dropped. Aware of her breathing—hell, she was aware of everything—Cassidy wanted to say something but didn't know what. He gave her a silent squeeze that sent shivers along her skin.

"Why?" she finally worked up the nerve to ask.

"Because I'm selfish when it comes to you."

It would be the worst time for an awkward silence. She should flirt. Be cute or sweet. Say something. Anything. Kiss him! But she couldn't because the nerves paralyzed her tongue.

Locke chuckled. "Flame?"

"Uh… n-no," she stammered, thankful Locke wasn't one to hang on to awkward moments where the career reporter was unable to speak coherently.

"Firecracker?"

"No!" That brought her back. Awkwardness gone, she play-pushed him—and Locke grabbed her hand as she clung, unsure of their fingers threading together before they fell apart. "That's ridiculous."

"Ginger." He ducked close but dropped his voice. "My personal favorite has been Flamethrower."

"I'm not a redhead tonight. Remember? See?" She held out her obviously black hair for his inspection.

"But, Cassidy, you *are* gorgeous." He cupped her face. Those were the same palms that had held her semi-innocently—enough that she could pretend this moment wasn't upon them. He'd swept under her hair, and his thumbs worked slowly back and forth across her cheeks. But a move like this? There was nothing semi-innocent about it.

The moment when a guy could kiss a girl and she couldn't care less about anything other than them… that was this moment. Except they were there for Alex and had stopped looking for him the second they'd walked in. Was she ruining her career rebound over Locke?

"That's not a nickname." Breathless, she tilted her head away, free of his hands, her blushing surely evident on her cheeks. Every part of her body was on fire, and—

He stepped to the side, staying in line with her turning. "Are your eyes blue or green?"

She cast a look at him, and they said simultaneously, "Both."

Cassidy could hear blood rushing in her ears louder than the music. Silliness was a schoolgirl crush on the big, broad man before her. Alex Gaev and the Mikhailovs—they were a career-saving story as soon as she figured out what was happening. There wasn't time for… whatever this was.

But God, there must have been pheromones pumped through the air vents, because she was going to choke on the sexual tension and dirty thoughts.

"Do you think we should… go…home by ourselves?" She gestured and couldn't finish.

Locke's blond hair fell over his forehead. "No. I think we should stay here."

"Why?" Maybe if she put bravado into her words, she'd have a stronger spine. Maybe he'd be convinced, because her traitorous body was willing to give up a career as long as she rubbed against him.

"Because of…" He stepped even closer. "These minutes before I kiss you? I'm loving every second."

"You didn't just say that," she murmured, melting under the heat of his stare. "Locke…"

The butterflies that swarmed in her stomach were rabid and sighing. They weren't a good barometer of how she should feel *while at work.* Which this was supposed to be. But she'd known that walking in…

"I messed up before, Beauty. I bit your lip, and you think all is ruined between us."

Beauty. That worked. There wasn't a better nickname that he could bestow.

"What's that look?" he asked.

"I like *Beauty…*"

Locke dipped his head close but danced his mouth over her cheek and up to her ear. "Good. Because it suits you. Inside and out."

The world slowed and spun. He dipped his head closer, and the club tipped to a dull roar as Locke's lips brushed against hers. Music pounded with her pulse, and he pulled her firmly, urgently, closer, as if he needed her mouth against his too.

Locke groaned, satisfaction vibrating from his chest. Just like before, he opened her mouth. She shuddered in his sturdy hold as his tongue forged past her lips, dipping into her mouth. His rough hands threaded into her hair, tilting her back, exposing her neck and the vee of her dress. The heat tore through her, debilitating arousal making her senseless as she fed at his lips, letting their unspoken desperation come out. Damn it—she fell apart, needing this, not giving a damn about anything anymore.

"Locke," she moaned, his name caught in her throat, her mind, *everywhere.*

The rough denim of his jeans scraped against her bare inner thigh as he pushed his leg against her. Oh, she grew drunk on him, and this was just a kiss. A sweet intensity, sexual and primal, grew deep inside her, igniting her core. She needed friction against her clit. The tight clench of her vaginal muscles screamed for far more attention than their lip-lock could bring, but his tongue, exploring and teasing, was dead set on testing the limits of her need. Cassidy rocked on his powerful thigh, and he groaned. His fingers flexed against her scalp, and she wrapped her arms around his thick, corded neck. Her pussy was tightening with awareness; her breasts were beaded and swollen, brushing against him. "Oh. Please."

For one heart-stoppingly long second, she imagined just them. No club. No clothes. He was consuming her kisses like a man meant to discover his new woman, and mixed with his possessive hold, she let him brand her with kisses in public. His hard body couldn't have been harsher, and his sweet lips couldn't have been plumper, devouring her, making her mind spin—as if a kiss could be like sex, and sex could be like a dream.

Her breath hitched as they slowed. Whatever that had been, it was savage, and she would remember the white-hot desperation behind each stroke of his lips because it mirrored everything she'd felt in her Locke-crazed mind.

His lips lingered, his thrusting tongue now just teasing, slipping languidly along hers until he abandoned her mouth and trailed wet kisses from her swollen lips, moving along her jaw line, to her ear. He took his time, and with every lick against her skin, he claimed her with pure male possession as the best shivers sparkled across her skin, surging her hunger for him to a level of intoxication she hadn't known could exist. There was no subtlety between them anymore, and her needs were his. That was how it seemed.

"Beauty." His fingers touched below her chin, tilting her to face his brilliant eyes. "It's a good nickname. We can go with that."

LOCKE FOCUSED ON Alex Gaev, Ivan Mikhailov, and crew as they walked by. Trying not to ruin yet another time his lips were on Cassidy's, he ran his fingers over her cheek, lost in the sweet addiction that was starting to consume his every thought.

Starting to? Anger had consumed his thoughts and actions for years. He'd been drowning in it, breathing in the rage every day his feet hit the ground. He didn't enjoy life like he used to. He didn't even talk to friends and family like he used to—because his friends were dead. When he saw her again, that overwhelming wave of hatred curled and drew back, ready to strike like a snake. Except everything changed. How and why—fucking hell, he didn't know, didn't care as he drifted the pads of his fingers down her chin, hating that the two of them had to work and he couldn't just revel in how she tasted like honey and sugar.

Maybe they didn't really *have* to—there wasn't a paycheck assigned to hunting Alex and figuring out what he was doing. Jared and Rocco weren't breathing down his neck, issuing orders—but Locke couldn't just ignore the Mikhailov group. For Cassidy's sake.

Against his better judgment, Locke tamped down his need. "We should work."

She hummed, sucking her bottom lip into her mouth and raising her eyebrows before releasing it. The woman didn't know, she couldn't know—or hell, maybe she did know how badly he wanted to lick that lip. He liked to use his tongue. There was something about licking a woman, sucking her, kissing her—whether it was her lips or her pussy—that made Locke drunk on who he was with. With Cassidy, a simple touch of her lips was like a shot of sweet whiskey, and when her tongue tangled with his, need like he hadn't known wove with the newfound reasoning he'd found when Parker made him watch her work.

She was as tenacious as she was beautiful, and fuck… now, he was as hard as fucking stone, juggling priorities, and that little lip trick she had going on did shit to help.

"He's behind me?" Cassidy's gaze jetted right and left without turning.

"Affirmative." He nodded and wrapped his hands around her waist as she kept her body soft and relaxed, then he turned her around, taking advantage of the move to feel the slide of the silky fabric against his skin. There was still a cover to maintain, still a daring woman who had his blood racing, and he'd use whatever excuse he could to keep her close as they tried to see what they could.

Parker had equipped him with a few low-tech gadgets to sweep conversations, and if they could get close enough, maybe Locke could get a bead on what the Russians were discussing. If the topic of the evening was cars or racehorses—something completely boring and legal—then Cassidy could calm her hunt and divert her attention back to him. They were here, the lights were low, and her dress made his dick hard as much as her mouth made his mind race. No telling how the night would end up, but he had his fingers crossed that the Russian criminal and his former target were the best of friends with no ill agenda. If there was more, then she would have something to go on, and they'd have to table the kisses they'd just started.

"Let's get closer." They pressed forward, surging through the dancing crowd in the direction Alex had gone. Cassidy swayed her hips, and Locke gritted his teeth even though he enjoyed each time her ass bumped against his swollen cock. His mouth watered, and the urge to confirm that she was as turned on as he was dictated every step. Control was the name of the game, and he focused on the sugary scent of her body.

"There he is," she said, turning around.

The Russians and Alex were in a velvet-roped section. Locke nodded sharply. The earpiece was already in place, well hidden by his too-long hair.

"Let me get a picture." Cassidy positioned herself to take a selfie, making the obligatory duck face but dropping the focus on the background to photograph the people Alex was with. Locke—and, he guessed, Cassidy—had a hard ID on Ivan but not the others. Titan could work on that, and Cassidy knew what she was doing even if she didn't know he could help with facial recognition. She was a reporter first. Locke liked that she was doing her own thing and that they each brought something to the table, though he hadn't told her much more than that he'd accompany her. She didn't know about the earpiece, which was good because he wasn't picking up anything as he turned a dial in his pocket, filtering out music and nearby ambient noise as he watched her take another selfie. Those lips...

they were kiss-swollen. He wanted to watch that sweet, pouty smile work its way down his stomach.

"I'm good—what's that look for?" Black hair fell over her cheek, and she brushed it off.

"Don't worry about it." He winked, shifting his weight and trying to discreetly re-adjust his bulging cock that was starting to edge on the line of uncomfortable. "Let's try a little closer."

They eased closer, still out of eyeshot, and she tossed an arm over one of his shoulders as someone pushed by. "Damn, you smell good."

Her fingers kneaded into his neck. "I was just thinking the same thing."

Even surrounded by the booze-filled crowd, she still smelled sweet as honey. He rubbed up her back, but more and more, he wanted his hands under that dress. Cassidy rested her chin on his chest, blue-green eyes looking up. Maybe she had the same idea. She lingered, and it hit him hard—from not wanting to be saving her off a mountain to being unable to keep his hands off her, that was a wild rollercoaster.

"I hate that I can't read you," she said. "What are you thinking?"

"Oh, Red Riding Hood…" He groaned and dropped his head back, taking a deep sigh, and coming back again. "You look good enough to eat."

Locke dropped his lips to her neck, and she made a soft noise that broke through the pulsing music and vibrated through his limbs. If she mewed like that when he kissed her neck, he needed to know how she'd writhe when his stiff tongue fucked her pussy.

Cassidy, unaware that he was more interested in sliding his fingers up her thighs than finding out what the Russians were doing, turned her head. "What if he sees me?"

Locke swallowed the unsatisfied urges. "The wig covers your hair; I cover the rest."

She cuddled him. The move was needy and heated as she knotted her hand into his shirt. "What if he sees you?"

Shit, woman. Locke wasn't worried. "No one's paying attention to us right now." Or if they were, they were voyeurs. "Plus, I'm a generic white dude Alex has seen in passing. Dime a dozen. He won't."

"Nothing about you is generic." Cassidy's husky laugh was sexy and rasped his senses in all the right ways. "But me? He knows."

"Don't worry—" He flinched as the earpiece squealed, then reached into his pocket to make an adjustment. "A little closer, okay?"

If that wasn't a sign they had to work, he didn't know what was. She let him lead, and finally, Locke could break past the white noise in his earpiece and dial in on a conversation, but it wasn't their targets. "Over this way. Come on."

What they needed was some high-tech spy toys. But he needed major convincing of Titan's head honchos to get his hands anywhere near those. What he had were essentially throwaways. Good thing he and Cassidy were only a few tables away, as far as Locke could tell, from their targets in the VIP section. It was hard to see without being too obvious.

"We're getting a little risky," Cassidy said.

"I think we're okay." Alex and Ivan were on the other side of a partition, on a raised dais. There was a pillar, so he leaned against it, drawing Cassidy to him. Security cameras likely scanned the crowd, but they wouldn't have an eye out for Cassidy, and with her disguise, he felt fine unless the club ran facial recognition and they had a flag for her, which was a stretch.

He pulled her closer and watched as she tilted her head up. Towering over his favorite redhead—even if she wasn't red that night—was fun, mostly because he liked to watch her blue-green eyes dance the way the people in this club moved.

She bit her lip. "Okay."

Christ. That lip thing would be his death. "I'm *this* close to losing control. It's not a good thing."

She inched forward. "What's not a good thing?"

Damn. It was. It really, really fucking was a good thing. The way her lips tasted, the way he imagined how they'd look wrapped around his cock, her dark-red hair falling around her face as her hungry, sassy mouth took him inch by inch—they were all good. He looked away and then back at her. No, he couldn't work like this, thinking about her sucking him, her tongue sliding along his shaft. He sucked in a breath. "Cassidy, don't bite that damn lip right now."

"Why?" she whispered. "I like the way you look at me when I do."

The time for gentleness was gone. He took her face in his hands, loving every bit of shock and surprise that was written all over it. "I'm going to love every second I suck on that tongue." His nostrils flared, and his chest expanded with each rapid breath. "Every moan you give me, from every second I kiss you, Beauty."

"*Locke—*"

He took her mouth, tasted it—damn, he owned it. Wanted it. Needed it. Locke struggled for a semblance of control as she fought for more of the kiss as much as he did. Her tongue tangled with his, slipping into his mouth, stroking and teasing.

Cassidy grabbed his shirt, and damn, he liked how this vixen knotted her hands in the button-down before sliding them up his chest. Like she needed to hang on tight, and every time she grabbed him, it went straight to his dick.

"We're still working," she panted.

"You think I can't do two things at once?" Though trying to listen to Alex's table was nearly impossible, he held her close with one arm, and the other hand traveled toward her full breast. Her hard nipple stood erect. "Three things. I can listen. Kiss you. And tease you."

In the crowded club, he grazed her breast, and she arched her back. Cassidy's dress cloaked her body like tailored-leather perfection, perfectly curving over her mounds and reminding him she had sexy hips he could hold onto and an ass that he wanted to see on his bed and raised in the air.

"Fuck," he groaned into her mouth, moving them so her back was to the wall and they had a faux semblance of privacy.

Locke teased two searching fingers down the vee of her dress, and his mouth watered over her breasts, knowing the peaked tips of her nipples were so close.

Her hand dropped, and Cassidy groped for his erection—he sucked air between his teeth.

"Beauty," he growled. What did she want him to do—unbuckle and free his throbbing cock? Slide her panties to the side so he could fuck her here? So many times had he imagined doing that. The night at the restaurant had almost killed him. He went home and jerked off to the thought again and again, knowing how his length would fit perfectly in her tight pussy. Inch by inch, he'd take her and would watch her lips part and eyes go wide.

Her hand grasped him—tightly. "You're very… remarkable."

"That…" He couldn't breathe as she stroked over his pants. "That sounds like a word a journalist would use," he whispered, grinding his back molars. "You are going to kill me."

"Then you know how I feel."

"No, Cassidy. You have no fucking clue."

"Locke." She caught his eye. "Touch me."

He stilled.

"Don't stop on me now. *Please.* I need that."

She was nuts if she thought they could play this little game and not explode from the tension, but he was game to try. Slowly, he let his hand crawl down the front of her dress, and then his fingertips danced across the soft inner flesh of her thigh. She sighed, leaning into him, and at the top of her legs, his knuckles brushed against her damp underwear. "God, Cass—"

Suddenly, Locke heard Russian-accented English. It came in spurts. He pulled his focus from Cassidy. As he tried to track the back-and-forth between the men, it became apparent that they weren't talking about ho-hum topics but instead were mentioning names of US senators and members of financial agencies.

"What?" she asked as his hand froze.

US senators Locke couldn't ignore, and he adjusted her skirt back in place as his head dropped back, hating the timing. His hand covered hers. "Hang on a sec."

"What's the matter?" Cassidy asked.

He gritted his teeth. "If I could hear them, would you want to know what the conversation's about?"

"Can you?" she asked, eyes narrowing.

"Maybe." The music shifted suddenly and boomed. The cool blue laser lights turned red like fire and exploded like fireworks. The bass dropped, and the crowd danced harder. The harder he tried to concentrate on the conversation in his earpiece, the worse the music grated his senses.

But it was more than that, almost like each note had a stranglehold on him. Locke's eyes pulled away from Cassidy, the pinpricks of a cold sweat popping on his neck.

Boom. Boom.

Damn it. He couldn't breathe. The DJ brought the music up, and the light show became brilliant. Yellows and red exploded on the walls. Locke's pulse escalated, and it was as though the Red Star club had been replaced by Sadr City, each explosion striking in his ears.

"Hey—Cass—" But he shook away the loss of control, the idea that he couldn't see straight, even that he wasn't the master of his reactions. The music was nothing more than a wailing siren, disguised as techno music, and it bled into the suddenly stifling air. It choked him. Crushed him. He couldn't breathe. Couldn't see. Locke had to get the hell out of this club.

"I need a drink. Come on," he said, tugging her away. "And air. Just need..."

"Hey, wait—I thought you could hear something," she said as he pulled her away.

Yeah. He could hear war. Death. Destruction. He could hear the hell he thought she caused, the world he'd been suffering through—would someone turn the goddamn music off?

"Locke?" She clung to him even as he rushed them through the dizzying crowd. The temperature must've risen a thousand degrees.

"Hey! Hang on." Cassidy pulled, but he didn't slow.

By the time they reached the bar, the DJ had transitioned the red-glaring music to the techno-Russian blue-lasered beat from before. Cassidy's stance was harsh and her eyes assessing. "What is going on?"

"Thirsty?" The rapid rise and fall of his chest matched the sweat tickling his temples. Locke flagged the bartender as his pulse slowed a fraction. He ran a hand through his sweat-dampened hair, getting his bearings.

"Locke?" She tried again. "What's your problem?"

"Nothing. Shitty music."

"The music?" Cassidy's demeanor was cool as the ice display that they offered vodka shots from behind the bar.

How grossly unaffected she was, and still, he couldn't shake the panic attack that rolled over him as if the Night of Fire descended all over again. Red and orange lights. The booms and sirens. And there Cassidy was, completely no fucking reaction. She'd watched everyone die too, damn it! Still no reaction? Locke stared, studying her.

No. Nothing. Maybe because she was guiltier than hell… "We should leave." Locke couldn't handle all the memories flooding his mind. All those bodies. All that blood. In his hair. His nose. His mouth. His hands—as the fires screamed around them and he couldn't find his friends, his brothers.

Fuck. The sound of explosions flooded his mind, punctuating it with wailing cries and death.

"Sure." Her look was overly assessing. "I'm ready to leave."

After waving the bartender away, he rubbed his temples, trying to make sense of the last few minutes and needing to block out the sound. Cassidy was his problem? He liked her, and hell, he wanted her more than he could recall ever wanting a woman. Maybe he shouldn't. But she was smart and beautiful and smelled like something he wanted to remember. Except that his mind *did* remember. He always leapt back there, even when it wasn't warranted. She was forever in his memory, tied to an awful tragedy.

"What's going on with you? We were just… and we're here." Her hands landed on his biceps, and he jumped.

Locke tried to play it off, turning and slipping the earpiece free and eyeing the club's exit.

"What was that?" she snapped. "What the hell is happening here?"

An icy-cold sweat tickled the back of his neck, and its uncomfortable fingers reached down his shoulder blades, reminding him that they had seen so much death between them.

"Nothing. Let's go." He put his hand on her back, trying to guide her to leave, but she sidestepped.

"Yeah, I don't think so." Gone were the good mood and the smiles. "Sure. Got my pictures, tried to see what they were up to. Nothing particularly shady." She cleared her throat. Taking a step back, she adjusted the black wig. "He didn't cancel on the Mikhailovs this time. That says something to me. I'm glad I came for the confirmation. Thanks."

She walked away from him, shoulders back with no indication that there was music or that her body had been dancing, wrapped against his as they groped and kissed. She could've been walking out of the Metro station on her way to work, head forward, shoulders back.

Locke swallowed the knot in his throat. The attitude problem walking away from him was fine as long as he got out of this place. Cassidy was back in business mode, and he had put her there. To hell with it. Locke shoved past another person and made a beeline for fresh air and freedom.

CHAPTER EIGHTEEN

FOR AS MUCH as Sadr City had consumed Locke's thoughts and as much as he wanted to hate her and blame her, he couldn't let Cassidy go. It probably had something to do with how frigid she became. That pissed him off. *He* was the one who could be upset. What the hell did she have to get worked up over if it wasn't the attack? Then he couldn't let her leave like that, which meant twenty minutes of awkward-angry silence because he'd nearly demanded to drive her home. She took up his offer though, which said something because Cassidy didn't take anything she didn't want from anyone.

"That's me." Cassidy pointed to a driveway.

He cut the turn and pulled in. Damn it. Right now, he wanted to hate her, and hell, he also wanted to tell her that he'd been partially able to listen to the Russian conversation. He even wanted to admit to having a partial mental meltdown. But fuck it, how to explain what he didn't have words for? That was impossible.

"What the hell happened?" Cassidy snapped.

Where to begin… He shifted into park and turned to stare as she pulled off her black wig and the odd little cap that had her red hair tucked into it. The next minute was nothing but hair fluffing while she focused on the wig rather than, he was sure, yelling at him.

He wanted her to. Really. If she screamed and ranted, he knew how to handle that. But a silent Cassidy? No, that sliced him.

Locke wanted her out of his truck but didn't want her to go. He wanted her back in his arms as much as the idea terrified him. Instead of doing either, he gripped the steering wheel, letting his knuckles turn white. He glanced over and saw that she wasn't going anywhere. Thank God.

His mind was so fucking jacked up even as he was calming down. "Do you ever want a fresh start, Cass?"

She didn't answer.

"One where you don't have a memory, a nightmare, that crops up when you don't want it to? Where you don't blame people in the darkness? Don't hear things that haunt you?"

She tilted her head his direction. "I don't know what you're talking about."

"Right." Alone in the darkness. He twisted his grip on the steering wheel until his palms hurt. His chest ached. His woman was hurt. *His woman?* He'd hurt her. Not that Cassidy was his, but fucking hell…

His mind hated them both, him and her and everything about that evening. Cassidy succumbed to the silent treatment the entire way back to her house. There she sat, one the most beautiful people he'd ever had the privilege to meet, with lips pressed into a thin, pissed-off line and so much ire pouring off of her that he could chisel the tension.

"Thanks for the lift." Mechanically, she unfolded herself from his truck and pushed the door open. Without so much as a wave, she slammed the door, and its echo reverberated in his head like a prison gate repeatedly locking.

Slam.

Slam.

Slam.

Cassidy marched toward a modest house perched atop a large brick staircase. She had flowerbeds and a cute lawn. How long had Cassidy been in prison? It couldn't have been more than a few days, but was she forced into the general population, or was it more symbolic, with her kept safe in a holding cell?

He wondered if she'd been scared. What was worse, the unknown of war or going to jail? She'd been protected in Iraq, as much as she could've been considering that death was an expected part of war. But in prison, no one expected to die, yet prisoners weren't exactly protected, either.

Slam.

Locke's hands went to his temples. He was lying to himself if he didn't think he cared about her or appreciated what she'd gone through, and fucking hell, he couldn't keep blaming her for Sadr City.

His fist balled, and he wanted to punch the ceiling—but he forced it open. He wouldn't take more pain or another blast of adrenaline to hang onto the past. "What the hell is wrong with me?" Cassidy. That was what was always wrong with him.

But at the moment, she was climbing a long brick staircase, getting farther away from him. Maybe that was the problem. On her front porch, she didn't turn around but only unlocked the door quickly—and she turned off the front-porch light.

"Got it, Beauty. *Go home.* Understood." She couldn't have been clearer. He'd been clear too. Before he'd pushed her too damn far away, his hands had been all over her; his mouth had been on a mission to create a thousand moans. Then… nothing.

The urge to go after her needled until he could think of nothing except what she might say if he opened the door. He chortled, dropping his head into his hands. She'd probably hit him in the chest and yell that he needed to stop opening doors that she had shut.

"But I never fucking learn." Locke jumped out of his truck and jogged to the long flight of stairs and up to the porch. Hand on the doorknob, he caught himself before trying to walk in.

Slipping into the back of her car outside the Russian embassy had been him watching out for her.

Getting into her car at St. Andrew's? Inserting himself into an investigation never hurt anyone.

But walking into her house unannounced could be crossing an unforgivable line.

He yanked his arm back like a scolded child and didn't know what to do. For the first time in his life, he just stood there, unsure and unsteady. He needed to knock.

So he did. Twice. No answer…

"Come on, Cass." He knocked again.

Warily, Cassidy opened the door. "Do you have a flat tire?" Her chin rested on the doorjamb. "Or maybe you'd like to continue playing games?

I'll save you the trouble. Not interested."

Man, he had screwed up. It was painful to see that sweet mouth spewing venom.

"Are you going to invite me inside?"

"Not a chance, big boy." She moved to slam the door, but he put his foot in the way. Her angry eyes narrowed.

Locke stepped back, throwing his hands up. "Jesus, shit. You're mad. I fucked up. I get it."

"Good. I get it too. You're an asshole. Go the hell home."

"Actually, no," he snapped. "You don't get it *at all*, but what the fuck ever."

"What don't I get?" She let out a small laugh, and her expression went back to stone. "Hot, cold. Helper bee. Huge freaking hindrance. All in all, *asshole*."

He scrubbed his face with his hands and ran them through his hair, blowing out a frustrated breath before dropping them to his side. All of him felt as though he was too large to be standing on her front porch having that conversation. "Are you going to let me inside, Cassidy? Because I don't like being out here."

"Are you mad at me?" she asked.

He had no idea. "I'm not sure."

And that answer sucked to give because he could see the innocent hurt in her beautiful eyes. It was as though the blue-green sea of her irises wilted and died.

They didn't know each other very well, and they hadn't spent much time together. But their interactions were intense. He wasn't even sure how he felt about that word. *Intense*...

"Well, get over yourself." She took a giant step back and slammed the door.

His jaw fell. "What?"

Nothing about what Cassidy Noble did was ever as he expected. Locke used the back of his fist and banged on the door three times. "Damn it, Cassidy, open the door."

"Go away," she yelled.

"You're ridiculous." He turned for his truck, but two steps down the steep length of stairs, he heard her door fly open and the sound of charging steps.

"Wait." She poked him in the back with a talon-like finger.

He turned around, and they were eye level.

"No, sir." Her red hair fell over her shoulders, framing her face wildly. "You don't get to call me ridiculous. You don't get to be like you were at Red Star and then act like that."

He took two steps onto the front porch and reclaimed his height advantage. "And how is that?" Though he knew exactly how hot and heavy they were, and it was one of the best nights he'd had in so long—until he screwed it up.

"*And* you don't get to call me ridiculous when you're the king of mood swings."

Her words reeled through his mind. The two of them stepped from her porch and crossed the threshold into her house. "If I'm the king of mood swings, Cass, you're the queen of evasion."

"You're out of your mind." Cheeks flushed, she scoffed. "All I've wanted to do was tell you everything. But you don't listen."

"I don't listen?" His lip pulled up, and he looked away before leveling her with the truth. "All you do is wait to talk."

"I do not!"

He stepped closer. "Whatever it is that you're so hell-bent to report on, that's all you care about."

"Bull!" She poked him in the chest.

He pushed the poking hand aside and came closer. "And you give no fucks what anybody else says."

"For someone who never has much to say, that's a whole lot of *bullshit.*"

The lights were dim in her foyer, and his breathing was heavy just like hers. He looked down. There wasn't much room between them. She did the same. Neither stepped away. He couldn't tear himself from her, even when they were fighting.

"Cassidy." Her name shook in his throat and rumbled in his ears.

"What do you want?" she pleaded quietly. "Because you said I was killing you. But you killed me."

His eyelids sank shut. He didn't know what he wanted to say. He wanted everything to go back to the way it was before. He wanted to take the pressure away and make them a good thing.

"I took it too far in the club," he lied. "All right? I shouldn't have… we shouldn't have. I don't know. Maybe that was too much."

Her chin dropped an inch, but worse, the spirit in her eyes seemed to extinguish. "Yeah, sure. That makes things easier."

She pulled away under the immense pounding of disappointment.

"Fucking hell." He couldn't handle that bullshit. "Beauty, wait."

"No." She wouldn't turn back, shaking her head as though that were the last thing she could handle between them. "Don't you dare say 'Beauty.' That was a sweet thing. I liked it. I loved it. You can't ruin it now."

"Beauty." He sidestepped and put his hands on her soft cheeks. "I'm broken."

Pain covered her face, fluttering her eyelashes shut. "No, you're not."

"I promise I am." He leaned forward and put his lips on her forehead. "I don't want to be."

"Then don't be."

"It isn't that easy," he murmured, dragging his lips into her hair.

"No," she murmured, draping her arms around him, holding him in a loose hug.

"I want to try. I missed you even before I got down the stairs."

She sniffled and tightened the hug.

"Cass, don't cry. Okay?"

Holding him tighter, she muttered an agreement, and when he was sure he wouldn't see tears, because he couldn't handle them, Locke tipped her head back and sweetly kissed her lips.

He'd bitten her. He'd taken her mouth, hot and heavy in a club. But when this sweet, sad, damn-near-tears Cassidy kissed him, Sadr City didn't matter. The lights and sounds he wanted to run from didn't matter either, only every fresh start he'd ever dreamed might be possible.

As much as he'd been running from her as the villain, maybe she was the key to his future without the nightmares.

CHAPTER NINETEEN

THE FRONT DOOR shut, and Cassidy kept her hands splayed on the wood.

One sweet kiss, and then he left without a word. Locke seemed almost strangled in thought. Scared and hopeful, apprehensive and needy.

But he'd left after a kiss so beautiful and careful he might've restored her belief in fairy tales. She wasn't giddy or beside herself, but the sadness was gone, and there was hope. Silly how a heartfelt lip-lock could remedy such a strange night, but it did.

He hadn't been gone for more than five seconds when Cassidy pressed her eye against the peephole and watched Locke walk down the path until he was out of sight. Her forehead fell forward and tapped against the wood, where she let it rest.

This night had just happened. Locke kissed her, finally, and then they somehow fought and made up, ending with a kiss again. But that was more than a kiss, more than an emotional moment they'd had. It was straightforward and surreal. It reaffirmed her belief that there was such thing as a "best" kiss, and the best one didn't have to end in toe-curling orgasms. Just a belief that happiness was possible.

She pressed her fingers to her forehead where his lips had rested and let them slide to her lips. He hadn't said much either, but it seemed as though he'd confided in her.

She let out a sigh that left a reassured smile on her face and deflated as she gave herself a hug, leaning against the door. Slowly, Cassidy slid down until she was squatting at the base of her front door as his voice danced in her head.

Beauty.

Cassidy wrapped her arms around her knees and squeezed into a hug. Nothing had ever felt like that before. "Oh boy."

She ran her tongue over her bottom lip, which was slightly swollen from how deeply Locke had kissed her that night—

Knock, Knock.

She shot straight from the floor, her heart racing and her hands trembling from the adrenaline of the surprise. She peered back to the peephole—*Locke.*

Her stomach somersaulted. A smile that she didn't think could get any bigger went straight to her ears. She tried to calm down but couldn't. She took a deep breath and failed at subtlety when she opened the door, blushing. "Hey, hi."

With one sweeping step, Locke came back into her house. "Hey, hi."

He had her back in his thick arms, her head tilted back and his devouring mouth on hers. His greedy tongue touched hers, and it was *fire.* Flames burned, hungry hands groped, and Locke's sugar lips melted her in the right places. If she could've flown, it would've happened.

"Locke..." Cassidy whispered her favorite word as he slowed the strong slip of his kiss. "Mmm."

They parted, and he barely let her take a deep breath. Still, she swooned at how careful and all-consuming he could he be at once.

"I didn't know how addictive goodnight kisses were." He dropped his mouth to her ear, gently breathing and teasing. "Beauty."

Swirls of sensation spiraled through her as she shuddered. "That word does dangerous things to me."

"Good to know."

"I like goodnight kisses from you." Her eyelashes fluttered, and she focused on him. His intensity bore down. "I like a lot about you, Locke."

He swiped his thumb over her cheek, letting it run over her lips, pulling down the bottom one slightly. "I'll call you tomorrow. Sleep tight."

CHAPTER TWENTY

THE DAY HAD started early at Titan HQ, yet he was nowhere near the first person onsite that Sunday morning. Locke wondered if some people ever left. The likely answer was no, as long as there were people who worked odd schedules and came off and on jobs, debriefing and rotating with other teams.

He needed to return the earpiece to Parker and find his boss in order to make a bigger request for resources and further assistance for Cassidy, but the wording hadn't come to him yet. Maybe Locke could throw ideas to Parker and get his thoughts.

Though… Locke was already up shit creek with Titan. What did it matter if his requests seemed nuts? Jared and Rocco had coined the term *intel-therapy*, and the entire company had decided that he needed to make peace with *it*, and by *it*, they meant *her*. Locke didn't even want to know what their thoughts on that were.

So, yeah, Parker was the best bet for hashing out the conversation on how to help Cassidy because, at the very least, he'd already given Locke some techy gadgets without asking many questions. Though if push came to shove, Locke could explain that not only had he made peace with *it*, he had kissed the ever-loving shit out of *it* and then gone back for more. How fast would that travel through Titan? The guys talked more than the girls.

What did Locke care? Since he woke up, Cassidy had been on his mind. But also, so had Alex and the Mikhailovs. Something was up, especially with the bits of conversation he had picked up. Senators. Banking. All in all, sketchy. But it also proved nothing.

Cassidy had one hell of a journalistic nose, though. His interest was piqued enough that as he entered Parker's office, Locke decided to hang tight for the guy who always looked far too busy to bother.

"I see you hovering," Parker muttered from a keyboard across the dark room. "Get in here, or get out. You're distracting me at the periphery."

Several flat screens had a replay of an old job from a few weeks prior. They were getting ready to do a very similar job. Locke guessed that Parker was autopsying the footage for what could be done better.

"If you have a minute."

Parker lifted a shoulder. "I never have a minute, but I always do. If it makes sense."

"Thanks for the comm piece." Locke stuck his hands in his pockets. "If I wanted to get more... involved in a project, how would I go about doing that?"

"More involved how?" Parker's hands stilled over the keyboard, and he twisted in his chair, rolling back from the desk.

"I have other Russians, and they're talking about members of Congress. Cassidy is onto something, and—"

"Cassidy?"

Locke nodded casually.

Parker, mockingly casual, nodded as well. "More intel and profiles would be doable."

Locke shrugged, not exactly sure what he was asking for. "Sounds like a start."

Pushing back in his rolling chair, Parker scooted across the office area to a table, where he leaned over and pressed his thumb against a lock on a filing cabinet and, after a beep, proceeded to put in a long series of numbers on a numeric keypad. A red light next to the keypad flashed to green, and Parker opened what looked like a filing cabinet. Only Titan would have a filing cabinet with thumbprint recognition. Parker pulled out a folder and opened it up, and Locke stepped forward enough to look interested but not to be a jackass and read over Parker's shoulder.

"Here you go. Your Russian assholes."

Locke's gaze dropped to the folder and then back to Parker. "How?"

"You think I couldn't hear what you could?"

His stomach dropped. How much of the conversation with Cassidy had Parker heard?

"Relax. I picked up what you mic'ed. Not *your* conversations." Parker gave him a sly glance. "Though you have me curious about what else you were up to. There was voice confirmation on Ivan and two other former KGB—now FSB—officials."

"Damn..." Titan had insane capabilities that Locke didn't know existed. "I didn't expect this." He took the folder Parker shoved into his hand.

"You should have. This is Titan. It's what we do."

This is Titan. Fuck yeah. And there was his opening. "About that. What's the next level when it comes to an off-the-books job?"

Parker leaned back in his chair, bouncing back and forth slowly, and studied Locke. "We don't have a company policy on doing what's right. I'll just leave it at that."

Not exactly the answer he was going after. "And resources? Say I want to know more about what these three are up to." Titan had every security clearance known to man, even ones that boiled all the way down to the basic state-level private-investigation clearances, and up to the White House. They could get to just about anybody. "The partnership between Alex Gaev and the Mikhailovs—there's something there."

"What is it?" Parker rubbed his chin and then unhurriedly pulled his arm away in thought.

Locke shrugged his shoulders. "Maybe something to do with Congress. I have no clue."

"You're gonna have to run it up the chain. If that's what you want, you'll get it. But you can't just ask me."

"Yeah, I'll talk to Roc. He was next on my list. I just wanted to feel you out, to see if it was a thing."

"It's a thing. I'll do it. They'll let you do it. But Roc has to tell you."

"I read you. Thanks." He turned toward the door. One step away, and Parker cleared his throat in a way that said the conversation wasn't over.

"Connect the dots for me," Parker said. "You sat in my office, not too long ago, and got a huge helping of in-your-face-intel on Cassidy Noble."

"Yeah."

"Then you started working something with her on Alex Gaev. That has you jumping from hating her to working with her?"

"Pretty much. She's onto something and didn't know who the Mikhailovs were." Locke shrugged. "I did."

"I'm still missing something." Parker's eyebrows went up.

Locke mimicked Parker's expression. "Maybe you are. I'm off to talk to Rocco."

As Locke left, he heard Parker's quiet laugh and a deliberate clap. "Fucking A. Score one for intel-therapy."

CHAPTER TWENTY-ONE

LOCKE PULLED OUT his phone and texted a quick message to Rocco, asking where he was. A few short seconds later, the response popped through on his phone's screen.

ROCCO: *I need to talk to you. War room. Now.*

Hustling to meet his boss, Locke passed checkpoints and found the door already open and Rocco waiting. The table was covered with papers and open folders. A tablet and a laptop sat in front of Rocco as though he had been working there for hours, and a trashcan sat close by with remnants of fast food. On a Sunday morning. People never went home from HQ. Until they did, and then Titan had tons of time off. But for the moment, an abandoned coffee cup and a fresh cup of coffee sat by Rocco's right hand.

Locke took in what could've been a college all-nighter. "Working hard, boss?"

"We had a couple of contracts come in, and I'm trying to see who's best to farm out to."

Locke pulled up a seat and sat down.

"This one"—he tapped the tablet—"Delta team is all over. What's written here should never see the light of day. Anything that has human traffickers, that team can't get there fast enough."

Locke had heard that about Delta and knew them in passing. He hadn't worked a job with them in person. A few of them had come through the building or been to Titan gatherings, but nothing official. Delta did "ghost" work, but this new team had quickly become renowned in the intel community for knocking out traffickers. Not a bad reputation to have.

"Then we have a small job that I think Cash and Roman will go knock out."

He nodded. "Those two are amazing to watch."

"Yeah, they'll be fast, in and out." Rocco leaned back in his chair. "Then we have you. What's going on with you?" He crossed his arms over his chest.

"Me?" Locke blanched, not expecting that.

"Do you have your act together? Because if you do, I can take on some of these jobs. If you don't, I'm going to be a man down because I don't have time for your bullshit."

"That's why I'm here."

"No, asshole." Rocco's brows furrowed. "You're here because I told you where I was."

Well… true. He leaned forward, resting his elbows on his knees, and rubbed his hands over his face. As someone who had made his name within Titan as a man of few words, and those words being the right ones, Locke had not done a good job of articulating his thoughts lately. "I have a favor to ask."

Rocco tipped back and roared with laughter. "Try again."

Locke pinched the bridge of his nose. "I'm serious. I need to run this crazy shit by you."

His boss stopped laughing. "Yeah, yeah. All right, Ballsy McGee. I'll listen."

He then took the next two minutes to explain everything: Alex Gaev, Ivan Mikhailov, and the odd, chummy meeting where they mentioned US senators while clubbing—after Ivan had so recently wanted Alex six feet under. Locke tried his to best to describe Alex's encounters with that woman in Russia, which Cassidy had witnessed and the teacher had denied. The entire oddly unconnected situation just stank.

Rocco had completely sobered, and his expression said he agreed that it stank. When enough odd-ass things didn't make sense, people needed to start asking questions.

Locke pursed his lips. "I don't know what I'm asking you for, because frankly, conspiracy-bullshit crap is not my specialty. But something's up." He shook his head. "I'm a little lost, but I'm smart, and Cassidy Noble? She's on point."

Rocco turned back to the table, ignoring Locke. Either his presentation was all wrong, and Rocco was a dick, or Rocco had a thought and didn't want to lose it.

His boss wasn't idly working. As Locke eyeballed him, he noticed that it was almost as if he was searching for something. Then Rocco slapped the table.

"Good news?" What else was he supposed to say?

Rocco pushed back. "Let me see the folder from Parker. I want to compare something."

Of course Parker hadn't given Locke a folder without Rocco knowing. Locke handed it over and watched as Rocco paged through the files, quickly going from one page to the next page, to the next—and then he stopped.

Locke leaned over to see that he was on Ivan's page. He shifted his weight in his chair as Rocco tossed the file onto the table and went back to his work. He pulled up a screen on the tablet and then moved over to his papers, moving back and forth, until he turned back to Locke.

"Do you believe in coincidence?" Rocco asked.

Tricky question, because it depended on the situation. Had Locke decided not to drive to see Bishop, he would never have seen Cassidy, and then he wouldn't be at this table having this discussion with Rocco. That was a solid argument that everything happened for a reason.

If he hadn't jumped in her car, and she hadn't called him a sexist asshole, then they would never have ended up at that club and seen Alex with Ivan. But for intelligence and military spec ops, Locke accepting coincidence was probably was not high on the list of things that Rocco wanted to hear about.

Still, honesty was the best answer. "It depends on the situation."

"Fair enough." Rocco took his tablet, slid it across the table to Locke, and gave him a chin lift to go ahead and look at the screen.

Locke picked up the tablet and settled back, reading the name Ivan

Mikhailov at the top of the screen. It was the same bio that Locke had in his folder. He didn't understand why he was looking at it. Raising his eyebrows, Locke asked, "Isn't this the same guy?"

"Now swipe to the next page."

Locke did so. At the top of the page was the same last name, different first name. *Taisia.* It was a woman's name. That was interesting. The bio listed her birthday, making her slightly younger than him, and referenced her education in the United States at the University of Maryland. Listed under Unconfirmed but Probable: "One pregnancy, assumed live birth. Unknown father. The child is believed to be living with the mother."

"Ivan's a grandpa?" Locke mused aloud.

"Bet he's stellar," Rocco spit sarcastically.

"No kidding." He'd just seen Ivan with women who had to be the age of his daughter—or younger.

"It says she didn't graduate from college." Rocco tapped the screen, expanding the intel report. "Dropped out junior year, spring semester."

"Huh." Locke wondered why she would be in the US to begin with. He knew the KGB had successfully planted Russians in America over the years, but his daughter would have been too obvious. But… his wheels began to turn. If the daughter was about the same age as him, Locke guessed Alexander was about his age also. What if…? He furrowed his brow, giving Rocco a hard look. "Did we ever get a follow-up from St. Andrew's or their insurance company?"

Again with the sarcastic laugh. "Did they want details on the asshole teacher screwing the locals? Yeah, no."

"Fucking A, man." Locke blew out a breath.

Rocco raised his brows. "You want to clue me in on your thoughts?"

"Cassidy saw Alex with a woman."

His boss's brows rose higher. "The teacher didn't screw just with the locals. He actually *screwed* a local. *The* local."

"*The?*"

"Taisia Mikhailov. She's like royalty out there. A protected, hidden princess. No one knows anything about her, but because of her last name and her father's reach and power? Yeah. *The.*"

"Daddy Russian wanted to blow Alex's brains out for getting back in touch with his daughter. He runs, they chase. We go in, thinking it's a typical private contract job…" Locke let his mind run.

Rocco hit the speakerphone button on a console on the table. "Parker?"

A moment later, "Yeah?"

"Where'd Alex Gaev go to college?"

Keys clacked. "University of Maryland."

"Thanks, bro." Rocco raised his eyebrows. "Coincidence again?"

"Not a chance."

Rocco slapped the speakerphone button again, and this time Jared growled, "Yeah? What?"

"War room needs your eminent presence."

"Jackass." The line hung up.

"Who knew this would become something," Rocco mumbled as he shuffled papers around.

Locke sure as fuck hadn't known. Maybe Cassidy knew, but even she didn't know how big, not if she didn't initially understand who the Mikhailovs were.

Jared walked into the room.

"Hey, Boss Man," Rocco said. "If some guy upset one of your daughters enough that you kicked him out of your house, why would you go meet with him again?"

Jared grumbled and smirked as he also took a seat. He cracked a couple of knuckles. "Just to kick the asshole's ass. Simple."

"What if you didn't touch the guy? What if you just hung out?" Locke asked.

Jared shook his head, his lips pursed. "Then there was never a problem with Asal or Violet. Simple. Their integrity isn't for sale."

"Ding motherfucking ding," Rocco muttered. "Ivan Mikhailov has no integrity."

"None of those fuckers do. What's going on?" Jared popped another knuckle and grumbled at Rocco.

Rocco looked at the folders, his tablet, and then at Locke. "I was reviewing a couple of up-and-coming contracts, but also, I happened to have the after-action report from Krasnaya Polyana over here when Locke walked in."

Jared nodded. "Got it. So?"

"It looks like the FSB involved in ordering the hit on Alex Gaev was none other than Ivan Mikhailov—"

"One of my favorite former KGB hardliners," Jared grumbled.

"But now they're all friends. Ivan's been in DC for the past few weeks, seen around town with Alex," Locke said.

Jared's eyes narrowed as he rubbed his hands together slowly in thought. "Interesting. Gaev became worth more to Ivan alive than dead."

"He was possibly seeing his daughter while in Russia."

"Doing the man's daughter would cause a hit, so Gaev negotiated his way out? Smart." Jared rubbed his chin. "Not all that surprised Ivan would trade for his daughter. But… how? Why? I don't see the connection."

"The daughter and Gaev went to college together."

"Where?" Jared asked.

Rocco tapped a finger on his coffee cup's lid. "University of Maryland."

"Not a small place," Jared said. "Could be coincidence."

"Last night, Gaev and Mikhailov were discussing senators," Locke said.

"And you're leaping to—what?" Jared shrugged. "They're talking politics? Who cares?"

"It's weird," Locke pointed out.

"I've seen a lot of weird shit in my life," Jared said. "Enemies becoming friends at a bar isn't weird. Even after they've tried to kill each other. That's the fucking story of my life."

Rocco nodded. "Yeah. We're missing something."

Locke rubbed his hands together. "Cassidy Noble, the reporter who was with Alex Gaev—"

Jared laughed. "I think we all know who she is. You've made a big enough deal out of her that we'll probably never forget her. Speaking of which, how goes intel-therapy?"

Locke bit his tongue and recalibrated his approach. "It goes so well that I'm going to ask you if I can work with her on something." He didn't know what they were missing, but hell, it was out there, and this was important. "She was with me when we saw Alex and the Russians. She's been following Alex, and I've been checking up on her, and the woman thinks some seriously hinky shit is going on."

"*Seriously hinky shit.* There's a first for me," Rocco muttered.

Locke ignored him. "There's no telling what Ivan would do to exploit others."

Parker walked in. "I agree."

Jared glared over his shoulder. "And why is that?"

"Because Ivan Mikhailov has come in and out of the US more times in the last six months than in the last two years, and because I threw some feelers out to see what's out there. The chatter is fierce."

"What's going on?" Jared asked.

Parker grimaced. "He's opening a new line of business, and it ain't pretty, and Ivan wants an insurance policy in the United States."

CHAPTER TWENTY-TWO

CASSIDY'S PHONE RANG, and she jumped for it. Not that she had been waiting for it to ring all day, but she had. Locke's number was on the screen. She swiped the screen to answer and in her most casual voice said, "Hey, how you doing?"

"Hey, Beauty. I'm good. How are you?"

Dang it to hell. How was she supposed to play cool when he dropped things like *Beauty*? "Oh, you know, I'm good."

An awkward silence hung there for a second, and she couldn't gather her thoughts, which was so unlike her.

"I found some information for you." Locke cleared his throat quietly. "I mean, it's shady. I'm not trying to insert myself into your work, but if you want information, I have something to offer."

"Really?" Information was far sweeter than roses and chocolates.

"Backgrounds and a folder full of connections for the folks he met at the club."

"Wow, yes." Her silly grin from earlier was gone. Locke's news just made her happy. "I'd love to see that."

"And..."

"And?" He couldn't leave her hanging.

"We have access to Titan's resources."

Her jaw dropped. "We do?"

"To nose around a bit. See what else there is besides a few one-off coincidences."

Cassidy couldn't believe what he was offering, and as her mind reeled, she wondered what the hell was in the folder that Locke had. "I'm right, aren't I?" she whispered.

"Is he a spy? I don't know." But Locke took a deep breath, and she could picture him stretching or rubbing his hand into his hair, deep contemplation marring his perfect face. "But I was right when I said to stop following them all over town. Not good people, Cass."

Damn. Alex was in bed with the Russians. It wasn't just that he upset someone in Russia and they chased him back to the US. "A journalist just knows where there's a story. Haven't you heard that?"

He quietly laughed. "No, I hadn't heard."

"But…" She plopped down on her couch and grabbed her notebook full of half-thought-out guesses and arrows that led to nowhere. "I'm missing something."

"I might know what that puzzle piece is."

"Yeah? Want to share?"

Again, he chuckled quietly. "You could wait for gut instinct to tell you."

"Locke!" She slapped her notebook shut. "Don't you trust me enough to share?"

"Draven trusted you; I think I can too."

The mention of Locke's CO caught her off guard, and her throat instantly tightened. It was easy to think about the loss of her good friend when she was prepared for it, but not when it came out of the blue. She might never get over Sadr City, and it still consumed Locke, dictating his thoughts on almost every conversation, even the easygoing teasing ones.

"Buzzkill. Sorry." Locke took a deep breath and blew it out. "I'm still working through that shit. It fucks me up sometimes. I don't like that I can't say his name without feeling gut-shot."

She got it. Mentions of Mike left her raw, and in general, she thought Locke didn't trust her on Sadr City. "Me too."

"And I wanted to mention…" He paused, letting an uncomfortable silence join them on the phone. "Look, you gave me a pass the other night when I came back. I get that, and… I can't explain it other than the music got under my skin at Red Star." He laughed, but this time, it was a shameful, scornful sound that hurt her to hear. "Sounds whacked, right? The music fucking got under my skin…" His voice became a whisper, then he cleared his throat. "But some things do that. They trigger a memory, and I'm there again."

She wished like hell she could hug him and had no idea what the right thing to say was, but instead, she just let him keep going.

"Kind of like PTSD. Just hits, then I calm down. But before that? Hell of a night."

"Yeah, it was."

"Who would've guessed I'd ever be on the phone with you talking about feelings," he muttered. "It just feels like—I can't control what I should be able to."

"Give yourself a break." She wasn't sure what he needed from her, and she knew that one heartfelt confession wasn't going to be the end of it. "Healing isn't linear, Locke. It jags up; it tears down. Don't confuse that for weakness."

Silence…

"Damn you, Beauty. I wish you were standing here right now."

"Why?" she whispered.

"Because." He breathed deeply into the phone and cleared his throat. "Never mind. Look, there's a kid. That's your missing puzzle piece."

She tried to follow his thoughts, realizing he'd changed subjects. "Alex?"

"Yeah. He might have a kid. And—"

That was as close as she was going to get to a heart-to-heart with Locke, and it was good, if not abrupt. But that was okay when he was connecting major dots and finding huge missing pieces in her investigation. "With the woman in Russia. That's the mother?"

"It's a chance." Locke hummed in thought. "Look, I have a folder that's begging for you to read. Interested?"

"Tell me where to meet you."

"Can you be ready in an hour? I'll be there."

"Yeah, of course. Hey, Locke?"

"Yeah, babe?"

She wanted to say something more about PTSD. Something about bruises that couldn't be seen and how exhausting it was to look impenetrable when, on the inside, the scaffolding shook. Instead, she closed her eyes and vowed to hug him the second she saw him. “Thank you. That’s it. Just thanks.”

CHAPTER TWENTY-THREE

THE DOORBELL RANG, and Cassidy jumped up off her couch, having lost herself in the world of ZNN and on-air reports that she thought maybe she could do different, better, faster, slower. It didn't matter how—one day, she'd be back on primetime TV. But she also must have lost track of time. "Wow. Locke was fast."

She shouldn't have been nervous about visiting Locke's work. But it was the good nervous that made butterflies run into each other and bump heads. She'd quickly dressed and looked casually professional enough to walk into his work, yet she absolutely picked out a pencil skirt and fitted blouse that drew attention to where he most liked to put his hands—over her curves.

"Coming." She slipped on her heels and fluffed her hair, then she stopped by the mirror near her door. No fuss hair and her makeup looked fine. If he was going to fall for her, he should see the real deal anyway, not the party girl dressed for the club. She threw the door open—

Her eyes peeled back as her stomach dropped with uncertain dread. "Alex." *And a friend.*

"Hi." Alex's eyes were sunken and dark. He hadn't shaved. At the club, he'd had a five-o'clock shadow, but now his facial hair was substantially overgrown. The smell of vodka and stale cigarettes clung to his clothes even though it was late in the afternoon. Cassidy wasn't sure if he'd been home from the night before to take a shower. The man with him looked roughly the same and seemed eerily like the people in Ivan Mikhailov's circle of friends.

"Um, Alex? Are you okay?" The other man hung to the side as though he weren't even on her front stoop, and her gut instinct screamed that there was a problem. The way he stood awkwardly to the side made her uneasy, and Cassidy wasn't sure if she should address him, ignore him, or what. But then she glanced the man's way and gave a flat smile and a confident, "Hello."

The man narrowed his eyes but said nothing.

"What's going on?" she asked Alex since he hadn't bothered to answer if he was okay.

His face darkened as his eyes swept her attire. "What are you doing? Where are you going like that?"

True, it was a bit much for a Sunday. Too work-ish to claim as church clothes. "Work."

"On a Sunday?"

"The news never stops. Why are you at my home? How do you even know where I live?"

"What did you do last night?" His scouring brow tightened.

"I think you should leave." Her stomach dropped again. Cassidy stepped onto her front porch, not wanting them inside and suddenly far more uncomfortable than she had been moments before. Apprehension squeezed bile into her throat. Did they know that she'd followed Alex? Was this a Mikhailov? "You could have called. I thought your schedule has been…"

"Complicated, Cassidy. It's been complicated."

"I've been trying to work with you," she said, flicking her eyes to the other man, who stepped forward. "*Can I help you?*"

The man didn't say anything. Shit, Cassidy wished she had a dog. A big, angry dog. Where was Locke?

Alex's eyes narrowed, tracking her assessment of the man. "Why?"

"Why, what?" She tried to recall what she'd just asked.

"Why?" he snapped.

"Is something wrong? Obviously, I've upset you. But… look." What had she done to cause them to show up? "There's a lot of pressure to get the articles and the op-ed done, but don't worry about it. Not if it's going to make you this troubled."

The other man stood next to Alex. She backed away, inching away from her front door, to the side of him. "Why don't you both leave?"

"Were you at Red Star last night?" the man asked, his Russian-accented English dripping with venom.

Lie or not? *Fucking hell.*

"Cassidy!" Alex shouted.

She jumped.

"Truth. Now," Alex pushed her again.

"Yes," she admitted, panicking.

"Why?"

Her mind raced for the safest reason. "Because I've been trying to get you to help me, damn it. I can't get my job back. Look at me; I'm doing stupid interviews at low-level reporting jobs that might not air. On a Sunday." She threw her arms out, hoping to God she had acting skills. "I used to have a major-network primetime gig that people would *kill* for. And now I'm reduced to trying to land op-eds and high school articles that are on hold because my teacher *friend*"—she used air quotes—"wants to go party it up. *Forgive me* if I want my goddamn job back!"

The unknown man leaned inches from her face, rancid vodka breath festering. "You have no idea what you are doing."

Cassidy slammed her hands into his chest. "Get off my porch."

The man's backhand flew swung back high and fast. She saw the knuckles coming as she reeled back on her heels. The impact snapped her head. The crack reverberated with the lights crackling behind her eyelids. Her body twisted violently.

Shock stunned her, paralyzing her mind. Her balance was gone; her balance in high heels gave out as she reached for anything to catch. Nothing. Nothing but air, inches away from a railing she couldn't grab onto.

Her fingers clawed as a blur of the world spun. Her body hit as she fell, landing and tumbling, falling and rolling. Her knees. Then her neck. Head. Then hands. Stars sprang—the violent, dark, and spinning kind—and her jaw snapped shut as white-hot pain hit the back of her head.

An earthquake of agony ricocheted again. Her back screamed, and her shoulder blades wept in pain as she replayed the fall. Stairs. Railing.

Sidewalk.

She tried to open her eyes. Tried to call for help.

Nothing. Until she realized she was on the brick sidewalk, vaguely aware she'd half-landed in a mulch bed, the flowers in her face. All the way down the brick staircase.

Cassidy gagged, spitting out dirt as it mixed with her blood. Every bone felt as though it had shattered. She squeezed her eyes shut, sure she was hemorrhaging blood. Dying. She couldn't breathe. There were no gasps left to let her scream for help.

"Shit, Cassidy!" Alex sounded so far away. His words spun, mocking her, making her want to vomit. "What the fuck did you do?"

Cassidy gasped—finally able to take a breath. She pushed up. Trying. Trying… no. She couldn't. Gasp. Cough. Oh, she sputtered and inhaled. The air had been knocked out of her lungs. She wasn't dead. But her temples… they pounded, and painfully, she dropped back as a headache barreled between her ears.

These steps are going to kill you. Softly, she began to cry, and not just because everything hurt. But that was the moment that everything caught up with her. She thought about how her career had come crashing down. She'd been in war and in prison, the laughingstock of politicians, of a country. And hated by a man who maybe didn't dislike her so much anymore but still ran from her when things became hot and heavy.

She was too exhausted—physically, emotionally, mentally. Cassidy hurt… so… many ways. Soft tears fell, and she didn't have the strength to get up and wipe them away. She was broken, absolutely shattered. She hadn't known that she was so close to falling apart or that a little pain would destroy her carefully constructed façade.

"Cassidy!"

Her eyes opened, and disoriented, she blinked through tear-soaked lashes as Locke's face was suddenly in front of hers. His palms were on her cheeks. His blue eyes were intent with worry—and anger.

Oh no. Wilting behind her pathetic parade of tears, she tried to sit up and wipe her face.

"Easy, don't move."

She agreed but moved anyway, burying her face in her hands and sobbing.

Locke ran his hands over her. "Easy, Beauty."

The lull of his voice and hands brought a calm. He whispered her name over and over like a spell until she crawled into his arms. Locke's solid body turned to a warm pillow. All she needed was to be wrapped in his cocoon, safe from the shock that had held her.

"I'm sorry," she whispered, hearing her voice echo in her head.

"Sorry? Don't be. We'll head to the hospital. Get you checked out."

"No, no." She wanted to shake her head but couldn't justify how badly her headache would hurt. "I don't like hospitals."

He held her closer. "You need to see a doctor."

Cassidy straightened. "I have a high pain threshold."

"Beauty, you're sobbing in your front yard."

She looked around, stared up the stairs, and then realized that her high heel had come off and her skirt had hiked—not that it mattered, since she was curled in a ball in Locke's arms. Slowly, she unfolded herself and sat next to him. "He pushed me."

Locke's caring face morphed. His blue eyes boiled, and his steely jaw flexed. "Excuse me?"

Cloudy-headed, she tried to recall how it had all happened. "Or he hit me. With his hand. Drew back and…"

"*Who?*"

"Alex was here—"

"Alex hit you?" Locke's deadly growl curled with the vicious, simple question.

"No," Cassidy whimpered. "He was here. With a man. And… they knew I was there. I pushed him, and he smacked me. I fell."

She focused on Locke as he tried to make sense of what she was saying. How they'd figured her out when her disguise covered her features was anyone's guess.

Locke shook his head. "Doctor's. Let's go."

Cassidy wiped her face. "This was more a mental breakdown than a broken bone."

His tight face showed that he didn't agree. "You might have a concussion."

"Then ibuprofen and no nap."

A car slowed as it passed to look at them sitting at the base of her front steps. "You're probably bleeding, Cass."

Probably so. Her knees were, and she shifted next to him. "Do you have a first aid kit in your truck? Because I'm not the type to stock Band-Aids."

Locke's inner war played on his face. Again, she could read one of his expressions, and it was a big fat *I don't wanna.* "Yeah… in my go-bag."

"Then bandage me up, because I don't want to go to a hospital. They'll want a report, want to press charges, and that will mess up what we're working on."

He looked at the base of the stairs where she had landed and let his eyes drift up, up, up.

"You know I'm right, Locke. Greater good here."

Locke reached for the rogue high heel then took her foot and slipped it on. His hands lingered longer than they should, and a sliver of goosebumps traveled up her calf, stopping short of her newly scraped knee—there was something so wrong with her if, in pain and in shock, she had a semblance of carnal interest.

But it *was* Locke, and who could deny that his strong, large hands smoothing over her skin wasn't some special kind of medicine. The act of slipping her shoe on seemed so chivalrous, possessive, protective.

"Please take me inside. The ringing in my ears has already stopped, and my purse has some headache medicine. I'll pop those, and it'll help with the soreness too."

Locke's features faltered as though he couldn't decide.

"Please, Locke. It's important to me that I keep going. Don't make me beg."

He rolled his lips together, and the tendons in his neck strained. "Give me a second to grab my shit."

"Okay."

"You sure you're okay?" he asked.

"What am I going to do? Fall again while I'm sitting down?" Locke took that moment to tip her head back and kiss her uncertain laugh off her lips.

Just like his protective, possessive hands, his lips were tender and said a million things as caring and calm, but when he pulled away, he twisted a strand of her hair in his fingers. "I'm going to kill that Russian fucker, Beauty. Just so you know."

She would've laughed if it wouldn't have hurt. For how singsong sweet and romantic he'd sounded, the man worrying over her was deadly lethal. "Thank you, baby."

His worry lines softened for a moment. "I know you're patronizing me."

"Not as much as you think, but I know you're not going to murder someone."

Locke grumbled, raising an eyebrow. "And if anything doesn't look right, I'm taking you to the hospital. Deal?"

Her lips pouted.

"Or no deal. Those are your two options."

"You wouldn't ruin an op for my well-being."

Locke's hard glare broke. "You have no idea what I'd do when it comes to you." He pushed off the ground and headed to his truck, quickly returning with his go-bag, pulling it across his chest like a messenger bag. She held her hand up for help off her butt, and—oh, her muscles were so dang sore—it was as good a time as ever to stand up. He leaned over—but scooped her up as though she were the flowers she had lain in.

"*Locke.*" Her feet dangled in the air as she wrapped an arm around his neck.

"Yeah?"

"I can walk, you know."

"Then I wouldn't have your ass in my arms. What fun would that be?" He chuckled, and she relaxed and dropped her head against his shoulder.

The man had a good point.

CHAPTER TWENTY-FOUR

CRADLED IN LOCKE'S arms, Cassidy had an altogether different point of view of her home as they entered. Mostly because she was floating, in more than one way, and trying to put on a brave face as her headache waned but the cuts and scrapes screamed for attention.

"Over there, please." She directed him toward the kitchen, where the nearest bottle of pain relievers was likely stashed in her purse.

They passed awards and newspaper clips that she had framed and hung on her wall. She wondered if Locke would react if he saw any of the clippings from Sadr City. They were a source of pride—as much as they were her downfall—and she'd decorated with them after she stopped winning awards for her writing and broadcasts as a reminder of where she had been and what she had survived and attained, so she could achieve all that again.

"Easy does it." He placed her on the counter and went to a cabinet, on his first guess finding the glasses and then filling one with water.

Locke's eyes lingered on the wall. He stood in front of the framed front-page *Washington Journal* spread on Cassidy's sentencing. It was a source of pride, though Locke probably was of the group that thought she'd committed treason for journalistic integrity.

He didn't mention it, though.

She reached for her purse and popped out the headache pills and then took the water he offered. She swallowed them down, semi-able to read his face. It didn't have to do with the clippings or Sadr City reports. He was upset about her injuries. Or maybe a combination of the two things. "What is it?"

"You have mulch in your hair." He picked a piece or two out, flicking them into the sink. "Ready to get cleaned up?"

She nodded, knowing that anywhere they went in the house would be like walking through a museum of her reporting. Not likely his favorite thing.

"Here? Where at?" he asked, not mentioning the magazine cover that her mom had framed and displayed across from the fridge. Cassidy couldn't make a cup of coffee in the morning without the reminder that she'd been on top once and would get back there.

"I can run to my bathroom and bandage myself up."

Locke's brow lifted and said *nuh-uh* without him having to say a word.

"I want to stare at myself in the mirror. You don't need to be party to that." Cassidy half-laughed. "The cuts and bruises—I don't know. They're going to be like a badge of honor. I want to see them. Ugly and all."

He stepped closer. "Nothing's ugly, hon."

The way he said it… Cassidy swallowed hard. Sometimes he didn't say much, but he said *everything*. His voice rumbled, and his intonation was measured. Locke could hide a thousand meanings in a simple phrase. Warmth crawled up her neck. "Help me down."

Just a nod. No words—just his capable hands on her waist—and still so much was said. He gently set her down as though she still had her dignity and wasn't mulch-covered and scratched.

"This way." Cassidy's high heels clicked on the hardwood floor, and she smoothed her hands over her hips, suddenly nervous that Locke was entering her sanctuary, however clean or messy she'd left it. If she'd had any idea he'd be near her bedroom and bath, a quick tidy would've been nice. "If we step over rogue panties on the floor, I have no problem admitting I'm not the greatest at laundry. Or using my hamper."

He chuckled. "Do you routinely leave—"

A bra hung on her doorknob, and she grabbed it, tossing it toward the closet. "Nothing to see here, folks."

His laugh gained gusto. "My eyes aren't even open."

Cassidy spun on her heel. "They so are."

He hitched half a smile and tilted his head but didn't give her much to work with, and she spun back around as they stepped into her bathroom.

She flipped the light on, thankful the room was neat, and Locke extracted a first aid sack from his bag as she stared in the mirror. There was a purplish bruise on her cheekbone where Alex's friend had backhanded her. "Does this qualify as a shiner?"

"Maybe a little low."

"Aw, shucks. Maybe next time."

"There won't be a next time." Tension flexed in the tendons in his neck as he placed items on the counter and rummaged through her bevy of lotions, sprays, brushes, and makeup. Locke rolled his lips and let out a breath like he was trying to let go of the anger. Maybe she wouldn't joke about black eyes.

"You have a lot of girl crap not to have any first aid crap."

She shifted next to him, toying with the bottle of her favorite lotion, and then popped the lid open, smelled it, forced it under his nose, and pulled it back. "I plan on spilled nail polish, *not blood*, and have a secret thing for sugary-scented lotions and sprays."

He made a face she couldn't read, as always.

"Tell anyone I'm not a cutthroat reporter and can be bought off with body lotion, and you're a dead man."

He flashed a quick glance but focused on the first aid supplies. "Your secret is safe with me." Setup complete, Locke turned his full attention on her, stepping closer.

Instantly, Cassidy's pain lessened under his silken smolder with him close, so protective, so gentle, yet so focused. That lethal powerhouse of brawn and brute force was housed in one man, and he was taking care of her. Her throat tickled with emotion and need, something entirely different from what had built inside her at Red Star.

"What's that look?" he asked. "Headache getting worse?"

"No. Better." She'd never confess that the look was her going far too deep.

"What hurts the worst?"

Quickly, Cassidy took an account of her injuries. She was much less achy than she expected, though maybe the double dose of pain relievers had helped. Her back hurt more than her knees, and the more she tried to ignore the pain under her hairline, the more that spot on her neck hurt.

"What's bothering you?"

"This is getting worse, but the rest isn't so bad." She lifted her hair. "See anything?" She twisted, trying to look in the mirror simultaneously. "I think I scraped it."

Locke sucked air through his teeth. "Damn it, Cass. That didn't just start hurting."

"No…" She dropped her hair and took a hand mirror from a drawer. He scowled as she turned to face him. "That bad, huh?"

"No," he said, but she was getting better at reading his BS.

Cassidy looked in the hand mirror and saw the reflection of her neck in the bathroom mirror. "Oh."

"Oh," he repeated. "The edge of a stair caught your neck, maybe?"

"I don't know," she mumbled.

"Looks like one of 'em took a chunk out of you, babe."

Cassidy bit her lip. "Looks like."

"Okay, back around." His cool fingers skimmed over her skin. The touch was methodical and precise, only meant to help, yet still she found her skin prickling with goosebumps. "Some hair dried in it."

It was the wrong time to react to his caress. "Gross. I'm sorry."

"I'll pretend you didn't just apologize to me for bleeding." Locke's concentration deepened. He was in work mode. He ducked closer and carefully dislodged strands drying in her scab.

Not meaning to sway in her heels, she watched him, drunk on the idea he was doctoring her. It was erotic. She couldn't figure out how or why. It just was. She knew how his tongue felt in her mouth, how his words could get her wound up, and his mind could challenge her—but Locke was physically taking care of her—even if it was just a scratch—and he was throwing his entire focus into it. Into her. She swayed again because, damn—had anyone ever cared that much about her well-being? No.

"You're steady on your feet?" He stood upright and eyed her suspiciously in the mirror, not having a clue he was whipping her into a frenzy. "Because even on the best of days, those heels are…" His lips pushed together, and he let the moment hang as she blushed in the mirror. "Hard to walk in."

She wasn't taking her shoes off if Locke looked at her like she'd struck a match to gasoline and lit him aflame from the inside out—not for all the pain pills in this house. "I'm good."

"You are?" His dexterous fingers danced over the fabric of her fitted blouse, running along the seam on her shoulders. He sucked his cheeks in, and his tongue dipped out over his lower lip before he dropped a long glance at her heels, letting the lazy gaze drag up her legs and over her backside and meet her face in the mirror again.

"Yes. Fine." Oh, no she wasn't. She needed first aid ointment and a Band-Aid but was painfully aware that his blue eyes could caress her in a way that ensured she would need a follow-up with his hands.

When he couldn't look away, she couldn't either. Did he see how she was losing control? Her bed—where she had thought about him so many nights—was a few feet from where they stood. At Red Star, before the PTSD hit, they'd been wild. Touching and teasing. In public… at her front door, after their fight, they were on a path to regroup and restart. Now, they had their privacy, but this wasn't sexy. She was a mess—though who cared about a little mulch and bruising?

He trailed a dangerous finger along her jawline, not knowing how little she cared about her injuries. "Knees. Neck. Where else were you hurt?"

His finger stilled, and she could feel the riot of pleasure quaking within her, starting at her knees, trembling up her thighs until she was sure that her panties were wet just because his fingernail scraped along her jaw.

"Cassidy?" His husky voice raked over her senses.

"Oh, you know." The driving hunger that stirred inside her now pounded in her lungs, making her hitching breaths evident. Cassidy licked her lips. Her casual words shook, to a discerning ear. Likely to *his* ear. "My pride."

She wanted nothing more than for him to touch her, but he seemed unflappable. Then he stole his fingers away, and she wanted to moan in complaint. But that was good. Responsible. Very Locke. Medical treatment and Alex Gaev were the things that should be in her mind. Not need and hunger and a deep desire to see if he could kiss away all her pain.

"Where else, Cassidy?"

"My back."

"Got it." He ran his hand into his unkempt hair, and she wondered how it would feel in her hands.

It was perfectly chaotic, as though the right length and imperfections had converged in blond hair thick enough for her to grab onto. How would his hair feel brushing against the inside of her thighs while he kissed her to orgasm? *Hell…* She rubbed her thighs together. Now wasn't the time to imagine that. Nor was it the time to think about how his fingers might feel if they plunged deep and his lips sucked her clit.

Her heart raced. This was too much, and she needed so much more—

"You okay, Beauty?" Locke asked.

She sucked a breath, stammering, "Yes."

"Thought I lost you for a second to a daydream."

A hot blush colored her cheeks, and she followed his gaze down her blouse, where her nipples pressed the white fabric. It wasn't cold in her house. Between that and her visibly rising chest…

He gently caressed her arm as she lifted her face and watched him in the mirror. "I'm glad you're here."

Their bodies touched. Her back was to his front, and she stood in her scuffed white shirt and black skirt.

His hand touched her elbow, running up her biceps. "Cassidy?"

The hairs on her arms stood at attention—her whole self did when he dropped his voice low and commanded it. "Yes?"

"Roll your sleeves up. Let me check your elbows."

Cassidy held his eyes in the mirror. "Are you… mad at me?"

"About?"

"I yelled at Alex. You know I have that little habit of pushing people, getting in their faces, and maybe I egged them on."

"No." His gaze dropped to the ointment tube. "I'm not mad *at you*."

"What's that mean?"

"*At me*." He blew out. "I'm mad at myself. If I was here earlier… I don't know… this wouldn't have happened."

"Oh." That wasn't what she'd expected. "Locke, don't be."

He shrugged. "Yeah, well. That's the truth, babe. You asked. There's the truth."

Maybe that was why she was drowning in sexual tension and he… wasn't?

"Let me see your elbow, babe."

She tilted her head and decided to ignore him, needing him to feel the sexual tension as much as she did and *not feel* one ounce of guilt for when he arrived. Cassidy undid the bottom button of the front of her blouse instead. Shocked at what she was doing, she looked up, and she could hear her breath. His blue eyes watched her fingers skip to the next button on her blouse before they met her gaze in the mirror.

"What are you doing, Cass?"

Oh, hell. She didn't know, but with every button, she felt the wave of arousal grow stronger. Cassidy unfastened the third button. The shirt was loose under her heavy breasts, and then she couldn't be clearer about what she was doing.

He stepped closer, aligning his body to hers, his hands resting possessively on her side. Now, her fingers trembled. She didn't know why the heat of his palm scorching though the fabric on her hips made a difference. They'd been running down a road of deeply sexual moments since they'd met each other. But still, the rise and fall of her chest was shakily evident as she worked free the button directly over her lacy white bra.

Her tummy showed. It wasn't flat—nowhere near perfect—but Locke squeezed, and a deep growl of approval made her slick with need.

"I want my face buried in those tits." His grip constricted again. "Do you know that?"

Her lips parted, a quiet gasp falling free. One button left, and her hands hovered over it as they both watched in the mirror.

"Let me see, Beauty," he rasped.

Her fingers fluttered over the final button. The fabric bowed away, framing her tummy and breasts. Cassidy's arms drifted to her sides slowly, and finally, his large hands stirred. He lifted away the loosened blouse, dragging it down her arms. The soft fabric seemed to scrape along her heightened senses, and goosebumps danced.

The dark pink of her puckered nipples pressed into the lace as the shirt slid to the floor.

"Gorgeous." He teased the pads of his fingers up her arms, skimming over the hairs standing on end.

"So are you." She stood in only a white lace bra, black pencil skirt, and high heels. She had darkening bruises, crazy red hair, and the wild, wild want of him coloring her cheeks pink.

"The places I'm going to kiss you…" He leaned close and ran a hand over her belly, across her panty line, to the vee at top of her leg, rubbing her mound through the skirt. "Ask me again. Like you did at the club."

Her legs went weak, remembering that night. "Touch me."

He curled his body over hers, pulling the skirt up, stroking her inner thigh. "What do you want, Cassidy?"

You. His erection was evident. *Hell.* A flush ran through her again. She was wet, wanting with him this close, wanting to explore him too, maddeningly enough, suddenly surprisingly enough, more than she wanted him teasing her.

"Tell me," he said.

"You," she gasped. "I want my mouth on you." Her inner muscles clenched when she voiced the idea, her lungs stuttered. "I want to kiss and suck you too."

His eyebrows rose in the mirror. "That's what you want?"

Nodding and mouth watering, she nodded then arched back against him as he slipped his fingers higher up her thigh and dropped his mouth onto her neck, nuzzling at her ear as she watched in the mirror.

"You taste good." His eyes were closed, and she fought to keep hers open. His free hand covered a breast the moment the other hand met the apex of her thighs. "You feel good."

"Ahhh." His thumb strummed over her tit, her panty-covered clit. "Locke."

"You sound good," he said against her neck, eyes watching everything in the mirror.

"I'm just standing here," she whimpered. She felt the natural juices of her body lubricating her passageway, wetting her underwear, and damn, how she wanted his deft fingers to slip under the fabric.

"Good, babe. Keep doing that." He massaged her breast, rolling his hands firmly, making her ass squirm, but his fingers wouldn't let her most needy area escape. Locke switched to the other breast, plucking at her nipple, thumbing it, and easing back.

She arched, needing both his hands. Could a nipple make a woman orgasm? *Hell.* Her hips swayed. "Touch me," she pleaded.

He strung her tighter and tighter. Yes, she could have an orgasm strictly from nipple stimulation—she was sure of it because it could happen soon. "Oh…"

His lips tugged at her earlobe, and he pulled the fabric of the bra cups down as she watched their show play out in the mirror before them. There was a chance she could. "Locke… *please.*"

Coolness teased her exposed skin, and he cupped her breast and rolled her bare nipple between his thumb and forefinger.

"Shit. God. I might…" She was so close. Almost there.

His mouth connected with her shoulder, and hot kisses trailed toward her neck, and his fingers swept under her panties, slipping against the wet folds.

"Yes," she groaned. "Really, I'm… Oh."

The pad of his thumb circled the bud of her clit, and he slid two thick fingers inside her, pumping with the rhythm of her hips, twisting and plucking the nipple in her hand. His teeth grabbed onto her shoulder, and she bucked, crying and riding his fingers. "Yes," she moaned. The climax hit her like a hurricane.

His mouth moved to her ear. "Do it again."

"A minute," she gasped, barely able to see straight as his hands moved to hold her waist and he kissed down her back.

She heard the sound of her skirt's zipper before she realized he had it down.

"Turn around for me, Cassidy."

She did as Locke bent onto his knees, dragging the pencil skirt down, kissing her stomach, hips, thighs as it fell to the ground.

"High heels and these?" Locke snagged a finger under the edge of her panties. "Fucking hot."

She might be able to come again from this powerful man on his knees saying that. He wrapped his forearm behind her thighs and lifted her onto the counter, spreading her legs as she instinctively snapped her knees shut. He slid his hands up her legs and dragged her underwear to the side, exposing her folds.

Stunned and blinking, she looked down at him. She had never been with someone so alpha strong and primal, so needy, and it was fucking insane. Erotic. She was on display. Her pleasure was his, and her body hummed, more aroused and alive than she'd ever been.

"This is crazy."

"What is?" He scooted her closer to the edge of the counter and nuzzled his nose against her pussy. "Because this?" He rubbed her slowly. Methodically. "This is sexy as fuck."

"I thought *this* was a task."

He drew his fingers back, stroking against her slit. "If that's what you thought, you've been with the wrong guys."

Her mind froze. Had she? Hell, she didn't know. Didn't matter—Oh, God. He was making her insane as his sweet tongue traced the same strokes as his fingers.

"Locke," she cried as her knees shook.

He shouldered her legs wider, and both of his hands went to work, exposing her innermost skin with a gentle touch. His lips, tongue, the stubble on his cheek—the combination made her moan, and she let her fingers thread into his hair, feeling each move his head made. Sweet Lord…

His stiff tongue fucked her, fingers taking their turn. She couldn't make sense of it all. So many sensations—too many to love. She closed her eyes, rocking and writhing as he made every vibration work in the right way.

Locke pulled the fabric of her underwear farther to the side. "Fuck, I want this." His lips feathered along the patch of trim hair, and he squeezed her ass. "All of this."

"God." Each word sent a shockwave across her nerves, and he never stopped the onslaught of rhythmic thrusts into her body.

Cassidy buckled. "I need this..." She gasped, knotting her fingers, knowing she pulled too much, unable to help herself. "So much."

Panting, shaking, she wanted more and couldn't move. He curled his fingers inside her body. "Locke!"

He rasped his five-clock shadow along her skin. "Come for me."

God. She fell apart and bucked against his mouth, on his hand.

"Good, Beauty. Good." He nuzzled his lips back and forth, and she jumped as he pulled back, kissing up her hip, her stomach. "Goddamn, good girl."

Spent. She couldn't even remember how to move—

But she didn't have to. Locke wrapped his arm around her, lifting her off the counter. "You did so good."

Her pussy still twitched and quivered as he carried her in a star-struck daze. A flush coated her limbs, a smile lingered on her cheeks, and she leaned forward, kissing him wherever her lips landed—against his neck, mixed in with his hair. "I pulled your hair."

"Battle scar I'll gladly take." He crawled them onto the bed.

"I don't think I'll ever look at my bathroom the same way again."

LOCKE'S PHONE RANG, and he ignored it. Staying in bed with Cassidy was the only thing on his agenda. Deepening the kiss, he flexed his cock against her, and she groaned. One of her legs wrapped around his, and her hands had found their way under the back of his shirt, scratching in a way that made his dick harder than he could ever remember.

The fucking phone rang again. "Ignore it," he said.

It kept ringing, and if he could have reached it without taking his hands off her and thrown it against the brightly painted wall, he might've.

"I'm not trying to be a buzzkill," Cassidy mumbled against his lips, "but someone's *really* trying to get a hold of you."

Jesus Christ. There had better be a five-alarm fire, and every other man alive had better have disappeared off the face of the earth. "Damn it. Hold on."

He rolled off her and grabbed the phone from her nightstand, where he'd tossed everything from his pockets: keys, phone, and goddamn condom.

Rocco. Locke gritted his teeth as he pulled his act together—he could handle a two-minute conversation with his boss—and tried to sound like he hadn't been two minutes away from diving dick first into the sweetest pussy to walk the planet.

He swiped the phone. "Yeah. Hey, Boss."

Locke turned to face Cassidy, who had wrapped her pale body around a turquoise body pillow, high heels *still on.* Her hair stood out starkly against the white comforter as she waited near a backboard of boldly colored, randomly sized pillows.

As Rocco talked, Cassidy patiently waited for him to come back. Was there a better sight than that? Fuck, he didn't think so.

"Hey, asshole," Rocco snapped. "Yes or no?"

Well, fuck. "Say again?"

"You want the intel or not?"

"Yeah, of course."

"The reporter probably does too. You want her read-in on this too?"

Locke paused. Hell. Because as much as he'd have liked to avoid a fucking ass-chewing from Rocco, he didn't want to put Cassidy's life in danger just to have a less bumpy conversation.

"Rapunzel, did you hear a fucking word I said?" Rocco snapped.

"Shit, sorry. I was—"

"*Traffickers.* Delta team," his boss said, interrupting a distracted inability to pull together a bullshit excuse. "They picked up new intel. The Mikhailovs are expanding into human trafficking."

What. The. Fuck. "Paying attention now." Locke pinched the bridge of his nose. "What do we know?"

"They have eclectic taste, and we got our hands on what they're calling the *shopping list* for their oligarch buddies."

"And Delta's going in?" Locke asked.

"We don't know who's doing what." By Rocco's tone, that wasn't a satisfactory situation. "But with a break like this, something's sure to come in soon. Get your ass to HQ. Talk to the reporter. See what she knows and what her interest level is."

He muttered. "I can already tell you her interest is high."

Cassidy's eyebrows rose.

"I'll head that way," Locke said.

"How high?" Rocco pushed.

"*High.*"

"Good. Parker's working his angles. Hell, grab her if you think she's interested. But get her fast. We're not waiting around."

"Roger that." The call ended, and Locke stared at the blank screen. "So…"

Cassidy sat on the bed, turquoise pillow folded over and tucked to cover her. The mood was effectively over—*thank you, Rocco.*

"So?" Cassidy couldn't have looked more interested if she'd painted a sign that read Spit It Out.

He weighed the idea of asking for a quickie before deciding that the blue balls he was about to suffer was worth having if he could orgasm with her the way he'd just made her come. That might not happen if he tossed out the idea of a thirty-second hump-and-run. Fucking hell, he was hornier than he'd ever been in his life, and knew she might be too, but they could wait a few extra hours.

He gritted his molars together. "Change of plans, maybe." He shifted uncomfortably in his jeans, frustrated but hoping he was making the right decision, and cleared his throat. "Have you ever been to Titan Group?"

CHAPTER TWENTY-FIVE

THE PHONE RANG, pulling Alex from sleep. He blinked in the darkness and looked around. His hangover was gone, but not the nightmare, though he was clearly awake. Mikhailov's people were calling him, and hell, he needed to get control of the situation.

Alex took a deep breath as the phone continued to ring, and he tried to ignore images of Cassidy piled at the bottom of her stairs. He wanted to throw the damn thing across the room and let it shatter in the dark shadows.

Hell. It wouldn't stop ringing, and he suffered through another worried thought that Cassidy was seriously hurt before he took the phone off the charger and stared at it—a Russian phone number.

His heart stalled.

That was not like the Mikhailovs. They used US phone numbers, rarely calling direct from Russia, and that number didn't seem familiar. Uneasy, he swiped the call to answer it, a slice of hope daring him to become more awake. "Hello?"

Dead air hung. He pulled the phone back to see if the call was still active. It was. "Hello?"

"Alexander." Taisia's whisper hugged his heart. "*Sladkiy*?"

He bolted upright in bed as *honey* fell from her tongue, clinging to the phone as though he could hold her, terrified that something was wrong with their daughter, and in tears that the woman he loved had said his name. "Is Alyona okay?"

"She is…"

Then why was she calling? This was too risky! They'd tried to make things work in person, and it had almost killed them all, and he was so close to bringing them together. She didn't even know about that, but they had a plan, and that plan was to trust him to do right.

"Alexander…" The way she said his name made him worry. "Could you—I don't know how to word this… If I asked you to research something." Taisia's voice trailed again. "It might not sound safe, and you will want me to explain why, but I can't."

His stomach bottomed out. Of course there was a reason for the middle-of-the-night phone call. His first worry was always their daughter, but that wasn't it. "Please tell me if you're putting yourself in danger."

Taisia's hesitation was the answer. "A complication has arisen. I'm not sure how to put it into words, but I'm taking steps to fix it—"

"On your own?" Panic fueled his skittering heart. If there was any chance that she could do anything as dangerous as he was doing, he had put a stop to it. "No. *No*."

"See, Alexander? This is why I can't talk about specifics. I'm not even sure what I'm asking. I'm laying the foundation"—she gave a sad laugh—"almost quite literally. And when I figure out what it is that I need, you will be the first person that I turn to. I know that you will help me. I know that this will help us. Alexander, please. I'm letting you know I have no choice."

"Taisia, *chyort*."

"Please don't curse—I miss you. I miss you, I miss you, and if my hand wasn't forced…"

Tears slid down his face. "I miss you both."

"I love you," Taisia said. "*We* love you."

"I love you and Alyona too."

But as good as it felt to hear her, as much as he wanted this, he wanted her safe and taking care of their daughter more than any selfish need.

"Alexander…"

"No. We can't argue again." Not after the other night when she cried over the phone and he had to cancel a meeting with her father. It had ruined plans for that night and forced other plans to happen. "We have to stick to our plan. Let me do what I need to."

She hissed her disproval in the phone. "I know what you're doing."

"You do not." And now his plan had to work faster than she could do whatever she was up to and get herself killed. "But it will work. I promise."

"There has to be a different way. For both of us."

"We've been saying that for years." Even though no one around would hear him and he wasn't waking up his mother, he needed to control his emotions for no other reason than not to worry Taisia. She'd panicked and was taking actions into her own hands. That couldn't happen! "You have to trust me on this."

"Don't do it, Alexander," she pleaded. "There are other ways, and the risk is too much. Let me do what I need to, and—"

"We have come up with nothing over the years. We couldn't see each other before. And Alyona? I just want to see my daughter! I can't go on like this. I'll do whatever it takes to get to you and her, and if that means doing this, I've seen much worse happen."

"We are not those people! You have never been. When we were young and surrounded by all of them, all of the time…"

"Times change, Taisia."

"You were different, and that is why I love you."

"No, you love me because I promised you a family. To love you like our fathers didn't know how."

Taisia sniffled. "I know, I know… family chooses family. But you don't know how it is here. I'm *not* choosing my father, his hatred or disgusting choices…" Her shaking breath tore his soul. "I will fix what's wrong here, and I choose you."

"Taisia, what are you talking about?"

"We choose you. That's all that matters."

His head dropped when he could tell that the call had ended. Whatever she was up to, he would get to her first. The Mikhailovs were too dangerous for her to fight alone.

"*Ya veryu v tebya, Taisia.*" He put the phone next to him in bed in case she called back, repeating, "I believe in you, Taisia."

CHAPTER TWENTY-SIX

THE SCREEN SHOWED that forty-seven of Alexander's AP students had used the download link and given him a portal to their home networks within the last two weeks. He scrolled through their files, focusing on the students whose families the FSB were interested in.

The priority list contained five students. If he could get into their parents' cell phones, Alex could wrap this job, trade the intel for Taisia and Alyona, and call it a day.

The plan was easy: parent-teacher conferences. They were coming up, and everyone hated them, especially parents whose schedulers made arrangements for such inconveniences. But he'd already notified parents that the in-person meetings were off. They might as well have dubbed him a saint. The suggestion to use the online and teleconference resources was met with huge approval. Even the principal told other teachers to look at Alexander's program.

He tried not to feel like a braggadocio. His plan was for his family, not career advancement. As his fingers flew over the keyboard, he knew there was enough information in his hands or on the way for Ivan and the FSB to be very happy.

An email came on-screen. The subject line used Ivan's code word that requested Alexander to meet a Mikhailov flunkie. Perfect timing. He could now confirm everyone on his list, including parents who worked at the IMF, the United Nations, senate leadership, and the two front-runners for the White House.

Alex stood up, grabbed his wallet and his keys, threw his cell phone into his back pocket, and shouted up the stairs, "Hey, Mama. Do you need anything?"

"No, are you going out?" Her weak question tilted downward.

Mom's frailty killed him, and he cringed. Tanya would have to step up when he left for Taisia and Alyona. He jogged up the stairs halfway to continue the conversation. "I'll be back in a few hours. Go to bed."

"Okay, Alexander. Don't stay out too late. I'll wait up for you and your sister."

"Tanya…" She was never there. "She'll be home late too."

His eyes sank shut. He couldn't handle the responsibility of his mother's dementia that night. More and more, she was lost in the past and unable to complete basic tasks—the woman who'd taught him how to grift!

Tanya didn't believe Alexander when he said Mama couldn't remember their past, how they grew up, the crimes, the hunger, the cigarettes, the booze. His sister wouldn't come, not with her kids. She didn't want them exposed to the life they'd abandoned.

Maybe Mama would fall asleep waiting for her husband. Alexander cringed, holding on to that hope and disgust he felt for his parents' never-ending affection for one another. Maybe that was devotion. He thought about Taisia—so different yet similar.

He could never understand the relationship between his parents, but they had some sort of love. They were partners, and maybe once upon a time they'd been in love. Finances and hardship and life had made them drunk and criminal. Now Mama was just an old lady with dementia, no husband, and false memories of a nice family life.

"Take care, Mom. Everything will be okay."

Come hell or high water, come traitors or treason, come whatever obstacle he ran into, Alexander would make everything all right. Eventually.

ALEXANDER PULLED INTO the parking lot as the cell phone rang, and the Russian number caught him off guard again. His pulse jumped. "Hello?"

"Alexander, it's me again." Taisia's voice set his heart soaring.

He threw his car into park. "Is everything okay now?" One phone call on top of another was extremely risky, and he was apprehensive about what she wasn't telling him, and she was concerned enough to use burner phones or a new phone number every time.

"It's fine."

He paused. "Tell me the truth. What else is happening?"

Taisia let out a small sigh that stabbed him in the gut. More was happening. Even if she used a throwaway phone, that sound meant she probably wouldn't tell him what it was.

"Is our daughter okay?" Alexander bit his fingernail, worry eating at his mind.

She didn't respond.

"*Taisia, the truth!*"

"Yes, yes. I take care of Alyona; she has more security than you can ever imagine. But the family business has expanded, Alexander."

"Meaning?"

Again, another breath, this one worn and weighted. "There are women. Girls. All ages."

"I'm sorry?" Alexander tried to understand. *Girls?*

"They've even talked about young ones. Girls not too much older than Alyona, and I have to stop it. I can. I am…"

Girls. Like Ivan had at the club. A new business venture. The information that Ivan wanted from the US… If he was pulling women and girls from various countries, he would likely need to cover his tracks, and blackmail was the most efficient way to get around bureaucracy.

Nausea ran through him. But maybe he was making this a bigger thing than it was. Maybe the two things weren't connected—Ivan needing access to intelligence, and this new business. At home, the Russians had always had their fingers in petty crime, alcohol, drugs, gambling, you name it. But never prostitution and pedophilia. Prostitution existed, but he hadn't seen it. His mind reeled. "Is our daughter safe?"

"Yes, but others aren't. I can't allow that."

He couldn't either. "Damn."

"It's… sick," she mumbled.

Taisia's words repeated in his mind. *I can. I am.* Maybe this was wrong. He'd heard incorrectly. "How are you involved?"

"It's complicated. Father has me… working—"

"*What?*" Alexander exploded.

"No! Not in that manner! But what you might call *management.* And I think this is a way that I can stop this."

"Wait, one thing at a time." Alexander's molars gnashed together with a force that could break his jaw. "That son of a bitch."

"I didn't think he had something like this in him. The greed, though. Always the greed. You know, living like we do, I have no choice."

Alexander cringed. He couldn't have failed as a man and father more than right at that moment.

"But I can't let it go on. I can stop it," she whispered so faintly he was sure he misheard.

"What? How?" Alexander shook his head. He couldn't *not* help those girls. But yes, he could. If it kept *his girls* safe, he'd man the hell up and say no. His stomach turned. He wasn't sure there was a right decision. Maybe he'd misunderstood. "What are you talking about?"

"I can help them," she said. "I told you I needed research. If we can get them off the property—"

"Then what?" he spat out. "You're going to hide a couple of girls in your closet? You'll feed and clothe and house grown women in your part of the Mikhailov complex? Think it through. Your father will kill you!" This escalated everything. He needed to go there *immediately* and bring them home.

"Someone came and got them!" she cried. "There must be people missing these girls."

He dropped his head back. "Taisia… the world isn't perfect. God, I love you. But there's not always someone to save them."

"What if there is?"

"What if there isn't." He broke down. "You're going to risk your life—and our daughter's—to help people you don't know?"

"Alexander Gaev! You fell in love with a woman you weren't supposed to! I was a death sentence! I was someone you didn't know, and still, you stayed by my side all these years."

He crumbled on the inside. God, he knew that and loved her anyway. "You do whatever it takes to stay safe. I am coming for you."

CHAPTER TWENTY-SEVEN

THE PLASTIC BEACH toys lay on the expensive handmade comforter. Taisia's heart rate had finally reached a baseline in which she could glance at any of her makeshift tools and not have a panic attack.

Alyona dressed quietly in her nearby bedroom with the radio playing in the background as Taisia questioned everything about her skills as a mother. They were lying to everyone they knew. But everyone who lived and worked on the Mikhailov complex functioned at some level of complicity. They were all on payroll and following orders. Some were even dedicated to keeping her safe and protected.

Taisia and Alyona had had the same bodyguards for years, and lying to them was an act of betrayal. The thought stabbed at her, but she shook it off, trying to ignore the disloyalty that clouded her judgment and made it all confusing. Given a simple nod from her father, the men who'd protected her for decades would turn on Taisia and her daughter. One order, and she and Alyona would be dead.

Add that to the long list of reasons for leaving. Humans couldn't be for purchase. The new prostitution and pedophilia ring was the final straw. There were too many things she'd ignored with a blind eye, and she could wage war internally about that for the rest of her life. The criminal and government worlds had never before affected her, a protected Russian princess living a lavish lifestyle in a beautiful prison.

Alyona walked in, her hazel eyes—just like her daddy's—dropping to the beach toys on the bedspread, and in English, which they always practiced, asked, "Are we going to work on the door?"

Taisia's pride grew. "We are."

Alyona wouldn't be able to comprehend how women and girls could be for sale. There were children arriving soon, according to her father, who were only a few years older than her daughter, and Taisia would save them first. She'd kill any man who got near them, be it an accident or full-fledged murder. She would save all of them, starting with the youngest ones. They would go out the door that she and Alyona were tearing open.

The antiquated Mikhailov compound was steeped in their history, passed from generation to generation. The rich architecture of each mansion on their property towered, facing one another across a courtyard. There was much history between the great houses on the property. But to build dynasties like this meant there were people in pain, being abused, and in servitude, particularly to her family.

And when there was tyranny and a destructive wielding of power, there would always be resistance—even if the Mikhailovs couldn't see it. Except that she was Taisia Mikhailov, and she was there to bring it down from the inside.

Taisia had heard the rumors of the secret passageways between the houses. There were the paths that everyone used and knew about—Russian winters required it—but her mother, whom her father had killed early in her life, had told her there were *other* pathways as well.

She and Alyona had found one. That was all they needed, though there were probably far more than she could imagine. The passage had been cordoned off, probably many decades earlier, but the barrier was made of what could only be described as a papier-mâché-drywall material. It wasn't guarded anymore. That was how Taisia would get the girls out of the main house, though she still had no idea where they would go next. Still, the first step would be to remove the barrier.

She and Alyona had started digging, tearing, kicking, clawing to break down the barrier the moment she found it. Their smuggled tools were silly—kitchen knives and now beach toys. The bodyguards had to wonder what game they were playing. And the maids? Taisia had come up with interesting explanations for why their clothes came back dusty and dirty after she and Alyona had been playing in the house. No one followed them, and it was easy enough to fade away in ten thousand square feet. No one had reason to assume she was doing anything scandalous. They just let her be.

CHAPTER TWENTY-EIGHT

JARED HAD CALLED the late Sunday meeting and now sat at the head of the table, taking in his team plus the reporter. Most eyes were on him with the occasional sideways glance at the newest addition, who stood at Locke's side.

"We're waiting for a couple of others," Jared said, checking the time.

A few of the team who hadn't been in Russia had figured out that Cassidy was the cause of Locke's issue last time they had all met in the war room, while others recognized her from the rescue mission a few weeks back.

Brock, Delta Team's leader, walked in, followed by Parker.

"All right." Jared clapped. "Now that we're all here, if you don't know Cassidy Noble, she's the reporter we found in Russia."

Parker hovered by his seat and motioned toward the door. *Damn it to hell.* When Parker had that look, Jared got indigestion. Then Parker gave the same gut-churning glance to Rocco.

Jared pointed at him. "You too."

Rocco hit his feet.

"Everyone else, hang tight. We'll be back in a motherfucking jiffy," he grumbled and met Parker and Rocco in the hall.

Parker gave them each a piece of paper, and Jared perused the list. "What am I looking at? This is what the Mikhailovs are shopping for?"

"Affirmative," Parker answered.

"Why does it require me to leave… the…" *Fuck.*

"Room," Rocco finished. "How about that shit?"

Jared stared at the high-dollar request for an American with dark-red hair, explicitly detailed as a "blue-red" redhead—natural only.

"I know someone who looks like this," Parker muttered.

"We're talking about Cassidy?" Rocco asked. All three were jumping to the same conclusion, though none of them would sell themselves as hair-color experts.

"Yeah, I asked around to be sure."

"Who'd you ask?" Jared chewed the inside of his cheek.

"I gave generic screenshots of redheads, including a couple of Cassidy, with their faces blurred, to Nicola, Beth, Mia, Marlena, Caterina—"

"Basically"—Rocco leaned against the wall—"everyone who might know?"

"Yeah. They picked the blue-red hair as Cassidy."

"Sugar did?" Jared raised an eyebrow.

"Well…" Parker rolled his eyes. "No. She crumbled hers up and threw it at me."

He nodded. That seemed right. "Back to Cassidy. She's been embedded. Her résumé says *investigative*, but what the shit does that mean?"

"The girl has gonads," Parker said. "I've watched enough footage on her. Embedded in the Middle East a few times, chased drug cartels with the DEA. She has no fear."

"Is that a good thing?" Rocco asked.

"She's Titan."

Jared nodded. "Where are we with the Locke dynamic? He going to try to kill her out in the field?"

"Fuck if I know," Rocco said. "But where can we get an in that good? On a project that Delta's going to want to go after, hardcore?"

"Nowhere." Statistically, a woman who looked like Cassidy had to be very rare, and judging by the value assigned to such a person as compared to the girls on the rest of the list, it was clear that she was a more valued commodity. "She's a solid ticket into this operation," Jared muttered. "But damn."

Uncertainty marred Parker's forehead, and Jared tried to get a read on Rocco's blank face, but nothing showed.

"She won't have a problem going. Hell, I'd say if she saw this list, she would come up with the idea before anybody else in the room." Rocco rubbed a hand over his chin. "The question becomes—"

"Locke," Parker said.

Rocco nodded, rolling his lips into his mouth, and this time his expression was easy to read. Uncertain. Uneasy. Unpredictable. "Again, what's their dynamic?"

"I'd say it's... evolving," Parker said.

"He trusts her," Rocco added. "That's a step in the right direction. He's invested in this project that they're working on, and I don't know if he feels as though he owes her assistance for being a complete jackass or if there's more."

"Yeah, *more* worries me." Jared crossed his arms.

"I don't think it should worry you. You're thinking like an old man, Boss Man. Sorry to call you that." Parker laughed. "But honestly, think back to your single days. There was a whole lot of fraternization. It happens. He's a smart operator, and even if his head wasn't in the game, he's trained well enough to compartmentalize."

Maybe. Then again, Jared had been through hell with Sugar, and every time his woman went on a job, even though she was trained and knew she was the best, it still made him uneasy. That was one of the reasons why he would put Rocco as the first line of defense between making any strategic decisions and Sugar's safety. Rocco wouldn't think emotionally—he'd just bring her home safe like any other member of the team. Then again, the reporter and Locke? Who knew?

"We were in Chicago a few weeks ago," Parker said. "There was a girl on the job, and he kept it totally separate. I don't know what happened there. Maybe they went out for coffee, maybe something more. But regardless, Locke clearly didn't let it affect his work."

"Did he sell the Chicago girl to Russian pimps?" Jared grumbled.

"You know what, guys?" Rocco interrupted. "Locke is solid. We're focusing on the wrong thing."

"And what should we be focusing on?" Parker asked.

"How we're going to sell what used to be an internationally known reporter with dark-red hair and not get caught."

Parker and Rocco both looked as though they realized that they weren't just dealing with any redhead, but one who'd been on TV, in front of congressional depositions and, most recently, in Russia. Not that the place wasn't huge, but they had a lot of what-ifs to account for and needed to cover their asses.

CASSIDY GOT THE immediate sense that something wasn't normal when Titan's boss stepped out of the room for a discussion. She also had a feeling it might have had to do with her.

This group didn't hold back judgment in their freewheeling conversation, and the only time any small amount of decorum was shown was in deference to her when Locke made introductions to anyone who hadn't been on her rescue op as they walked in—after she had jumped through every hoop Titan Group had required. They'd done scans of her hands and eyes and had a video camera follow her from the moment she and Locke exited his truck in the garage and entered the labyrinth of hallways. Hoop after security hoop.

Jared walked back into the conference room that they called "the war room," flanked by Rocco—Locke's boss—and the dark-haired guy. Rocco returned to his seat, and the dark-haired guy took a seat near Jared. A few of the people she had met flicked glances toward Cassidy. Most definitely, that hallway chat had been about her.

"Cassidy." Jared motioned to the man with dark hair. "This is Parker Black; he runs IT and intel."

Ah, that was the man who'd provided Locke with information. She liked this Parker Black.

"Nice to meet you," Parker replied.

"Likewise." She smiled courteously and took note of the manila folder that rested under his hands.

"As we were talking about," Jared said, "between Delta's intel on the new sex-trafficking ring and this"—Jared waved a piece of paper—"we have a solid entry point."

Parker opened his folder and shuffled out a stack of papers that slowly began working their way around the table. Papers crinkled in the cold room. She watched each operative study the sheet until Locke handed her the stack. Cassidy took hers off the top and handed the pile to Jax.

A Classified label was slapped at the top.

TO: Jared Westin
FROM: Parker Black
RE: Mikhailov Expansion—Human Trafficking and Exploitation

Cassidy's stomach recoiled. *What?* She read further. This new Mikhailov arm was actively and aggressively *shopping* for new women to sell. They called it a *product list.* Blood pulsed in her temples, and—her stomach lurched as she took in some of the ages.

Her head shot up, eyes sweeping the room, and she tried to remain calm. This was what people like this did. They saved little girls who were *exploited.* A fucking generic word for atrocities that would, could, maybe already had happened to them—crimes that happened to other little girls all around the world every day.

And Alex was associated with this?

Jared cleared his throat. "Looks like another pimple on the ass of the unthinkable is trying to sprout."

Her eyes blurred as she tried to read the *shopping list* again, and Cassidy discreetly pulled it together. She was there as a professional, and if she cried—or screamed or puked—then no one would let her help.

Adequately calmed, she continued to read—and her eyes stalled.

American. Dark-red hair. Blue-green eyes. Few to zero freckles. *Dark-red hair.*

Holy crap—that was her. Cassidy's chin shot up, and she surveyed the room to see if anyone else saw what she did. Adrenaline began to race in her blood at the thought of becoming more involved than she already was. She didn't know the extent of her invitation, but she'd thought they strictly wanted to use her for info. *I could do more…*

Her pulse jumped. Absolutely—volunteering was stupid-dangerous, and yeah, maybe she would finally admit to being an adrenaline junkie. But there was more to this: the idea of not just reporting, but helping. Nobody in the room could offer what she could, simply because of how she looked. One foot bounced under the table, and she put a hand on her knee to stop it.

Jared's gaze landed on her, and she knew they were on the same page. Then he shifted his stare. "Now that we've all perused that list, we know a couple of things." He bounced slowly back and forth in his seat.

Cassidy caught a glimpse of Locke. The man was a frozen statue. His grip was white-knuckled on the piece of paper, though otherwise, he seemed casually attentive. To maintain the deception, all he had to do was put down the shopping list and not throw the table against the wall.

Between Locke and the painstaking slowness of Jared's conversation, the anticipation was going to kill her.

"Mikhailov's moving faster than we thought. They're working to feed their connections into a niche supply-and-demand market, possibly in some cases acting as a broker, maybe housing and holding women." Jared tapped the paper in front of him. "A shopping list has hit the streets. They already have scouts and buyers. If the requests are this damn long, then there's already a stable somewhere."

Her stomach bottomed out. A *stable*... of women. The lingo was sickening. She had heard it before and had to toughen to it if she wanted in. She couldn't dive in if she was cowering, green in the face.

"It validates what Delta has turned up on a new supplier," a man said—Brock was his name. Locke had mentioned that he ran another team.

Jared leaned back, rubbing his forehead. "Yeah. It does."

"Just been waiting for an opportunity to surface," Brock continued. "The whispers, the shadows. You can follow them only so far."

Everyone either nodded in agreement or glimpsed at her. Except for Locke. He simply placed the paper down and waited without any discernible expression.

"Right." Jared tapped the paper. "We have confirmation. They are not only up and running, but they are going big. Delta's going in?"

"Fuck yeah." Brock nodded, no hesitation.

She wanted in! Where was this Delta team? How did this work?

"Good." Jared's approval only exacerbated her need to join in.

Hello! Cassidy wanted to scream.

"Now..." Jared mumbled. "Couple of options regarding product placement. A couple of blondes and brunettes. Nic and Beth, you two could generically fit the bill."

What the fuck? Cassidy's head would explode. She wasn't the least bit generic. A perfect match.

"How old's this list?" Jax asked.

"A few days," Parker answered.

"What's so special about the blondes and brunettes? Low dollar, low value. Nothing but stable girls." Jax shrugged and turned to Cassidy. "Here's your bait."

CHAPTER TWENTY-NINE

CASSIDY BET THE statistical chance of Locke's head exploding would've been less if she'd raised her hand. But no—he looked like he was plotting an untimely death for Jax for merely suggesting she step into an operation as a lure.

"I *could* be bait," she said.

"Lots of things you *could* do," Locke grumbled. "Doesn't mean you should."

But Jared was nodding. "You fit a stone-cold description of an uncommon request."

"All right, then," Cassidy said, her gut in her throat and every nerve skittering on adrenaline like she'd downed a gallon of energy drinks.

"Hang on a second," Locke interrupted. "If that's all the screening we're going to do, then it's a hell no from me. What's it entail—what is she going to do? What the fuck does 'bait' mean?"

"What do you think it means?" Jax laughed.

Cassidy glared at both men. "I can speak for myself, and I said okay."

Jax scoffed and smirked. "They'll love her."

"Dude." Locke snarled. "I will end you if you don't shut the fuck up."

"Jeez already," Cassidy mumbled.

"Shut the hell up," Jared boomed from the top of the table, and she jumped. There was something about how Jared could grouse and growl all at once without moving that made him scary. Yellers didn't normally command respect. But somehow, when Jared raised his voice, the building listened. Both men on either side of her did. They decided to turn and behave, or at least chill.

Jared's black eyes darted from Locke to Jax and back. "Neither one of you will get anywhere near this job if you can't pull your heads out of your asses—" Wheels turned as she could all but see the operation planned. "*Actually*... both of you will be by her side."

"Excuse me?" Locke asked, his voice bottoming out.

"Parker"—Jared ignored Locke—"put the word out to the Mikhailovs that we have middlemen with product to move, and build out a history for our two entrepreneurs."

Locke threw himself back in his chair. "Christ, nobody in this room will let that happen."

"Back to Russia," Jax said, rubbing his hands together. "Logging the frequent-flyer miles lately. Let's stay long enough to enjoy the scenery this time."

Jared muttered about a thousand curse words rolled into one. "Brock, get your team ready. Soon as we figure where and how deep their network is, it's yours to take down. Rocco, you work with Locke and Jax to plan the sale. Parker, build the history. Nic and Beth, work with Cassidy and get her prepped for this program."

Locke snorted. "Program."

Rocco shot Locke an angry stare. "Or you're benched, and Jax is her body guy. Your call, asshole."

"Not a fucking chance," Locke snapped back.

"Then shut up and listen up. Understand?"

Locke turned her way, and the possessiveness marking his brow almost worried her. "Yeah, she's not going there without me."

"All right, then." Jared cracked his knuckles. "Any questions?"

"Wasn't she a reporter?" Bishop asked. "What if someone recognizes her?"

Jared rubbed his chin. "A couple of thoughts—"

"No one will care," Cassidy said. "I'm fallen. Won't be missed. If they do recognize me, then bonus points to my new *owners* for getting a great deal on someone who used to be important." It hurt to say that. "But they won't. I'm forgotten, and it's the hair and face they want. Not a lot of freckles. I'm filling the need of a fetish. No one cares about anything else."

Jared seemed to run her assessment over in his head and, with a quick look at Parker and Rocco, came back with a nod. "Agreed." He pushed forward in his chair and stood up. "Let's sell Cassidy and take down a new network."

A room full of grunts and claps and table slaps—except for Locke—echoed as they pumped themselves up. As everyone filed out of the room, Locke simply sat there, staring straight ahead, his lips in a thin white line. His hands rested on the table, and the muscles in his forearms twitched.

"So help me God, Beauty," his hoarse voice whispered. "If someone touches you?" His fists clenched, and he unfolded himself from the chair in a manner that was so calm it was eerie. "I won't be able to handle it."

Pinpricks of panic spiraled down her spine. "Locke..."

"If I had known this was where the meeting would go today?" He shook his head. "If only I had known... I already thought once today, 'If only I was there,' and now I brought you here so that I could give you to the Mikhailovs? My regret list is making me sick."

"It will be okay," she promised.

"You don't know that."

"There are some things we have to do."

Locke closed his eyes. His chest expanded, and finally, he blew out a slow breath. "I know, and I think it makes me care about you in a different way—I can't explain it. Just... damn it, Cass. This job, you and me—let's fucking do this in a way that works for us. Okay?"

She knotted her fingers together. "I don't know what that means."

He leaned over and kissed the top of her head. "Yeah, Beauty. I think you do."

CHAPTER THIRTY

WITH EVERYTHING THAT Locke had said, coupled with the smallness of the new room she had moved to, the weight of the decision to be *bait* was starting to overwhelm Cassidy. But with Nicola and Beth on either side of her, she at least seemed to have somewhat of a life raft to hang onto in the chaotic ocean that she'd just thrown herself into.

Nicola and Beth knew their shit. Period. End of story. For the last hour, they'd volleyed information about Eastern European sex-trafficking rings, more than Cassidy had ever thought she could know.

Piled in front of them were folders so that Cassidy would not only understand the business, but know the players, possible buyers, and what this wing of the intel community knew about *property*. She needed all the information just in case things went wrong and Titan-Delta had to leave her alone for longer than they anticipated. Apparently, different factions had varying levels of respect for their purchases.

Cassidy's summary could've been simple: they were all disgusting assholes. She hoped they would burn in hell and couldn't wait to help stop what was happening.

Nicola also seemed to know every language under the sun and was trying her best to pass some knowledge along. If Cassidy walked in knowing some of what her captors said, she had an unknown advantage. No amount of defense would be too much, and if she had time, Cassidy would learn Russian in a heartbeat. Impossible, but she'd sure try.

The door flew open, and in walked big hair and bright lips, a woman who said a lot before she even opened her mouth.

Then she did. "You're the redhead causing Locke a mental breakdown?" Her dark eyebrows arched, and her sweeping, smoky eyes narrowed. "I can't tell if I like you for making that guy work a little harder or hate you because Locke is such a fucking sweetheart."

Um... Sweetheart might be a bit much, but Cassidy agreed he had a sweet side to him. Definitely a sweet tongue. But that wasn't for the public to know.

"There's a difference between a gentleman and a sweetheart, Sugar," Nicola replied on Cassidy's behalf, tossing a solid dose of side-eye.

Beth shook her head, rolling her eyes. "Yeah, Locke's a real saint."

Well, Cassidy wasn't just going to sit there in silence. "He has a rolling list of people he wants to kill on my behalf. I would agree. Not a saint."

Sugar beamed at the revelation.

Beth laughed. "Are you here to help or solely for the purpose of distraction?"

After her initial hesitation, Cassidy had a good feeling about Sugar. Maybe it was the blood-red lipstick—which few people could rock that well—or the pile of black hair that would've looked haphazard if Cassidy had tried to imitate it. All in all, the whole look was kind of like a rock star. Complete with leather pants and—Cassidy tilted to the side just to confirm—pointy-toed boots that curved over her knees. Solid rock star package deal.

"I'm Cassidy. If you aren't here to help, what would you be here to do?"

Sugar tipped her head back and laughed, then joined them at the table, sitting across from Cassidy. Her black shirt had a distressed American flag waving across what looked like an ocean, and her fingernails were painted gray—except her pointer fingers were fuchsia. The whole look would have been odd, but she nailed it.

Sugar held up her fingernails and wiggled them. "The pink works, huh?"

"Yeah. It works." Cassidy nodded.

Sugar looked at her fingers. "Sometimes I do little things like this to drive Jared batshit. She wiggled her fingers and then pretended to shoot off into the air.

Cassidy snort-laughed. It couldn't be helped. Well, there was something to be said for a woman who liked to drive Jared Westin *batshit.* "Sounds like a fun hobby."

Beth pushed a piece of paper in front of Sugar. "If you have an opinion on this, that's what we're on. Otherwise—"

"Are you sleeping with Locke? Or what's going on there?" Sugar picked up the piece of paper but didn't look at it.

"Should have seen that coming," Nicola muttered. "Sugar..."

"Not sure who I'm sleeping with is your business." Cassidy laced her fingers together and grinned. Sugar liked to play games. Good thing Cassidy had no time for bullshit. Or batshit.

"Even if she was, Sugar, darling," Beth added, "it's not your business. And as I was saying—"

Sugar laced her fingers together also. "It's always my business."

"Then take it up with Jared." Beth flicked the piece of paper. "*This* is what we're talking about."

"While I appreciate"—Cassidy turned her head to look at Nicola and Beth—"you both defending my delicate honor, I don't need you to." She narrowed her eyes. "Whether I'm sleeping with Locke isn't your business. Whatever he does outside this building and these jobs, including me, isn't yours to know, whoever you are. You want to reword your question, try to explain how I'm wrong, I'll just explain to you why you're still wrong." Cassidy folded her hands one over the other, mocking Sugar mocking her. "But, by all means, Sugar. Come at me. I'll play for a few more minutes."

Sugar flattened her hands, eyes dancing, and the corners of her lips curled. "Come at you?"

"Sure." Cassidy bunched her shoulders. "I don't have time for gossip. I literally just signed up to be a sold as a prostitute in Russia. If you're worried about Locke, he's fine. He's a big boy. He's smart. He's lethal. He's not gonna let me bring him down. And if you came in here to test me? *Come. At. Me.* With more than a little gossipy bullshit about who I might be fucking. Because, lady, I've been through congressional inquisitions, I've been deposed, I've been to prison after sitting in war *without* a weapon. So, sitting with you in a little conference room?" She shrugged. "You seem awesome—like you want to test me and you're going easy. So get it over with." Cassidy nodded to Nicola and Beth "And same goes for you two. If there's anything you're holding back, I'd appreciate it if you wouldn't. Because I'd like to not get raped or die. Are we all on the same page?"

Sugar grinned, seemingly pleased with her assessment. "Jesus fucking Christ, I hope you fuck his brains out. And then stick around for a while." She winked at Beth. "That's all I got."

Cassidy laughed, shaking her head. "All right, then."

Sugar dragged her pink nail down the piece of paper that Beth had given her and seemed to agree with what was on it. "If you need something to shoot and kill people with, find me. I'm your gun girl."

Then Sugar jumped up and left with the same explosive style that she'd blown in with.

"So that's Sugar." Beth made big eyes as she laughed.

Nicola had the same laugh, smile, and expression as Beth. "She and I had a rougher start. But she's good people. Promise."

Cassidy lifted her shoulders. "I don't doubt that, and I'm the guest. Vet me. I get it. You want to make sure that your team comes back safe, in one piece."

Nicola leaned back in her chair. "She's also married to Jared and tortures him daily."

Cassidy laughed. "Ah, the pink trigger fingers—"

The doorknob began to twist, and for a moment, Cassidy thought Sugar might come back, but it was Parker.

"That fast?" Beth asked, reading his face.

"Way more so than we expected." He turned to her. "How are you?"

"Fine," Cassidy said, ignoring the jump in her stomach.

"What kind of bite did they take?" Nicola asked.

Parker slid his tablet onto the table "Hook, line, and sinker. Cassidy is a go. They've not only bought the idea of Locke and Jax as business partners, but are quickly trying to secure a few big purchases to make a name."

"I am one of those?" Cassidy bounced her heel under the table.

"I doctored a couple pictures of you *in the wild*. Locke and Jax sent it to the Mikhailovs, who sent it to their client. We don't know who that is yet—still working on it. But he gave his approval for the purchase. You're good to grab. They have five days to bring you to the to-be-determined location."

"What if it's random?" Cassidy asked.

Parker shook his head. "Big oligarch, and they're trying to establish footing in a new market? Nah, you'll be paraded out. Expect pomp and circumstance. Hair, makeup, et cetera."

"Locke and Jax won't make a deal unless they're where Delta can clean house," Beth added.

"You good?" Nicola patted her hand.

Not really. Yes, Cassidy knew it was coming, and she wanted to do this, but she'd have to be insane not to have a reaction. A Russian oligarch had purchased her through a sex-slave trader.

Her mouth felt dry while anxiety and adrenaline were making her blood rush. This was something that she was familiar with. When she first touched down in war zones, when she first walked outside of green zones, whenever she had been testing the line of her safe areas for the story, she had this feeling. But there had always been a safety net. The people in this room were her safety net, as were Locke and Jax, but they were going to let her go eventually.

If this job was bungled, there wouldn't be a congressional investigation. She wouldn't be a reporter who'd fallen from grace for airing military secrets. She would simply be a woman who had been trafficked and disappeared. A cold shiver ran over her body, prickling the hairs on her arm. They had no choice but to get this right, or everything that Locke was worried about would happen.

CHAPTER THIRTY-ONE

IT WAS THE middle of the night, and Cassidy had fallen asleep as Locke drove her home from Titan. She must've had a long day. Hell, it'd been a crazy weekend, and as he pulled into her driveway, it hit him that the last time he pulled in, she was lying on the ground—in the dirt, half on her plants—and he'd about choked on his own fucking spit trying to get his truck in park and jump out.

Quietly, he parked, and she woke, groaning as she stretched her muscles, as if the pain pills were wearing off.

"Sorry, I didn't mean to wake you."

"No big deal." Her sleeping had given him time in the dark to think. "I haven't given you enough credit for what you do, Cass."

She laughed quietly. "You've never given me *any* credit."

"Hey now."

"Joking, joking."

Locke laughed too, but the truth was, her words cut. "No. You're right, and I'm sorry. I've been hard on… the situation, hard on you." He cut the headlights, content to sit and talk in the dark. He needed to go and sleep. He was honestly just as wiped as she was, but he didn't want to let her go yet. Somehow, Locke knew that the moment she stepped out of his truck, he'd be that much more exhausted, that much lonelier. He leaned against his door, taking her into view. "Back to where we started."

Cassidy gave a flat grin and turned to stare at her front door like she dreaded heading inside.

"You okay?" he asked.

"Sure," she said, turning back to face him. "I just have a lot on my mind."

He understood the sentiment. He'd had years of mental preparation to battle the stress she was about to endure. He'd long ago accepted the idea that he could give his life for a greater good, and while he had no doubt in her patriotism, she'd done little more than accept someone else's offer when she stepped into a danger zone. She'd been in dangerous situations before, but this would be her first time acting as bait. "If you couldn't handle it, I wouldn't let you go."

"I wouldn't let myself go."

"You'd push yourself until you were able to. That much I've learned about you. You don't stop until you get what you want."

"Ha. I don't know if you said that like it's a good thing."

"It is, Beauty. You're passionate and determined. Hell of a combination."

Her hair fell from behind her ear as she tilted her chin. "Thanks, then."

He lifted his chin to say welcome, and damn it, Locke didn't want to be without her that night. Selfishness was a driving force, but the idea of her in his arms all night long, where he knew she was safe, where he could memorize the feel of her body, every peak and valley, every soft curve—that seemed like a much better idea than dropping her off alone.

Cassidy murmured, but it sounded like something sexy. Everything from her did.

Fuck. He shifted, his cock hardening at the thought of sliding inside her tight pussy. There were rules of engagement. Surely, there were Titan rules. He didn't know what they were. Titan, for all their protocol and security measures, let its team operate as a unit how they deemed fit. But spending the night in bed with her, now that she was essentially another ops member, didn't seem high on the list of appropriate actions.

He drew in a sobering breath. "Good night, Cassidy."

She unfastened her seatbelt and leaned over. Her lush lips pressed against his cheek. Everything about her was too much. The rush of her creamy, soft thighs wrapped around him came roaring back, reigniting the memory of her nectar-sweet taste as he kissed her pussy until she came. He thought of how her body quaked and convulsed, a wild woman on his tongue. Every sensitive, intimate muscle vibrated with his face buried between her legs. He wanted that convulsing moment on repeat.

"Cass, wait." Locke snaked an arm around her, holding her place, drinking in the surprised gasp as she tensed in his hold.

He nuzzled his cheek against hers, letting the shadow of his whiskers rub on her jawline, then hungrily kissed her, sucking her bottom lip, the one he loved to bite, before slipping his tongue into her greedy mouth. Her velvet slashes plunged with his as she leaned over, hands knotting into his shirt.

He moved down her chin, passion thick in his chest as he licked to her ear, owning every muted cry. Cassidy mewed, pulling herself across the center console.

Roughly, he grabbed her waist, dragging her into the awkward space between the steering wheel and his chest. Her knees were by his sides and her forearms wrapped around his neck. Cassidy ground against his rock-hard shaft, making his jeans feel like hell.

"Come inside," she said.

Her needy request tore through his concern that they were about to leave on a mission and needed sleep. There wasn't a gentlemanly bone in his body about to pretend that it wasn't a good idea. His hand found the handle, and the cool night air rushed over them as he pushed the door open with his knee.

He helped her untangled her legs and step outside.

"My purse, please."

Right. He grabbed it, unfolded himself, handing it to her, then grabbed his woman and half allowed her to lead the way, without letting go of her, to her house and up the stairs to the front door.

"Wait, Locke." The words and her tone were like screeching brakes and an ice bath, spun into one. "Before you come inside, there's one thing we have to clear up."

It was like his mind ran into a brick wall. "*What?*" About thirty seconds earlier, he knew what was going on, and now… he didn't.

Cassidy ran her hands along her hips, almost nervously. "It's important before we leave with Jax in the morning, but even more important before you come inside."

He tried to figure out what the hell she was talking about and came up blank. "Okay. What?"

"Do you still think I slept with Mike Draven?"

He pulled back, and unexpected shock ran through him at the thought of his CO. "What? What's that have to do with it?"

"If I'm going to sleep with you, and we're going to go on this job… you thought maybe I'd slept with Mike and was the cause of what went wrong in Sadr City. I'm not trying to bring up a bad time for both of us, but yeah. Hell. It has to be brought up, because you and I have to be on the same page."

"Why?" Damn it. He never wanted to think about that and certainly not at that moment.

"Because you thought—think—I don't know, that I slept with Mike. I don't want you thinking that—I don't know—that I sleep around at work. Or that I'm a bad omen."

His jaw fell. "It never crossed my mind that your pussy was a bad omen."

She shook her head and stared at the sky. "Well, good."

"That's just me being a red-blooded asshole and you being beautiful."

Her eyes dropped to his, and a tiny smile curled on her lips. "Okay. I wasn't searching for a compliment or trying to kill the mood or whatever…"

"For that matter…" Damn it, he hated thinking about Iraq. "I know you weren't sleeping with Draven."

"Good." She nodded as if all had been said, and she opened her purse.

"Look… shit. I don't know." Locke shifted his weight. "Truth is—not that it matters—I don't think he dug chicks." It wasn't his business to talk about, nor was it his to comment on post-mortem. Draven hadn't taken a stance one way or the other about his orientation, so Locke was in the wrong to do so now. But in a way, he was trying to offer an apology to Cassidy.

"I know," she said.

His eyes bugged. "Wait, what? You know? You know *what*?"

Cassidy's blue-green eyes held his. "*I know*."

"I'm lost. You know..." Locke himself barely knew. He gestured blankly. "You can't know."

"I do," she whispered. "I knew his partner too."

"You do?" Locke's mind reeled at the consequences of what she'd just said. "Did?"

He couldn't think. Forget the fact that someone didn't get death benefits or the respect deserved of the partner of a fallen soldier, but Cassidy could have easily taken the heat off herself if she'd said that, invalidating any number of accusations that she'd slept her way to information.

And if she was close enough to him to be trusted with that kind of secret, what else did Draven tell her? "He was your source?"

Cassidy didn't speak. She just stood there, holding the key to her front door.

Then again, Cassidy never spoke when questioned. With all the names of men—dead and still serving—who had been thrown at her under deposition and threat of imprisonment, the woman hadn't divulged her source. Never once had Locke thought that Mike Draven would do that... but it had been him. "Why?"

"I didn't say it was him."

Locke dropped his voice lower. "Why?"

Her blue-green eyes turned to fire. "Because sometimes it is more important for Americans to know the truth about what is happening than what the politicians deem appropriate for their delicate sensibilities to know."

Fuck. Fuck. Holy fuck.

Michael Draven had been her source. Who some people, like him, called the leak. Everything made sense now, even if it had taken Locke this long to put all the puzzle pieces together. Hell, what Cassidy just said about truth and delicate sensibilities sounded like something Draven would believe. That cocky, badass motherfucker. Tougher than screaming Apaches. Harder to break than titanium. Draven was the toughest asshole who Locke would ever respect in the Iraq war, and he had to say the truth out loud. "Your reports didn't cause the insurgent attacks."

"I know," she whispered, biting her lip and staring hard, as though maybe trying to read if he really believed what he was saying.

"They were coming at us from all directions. There weren't enough boots on the ground, and we were sending more home every day."

"I know."

They all knew that. How didn't he connect the dots? Jesus shit, he'd been so angry and so hellbent on finding someone to blame for the attack that he hadn't looked at the obvious. "I'm sorry. For everything that I've said. And that I've thought."

She lifted a shoulder, downplaying what she'd done, which was heroic as fuck. Dissent could be a rabid form of patriotism, and damn if he wasn't staring at a hero. "You're brave, Beauty."

Cassidy blushed, and right then and there, he fell hard. "Cassidy, keep acting like it's nothing, and you're not going to be able to get rid of me."

Her face melted into a genuine grin, and whatever barbed wire had encircled his heart in Sadr City unwound itself and disappeared. Cassidy inched toward him until he grabbed her into a hug.

"You're one of those guys who always knows the right thing to say, aren't you?" Her lava-hot lips latched onto his neck, and his mind was lost to oblivion.

"Remember what you just said, and hold onto it whenever you want to kill me."

"I'll try."

"We good?" he asked, nudging his face against hers until he had her mouth.

"We're good." Cassidy ran her hands along his biceps.

"Let's go inside. I only have a few hours until I have to share you with the world again."

She made quick work of the door as his fingers played with her shirt, teasing along the valley of her spine. Locke retraced their path from earlier until he took her hand, leading into her bedroom.

Earlier, Locke wasn't sure what he thought Cassidy's bedroom would look like. But the second look around confirmed that this was where a journalist who made an impact lived. Awards. Clippings. Photos.

"I haven't hidden from my past," she said as though reading his mind. "I thought you might've taken issue with my decorations."

"I don't care how you choose to celebrate what you've done." He lifted his chin. "All a bedroom needs is a bed."

"And pillows."

True. The girl had lots and lots of pillows. He might never forget her curled around the long one with her high heels on earlier that day.

"And a closet," she added, laughing, and he noticed the shoes spilling out of the walk-in.

"You should see mine." He threw his hands into the air. "Out of control. Shoes everywhere."

"Oh, shut up." She faux-hit him, and he pulled her in for a kiss.

That was the kiss he needed—one that brought them back to the business of getting into bed. She loosened in his arms, and he lifted her onto the comforter. Locke crawled over her, pinning her down, caging her head between his forearms and holding himself over her body.

This was his woman…

Cassidy walked her heels out, wrapping her legs around his, and hell, even if they stayed like that for the rest of the night, he'd be fine with it. He tore his shirt off, and her hands ran up his bare back, dragging her fingernails into his skin.

Needing a woman this badly wasn't normal, but nothing about her caused regular reactions.

He rolled over on his side.

"I'm not one to gawk, Locke. But you're gawkable." She eyeballed him.

"Is that official journalist lingo or—"

Her eyes cemented to his side, the color draining from her already pale face, and his blood stopped.

"Your tattoo…" Her face fell, and her blue-green eyes dulled behind eyelashes that dropped.

"Hey, wait." He shifted, dropping to stare also. Locke almost couldn't. Not one woman ever asked about it; they'd never react unless they got off on ink, because they weren't clued in to the tattoo. But, of course, Cassidy would be.

It was military in design like the others on his back. But the one on his side, the Roman numeral twenty-six—XXVI—was almost like a secret, a sign of respect that he could carry with him and no one would be the wiser.

He tore his eyes away from it and looked at her. Tears welled in her eyes. One slipped free. She wasn't crying—just letting go of what was too much to keep bottled inside.

"Cassidy. Cass." He gathered her into his arms, and she was limp and loose. Sad. "Shhh. Baby, let it go. It's okay."

Cassidy came back to him, gasping for a breath like maybe she hadn't taken one in a long time. Then she let out a long, miserable, swollen sigh. "I didn't expect that. Sorry."

"It didn't occur to me to warn you. No one ever knows what it means." He hugged her tighter. She shared so much of his pain. "C'mere."

Nodding against his cheek, she whispered, "It's fine. Buzzkill. I'm sorry. God."

Fighting to get her hands in between them, Cassidy buried her face.

What? She was embarrassed? No. Not going to happen. "Come on. Put your hands down. Cassidy, *Beauty*." Her eyes peeped out from between fingers. "There you go. Don't make me start all the redhead names again. That one suits you the best. Flame, Red Riding Hood, Strawberry Shortcake."

"You kill me."

He kissed the back of her hand, which half-covered her cheek. "It's all self-serving. I can't handle the tears."

She laughed, pulling her hands away, and he found her lips. The dampness from her cheeks touched his own, but her kiss came alive more than before. Deeper too. Her palms ran over his hair, fingers threading into his locks, and he breathed every breath that she took, each one easing as the passing memory of hell left her.

"That's my girl," Locke crooned against her sweet lips.

She hummed, and he broke free long enough to steal her shirt. Her nipples were outlined behind a silk bra. Locke pulled the bra cup down and sucked her dark-cherry nipple into his mouth.

His cock ached. Rolling the tight bud of her tit on his tongue made her moan, and he unfastened the top of her pants, sliding his hand down under the panties to her pussy.

"Oh, that's..." His fingers passed the clipped triangle of hair to her slick folds. He released her nipple and finished the thought. "Sexy. How turned-on you are."

Cassidy's sultry gasp rocketed through him as he penetrated her entrance with teasing strokes. The base of his palm pressed against her swollen clit, and his fingers danced in and out of her tensing body. Locke flicked his tongue over her perked nipple.

"That's so good," she moaned.

"Good, Beauty." He unclipped her bra, letting her breasts free.

The more she writhed on his fingers, the harder he concentrated.

"Deeper," Cassidy begged, flexing her hips for increased contact, and he did, adding a circular motion as he pulled out. "Locke! That. Is. Oh..."

"Like that?"

"*Yes.* Locke. Yes."

He abandoned her breasts, kissing her needy cries. If she was going to make sweet noises and purr his name, he'd drink every plea. Locke curled an arm behind her like a pillow and finger-fucked Cassidy as her tight muscles milked him. Knowing his cock would breach this same entrance, sliding deep into her honeyed arousal, drove him to the brink of insanity.

Cassidy splayed her legs wide, tossing a knee over his. Her body shook and vibrated, her hips reaching to meet his every thrust. "I'm—going—to—"

"Good," he growled against the shell of her ear. "Cassidy."

"*Almost.*" Her eyes met his. Her mouth hung, breaths gasping, and she panted, mewing and moaning, as her lips searched for his. "Please."

"Got you. Let go."

Her back arched, and her vaginal muscles clung to his fingers, spasming in a way that made his dick ache. His molars ground, and Locke pressed his mouth to her forehead, kissing into her hair, easing the roll of his hands as she cried his name like a prayer.

Her hips still moved as she panted, but the sugary focus of her gaze narrowed on him. He pulled her into a hug, wrapping his arms around her. "You sound as good as you feel."

Cassidy kissed him, letting her tongue tease his lips.

"As good as you tasted," he murmured against her lips. "And I know how every bit of you tastes."

"I thought you were a gentleman," she teasingly chided, working her hand to the top of his pants, fumbling with his button and fly.

Locke stilled her hand. "Have no doubts about that."

"Kidding." Carefully, she moved his hand from hers. "Kidding. You're a gentleman." She hooked his loosened pants and underwear down, tugging them over his ass. "A gentleman who says perfectly appropriate things but does so in a way that gets me wet. On purpose."

"Beauty," he warned, because with a mouth like that, he was liable to rush things—and ruin all preconceived gentlemanly notions.

"Hmm." Cassidy pushed his pants to his thighs and encircled his erection with her hands. Locke sucked a hard breath when she stacked her hands, holding onto him tightly, and slowly worked his shaft. Twisting up, sliding down. Her hands were bliss.

"You're a gentleman with a wicked tongue." Her thumb ran over the crown of his cock as a drop of precum leaked.

Shit. Sensitive. His lungs faltered as she massaged the thick head, her hands carefully working a pattern that might be his undoing.

Cassidy leaned down with no preamble, no walking her daring tongue down his abdomen, and sucked the head of his cock into her mouth. White light exploded at the searing heat. He saw stars and sparks as the intense wetness ran to his balls, sizzling delicious electricity up his spine.

He threaded his hands into her hair, and Cassidy didn't bob her head down. No, fuck no. The woman was a torture operator. Slowly, she circled the thick ridge of his crown, tracing the head of his erection until she followed the vein running the length of his dick.

"Fuck," he whispered.

Her tongue ran back up, just as slowly, until she crested the top of him and then sank her mouth down, taking his length. Both hands massaged his balls, one hand drifting up to his shaft as she dragged her lips back up.

"Amazing." Locke's eyes were pinned shut, and he would've promised, if he could've found the words, that no one on earth had felt like he was feeling. Cassidy's mouth was like a life force. He'd live for it—sweet heaven, she sucked his cock again. "Cassidy. Beauty."

Locke pushed on his elbows and dropped his head back as her hands tugged his balls gently and she rhythmically bobbed her head. His hands knotted in her hair, the slippery, sucking sounds permanently in his brain, and he watched as her eyes set on his. "Fucking perfection."

Damn, he wanted inside her. "Condom, Cassidy."

She paused, eyes inquiring.

"Beauty…"

That. That fucking moment right there, forever in his mind. Damn it. With his cock in her mouth, Cassidy just smiled. He was going to die a happy man.

She slid up, and Locke had her by his side, head on the pillow and stripped naked, before she could say a word. He jacked the pants off, grabbed a condom he'd left on her nightstand, and rolled it on, tossing the wrapper.

"Locke?" Cassidy kneeled next to him, laying a hand on his arm. Her breasts swayed, and her dark-red hair fell over her shoulders.

"You are absolutely stunning." There weren't enough hours in the day to stare at her. "If you haven't been told that enough in your life."

Slowly, she shook her head and tossed her leg over to sit on top of him. "No, sir. Not me."

"I'll make sure you do, then."

With his sheathed cock in her hand, Cassidy began to tease the pussy that he couldn't get enough of, rubbing back and forth. Locke could watch that erotic show all day, though hell, feeling that push into her tight canal was almost more than he could handle. *Almost.*

Her pale thighs on display, Cassidy pressed onto her knees and centered his blunt head against where he wanted to thrust so badly.

"You want my cock, Cass?"

"Yes." She nodded, jaw hanging half-open. "God, yeah."

Locke pulled a sharp breath, needing to hear it again. "You want to ride me, Beauty?"

Trembling, her lips parted as she let him inch inside her tight body. "You have no idea how bad I've wanted this."

"Fuck. Good." His chest tightened. A strong will was the only thing saving him from delving into her delicious body. Sweet and slow. His eyes sank shut as she inched down and up and let herself adjust to his length and girth.

"Oh," she breathed out.

Locke's breaths came in bursts. His hands rested on her hips, fingers flexing into her softness, and Cassidy's hands dropped to his chest.

"You have all of me," he said. *Every single mind-numbing inch.* Hell. Sensations bled through him as she convulsed, adapting to his intrusion. Locke's eyes squeezed shut as he existed, for a moment, in a world where he was buried inside her. "You good?"

"Mm-hmm." She exhaled.

"C'mere," he said, needing his arms filled.

She collapsed, kissing his neck, catching her breath when they hadn't even started. That night was a marathon. Jesus. He involuntarily jerked.

"Oh, mmm—you're a lot." Cassidy arched but then folded to touch her forehead to his. She rocked her hips, her tits teasing his chest. "So… much."

"We're good." His chest heaved as he pulled back his hips and, achingly slowly, thrust, and she rocked against him too.

"Oh, baby." Her head tossed back as he withdrew, her moan almost inaudible. "Again."

They had a slow roll of precision. Locke thrust. He gave her more force, and she rode him harder for it.

"More, Locke."

Damn, Cassidy could move, giving all she was worth again and again. The sight of her over his hardened, war-torn body couldn't have been sweeter. Pale and innocent. Soft and seductive. The more he stared, the straighter she sat until he wasn't thrusting, just watching Cassidy ride him, her juices dripping down his shaft, covering his balls, as her breasts moved in time, her eyes shut and dark-red hair flowing wildly.

"Yes," he hissed. "Ride me. Fuck me, Cassidy."

Maybe she didn't hear him. Maybe he hadn't said it out loud. But then her blue-green eyes opened, blazing fire, and they latched onto his. His soul caught fire just by their laser stare.

"Yes," she purred.

Locke gripped her hips harder than he should, and somehow, she squeezed his dick tighter.

"I..." Her tits bounced, and her pussy began to quake on his throbbing cock. Cassidy's body begged. "Need you."

Locke pumped inside her, rocking her with an ironclad hold. He took over as the support she needed as Cassidy's head dropped back and she arched, whimpering like he'd never heard before. Cassidy dropped a hand to her clit, chanting his name. There'd never been a sexier woman fucking him. Ever.

Sweat teased his brow. An orgasm curled in his balls, begging for escape. Cassidy's promise to God that she might die sounded like she might come soon too, and—her body went ripcord tight. A hand clung to his forearm, nails digging into his skin. "Locke! God!"

Have fucking mercy. He came with her, throbbing and shooting his climax into her spasming chasm. Her legs crawled around him; she fought the heaven-sent relief that tortured them both into oblivion until she collapsed onto his chest, his cock still thrusting, her hips still moving. Their mouths connected, their erratic breaths merging into one storm.

Damn. Locke wrapped his arms around her back, hugging her still and holding himself deep in her, feeling every last drop of his cum release.

His harsh gasps burned. Her red hair covered his face, masking his hot lungsful to her ear, encapsulating the two of them from the world. He liked this girl. Needed her badly. Wanted to keep her safe. Wanted to keep her for himself.

"Cassidy, Cassidy. Beauty," he whispered, slowly coming back to reality. He stroked her back as she twitched and gasped, kissed him and shook in his arms. "Beauty..."

He stroked her hair, patiently catching his breath, listening to hers return to normal. What had just happened would happen again. There would be no question.

"I'm..." But she didn't finish.

"When we get back, you're in my bed again," he promised.

"We're in *my* bed." She laughed quietly.

"Beautiful girl, my bed is where I am." He kissed the top of her temple. She didn't get the magnitude of where his head was at, and hell, maybe the magnitude of what they were getting ready to walk into the next day.

There was always the chance a job could go wrong. She had stepped into the role of a woman sold for sex. Cassidy was property to be used for another man's desires. But not under Locke's watch. No one would have a chance. No traffickers. No Russians. *No one.* He'd die and take everyone out well before they got close enough to what she just gave him.

But that was a lie he told himself, because he and Cassidy had a lot more than sex. There was a connection and chemistry. They were playing on an emotional field he hadn't expected and couldn't ever have understood, until he'd experienced the woman in his arms. "Good night, Beauty. Sweet dreams."

CHAPTER THIRTY-TWO

OH, IT WAS too early in the morning to be in a car. Cassidy rolled the hot coffee cup back and forth in her hands once she was done picking at the lid. Locke was in the passenger seat of Jax's car, and she sat in the back, and they cruised onto the highway on the way to the airport. *On the way to Russia…*

She and Locke had a very late, very rambunctious night, and Jax had shown up at her house very early. Which meant she looked like hell, with bags under her eyes to match the bruise on her cheek from Alex's Russian friend. All in all, she looked ready to play the part of a trafficking victim.

Titan Group had somehow anticipated where Locke might wake up, and there was a bag waiting for him on her front porch.

With her lip tugged in between her teeth, she mentally chanted to not be overwhelmed, not to be afraid. Titan was the best. They had everything covered. They obviously even knew what to pack for a human trafficker who might need to hit the road. Cassidy was just having a hard time wrapping her head around the fact that Jax and Locke were fully outfitted with identification, clothing, and apparently, anything else one might need to peddle human flesh.

She, on the other hand, needed nothing.

After a quick phone call with Beth to answer last-minute questions, Cassidy was ready to be a victim of a kidnapping. All she had to do was act scared as shit. Semi-drugged. A little despondent. Which wasn't too different from how she was feeling.

And she was terrified.

She tore at the lid of her to-go cup. Her fingers couldn't stop fidgeting.

"You doing okay back there?" Locke asked.

"Yeah, I'm fine," she said, lying through her teeth.

"You sound like you're going to puke on my carpet," Jax said. "If you decide to do that, try to roll the window down and aim out there."

"You are such an asshole," she snapped.

"It's the only way I know to be, Cassidy."

"Yeah, yeah," she mumbled and decided to chew on her fingernail instead of further destroying her coffee cup or griping at him.

"You know how much I respect you for doing this?" Jax asked.

Cassidy raised her eyes and watched him drive. His facial expressions were far too animated for this early in the morning.

"Really," Jax continued. "I respect the shit out of you." He flicked his gaze to the rearview mirror and caught hers. "You believe me?"

She nodded, dropping her fingernail from her teeth. And she did believe him, since she saw the truth in his face—unlike Locke, whose expression she couldn't read. Jax was like a book, and that book was ten kinds of an asshole, but he owned it. Maybe he didn't set out to be a dickhead, but he just kind of was. It seemed like the things that popped into his head… well, those thoughts bubbled out of his mouth. People always knew where they were with him, and she liked that. No bullshit, always the truth. If he didn't like you, you knew it.

Truthfully, she was glad that Jax was working with them because she could use him as a solid barometer. If Jax flipped out or blustered with serious bullshit, Cassidy would know there was a problem. But as they drove to the airport, he swerved in and out of traffic, one hand draped over the steering wheel, and she knew there weren't any. This was like any other job. Jax gave no fucks, and that made Cassidy grateful he was in the driver's seat.

The phone rang, and Locke swiped the call and hit Speaker.

"Hey, all. Parker here. Ready for a quick rundown of what we have going on?"

"Anything change?" Locke grumbled.

"No, asshole," Jax grumbled back. "If something changed, Parker would've said, 'Hey, we've got changes.'"

"Jesus Christ, would you two shut up?" Parker said.

Jax threw a middle finger but stayed silent.

"If Cassidy doesn't quit by the time you get to the airport, it will be a miracle." Parker cleared his throat. "Everything's still a go. Jax and Locke, you are going to deliver Cassidy to the Mikhailov compound. They are expecting you at ten a.m. local time. That means you take the redeye, and ground transport will be waiting for you when you land. You'll be escorted into the compound, where we will lose contact with Cassidy."

Jax flicked a gaze at her in the mirror, assessing her, and she nodded.

"And our buyer?" Locke asked. "Where's that dickwad? Or do we have to hang with the Mikhailov middlemen and shoot the breeze?"

"We have a couple changes."

"Here we go," Locke mumbled.

"Simultaneous action is now in play," Parker said. "First, your buyer is coming from London. Anyone not read up on Cassidy's oil oligarch, just in case?"

They all had.

"Hey," Jax cut in. "I'm not up on the cool, rich Russian thing, but what's up with that? He's coming from London? And all these assholes you sent over the intel on—Middle East, London, the US? A small fraction of this network maintains a home base in Moscow. That means not a lot of Russia." He looked at Locke, shrugging.

"True," Parker said. "If you have all that money, you go where it's nice to live. But if you're moving merchandise, base it where it's safe to stage."

"*Merchandise*," Cassidy muttered, anger boiling as she listened to them banter about topics that made her homicidal. "I hate when we use words like *merchandise* and *product*. It really sanitizes the situation. These fucking assholes are buying *women* and *kids*. They are buying slaves to fuck. They are buying *me*."

The car became uncomfortably silent, and even Jax let off the gas pedal, decelerating somewhere close to the speed limit.

Parker backtracked awkwardly. "Hey, Cassidy. Sorry. You've got a good point. The man who… *purchased* Cassidy"—he paused as if maybe searching for the right words—"to fuck when he feels like, will be driving in later the next day. Jax and Locke, your Mikhailov point of contact believes that you're also picking up some stable girls, er, um—" Parker cleared his throat. "Or rather—shit. I don't know. A group of low-dollar women, who they plan to keep on-site and sell for sex... Fucking A, Cassidy. I don't know a better way to describe stable girls. Girls kidnapped and forced to live somewhere for the sole purpose of being rode."

"Okay." Tears slipped down her cheeks. She wanted to fight as much as she really did want to vomit on Jax's carpets, heartbroken that this existed for profit. "I see why you say 'product' and 'stable.' Nobody would get any work done if you had to say what you saw all the time. Or fuck it, you would just become desensitized."

No one spoke, and she wiped at her cheeks.

"But, Cass..." Locke turned in his seat. "You're going to take everything you see and you're going to write the shit out of it when this is all said and done." His angry voice was a battle cry, urging her to pull it together. "More people will know about the hell that is out there. When Delta team rips all these girls to safety, you will educate the public so there's less of a chance it will happen again. You know, babe?"

Cassidy smacked away a few hot, stray tears and tried to breathe through her nose. "True."

"We good there?" Parker asked.

"Yeah, we're good here," she said.

"Hang on—Rocco's jumping on."

"I'm here," Rocco said. "Sorry to come on late. We had a change of plans with Delta team, and Brock and I needed to touch base. All right, where are we?"

"About to touch on that and"—Parker clicked on his keyboard—"you just received some new information in your emails."

"Locke and Jax," Rocco said. "You do what it takes to slow down Cassidy's buyer. Delta team has a serious timing issue that we're trying to work out. There's an unexpected stable-girls delivery to the Mikhailov compound."

"When?" Locke asked.

"Roughly same time," Parker answered.

Jax blew air through his teeth as Rocco said, "If Delta can stop the delivery off-site and still arrive on-site for a full takedown, that's the ideal situation."

"Wait." Cassidy was missing something. What did that mean? They hadn't talked about on-site, off-site, Delta team. This wasn't what was discussed in their meeting with Jared Westin in the Titan Group's war room the day before. "I'm confused, and maybe this is one of those need-to-know things and you guys are all over it. But what...?"

"Mikhailov Enterprises is building their new arm so quickly that they have two merchandising operations occurring almost simultaneously," Rocco said. "Not only are they facilitating the commission purchases of the high-end retail like you, but did you see the shopping list of the generics?"

"Yes." The list had requests broken down by age, hair color, ethnicity, eye coloring, virginity, and experience.

"We have very new intel that says there's a truckload coming in, and we want it. Those are girls we can save and return home," Rocco said. "If Delta can intercept that before word hits on the street that the Mikhailovs have failed, then we can also help anyone they have on their property. We want the oligarch who has purchased you, and if we come in blind, they won't have time to destroy their records and clean house. We want their intelligence. To learn about their network, people, distributors, housing. Whatever information we can get our hands on. Then we keep cleaning house."

"Oh," Cassidy whispered.

"It's two operations, one on top of the other, almost immediately so as not to tip the other off. Make sense?"

"Yes."

"But..." Rocco's voice turned all business, and she knew the caring part of the conversation was over. "Locke and Jax, you have to do whatever you can to delay the oligarch."

"Delay the oligarch," Jax repeated in a manner that made Cassidy's bullshit barometer spark a level of concern. Jax turned to Locke with his eyebrows raised, but he continued speaking to his boss. "And I assume that the rest of Titan has already shipped off to Russia and will be meeting us there? Because I also assume that an oligarch travels with, I don't know, his people."

"No," Rocco said. "Nobody else has moved your direction."

"Right, so it's just Locke and me versus the billionaire. Cool, cool. We've got this." He turned to Locke as he threw on his turn signal and began to exit toward the airport. "I don't know, Locke. You think we could ask him to drive slower? Maybe he likes coffee? Hey, Parker, does Russia have Starbucks? There's one everywhere, right? Or do they drink something else? Russian tea? Is that a thing?" Jax slapped the steering wheel. "What the fuck am I thinking? Vodka. We'll stop and ask them if they'd like to have a nice vodka."

"For fuck's sake. Locke, are you there?" Rocco growled. "Would you please pipe the fuck up?"

"Jax has a point," Locke said.

"Parker," Rocco snapped. "Have you talked about their go-bags?"

"Nope."

"Talk." A smack that sounded like Rocco slapping a table punctuated the order. There were pros and cons to working at Titan, it seemed. One con would be grumpy-dude speak, though neither Jax nor Locke seemed to notice it.

"It's like you guys don't know me at all." Parker tsked. "In your bags, you will find all kinds of crap to the screw with the billionaire. Spy toys and gadgets, devices and things that will blow your minds. Things that will *actually* blow his mind. Without blowing up his mind."

Jax smiled and smirked at Locke, changing lanes for the fun of it, as though Parker had announced they were going to an amusement park instead of a human trafficker's trade compound.

"Whenever you check your email, jackoffs, you'll see the oligarch's anticipated schedule. You know he's not likely to travel alone. My suggestion is to tail his caravan at a distance and mess with his sick, sorry ass. Slow the bastard down. You have everything you need to make the guy hurt."

Locke raised his eyebrows back at Jax like that was the best plan they'd ever had. Cassidy was surprised they didn't pull over to chest-pound it out.

What on earth did Parker Black have that could blow somebody's mind without actually blowing it up? And… how were they going to get through customs?

But this was Titan, and she had to assume that Parker had thought everything through. Her job wasn't to think about their jobs; it was to be a kidnap victim on the way to hell.

"We good now?" Rocco asked.

Both Locke and Jack suddenly seemed very satisfied.

"Guess so," she said.

The parking-garage signs were ahead. "We're here. We're jumping off unless you need anything else," Jax said.

"Now, I think that's it," Rocco said. "Cassidy, thank you."

"We'll keep an eye on you as best as possible," Parker said. "Don't forget: the second you get out of this car, assume that somebody is always watching. Thanks, Cassidy."

"You're welcome," she said quietly.

"And on that note…" Jax reached over and ended the call. "Let's get ready to do this."

Locke muttered his agreement. "Done and back home."

Her mind finished his sentence: done, back home, and in his bed.

LOCKE STEELED HIMSELF as Cassidy came out of the women's restroom. He was sure she was worried. She was strong and professional. Titan had trained her as best they could, and she was heading into this with eyes open. But that training had lasted less than a day.

"Hi," she said, quieter than normal.

"Hey." Locke gave her a placating grin. "That was the last time I can let you be by yourself. I'm sorry. There's no telling if a set of eyes will start trailing us."

Cassidy's eyes flitted side to side, and she ducked her chin, which he knew was part of the act. Beth and Nicola had put her through the wringer, showing her how to act and look—broken down, despondent, frightened of her surroundings, wanting help but scared to leave.

"She knows," Jax said. "Let's roll."

"Screw off. A minute won't make a difference." Locke wanted to put his arm around Cassidy and comfort her in a way that he had never wanted to comfort anyone before. They were traveling overseas to leave her in a place where people were raped. Where they were sold. It was only on a businessman's honor that he could trust that she wouldn't be touched until *her* oligarch arrived—and that asshole would never get near her. But trusting people who sold other people? Locke's stomach turned. Not the kind of folks he wanted to leave his woman with.

Cassidy chewed on her fingernail, a nervous habit that seemed to have started that morning. "There's a sticker on the inside of all of the toilet doors. It says if you're trafficked, here's a number to get help. It's easy enough to remember, but who on earth in my position would have a cell phone?"

This was such an ugly world. She'd bring light to it when this was done, but it was hell having to drag her into the pits of those cretins. "Maybe you would have access to one eventually."

"I'm just gonna remember everything for my story. I never noticed it before, though. How many airports do you think have that, and how many people miss it because it wouldn't happen to them—or in their neighborhood? Or to people that look like them or…?"

He put his hand on her shoulder, letting his thumb slide back and forth. He guided her toward Jax as though she were a possession, when he wanted to tell her it would be okay, that it was too early to let the evil break her.

Their gate was ahead, and they had no room for error. Locke leaned close to her ear, far too personal for what she was supposed to be, and whispered, "I will bring you home."

Cassidy nodded as they kept walking, and he couldn't drag his lips away, even as Jax glanced back and the loudspeaker was calling for their flight to board.

"Nothing will happen to you, Beauty. Whatever you do, you believe in me."

CHAPTER THIRTY-THREE

THE RED LIGHT wouldn't turn. Alexander sat at the light, and finally it turned green, but Monday-morning gridlock had jammed traffic across the box. There was no way that he could get through even when he had the light. His fists slammed down on the steering wheel. "*Chyort!*"

He threw his head back against the headrest. His morning couldn't get any worse. That weekend's call with Taisia had been a disaster, and all he wanted to do was get the last bit of data off his computer and hand it off to her father for what they had negotiated on: their freedom.

Traffic broke, and Alexander gunned his engine, slipping through the intersection as the light turned yellow. A trail of car horns echoed behind him as though everybody was having as shit of a morning as him.

"Wrong." He glared at the angry commuters around him. "You know what? Fuck it."

He wasn't fighting traffic anymore. Alex pulled into the parking lot, grinding his molars. It couldn't get any worse. He didn't want to fight across the bridge into DC, didn't want to sit at St. Andrew's all morning and think about Taisia. He'd rather sit in this shopping center—he glanced out the window.

A goddamn toy store. "Fucking hell!"

He wanted to go to places like toy stores. He wanted a stupid, normal life with a beautiful wife and child. What was so wrong with him that he couldn't have any of it?

He couldn't breathe. Tears streamed down his face, and he couldn't say why. Sad, mad—he wanted to rage at the world. Chaos brought him to a panic, made him insane, made him cry.

Taisia was endangering her life. It didn't matter if she believed in him or that she could do whatever she was doing in a safe manner. Hell—Alexander clutched at his chest. Was this a heart attack?

He'd never gone into a toy store and bought a gift for his daughter.

Or rather, he had—his head dropped. But he'd never been able to send it. Taisia said she wouldn't be able to explain his gifts. They were rich beyond his dreams at the Mikhailov compound, but she was a prisoner.

The sobs fell without his control. Every gift… he'd donated eventually. Someone else needed it. Some other child loved it. That cut so deep that he could hardly see straight.

What did eight-year-olds like, anyway? Other dads knew. He wiped his cheeks, alone in his despair. He didn't even know what kids played with. Maybe he wouldn't be a good father. Maybe he would've been like his dad.

"Bullshit!" he yelled.

He would've been—would *be*—a good father. And toys didn't make a good daddy. Alexander dropped his head again and let the tears burn his eyelids. He was jealous of people he'd never met, would never see or know, all because they could walk into a store with their kids and buy something they wouldn't have to give away.

DEPLANING IN RUSSIA meant there was no going back. Cassidy knew this, and yet it wasn't until they were surrounded by the unfamiliar buzz of a foreign land inside the Russian airport and an armed man approached Jax that it became all too real.

Quickly, with a series of headshakes and grunts, the other man confirmed that Locke and Jax were the American business partners that he'd been waiting for, and then, with all the perverted disgustingness, right in the middle of the airport, she was *appraised.*

The man hadn't said that was what he was doing, but there was no doubt.

Her hair was touched. Rubbed.

He made her open her mouth, bare her teeth.

Her tits were inspected and squeezed.

Jax and Locke casually waited as their merchandise was authenticated—for lack of a better word—and she whimpered and pushed away from the grabbing hands. The man laughed. Faux amusement played on Locke and Jax's faces, and she wondered how many ways Locke was mentally creating to annihilate the man—because she had come up with several.

The inspector leered into her face, close enough that she smelled his tobacco-scented breath.

Locke coughed in that businessman way as if to say, *Enough*. "She's not yours. Can we leave?"

"Done." The man dusted off his hands and abandoned her as travelers filed by.

Nothing had happened, really. But *everything* had, in full view of business travelers and families, other women and airport security. She'd been inspected as property; it was more than obvious what was going on. Still, no one saw fit to say or do a thing.

Jax snapped his fingers, and her head swerved toward them. Locke's eyes demanded she walk forward, and Cassidy obeyed. Their foursome surged into the crowd, and she lost herself in thoughts. People. Police. Families. People. Men, women, and children.

Overcome, she became numb, trying to concentrate on occasional significant details to remember for a future report. They loaded her into a car like she couldn't do so herself, and Locke took the seat next to her in the back but never looked her way.

All of that, she was prepared for. Still… the reality was harsh.

The drive was long, the road was severe, and the sky hung low in the early morning. They began to climb the driveway of an estate, and there were mansions—plural—on it, a breathtaking complex of architecture that deserved to be photographed—minus the armed guards that awaited them as the car slowed. The guns made her heart climb into her throat even as she took in wealth on a level that she'd never seen before.

Strange, seeing such opulence, even from a driveway, when they'd been driving for what seemed like hours through a deep, depressive blanket anywhere she glanced.

Locke and Jax spoke to the driver, and she said nothing until her door was opened, and then she stumbled forward, mumbling into the frigid wind, "Thank you."

Manners. Even when sold and cold.

The harsh weather had caught her off guard before, and still, it stole her breath as they hustled inside the largest of the homes. The great door closed behind her, and grateful for the warmth, Cassidy took in her new surroundings as the men stepped away.

It was absolutely exquisite and ornate—nothing like she'd ever seen before but exactly what she would have imagined. There were thick tapestries hanging over each side of the windows, and the thick carpet was a deep red. Everywhere she looked held cabinets and curios, a thousand accent pieces in brilliant yellows and golds.

At the direction of their escort, Locke and Jax pushed her into a grand foyer. Locke stopped making eye contact with her. It was for the job. She repeated that over and over as she clung to the knowledge he wasn't a cold, human trafficking piece of shit who jet-setted around the world.

Jax seemed harsher. Shrewder. Always looking for a deal, appraising art, appraising her. All that she had expected. Still, Jax and Locke had each other. She had no one.

The foyer opened into a grand sitting area. "Here, come here." Their driver beckoned as women dressed in what looked like servants' uniforms—black dresses and starched white aprons—urged them to follow.

Cassidy's stomach dropped as she followed directions. Ahead, men in business suits with their hair slicked back entered from the opposite end of the hall. Locke and Jax surged forward. Her footing stumbled, heavy and unsteady. She searched helplessly for exits even as she studied the ornate statues that lined the walls. There was no way to leave, and even if she could break free of these walls, she'd freeze to death. They were a hundred miles from the nearest town, and she had no way to communicate with anyone. Damn, her pulse thundered. Unable to breathe, she felt as if all the art had toppled on top of her as everyone bustled around.

Jax snapped, and she jumped, her reaction completely real. His unforgiving eyes made her jog forward, and her fear wasn't an act.

Damn. This undercover operation was all too real, too much, and—Cassidy felt Locke's gaze before she found it and could breathe.

Thank the fucking Lord—she could breathe. A ragged breath cleared. She wasn't going to hyperventilate. Too much rode on the success of their job.

And for Locke's part, vengeance burned clear and angry in his blue irises. Any onlooker would've seen her as simple product waiting to be sold. Her very real response was important to the process. If any of them didn't feel as if the situation were real, and their covers were blown, they'd all be dead.

But he wouldn't screw this up. Locke was simply making a list of fuckers to kill. A calm ran through her. God, she loved him and was amazed that he could give her strength from just a glare.

Handshakes were completed. The business was done—at least, until her buyer arrived. Jax began the conversation in which he and Locke would have to step out for a few hours but return before the oligarch arrived. Everyone believed the man arriving to purchase her would be there in hours, and the transportation was graciously arranged for her only points of contact. All were merry and chummy as she stood there, ignored, waiting for Locke and Jax to leave.

CHAPTER THIRTY-FOUR

ALEXANDER BURST INTO his house and ran up the stairs. "I'm home from school, Mama."

Wrapped in the same shawl around her shoulders as when he'd left, his mother sat with a pencil in her hand, circling words in a crossword puzzle. "You should be in class."

"I'm the teacher. I *teach* the class." He'd glanced at her crossword puzzle books before, and the words she circled never made sense. But at the moment, he didn't have time to feel disheartened. "But, Mom, I'm going on a trip. I shouldn't be gone very long, but until I get back, Tanya is in charge of you."

She put her pencil in the crease of the book and closed it primly. "Alexander, no one is in charge of me. I'm your mother. Your sister is not, and you are not. And you should be in school, young man."

He ignored her conviction that he was still a student, and he focused on Tanya. "Well, she is. You two can bicker about who's the boss later."

Tanya would moan and groan and complain about her real life and family, how she was far away from them, but he was sick and tired of being responsible for Mama all the time. "When I come back, I'm going to have my daughter. The one that I keep telling you about. Remember her?"

"Hmm?" His mama's glassy eyes gave him the answer. She had no clue. "It's good to have goals in life, but you won't have a family if you don't go back to school. Did you eat breakfast this morning?"

Damn, that irritated the hell out of him. Where had *this mother* been when he was growing up, when he needed to hear about "goals"? Or maybe he needed her to say, "Don't do illegal things." Dementia had transformed his mother into fucking Mother Teresa. Fuck it. He knew he should feel bad about her slip from reality, but he couldn't. She was no longer the woman who stole and drank, the one who'd introduced him to petty crime and let their father take him from school to hang with the Bratva. That Mama was gone.

Yet that Mama had been so proud of him in the neighborhood.

A dull ache pounded in his chest. Abandoning Mama to Tanya, ignoring her upstairs as often as he did—that was disloyal. Mama had given him everything, or at least, as much as she was capable of.

So what if they stole together, lied together, worked with the Bratva? It was the only life he knew: crime and alcohol and the bosses… until Taisia came into his world.

He hustled back up the stairs. "Mom, I will do right by you."

Because even if she didn't know how to be a good mom, she had tried. Just like he'd been trying to be a good father for the past eight years. He would do anything for his family. "I'm going to go get my daughter and my woman. I will make you proud. I promise."

"Alexander…" She blinked, dumbfounded. "I'm always proud of you."

He froze, stunned into paralysis. Those words? That was his mom, not the lies of dementia or her pretending to be someone she wasn't.

"Always," she repeated.

Free of the surprise, he kissed her on the top of her head. That wasn't what their family did—affection, hugs, kisses, touches—and it felt awkward. But it was what he wanted to do for his daughter, and if his mother lived in a land of make-believe, maybe now he could too. "Thanks for saying that."

"But be home before dinner. Your father will want to see you."

"Sure thing." Alexander left to her trail of gibberish about his dead dad's plans for that night and tried to calculate if he had enough money to buy the ticket to Russia. In his bedroom, he decided against a phone call and pulled up a text message to his sister.

> ***ALEXANDER:*** *I'm headed out of town. I don't know when I'll be back. You're in charge of Mama.*

That was that. He moved through his room quickly, stuffing a few pairs of pants, underwear, shirts, and a sweatshirt into his duffel bag, and then grabbed his recently stamped passport. He wasn't coming home without Taisia and Alyona. This time, there would be no mistakes. Her father wouldn't stop him. No matter if he pulled guns, no matter if he threatened lives, no matter what that bastard did, nothing would stop Alex.

Alexander ran back to his laptop. "Almost forgot the most important thing."

On two separate jump drives, he had downloaded everything he'd found in his students' parents' emails and files. Some things were salacious; in other cases, the emails and information were scandalous, though ninety-five percent were boring. The remaining five percent, though, were newsworthy and very much of interest to Ivan and maybe to Russia's FSB. All of it was worthy of a trade for his child and woman. "Now I'm ready."

THE MEN CONDUCTED business, and Cassidy stood awkwardly to the side of the great room, cast as background like one of the pieces of art that lined the walls. Each piece looked expensive and probably held great artistic significance. She couldn't wrap her mind around how expansive the room was. Locke and Jax puffed on cigarettes that encased them with heavy smoke, and their jovial business chatter carried as if she were long forgotten. To the other men, she probably *had* been forgotten, set aside until her *owner* arrived.

"Are you hungry?"

Cassidy jumped, twisting toward the unexpected, strongly accented English question that came from behind her.

There stood a beautiful woman, not dressed like the servant girls, but rather, in impeccable clothes that made her look like aristocracy from another century. Cassidy shook her head, remembering to keep up the dejected, drugged-victim appearance. "I'm not."

"You will eat," the woman commanded. "Keep your energy up. Stay healthy."

Well, then. If Miss Prim and Proper in the Nice Dress was worried about the health and well-being of the poor sex slaves… Cassidy channeled her newfound aggravation into mental investigative inquisitions and did an appraisal of how she was actually feeling, comparing it to earlier. She was not as terrified—at least for the moment—and absolutely pissed off that there was a woman involved in this, one who was absurd enough to order her to keep her strength. Women who hated and hurt other women were the devil. That, Cassidy decided, was the truth and would be a highlight of her future article.

"Come, now," the woman said in a way that gave no question that she was in charge. Even the men seemed to react to her in a positive way. She was quite the specimen of a human trafficker. The bitch. "Don't fight it. It can be bad. Don't make it that way."

Locke had turned away again, as had the other men, and the woman adjusted her beautiful skirt and started away. Hell. Cassidy didn't want to leave Locke, but there was no turning back now.

Cassidy shuffled to keep pace with the woman. They left the formal areas and entered the working part of the mansion, moving in and out of halls until they came into a large kitchen. Two women with hair tied in buns worked quietly, never lifting their heads. They didn't speak, didn't acknowledge that Cassidy and the well-dressed woman had walked into the room. They just existed to work. Was it fear or desolation that made them that way? Cassidy would know soon enough. Each robotic woman chopped carrots, tossing them into large steel vats. She wondered why it was so impossible for them to even look up.

The woman in the long skirt pushed her onto a stool. "Sit." Her heavy skirt flared as she spun. She reached into a massive fridge and extracted what looked like butter or a spread of some type, clattered it onto a counter, and then went to a cabinet and removed a loaf of bread.

"Hello," Cassidy whispered to the carrot choppers.

They didn't acknowledge her existence. The well-dressed woman spread the butter over the bread slice as if Cassidy were four years old. With a final flick, she dropped the bread onto a plate and went into the refrigerator again.

Turning, she said, "You like soup?" Not giving a chance for an answer, she produced a gallon-sized container and proceeded to a counter to spoon red soup into a bowl.

"I guess."

After microwaving the soup, the lady put the bread-and-soup combination in front of Cassidy. "Eat."

"Thank you." Again with the manners. Who knew this would be a thing and that it would bug her so much?

The woman pressed her lips together. "It is important that you eat."

She couldn't be worried that Cassidy was hungry or weak. They needed to keep their product in the best condition possible, and that meant with food in her system.

Cassidy quickly finished off the soup and buttered bread. The two women who cut carrots never raised their eyes from their cutting boards.

"You have finished," the woman snapped. "It is time."

For what…? Cassidy glanced at the carrot choppers. No reaction.

Seeing that the niceties were gone, she hopped from her stool, quickly following the woman back toward the huge room. At least Cassidy would get to see Locke again. That was worth the smile that she tried to hide as they came closer to the male voices that traveled down the hall.

Or had they come another way? She tried to memorize the labyrinth. Yes. This was where the main area was. And Locke.

But they stopped. No… Cassidy's nerves fluttered. From ten feet away, she could even hear his laugh. But the woman stopped at a small doorway and took a key set out of her pocket, and unlocked the door.

Oh… they were close to Locke.

Gesturing that Cassidy should walk through, the woman said, "Go."

Searing disappointment scored through Cassidy. She wouldn't see Locke again. The distance between them was so small, and other than a partition of drywall and heavy tapestries, there was nothing between them.

"Go," the woman ordered again.

Cassidy nodded and followed directions, for the first time, feeling helpless. The lady followed right behind, and the door slammed, the key turning again from her side.

Locked in.

Cassidy's stomach sank as her eyes adjusted to the dank, musky, tiny hallway inside the wall, right next to Locke.

If she screamed, he wouldn't know how to get her—short of tearing through the wall. But he probably wouldn't get her. They were undercover, and this was her job. A move like that would find them all dead.

"Go." They walked down winding halls that opened to a wider hallway. Off that, there were what looked like small rooms without doors, each filled with cots. With people… women.

They sat in silence. Some slunk down. Others peered up nervously. Curiously. Uncertainty hung over them like a lead blanket.

"Stay," the woman said, and then she was gone.

"Hello," Cassidy whispered.

A few responded. Most did not.

Cassidy had her work cut out for her if she wanted to help Delta gather intel. People wouldn't hand over information willy-nilly. She wanted to know who they were, how long they'd been there, where they came from. But Cassidy needed to stabilize. There was too much despondency staring at her, and just standing there sucked the life out of her.

CHAPTER THIRTY-FIVE

N*INETY, ONE HUNDRED…* Insomnia sucked. Cassidy counted how many hours she had been away from Locke. She counted how many girls she had met—eighteen—and how many guards were on duty at night in the Russian sex trafficker's mansion, though that number was a total guess. No matter what she did, there was no going to sleep. She shivered and pulled the tattered, itchy blanket over her shoulder on the cot. Cassidy had guessed it would be like this, but still, a little bit of sleep would be a good thing.

Somewhere out there, Delta team was rescuing a truckload of "stable girls." How long would that take? She thought they would have finished and been here before nightfall.

Nope. Plans were meant to be adjusted, and she was flying blind. Other than one girl named Victoria from the Midwest, few had spoken to her. They were convinced, Victoria said, that people could hear their conversations. But she didn't think that was the case. Still, Victoria hadn't given up much information other than she was also an American and had been in the mansion for more than a week. Cassidy had the distinct impression that Victoria had caught the eye of someone powerful. Maybe even Ivan. Perhaps that was too much of a guess, but whatever had happened to Victoria had left shadows in her eyes despite the strong front she offered to everyone around her.

Cassidy had chewed her nails down until she'd finally given up on finding out anything, realizing that they thought maybe she was a plant from the woman who dropped her off. Who knew what kind of paranoia and awfulness some of them had seen?

Everyone was asleep. Maybe it was the new sounds and smells, though she'd never had sleep troubles before. Too much worry, maybe. Too many lives in danger—in this room and in the adjacent ones. They'd been hurt and were going to be raped and sold if Titan and Delta didn't get this right.

Those things might happen to her if Titan didn't get the job done correctly.

But Titan would come through… they would. Cassidy chewed another finger.

There wasn't much light from the few windows, and she pulled her finger away, trying to remember the layout of the mansion and the hidden hallways. Each square room slept a few girls, and no area had doors. There was a bathroom. No one was in filth, and before bed, the woman in the dress ensured they were sufficiently fed.

That woman… Cassidy couldn't take her eyes off her. Neither could Victoria, who had been assigned to hand out plates and dole out their food. Victoria seemed to be the woman's chosen one—a sort of house-mother's helper. Cassidy found it interesting that there was a pecking order within the dormitory.

She tried to get a good read on the woman the two or three times that she saw her. They were about the same age. Cassidy wanted to see evil in her eyes, wanted to hate her, to understand why she could cart girls in and out for sex and abuse at the hands of men. The woman herself didn't look used and abused. Actually, she was pretty.

Hell, Cassidy couldn't lie in bed any longer and map out the screwed-up complications that sent people to work in this environment. She sat up, hesitantly glancing around, but no one stirred. "Psss."

No responses. Either they were out, or they didn't want her kind of trouble. Cassidy peeled back her blanket and stood. Still, no one moved.

Maybe she'd take a quick walk around, head to the bathroom, see where she could get before she hit a locked door. No big deal. If she got in trouble, she could claim she didn't know the rules or something.

Carefully, Cassidy crept out the doorless room and passed the bath-room. She tiptoed in the dark, down the winding halls, trying to remember her way. The maze behind the walls had to have been built secondarily, and the expansive shadow of rooms was so odd. But still, she wanted to make sure she had as much information as possible—if not to help Delta, then for future reporting.

Footsteps walking down the hall pricked Cassidy's ears. Shit! She hadn't expected another person. They weren't the heavy ones that she'd heard earlier when guards checked on their merchandise. She had not heard those footsteps in a few hours. Maybe it was the woman again.

Who was she? If Cassidy was caught, she could simply look for a common ground. Was the woman once a captured girl herself? She didn't look as if she'd seen the horrors that some of the women in these rooms had. Did any horrors happen here, under the woman's watch?

Where was Delta? Titan? Locke… she missed him. And man, Locke was going to give her hell for getting caught on the first night. Cassidy bit her lip, tucking against an alcove—

A phone chirped and was quickly cut off.

"You can't just call me," a woman's voice whispered harshly. That was absolutely their house mom.

Silence ticked by. Cassidy couldn't tell which way the voice came from and if she should hurry back to her cot. Was this news of Delta's rescue of the other girls? Oh no… that meant something had failed. The woman shouldn't know about the rescue operation. Cassidy leaned into the hall, trying to listen, but the woman said nothing. Her heartbeat slammed in her ears.

"No!" the woman whispered again loudly, her tone panicked. "*Het!* No!"

Oh shit… Delta had failed. Bile burned the back of her throat, heartburn mixing with fear. How was that possible, and what kind of danger did that mean for Cassidy… and her oligarch? Cassidy's mind raced.

"*Do not come here.*"

Wait… what? She leaned forward, trying to hear. That didn't have to do with a failed rescue mission or Mikhailov girls.

"He will kill you." The woman's accent became much thicker. "Leave. Get back on the plane and *leave*!"

Then it struck Cassidy that she was speaking in English. Whispering in a corner, speaking about the danger, telling someone not to come. Something was going on. Cassidy inched out of the alcove, her ears straining to hear more, but there was nothing.

"You can't always use the excuse of our daughter," the woman snapped.

Daughter? Cassidy's mind rushed back to the classified intelligence report from Titan Group. Fuck. Was this woman Ivan Mikhailov's *daughter*? Did he have her working the trafficked women? And if so, was she talking to—

"Alex. No!"

Holy shit. Holy shit. *Holy shit!* Cassidy froze, replaying only one word in her head over and over and over. Alex. Did she just say Alex? This wasn't a dream about insomnia and futzing her way down the hall, was it? She pinched herself—literally twisting the skin on her forearm—and it most certainly hurt. She was awake, and this was far more complicated than anyone knew.

"He can't make us both do these awful things." A sniffle mixed with her words. "Go home! I love you, but leave."

Quick footfalls rushed away as the conversation trailed also. Titan and Delta were working on incomplete information, and no one knew Alex was in Russia. Cassidy knew he was working on something. Was the woman she'd seen from afar this lady? Cassidy closed her eyes and tried to picture the face from the ski resort before she and Alex were run off with gunfire. About the same size and hair color… but she'd been too far away.

Oh boy. If they were both working for Ivan Mikhailov, what did that mean about the daughter? Parents would do anything for their daughter.

Cassidy ran back to her room, searching for her cot. There were too many variables, but none of them mattered. Two parents were trying to please a criminal to help their family. Recipe for disaster.

CHAPTER THIRTY-SIX

"WE HAVE A serious problem." Parker walked into the war room, interrupting Jared—that rarely happened. Jared put his coffee cup down. Something on Parker's face made his gut twist.

"You weren't gone very long for everything to have gone to shit," Jared mumbled as Thelma rolled over on his feet and chewed on her rawhide.

"Yeah, well." Parker shook his head. "Another of turn of events, and you know how I feel about those."

"You like them about as much as I do." Which was not very much. He checked the flat screens and didn't see any updates for the team. Neither Parker nor Rocco had posted to Locke, Jax, or Delta. "Is Cassidy okay?" If something had happened to the reporter, Jared could understand Parker bringing it to him before it was blasted to the rest of the team.

"Alexander Gaev just cleared customs in Russia," Parker said, rubbing his temples, and then dropped into a chair next to Jared. "And he made a phone call. Back channels intercepted it, and my contacts say it was to Taisia Mikhailov."

"We know she's there somewhere. Not pleased with Gaev, though." Jared cracked his knuckles. "What's he doing with Ivan?"

"Her location was pinpointed on top of Locke and Jax's identical locale twelve hours ago."

Jared let that sink in. "She's on-site with the girls?"

Parker raised his eyebrows. "Seems like."

"Why is he calling her?" Jared gnawed on his lip.

"Exactly." Parker swiped his phone screen a few times and shrugged. "Alex is Alexander Gaev. We know the Gaev family has a loose history of connections with US-based Russian crime. It's a reach, but there's petty crime associated with a group called the Bratva outside Baltimore. There's a note in a file on Ivan Mikhailov. He had a gopher at a local college who he elevated from the Bratva, paying for college so that the Mikhailov organization could have access to whatever they needed on campus, but they eventually dropped him."

"What does a Russian crime boss need from a college campus?"

Parker shrugged. "Chem labs? Cheap labor? Distribution points?"

"Hmmm. No details on the gopher?" Jared asked.

"Not much here other than a note that he had access to the school. Teenage gophers were probably a dime a dozen."

He thought on that. "I bet. How long ago was that?"

Parker's eyebrows bobbed. "About… nine years ago."

"What am I missing?" he asked. "Why are you looking at me like that?"

"Alex and Taisia…" Parker tilted his head. "We have a visa on file with US Customs and Immigration from about ten years ago—where she lived and went to school in the US, and when she dropped out. I'm going with eight to nine years old."

"And?"

"Ivan drops the gopher and pulls his daughter? Both go to the same school, both disappear about the same time. Now, they are back in contact after Ivan tried to kill Alex?"

Jared whistled. "Fucking hell. They had a relationship—or, hell, Gaev knocked up the daughter. Bet that didn't fit in with any of their plans."

"A pregnancy would be a reason to make moves like that," Parker surmised.

"What do we know about a kid?"

"Nothing. It's all assumptions, and since we don't have access to Russian birth records—"

Jared glared and growled.

"Could a kid could be on-site?" Jared pinched the bridge of his nose. That was a total game changer. "The mother's on-site. Fucking hell." People did that batshit-crazy stuff for their kids. Throw in a lover or a father—whatever Gaev was—and they went off the reservation.

He would. He had before.

If some former KGB-FSB asshole had Alex by the nuts and had kidnapped his kid or his woman, there was no telling what he would do. That was not the environment he wanted when he had a Delta team op, Cassidy, Locke, and Jax walking around.

Thelma rolled over on the floor, groaning as though she understood the giant clusterfuck that was this international-family situation that very well might cause an incident of treason. "So why is Mikhailov meeting with Gaev? Or vice-versa? What's the endgame?"

Parker sucked his cheeks and shook his head. "No idea. Can you imagine a family with the commies' criminal king for a father-in-law?"

Jared couldn't imagine what kind of sick world Ivan Mikhailov lived in that made it okay for his daughter to exist near his trafficking activities, much less the possibility of a grandchild. Then again, Jared couldn't imagine trafficking. "Get word to our guys, and let's hope like all fuck Alex doesn't see Cassidy."

Parker pushed away from the table and stood. "I don't think Locke will survive if that girl doesn't."

CHAPTER THIRTY-SEVEN

LOCKE HADN'T SEEN Cassidy in more than twelve hours. His heart had been in his throat when he and Jax loaded into a chauffeured vehicle, off to a bullshit appointment. It took all his energy to focus on finding the oligarch who was coming in to purchase and pick up Cassidy.

After they ditched the chauffeur, they found the new ride that Titan had prearranged. It was nothing more than a souped-up clunker sure to blend in with their surroundings. He and Jax had been so busy locating and enacting the first part of their plan, to throw the oligarch off schedule, that Locke almost had a reprieve from worry.

But that morning, he had time on his hands to think about Cassidy's night. The gray sky didn't hide in the clouds dancing with the cold sun that crept overhead.

Locke rubbed his hands together after he readjusted the piece-of-shit heater in their nondescript clunker that still seemed to zoom pretty fast. But he wasn't driving, so what did he care?

"This glorious morning in Russia just gets better and better." Jax steered into a parking space, avoiding the pocked asphalt, and zipped his jacket. "If I weren't enjoying the hell out of fucking with this asshole oligarch, this wouldn't be nearly as much fun as blowing something up."

"Agree." Locke took a pull from his coffee cup as they monitored Cassidy's buyer from afar. All in all, they'd given this dude a bad morning. Their only responsibility was to make sure he couldn't go and pick up his merchandise until they received the all clear from Brock and the Delta team.

When Parker said he had provided spy toys for Locke and Jax to use, he wasn't kidding.

"Did I mention the heat in this rickety-ass car doesn't do shit?" Jax said. "What's next on our list to make this guy miserable?"

After adjusting their schedule to the traveling caravan, Locke and Jax had taken great pride in making his drive unbearable. It turned out there weren't a lot of travel options in Russia. An oligarch with a fear of helicopters—like this man from London—would have to fly into one of a small selection of airports within a few hours' drive of the Mikhailov estate and prepare for a tranquil drive—ignoring the road infrastructure. Because, damn, the pothole problems.

But no one had accounted for Locke and Jax, who thus far had blown out a tire, given a billionaire the shits, and disrupted his cell service. Locke and Jax had endless hours to crack fart jokes. How bad did their sedans fucking stink? Blown tires and needing to use the crapper? Locke still couldn't stop laughing when he remembered one of the security guards jetting from a sedan after they veered off the road and dropping his pants on the side of the highway.

"What's that thing that Parker gave us, over there?" Locke tilted his head toward the backseat.

Jax grabbed the duffel bag full of gear that they didn't normally use on their blow-'em-up, take-'em-down jobs. He rifled as Locke continued to check their surroundings. The vehicles were older, as were the stores. The Russian economy had to be awful, and yet, the man they followed had bought a *person* and was worth billions.

Locke couldn't wrap his head around that concept. *Millions* was a lot to understand. *Hundreds of millions* was a farfetched concept, but billions? What did one do with billions? If Locke had billions, he'd probably drop a million or two along the way and help some of these people. Jesus Christ, he was sitting in a car with the crappy heat on and a parka, and walking up and down broken sidewalks were people wearing what would be scraps compared to his down coat. "Dude, life is not easy here."

"Life is not easy a lot of places," Jax replied. "But I bet most of these people don't go home and decide to take cash in exchange for another person. That sick fuck." He extracted something like a radar gun. "This is some serious James Bond shit."

Locke smiled, knowing what that was. "Yep, that's the next one on our list."

Parker had explained there was a device that, if pointed at a room—or in this case, a car—would emit some sort of frequency. It could deliver the world's worst headache. Those targeted wouldn't hear it, but they would feel it.

"I wish we had eyes inside their car. To see them tugging at their ears, not saying anything." Jax smirked.

"I'm not one to relish in people's pain. But… yeah." The man driving to retrieve and fuck his woman? Locke would shoot a migraine his way.

"Fuck it, I am. They bought Cassidy. Don't tell me you haven't thought about doing awful fucking shit to those people." Jax turned the device in his hand, inspecting it from the top to the bottom and from side to side, and then offered it to Locke.

It looked just like a radar gun. "True." Locke turned it over. "These fuckers. I'd be okay if they suffered."

"So, you and her…?" Jax asked.

"Me and her." Locke shrugged, not committing to an answer. "Working together."

"Is that it?"

"Is that important?"

Jax had his hand out for the device, and Locke handed it back, immediately wishing that he had it still. Their Russian targets were regrouping enough to get back in the vehicles and hit the road. They had approximately three hours more if there were no more stops. Of course, there would be.

"All right. I've played enough. Take the mind scrambler," Jax said. "Blast the hell out of them. Make it hurt."

Locke didn't know why Jax dropped the Cassidy questioning, but he didn't care. He didn't want to be a dick about a woman who Jax seemed to get on nicely with—a situation that probably didn't happen often. "Good plan."

"There they go," Jax mumbled.

They gave the other vehicle a few car lengths' lead, and as Locke waited for Jax to go, he began to worry. Was Cassidy doing okay? Were all the assumptions about other buyers and deliveries still in place? Did she handle the unexpected delay? Of course. She was a trooper—as long as no one touched her.

Locke's phone buzzed with a call from Titan as it sat in the center console, and he swiped the screen then pressed the speakerphone button.

"Hey, it's Rocco, and I have Parker with me."

Locke and Jax said their hellos.

"We have new intel and a shift in what's happening. It may change your plans."

Stellar… Locke rubbed his trigger finger along the side of the radar-like gun.

"What's up?" Jax asked.

"Alex Gaev is there, likely making pace alongside you. That's a total game changer."

Locke's jaw fell. "Excuse me?"

"What?" Jax snapped simultaneously.

"We think he's coming for his kid and woman. Not sure," Rocco said.

Damn. People did crazy shit when they were working for God and country. But throw in kids, and decisions weren't rational.

"The problem is," Parker added, "we didn't intercept the call. We're working with third-party info. Alex will recognize Cassidy if he sees her. There's a chance Ivan Mikhailov's daughter is involved in the trafficking. No idea how this is set up or what the risks are to Cassidy."

Locke's stomach bottomed out. That would be a death sentence for her. Assuming that Alex saw her or even knew about the sex trafficking ring. "Maybe he doesn't know. They chased him out before."

"Maybe," Rocco said.

What they all left unsaid was that Cassidy's survival now relied on a maybe. There were too many variables to account for. All of it was bad, and Cassidy was blind, having no idea what was about to happen.

Jax's head pivoted back and forth as he eased onto the street, following the Russian billionaire's caravan, and silently mouthed. *What the fuck?*

"Yeah, so shit got complicated," Rocco said.

"Yeah, you think?" Jax muttered. "You said this probably changes our plans. I'd say so. They're going to slaughter her if Alex walks in and says, 'Oh hey, hi, Cassidy. I know you.' Locke won't be able to get in there as a buyer, and all the intel that Delta team is working on will be for naught."

"Thanks for the summary, Jax," Rocco said. "I got that too."

"There was no way we knew Alex was going to jump on a plane," Parker said.

Rocco grumbled, and his frustration was clear all the way from the United States. "We need to protect your cover and Cassidy's life."

"I need to get back to her before Alex does," Locke said.

Jax, still following the billionaire at a safe distance, mumbled his agreement. "We'll make sure that these assholes don't make it to her, and then we'll get back to Mikhailov's ASAP. And where the fuck is Delta team?"

"Waiting for the delivery, Jax. Chill your attitude," Rocco snapped. "They will be ready for you very soon after you get back to the compound. Put a stop to these dickwads, and go."

"Roger that," Locke said.

"Nonlethal. You do not have orders to kill unless they take direct action first."

"We understand, boss," Jax said. "We're not trying to cause an international incident. Even if the prick purchased Locke's girl."

Locke had nothing to say. "If you can't get there, or her extraction goes wrong, she's smart. Delta will get there. Take a breath, Locke."

"Got it. Thanks, Rocco." Locke caressed the device in his hand as the call ended.

Jax gave him a look that said they'd handle their shit no matter what came up. "Sometimes this spy-bullshit crap is a lot more work than I'm used to."

"It's an adjustment."

"Let's do this."

The rickety vehicle surged as Jax stepped on the gas pedal. Locke raised the radar-looking gun and pulled the trigger, not letting go. "Did Parker give us a time length on this?"

There was nobody else on the road, so Locke wasn't worried about frying anybody else's brains. Not that they were going to do permanent damage. He couldn't hear anything, and he couldn't feel anything. He didn't have even the slightest tingle of a headache.

"How do we know if it's working?"

Jax looked over at the gun and then back to the road, laying his foot on the gas and surging closer to the caravan in front of them. There were two cars that had been taking turns leading. Both were in their line of sight and within the distance Parker had specified for the device to work. "I guess we keep at it. See if it works. If nothing happens in a little bit, we go through the bag of tricks again. If that doesn't work, we run them into a ditch."

Locke liked that a hell of a lot better than *try, try, try again*. "Good plan."

After another minute, Locke released the trigger, and they watched the two cars for a few moments. There were no exits anywhere on this desolate road, and he checked the map for the next place where the Russian oligarch might find headache medicine and relax after a thoroughly shitty morning.

They passed a highway sign that confirmed that they were not too far from another exit, where there would be places to sleep off horrible headaches. Locke went back to the gun and pulled the trigger, not releasing it. "I'm just going to pull this baby until the next town. If they don't pull off, then we'll change tactics."

A motorcycle came out of nowhere and shot right past them, blowing by the three cars barreling down the road. There was enough space between them that Locke was sure that they could continue at this distance without causing much attention, even if they wanted to follow the billionaire off the exit ramp to ensure his party stopped at a hotel. Interesting how little traffic existed between towns. Commerce had to be dead. Their economy was just so exhausted.

One of the cars in front of them swerved slightly.

"Did you see that?" Jax asked.

Locke hummed his response. A few moments later, the other car veered over to the shoulder area and then back onto the main thoroughfare. "I think it's working."

They were fast approaching the exit into the upcoming town when the two-car caravan that carried Cassidy's purchaser pulled off the main road. Locke took his finger off the trigger.

"I'm gonna pull onto the shoulder right here," Jax said. "Let's give them a minute to pull down the ramp."

Locke agreed, and he jammed cassettes into the player, which turned out to be broken. "Really?"

"All right, long enough," Jax grumbled. He eased them down the road and into the small town, where they quickly hit a main street and lodging. The two vehicles they had tailed were parked in front, with the occupants long gone.

"That was fast." Locke chuckled. "Guess Parker's headache gun works."

"Poor sexual predators need to go nighty night. We should go slash their tires to make sure that they don't just take a quick nap then rock 'n' roll." Jax pulled into a nearby spot and shifted into park. "Do you wanna do the honors?"

Locke shook his head. "No, let's not make them suspicious. They've already had tire problems. Their road trip from hell needs to be a string of bad luck."

"Yeah, I guess."

"Go inside and make sure no prying eyes point my way. I'm going to add water to their gas tank."

"I feel like we should be earning pseudo Boy Scout badges for this shit. *Bill Nye the Science Guy* meets *How Does It Work* gone rogue." Jax smirked. "Score one for the good guys."

CHAPTER THIRTY-EIGHT

HIGH-HEELED FOOTSTEPS MADE everyone in the cramped bedroom fall quiet, but when the housemother walked into the room, her eyes fell on Cassidy.

That seemed all wrong. The housemother held a dress and what looked like a makeup kit and hairbrush. Cassidy's eyes flitted to Victoria, whose grim face and lips pressed together didn't bode well. Shit.

"Is that for me?" Cassidy asked, knowing it couldn't be.

"Come, time to shower." The woman lay the dress on the cot, lining up the hairbrush and makeup, and Cassidy froze, fully awake, wondering what the hell was happening.

"I'm not going to hurt you," the woman said.

But someone was. "No. I'm not going anywhere."

"If you don't come with me, someone much bigger will make you. You don't want that."

Nervousness rose as her stomach dropped. "Why?"

"No time for questions." She beckoned. "Now."

"No," Cassidy said, her feet growing anchors. Where was Locke? Delta?

The benevolent-housemother-slash-sex-trafficker act was wearing thin.

Heavy boots stomped down the hall as male voices carried until two large men with scowls large enough to match their guns flanked the woman.

"Ready?" the woman asked again. "Come."

Fucking hell. Cassidy hated the weak, unknowing feeling and hated that there was ever a time when she had been arrogant enough to think this was an assignment she could pull off without cold fear. But Locke wouldn't let anything happen to her. That was the only thing she truly believed. Cassidy would go wherever only to come back and put on the dress, though she'd do so slowly, giving Locke as much time as he needed to arrive. "Fine."

She unfolded herself from the covers, and a bar of soap and thin towel was thrust into her hand.

"Take this." The woman's thick accent was noticeably stronger now that Cassidy had questioned her. "When we return, you dress in that."

The two burly men parted as they walked through, and Cassidy bit her bottom lip as queasiness returned. This was a problem. They were dolling her up for her purchaser, literally, evidenced by the ornate dress lying at the foot of the tattered cot.

"Um…"

"Let's go," the woman said. "Now."

Cassidy shuffled forward, clinging to her bar of soap and threadbare towel. This had to be part of the plan. Titan had eyes on the situation, somewhere, somehow, and they wouldn't let it get to the point where she was in trouble. They promised, and she would trust them.

Trust Locke.

Still, her heart jackhammered in her chest.

"Faster."

"Sorry." Cassidy stumbled. "Crap. Shit. Sorry."

The woman held out her arm, steadying her. "Are you okay?" Her accent softened. "I do that sometimes."

The flash of kindness lasted only a fraction of a moment, but it was in that split-second that she believed there was still the chance the woman had a heart. "Thanks."

Cassidy didn't know what that chance would be or when it would appear, but it would happen. Or maybe she was clinging to hope like a fool…

No. Damn it. God had given her a journalist's instinct for situations like this, and it might save her life.

"In there."

The bathroom, even under these circumstances, was breathtaking, decorated in a mosaic style with a claw-foot tub, but Cassidy remained unsure of her next move as the woman turned on the water and awkwardly waited for her to undress and get in.

She slipped off everything and ducked her chin as the water hit. Oh... The lukewarm water was wonderful, even if the soap didn't make suds easily. It served its purpose. Her hair and body were clean.

"Shave, please," the woman said, handing her a one-blade razor.

Again, with her stomach in knots, Cassidy mentally chanted that everything would be fine. Titan had a plan, and while the early-morning rousting wasn't normal, they wouldn't let her *owner* take her away.

"Smooth." The woman pointed to her armpits, legs, and along her bikini line.

"Right," Cassidy whispered. They weren't dolling her up to be window dressing.

The cheap disposable razor did as good of a job as it could. She handed it back over and washed off one last time. Cassidy shut off the water, stepping out and into the towel. The woman handed her a comb and deodorant. They couldn't have a stinky, raggedy sex slave.

God, if she didn't know help was coming, this process would be hell, and—Cassidy caught sight of the woman's face, and she seemed to be upset too. Until she caught Cassidy watching her. Then her features went to stone.

"Good. Finished," the woman snapped in accented English. "Now, follow me."

They padded back to the room, and the other girls simply watched in silence. Cassidy wanted to promise them it would be okay, that her friends would come soon to help. But instead, she tried to focus on how she *should* act, which was nervous and not overthinking.

Not that she wasn't actually nervous. Where was Locke?

The other girls continued to stare as though they couldn't tear their eyes away from the impending doom. Cassidy supposed that other girls left to meet their owners and likely never came back.

She looked down. What a dress. The fabric was heavy. It was embroidered and made from yellows and golds, cinching around Cassidy's waist.

"If you listen," the house mom murmured, "it will go better. That's how these men work."

"Russian men?" Cassidy whispered, surprised to receive any advice.

She hadn't gained much intel on the network of buyers, other than what she had gleaned from the girls and, even then, only the basics—where they were from and how they'd arrived on-site. But how did the Mikhailov network spiderweb? Titan couldn't defeat the whole process unless they cut off all the heads.

The woman shrugged. "You need to know that to survive. Listen. Don't fight it. Try to relax." She turned her, dragging her out of the room, where the others couldn't see them, the rough treatment making Cassidy trip—and the woman carefully rested her hands on Cassidy's shoulders. That was when she saw the tears welling in the woman's eyes. "I'm sorry. This should not happen to you. I thought I could save you. Them." The woman tore her face away, and Cassidy was shocked, so confused she couldn't comprehend what was happening.

The heavy-booted steps of the armed men came down the narrow hall, and the woman stepped away, moving back into the room and returning with makeup and a hair tie, as though nothing had been said.

A knot lodged in her throat. She didn't understand who this woman was, but Cassidy knew they were getting close to being ready for her to meet her buyer.

"Why?"

"Shhh." The woman hushed her like she was a baby, and all signs of emotion and connection from before were gone. Then she went to work on her makeup.

It felt odd having someone prepare her face and hair and choose such a foreign, formal way of dress. When she was done, the woman offered Cassidy a small mirror as though she wanted her to see the work she had done before shipping her off as property.

Cassidy blinked at the reflection, not recognizing the made-up smoky eyes and pouty lips. She turned to the woman, unsure of what to say, so she didn't say a word.

"Remember what I said."

Gee. Fuck you, and thanks. Cassidy nodded. "I don't want to do this."

Her eyes stayed on Cassidy's, faltering, but she took a breath. "Let's go." The woman turned her head, her hardened edge softening. "Come now."

Together, they walked into a hall, and one of the burly guards who snarled and stank hurried toward them. Cassidy shrank back. Even the woman did, but they had a quick back-and-forth in Russian. Nothing Nicola had taught Cassidy was useful. The woman and the guards argued, and the conversation escalated.

"It's time," the woman said.

"What's happening?" Cassidy asked.

No answer. *No, no, no.* She didn't like this one bit.

She tried again. "I'm sorry. I'll listen. Follow directions. Everything you said. If you can just tell me what is happening."

"If they cannot come to us, we will have you delivered to them. Simple. You've been bought and paid for."

"I'm sorry?" Cassidy blanched.

The woman shooed her away. "It's time for you to go to your new home. Go."

The guard stepped to the side, and the woman pushed her through an alcove. The hallway had been so dark, and now bright lights blinded her as though she were merchandise on display.

Head held high, eyes as wide as she could make them, for no other reason than to see what was going on, she walked to what was a raised apparatus. A platform. A stage.

"That's her," the low masculine voice growled. "That's mine."

"*Nродан.*"

Sold. Cassidy knew that word. Nicola had taught it to her and said she hoped Cassidy never heard it.

LOCKE WANTED TO kill. His fingers curled into fists, and his jaw was fixed so tight there was the chance lockjaw would set in and Jax would have to take over any further negotiations. Everything should have been cut-and-dried at that point, but it wouldn't do shit to help if he couldn't speak.

Cassidy marched forward with her shoulders back, and come-fuck-with-me bravery emanated from the dolled-up attire. No telling what they had told her. All Parker had leaked to the Mikhailovs was that her purchaser couldn't make the pickup in person, and the source vendor should transport the woman to London.

Naturally, Ivan Mikhailov would be pissed because he wanted to showboat the process. The dais that Cassidy had walked out on was quite the step up. But what the fuck ever. They wanted to continue doing business, and by the time they figured out it wasn't real communication, it would be too late, and Cassidy would be free. Fuck 'em all—Locke didn't care.

They might've rolled her into some freakish, fancy, homegrown dress and made the woman look like a Russian doll—because what was a high-end sex trafficker without branding and high-quality clothes for their high-end products—but they couldn't take the feisty redhead out of the woman. Cassidy was a fighter—and she likely couldn't see him.

Jax spoke to someone on the side, and Locke stepped forward. Cassidy was called down, and he was sure he heard her growl—until she caught sight of him.

She gave an audible gasp.

His eyes warned her that all she needed to do was keep it together. He'd explain later. Damn, how he needed to touch her. Kiss her. He'd never missed her more than he did at that second.

It hadn't been that long since he left her side, and he'd imagined waking up next to her. She was so close he could touch her, breathe her in, and yet he wasn't able to.

"What else do you have?" Jax asked.

The man who greeted them, who they'd initially sold Cassidy to, came over, and the two of them began to discuss business.

"Come here," Locke called to Cassidy. "You remember me."

She nodded hesitantly as she walked out of the blinding lights. They couldn't break cover. She held her eyes to the ground as she walked over and came to a stop a foot away.

Locke lifted her chin, inspecting his merchandise for any onlookers, and the connection warmed him from the inside. Even though she was made up and dressed like someone he'd never met, he wanted to kiss her. It wasn't about how she looked—it was the person underneath all the window dressing.

"You good?" he mumbled.

"Yes, sir," she whispered, staying in her role. That was good. You never knew who was listening.

"Good girl."

"I'll be back." Jax motioned that he was leaving with the other man.

"This way." He led her back to a private area. Locke pulled a pen from his suit jacket.

"We have a problem," Cassidy murmured as she rubbed a hand over her mouth, trying to hide what she said.

"Alex"—he completed her mumble—"is on his way out here."

Her eyes went up and down as if to nod.

"Brock's people are right behind us. Too dangerous with Alex on his way out to have you here any longer."

Somewhere toward the front of the mansion, a commotion rumbled, and the distinct sound of a man yelling "Taisia" echoed in the grand room.

Cassidy's eyes rounded. "He's here."

CHAPTER THIRTY-NINE

BELLOWING VOICES ECHOED from down the hall, and Jax came walking back into the room with more purpose than when he left, accompanied by one of their business partners. Locke held a hand out, shielding Cassidy from stepping forward, and raised his eyebrows, questioning Jax as to what the fuck was causing the ruckus.

The only feasible reason was that Alex Gaev had just stormed into the Mikhailov mansion, but on a scale from one to stupid, that was mind-blowingly dumb. Locke's gaze shifted to Cassidy, and a possessive hold clawed in his neck and chest. He hadn't known her for very long—well, that wasn't true, he'd known her for years, but most of that time, he'd hated her.

Now, though, Locke was liable to act as stupid as Alex Gaev sounded. He tried to hear what was happening. If Cassidy had been his woman for years and he couldn't get to her, yeah, he might sound like that too, making the same wrong decisions. The added complication that there was a child wasn't something that Locke could understand, but he could appreciate it.

Jax closed the distance. "Confirmed the visual. It's him."

Locke checked his watch. By their estimate, they had another thirty minutes. They had to get Cassidy out of there without being recognized. Even Locke was a risk, but Cassidy would be dead.

"Cassidy, where's the bathroom?" Locke asked. "You have to use the bathroom."

"Um, back that way." She gestured back the way she'd come from. "But we've never gone unescorted."

"I'll stay here," Jax said. "In case anybody comes this way. I'll explain that you took your girl to the bathroom."

"Let's go. Come on, Beauty." Locke put his hand on her shoulder, guiding her. They moved around a corner and came face-to-face with the snarling guard begging to have his face beat in. Locke grinned. "Where's the restroom? She has to go to the bathroom."

The guard glared at Cassidy as though she had broken some golden rule. God forbid sex-trafficked girls ever had to take a piss. Jesus Christ. Locke wanted to hit the guy all over again.

"Where's the fucking bathroom?" Locke said again.

For all that dipshit bodyguard knew, Locke was some rich sex-trafficking business partner.

"That way." The asshole pointed, and they passed.

"Come on," Cassidy said as they threaded their way down the hall—and she abruptly stopped in front of another woman. "I had to go to the bathroom."

This lady. He'd seen her take Cassidy away. Locke took in the woman, who seemed anxious and unsure about what to do. Was she Ivan's daughter?

"Sir," the woman said in heavily accented English. "I'm sorry. You didn't have to escort her. It is not your job. Mine."

"Not a problem," Locke said as Cassidy fell back into her role. "She has to go to the bathroom."

"I can take her." The woman began to show Cassidy to the bathroom. "If you'd like to return. We will be back shortly."

"No." Locke stopped them. "One second."

The woman paused with her hand on Cassidy's back. "Yes?"

But he focused on his woman. "Cass, how did you know about him?"

"Uh…" Her expression stumbled as though she didn't know his end goal, but he needed her to trust him. This was a risk, and he needed the information without her saying too much.

"Cassidy?" he coaxed.

"I'm sorry?" the woman said, bouncing a look between them.

"About him. How did you know?" Locke stepped closer to them, dropping his voice low.

"I overheard a call," Cassidy whispered. "I went for a walk at night." She pivoted to Taisia. "And heard you answer the call. His call."

Fuck, this was risky. Locke's nerves were in his throat. "And does she want to see him? Could you tell by her voice?"

"Excuse me?" The woman's head ping-ponged between the two of them, maybe knowing what they were talking about, but not likely. There was no way she knew what was happening with Alex just down the hall. What they'd said was probably vague enough that they could get away with it, but there wasn't question of them knowing each other outside their concocted cover story. And the fact that they weren't who they said they were could put the woman on edge and blow their cover.

The woman was weaponless, and concern was etched on her face as she tried to figure out the dynamic between the two of them.

"She wants to see him, even if she told him to go home," Cassidy said.

The woman sucked in her breath, stumbling back a step as Locke turned toward her and leveled a stare that held all the intensity and honesty he could possibly summon. "*He's here.* In the front foyer, fighting like all hell to get to you."

Her bottom lip trembled, but she didn't respond.

"You're Taisia Mikhailov, aren't you?" Locke beckoned Cassidy to step to him. "I can't let Alex see her."

"Who are you?" Taisia gaped, all but confirming her identity.

Locke tilted his head toward Cassidy. "It'll trigger a chain reaction of bad shit that'll happen to her, and I won't let it. But he's coming for you and your kid. Not Cassidy."

Taisia's eyes brimmed with tears, and she glanced down the hall, worried and hopeful. "What's happening?"

"If you want to be with your man, if you want to be a family, you need my help," Locke said.

She trembled, her head disagreeing. "I don't know what you're talking about."

"Yes, you do," he said. "We're your only way out of this hellhole with your man and your child."

Her bottom lip shook. "I don't believe you." Again, she looked over his shoulder. "Help." But she didn't call loud enough for anybody to hear. Her forehead wrinkled, and tears slipped free. "Who are you?"

A commotion clattered down the hallway. "Taisia?"

Alex's voice echoed as Cassidy dashed to a nearby door. Tears flooded the woman's face, sliding down her cheeks as Alex's calls grew closer.

"He's not getting out of here alive. Your father won't allow it," Locke said. "We both know that." He didn't trust her enough to share about Delta, who would be there any time now… "Unless I help you. We talk to Alex, keep Cassidy hidden. You must trust me, and I have to trust you. We are trusting each other with the only things that we care about."

"I'm not sure…"

"There's a raid coming," Locke said, throwing it all on the table. "Any minute now. Alex's timing is awful. Cassidy's life is in danger. And unless you want to go down as a trafficker—"

Taisia's jaw dropped. "I just smuggled the girls out. I couldn't help your Cassidy. But… can you help us?"

Locke's chest pounded. They lost the girls? Everything that Delta was coming for? Shit! "They're not here anymore?"

"They are. But they aren't. I know where they are," she said wearily. "You can help all of them?"

"Yes. I promise." He nodded. "We good?"

"Taisia," Alex called from behind Locke, and there was no more time left in the dark hallway.

"We are," she said, stepping around him. "Alex! You're here."

And so was Locke. Fuck.

CHAPTER FORTY

LOCKE DROPPED HIS head, letting loose hair cover his forehead, but he saw through the strands. Two men trailed Alex with weapons drawn. Perfect. He had no weapons, as they were disarmed at the front door, a courtesy that he'd expected and now regretted. If they didn't have weapons either, he could take them, but damn, he'd take a bruising. But three with guns pointed at him, no chance. Add to that the fact that Taisia Mikhailov stood next to him. Locke didn't know if the guards cared whether she died or not.

Alex pushed down the hall, and Locke turned, stepping toward the egress Cassidy had escaped to. Taisia could make one wrong move, say one wrong word, and he was a dead man. But he had no idea what that word or move would be. How much power did she wield? More importantly, was Ivan Mikhailov at the compound? That would be the real kicker.

Alex slammed to a halt as Locke tucked against the wall, shadowed and unwilling to walk away from unfolding danger but needing to be able to intercept anyone who came Cassidy's way. Perhaps Alex couldn't see his face, or perhaps he didn't give a shit because he was with his woman.

"Why are you here?" She turned to the other men and shooed them in Russian.

A movement caught his eye—another woman stood with Cassidy. What the mother hell? Was she finding others? Collecting friends? Either way, Locke unexpectedly had one more variable to account for and still no weapon.

ALEXANDER HADN'T NOTICED his fingers—or his arms or his chest—until that moment. Wiggling his fingers and taking a deep breath, he felt as though his body functioned better. The weight of the unknown was gone, and Taisia was real and in front of him. She wasn't only a sound through a phone line. Seeing her was like a salve to every worry and problem, every one of his nightmares.

The dark hallway brightened as her eyes danced, even as she tried to order away the persistent guards who could've killed him on the spot—but didn't—because he had information for Ivan. Soon enough, Alexander would have his family. All it took was selling his soul and country to the FSB.

Taisia snapped again in Russian for the guards to take their weapons and go. The back-and-forth was harsh, but she won.

She always would. Even if she was forced to do the unthinkable for her father, she was still a Mikhailov princess, the daughter of a warlord. Her words were a command to anyone but her father.

With Russian curses, growling, and grumbles, they holstered their weapons and pulled back. They weren't far, and wherever Ivan was, he was no doubt on his way here.

Alexander stepped forward, taking her hand. "Let's go somewhere private—" The sight of another man farther down the hall stopped him in his tracks. Who was he, standing in the shadows, not a concern of the guards or Taisia? Jealousy ripped through Alex. Maybe in their years apart, she had not been alone. Despair wrapped a tangle of barbs around his heart. Not once had he ever wondered whether she had moved on. Never.

"Who is he?" Alexander gripped Taisia's fingers, desperate for her to answer with anything that would make the sudden ache go away.

She swayed as though she meant to see behind her but changed her mind. "One of our clients."

He sucked in a deep breath. Taisia sold people for sex. He'd never forgive himself. "I need to speak with you in private. Now."

This time, she pivoted, looking at the man, who was broad and tall, built like the bodyguards. An uneasy feeling clapped into his mind as Taisia slowly shook her head.

"We have to talk," she whispered. "But the situation, it's not what you think."

Was the man not a client? Maybe she'd taken a husband or had been forced to marry someone. All the negotiations with Ivan were for naught, and that bastard knew the whole time, using Alex. Sweat dampened his pits, his neck. "God dammit."

He still loved her. He'd never stopped.

"Wait. No. Stop," she whispered, taking a step back, motioning for him to come also.

One more step might kill him. Pain seared his throat, his arms ached, and his soul felt empty. Every dream he'd had about having a family was nothing more than dust, and each step she took was just blowing it away. Taisia continued to the man in the shadows, and Alexander was consumed by hatred.

"Come," she said in Russian. "Alexander."

His throat burned with tears that he would never shed. Maybe he could at least see his daughter. He wanted to hug her, hold her, tell her who he was. If talking to her meant meeting this bastard, one more layer to get to Alyona, he could do that.

Alexander followed her down the hall until they reached the corner, where the man in the shadows stepped forward. He had a hardened face that Alexander recognized but not from the meetings with any Mikhailov.

"I know you."

But where from? His mind searched, trying to distinguish between his confusion about Taisia and jetlag…

The rescue jet. From when they were here before and all hell broke loose. "What the fuck is going on?" He faltered back, eyes scrambling between his woman and the blond man dressed like a Russian businessman.

Taisia reached for Alexander, but he wouldn't take her hand. A tear slipped free. "What deal did you make with my father?" she asked.

He shook his head, swallowing his words. This guy worked with the *military*. The United States government! They killed people for what Alexander did. Or almost did—or had done but not turned over. No matter. He would not admit to anything in front of that guy.

Stubbornly, she grabbed his hand, clinging to it even as he tugged back. She wouldn't let go. "He can help us."

"You're out of your mind!" Pulling away from her killed him. "Taisia, let's go. Leave him here. Come on. Let's go."

"What does Ivan have already?" the man asked in a low voice that was so calm it stopped both him and her in their struggle.

Alexander snapped toward the blond man. "Why? You want it back so you can get a medal and hang me? Fuck you."

Taisia's head dropped as she whispered, "What did you do?"

Alexander snatched his hand away. "You saw what happened when I finally saw you! After years of trying! This was our price." He stormed back and paced the tiny width of the hall. "Everything has a price, Taisia. You know that. Especially for your father. And the price for my family was information. Simple."

"Did you give them that information?" the man asked.

"What's it to you, asshole?"

He calmly shrugged. "You're in a very interesting situation—"

Alexander surged to the other man. "Gee, you think?"

The man didn't flinch. He simply continued. "Ivan will be here soon. You're in possession of stolen US intelligence. In very short order, there will be a raid. The compound is likely already surrounded. You're not getting out of here with your woman and child."

"Fucking hell." Alexander whirled and slammed his palm against the wall, nearly falling limp.

"I need your help," the man continued.

He barely picked his head up. "Oh, yeah. And how's that?"

"My question first. What have you turned over?"

"Nothing. Yet."

"Good. And who, exactly, asked for what? In very simple, concise terms."

"The FSB wanted information that they could use against American politicians or to influence policy. It ranged from things that could be used for blackmail to insider information on American legislation and policy work."

"If you'd testify and go on record, anonymously, with intelligence officials and to Congress, then Uncle Sam would spring for new identities."

Alexander straightened. "Plural?"

"I think it could be brokered," the man said.

He blinked, trying to understand what was being offered. He was swinging from completely paranoid to highly optimistic and back again. The guy seemed to be suggesting that he could provide all of them with new identities without clearing it with the president or some shit. He could just come up with that in a hallway meeting? "Bullshit."

Alex's phone began to buzz, and he silenced it. The last thing he needed was a call. It rang again, and the roaming call wouldn't show the phone number.

"Maybe it's Ivan. Answer it," the man said. "Don't tip your hand."

Who was this freak show?

"Listen." Alexander silenced the phone to prove a point. "You're speaking out of your ass. I don't know who you are. I don't even think you can say or do anything that you just suggested—"

"He can," a woman said. The voice came from inside the room. "I can promise you that, Alex."

Cassidy Noble, dressed as a Russian slut, walked into the hall and came up behind the man. "His name is Locke, and he works for a powerful organization that probably does have the connections to do what he just said."

What the fuck was going on? Alexander stared at the three people in front of him. He didn't know what to make of the situation and—his phone rang again. "Damn it." He pulled the phone off his hip and looked at the screen. This time, the screen showed his sister's name, and he answered it. "What?"

"Alexander." Tanya's hollow voice sounded far away. "She passed away. Mama went to sleep and didn't wake up."

His mother had died? His hand went to his forehead, covering his eyes, as he tried to understand everything that was happening. "What? Are you sure?"

Not now. Damn it. They had finally had a family moment! She been proud of him, and he'd kissed her…

"I'm so sorry. I know you were close. I was over here. Making her dinner. Are you there? Alex?"

His mother died, and he wasn't there. "Yeah, I'm here."

"She was fine, though. The happiest I've ever seen her," Tanya mumbled. "Chattering on and on about a granddaughter, then she said she wanted to take a nap."

Alexander's heart shattered… but at least he gave that to his mom—a final happiness. He swallowed the painful ache in his throat. "Thanks, Tanya."

Turning away, he hung up the phone and pinched his eyes. He shoved the phone back in his pocket and again rubbed his eyes. He had nothing left at home. Tanya would disappear again.

Alexander wandered away from the three people in the hall. He was alone in the world with a decision to make, somebody to trust that he'd never met before, and the potential to possibly have his family to start over with, but he had to keep going.

CHAPTER FORTY-ONE

LOCKE STOOD NEXT to Taisia as they watched pain consume Alex. The dark shadows of the narrow hallway matched the veil of darkness that suddenly and completely hung over him. Whatever had been said on that phone call had sliced the man's soul.

Taisia moved to Alex, taking his arm and lacing their fingers as he numbly walked back to Locke. "Are you okay?"

Alex mumbled before he found his voice. "I'll be fine."

"Who was that?" she asked.

"My sister."

"Everything okay?" she asked.

Locke took a step back. There were so many family dealings happening with this man, and standing there felt intrusive.

"My mama passed."

"Oh." Her face fell. "I wish we had the chance to meet her."

The daughter hadn't met the grandmother. Worse, the only grandparent she'd known had been Ivan Mikhailov. That was horrible. Locke hated the torment on Alex's face and couldn't imagine losing his mother—who he needed to call when they got stateside. What if his mother met Cassidy? His mind jumped, startled at that huge leap. Or was it that huge a leap? Cassidy was fierce, and his mom was scarily similar... At some point, growing up, he'd heard that his mom had lived through hell and come out an angel on the other side. No, Locke wouldn't call the woman who raised him an angel—or at least, not one of those delicate, glowing, floating, ethereal types. But she could spout wisdom and knew how to bust his ass to keep him in line. Yeah, he wanted the two women he most respected to meet one another.

"It was her time." Alex turned to Locke, a solemn pledge in his voice. "I'll do whatever you need. My mother would have been my only hesitation, and now she's with my father."

"Okay," Locke said quietly. Before the phone call, he honestly couldn't tell what the man would do. Now, he could see Alex disappearing into an alias with his woman and child. He had no reason to say no. Locke turned to Cassidy. "Where's the other lady I saw you with?"

Taisia cut in. "Victoria. We have to make sure she gets help."

"Did you start already?" Alex asked, nervous energy suddenly changing his move.

"Yes."

"Taisia!"

"They are hidden. Safe." She scowled. "I told you not to come. It's an unexpected distraction."

Locke didn't need them fighting as he accounted for the many variables and inability to notify Delta. "They're not on-site, then?"

"What were you going to do with them?" Alex said.

"I hadn't figured that out yet. But Victoria…" Taisia cringed. "And then she was the first one they were removing off the property. I couldn't do that anymore!"

"All right. Stop," Locke said. Eventually, someone in the Mikhailov empire would realize that they were missing a bunch of girls. "We need to get you guys safe. The place with the fewest number of guards would be where?"

"My house," Taisia said.

"Let's go."

"That connects to where the other girls are too."

"Even better," Locke said. "Not a lot of time. Let's go."

"*Da.*" Taisia led their group, hand in hand with Alex. The long, dark hallways opened to ones that Locke assumed were for people who weren't trafficked and servants. Though bright, it held a chill that matched the mood of the mansion.

There was so much wealth. Beautiful drapes. Thick carpets. Things that he would never think about buying. Hell… Locke glanced at walls as they rushed past. The wallpaper and upholstery glinted as though gold had been woven into the fabric. He couldn't wrap his mind around any of it—women as things to buy, sell, and trade, or décor fabrics made from gold.

The back of Cassidy's hand grazed his, and Locke reached for it, threading his fingers with her much smaller, softer ones as they rounded a corner. He gave a squeeze, and she leaned closer as they silently trailed behind the odd couple in front of them.

"Where's Jax?" she asked.

"Likely terrorizing the Mikhailov assholes who think he's big money. They have to be nice to him."

Her fingers tightened on his as she laughed. There was something comforting in holding Cassidy's hand. His thumb dragged over her knuckles, his pad rough and scraped from a lifetime of living and working. He glanced down, and the only thing that came to mind was, *Damn, that is my woman.*

"Where's Delta?" Cassidy asked, picking up the skirt as they moved down a staircase.

"No fucking clue." By his estimation, Delta should have rolled through the door about fifteen minutes earlier. But since the moment they went back into the Mikhailov compound, he and Jax were blind on updates.

"Through here." Taisia opened an exterior door that spilled onto a sidewalk and driveway as a large SUV with tinted windows rolled up.

Locke's gut churned. That wasn't Delta. Fucking hell. Was it Ivan?

He squinted into the daylight, and his chest tightened at the sight of a child jumping out under the protective shepherding of a bodyguard and nanny. Alex staggered to a standstill as the vehicle's occupants noticed them.

"Mama!" The girl broke free of her gaggle, skipping forward to her mother.

The resemblance to Alex was uncanny. A cold shiver traveled down Locke's back as Cassidy squeezed his hand. Taisia waved the group away, saying something in Russian that Locke assumed gave the others permission to head inside.

After a wayward glance from the guard, they listened, and everyone shivered as the girl bundled in a coat ran forward. Locke pulled Cassidy close, tucking her under his arm.

Taisia hugged her daughter, exchanging a brief greeting, as Alex put his hand on the mother's back, then they rushed inside out of the cold. Locke stepped through the threshold, and just like the other mansion, the awesomeness and vastness was incredible.

"Welcome to my house," Taisia said, holding the girl's hand as Alex unabashedly gawked at his daughter.

Taisia's house was more like a home than the other one. It was still a mansion, still ornate and regal, expensive and expansive, but was smaller than where they just came from. There were pictures on bureaus and portraits lining the walls. The drapes were drawn, and the house had a feeling that someone lived in it, even if it was heavily armed and guarded.

That was not the most remarkable thing, though. Alex emanated a depth of emotion that Locke couldn't grasp as he watched the girl with a ponytail shuck off her coat. The moment seemed entirely too private to participate in, and even though Locke knew Delta was coming and there was so much to discuss with Alex, he wanted to give the man his time.

Even standing in the hall was intrusive. Locke dropped his gaze to Cassidy and saw that they were on the same page as they inched into the corner. The man was united with his woman and child. Locke wanted that—not the loss and recovery of someone he loved, but that joy. Wow...

The guard who'd arrived with the child walked into the foyer and paused, speaking with Taisia, and then he left.

"Everything okay?" Locke asked.

"My father is home now." Taisia squared her shoulders. "I hope that what you said earlier is true. He"—she motioned to the man who left—"was called to meet with the others. I suspect, to discuss Alex's arrival. And soon?" She shrugged. "Sooner or later, someone will find the girls are not there."

Locke was blown away by the strength in her voice. "You're not worried?"

She gave a flat smile. "Terrified. But it's been set in motion. It will work out."

Then her face brightened, and Locke couldn't believe her faux grin and bright eyes as she squatted to eye level with the girl. Taisia had likely changed subjects. She had more important things to talk about than her father, and maybe that kind of abrupt change was something she was used to, living in that family.

The intimate conversation between mother and daughter was too much to watch, yet Locke couldn't tear his eyes away.

Cassidy stepped in front of him, interrupting his trance. Locke pulled her to his chest, and they huddled in the corner. Her chin rested on his sternum, and staring down, he couldn't help but think of her and the future. "Hey, Beauty."

Cassidy's dark-red hair was styled but falling loose, and her painted lips were foreign. But she whispered, "I missed you."

Everything about her was his. Locke palmed her cheek, sweeping over the red rouge that marred her fair skin. "You have no idea how much."

Taisia interrupted. "We should move someplace farther into the house."

Locke's head shot up. He'd been lost in Cassidy. Taisia's eyelashes were tear-dampened, and she wore a smile that looked like it hadn't seen real happiness in years. "Sure," he said.

Alex put his hand on Taisia's shoulder. "Then we will confirm everything you discussed before. You can have anything you need from me."

Locke nodded—

The *womp-womp-womp* of a helicopter sounded as though it was right outside the house. Both Taisia and Cassidy turned toward the door.

"Time to move boots," Locke said.

Delta had arrived.

CHAPTER FORTY-TWO

Taisia and Alex's daughter rushed around Locke and moved to a window, pulling the drapes back.

"Who is here?" the little girl asked, giddy with excitement as though a new friend might arrive.

Locke had to temper his reality with hers. She likely had helicopters arriving on a regular basis—doting billionaire guests with their gifts and entertainment. The Mikhailovs probably used choppers the way Locke used a taxi. "Back away from the window, sweetheart."

Taisia called her daughter too, and Locke turned to the mother. "Where can I get my hands on a weapon? And are you sure there are no other guards in the house?"

"There aren't. This way." Taisia took the little girl's hand, and they moved up a grand marble staircase.

At the top of the landing, the hallway became expansive. Taisia pulled a set of keys from her skirt pocket, moving to a nearby door, and unlocked it. "Weapons."

As she sidestepped, Locke clearly saw this was the bodyguard stash. He stepped in and grabbed two handguns, checked that they were already loaded, and found a tactical knife. He tucked the guns into his pants and secured the knife in his boot.

There were no protective vests that he could use for the group's safety, and he didn't feel as though he should hand a weapon over to anyone else at the moment. "You know how to fire a gun?" he asked the adults, and the curious child wandered away, unimpressed. What a crazy life that kid must have.

None said yes, and truthfully, that eased his mind somewhat. Alex and

Taisia… he didn't trust them one hundred percent. "Ready? Where are the women?" he asked.

The girl gasped and shrank back. Fear shook in her eyes, but her mother reached out and grabbed her hand, pulling her close. "It's okay. He is one of the people I told you could help."

"Oh… oh." The girl smiled hesitantly. "We hid them. We made the tunnel, and we hid them."

Locke held out his fist, and she hopped forward, bumping hers to his. "You did a really good thing." Cute kid. Badass too. But little badasses didn't need to play in this kind of melee. Was there a chance the guard could find them? He glanced to Taisia. "Can you access where the women are hidden from both houses?"

"Yes, there are old passageways."

He needed to check on them, make sure that Mikhailov guards weren't using them as human shields or hostages. "Let's go." But again, he remembered the kid. "Do you have a safe room?"

Working with oligarchs and the megarich wasn't his background, and Locke was pulling a safe-room reference straight from the movies. But it made sense, and the last thing he wanted to do was put their daughter anywhere near a danger zone.

"Yes," Taisia said hesitantly.

Her body language was all over the place, and Locke realized that she'd been put in the position of choosing between leading him to the women and staying with her daughter.

"Taisia." Locke stepped forward. "I don't pretend to understand how you grew up or the threats you have lived with. But I trust Cassidy, and you trust Alex. They will be with your daughter in the safest place possible."

Taisia blinked rapidly and didn't speak, worry pinking her cheeks.

Locke tried again. "We don't know what we're going to find. I know you've been protecting your daughter since the day she was born. You've probably been by her side every moment. But this is the time Alex can be there for his daughter, and you need to come with me."

Alex put his arm around Taisia's shoulder, and she let out a breath that seemed to deflate her. "Yes, yes. We go this way first."

Locke let out a breath. He wasn't sure Taisia would agree.

She pivoted, changing the direction. "I will put you in, and then only you can get out from the inside."

Cassidy grabbed Locke's hand as they followed the family. He wanted her in there also, and he realized, as they moved through the expansive mansion, that Cassidy wouldn't love the idea of the separation either.

They came to a large portrait and curio cabinet. Taisia easily moved it with the slide of a lever. A light came on automatically as the heavy door slid. She wrapped her daughter in a hug, whispering in her ear, and then sent her to follow Alex.

"I suppose this is a pit stop for me too." Cassidy curled to his side, and he held her waist.

"It'd ease my mind." Even in that silly dress, she still felt like his.

Her lips tightened, but she kept all protests to herself as though she knew he had no time.

"You mean the world to me."

"That's what I was going to say," she said.

"No, it's not." Locke winked. "More like 'I'm coming too.'"

"Fine." Cassidy gazed to the side. "How about both? You mean the world to me, and I could come with…"

"Or you can stay in the safest place for you. Do this for me so I can work. Okay?" He kissed her forehead and then kissed her lips. Tearing himself away from Cassidy made his arms ache, but knowing that she was behind a door that was virtually indestructible soothed that hurt away. "In you go."

"When I come out, I'd like a hot shower and new clothes," Cassidy said. "And maybe a pizza."

"Whatever you want, Beauty. But it's time to rock and roll. Okay?"

"Okay," Cassidy said, backing into the safe room.

"I'll be back shortly," Taisia added, blowing one last kiss to her family.

"See you." He gave a quick wave, and his heart pounded. *Damn.* He was leaving her alone. Again.

Taisia showed them how to engage the door then stepped back to the hall as the steel frame shut. "My daughter is always by my side. Always. Whether she should have been or not."

Locke wished there were some comfort to give her other than the truth, but there wasn't. The truth would have to do. "Then you've already started giving her a better place in life."

"And that's what every mother dreams of," Taisia said as she hurried away.

They came to a dead end in the hallway, and there was a door that blended in with the wall. He wouldn't have noticed it if she hadn't stopped.

Again, she took out her keys, and again, they slipped behind the hallway, much as they'd done in the main mansion. This one was smaller but just as dark, and the halls they went through seemed like servant passages. They descended to the first floor and then below that. The basement level was cold and dank. Somewhere along their trip, the hallway had changed. What was obviously used on a regular basis became cobweb covered.

"Does this path connect to your father's house?" he asked.

"It does. But it's abandoned. There's another one still in use, but this one, not in ages."

Locke stepped over a barrier that looked as though it had been recently hacked apart.

"Psss," hissed someone quietly in front of them.

Taisia held out her hand for him to stop in the passageway. It had widened, but there was so little light by that point. The last of the sparsely hung, rudimentary lightbulbs had ended two-dozen feet back and—another face appeared next to Taisia. One of the women?

Locke's eyes had barely adjusted to the new darkness. "I have a flashlight on my phone. I'm turning it on."

He swiped the app and turned on the flashlight. The bright light didn't go far enough but did its job and illuminated the woman's face. She was the same one who had stood next to Cassidy upstairs and then disappeared.

"Hey." Shifting the flashlight over her shoulder, Locke saw women sitting on the floor, lined up one next to the other, at least a dozen deep.

How long they had been there in the dark and cold? They had what looked like thin blankets but no access to food, water, or a bathroom. Damn. But now he'd make sure they were safe—

His skin prickled. Echoes of male voices slid from the far side of the passageway. Gasps fell from the line of women on the floor.

Fucking hell. "Easy, no worries."

But he had a few concerns, and all ranged from not good to screwed. That was not how Delta would sound. Mikhailov might be trying to find an escape route. Whether they were aware of the missing women or not didn't matter so much. What mattered more was how many of them were there and if they were out of bullets.

Locke killed the flashlight and put his hand on Taisia's shoulder. "Who knows about this exit? How easy is it to find?"

"The old guards," she whispered. "The ones that have worked with the family for years. Maybe their sons who were told about them by their fathers. That's how I knew. My mother told me. And they're not hard to find. If you can access the servants' passages, you can access these."

Not exactly what he wanted to hear.

Behind him, Locke heard a noise. He pivoted, his ear straining to make out what it was while still keeping tabs on the drifting Russians echoing on the other side. "How bad of a rat problem do you have down here?"

The woman from earlier touched his shoulder. "Not bad enough to have caused that sound."

It was the first time he'd heard her speak. Interesting, an American.

The not-a-rat noise sounded down the halls, but not much closer. Was that Delta?

"That sounds like a person," the other woman whispered.

The idea that another person was creeping behind them while others were pressing forward... *fuck.*

"Do you have a plan?" the American asked.

He didn't, really. He couldn't see anything and, strategically, didn't have enough cover. His current plan was to take out whoever was quietly making noise and hope that the escaping bodyguards would choose a different hallway that ran straight into a flock of Delta. That was the plan at the moment. All in all, Locke deemed it a shitty plan.

"Are you armed?" she asked.

Who was this lady? He turned to her. "Are *you*?"

"No," she hissed. "But it would be a lot better if I was. Because you could take the forward approach, and I could take whoever's behind us and flank—"

He tried to figure out who she was. "I'm sorry, do you have some kind of background where you would feel comfortable doing this?"

Russian bounced off the walls, and he couldn't tell how close they were. Dread curled in Locke's stomach because they were closing in.

"Something like that, yeah. You don't happen to have an extra gun on you, do you?"

Jesus shit. "What's your name?"

"Victoria."

Ah, he'd heard her name before. The girl from upstairs. "Victoria...what? Have a last name?"

"Victoria. That's it."

"Got it. Victoria with no last name." There wasn't much time here. "Victoria with no last name, if I give you a loaded gun in the dark, are you going to accidentally shoot yourself, these women, or me?"

"No."

"Do you know what the shit you're doing?"

"I don't want to die. I don't want to kill you or these girls either."

At that very far end of the hallway, Locke saw the faint trail of a flashlight beam flash and go away. The Russian bodyguards were on their way down their passage. "Give me your hand." He reached into the dark and found Victoria's outstretched hand then pulled the PSM pistol from the back of his waist and put it in her palm, wrapping her hand around it. With his other hand, he moved her fingers and thumb over the gun. "No safety, no manual slide lock. Very thin weapon. Do you feel that?"

He couldn't see it, but he felt her move as she whispered, "Yes."

"These triggers don't take much, but they're not hair-trigger. Pull back here, and you get eight shots. You won't need eight shots. You shouldn't need any. There is a team of good guys on-site. Do not kill them. They are my friends. They are my family. Do you understand?"

"I do."

"Okay, anybody who is not a woman or with a child, not another American, and not on my Delta team—don't let them through to these girls. I'm going to do the same on the other side. That's our plan. Sound good?"

"Sounds like a plan," she said.

He nodded. "Thanks, Victoria with no last name..."

With that, Victoria turned to face the very faint light in the direction he'd first come from. Locke stepped over and around all the women who lay and sat on the floor, and he tried not to think about the hell that they had been through.

The farther he crept away, the more nervous he became that he'd just left them with a woman he didn't know, who was holding a gun. But the way Victoria had stood with Cassidy, interacted with Taisia, and pushed Locke to come up with a plan had inspired his trust. Locke had to trust his instincts while still hoping the noise he heard was a giant-ass rat. Or Delta.

God help them; let that be Delta making their way through the maze of passageways that seemed to be behind the walls of the Mikhailov compound.

He came to the corner and poked his head around it, not for the first time wishing he had equipment. No sign of the flashlight beam. No sounds of men walking or their voices rumbling. There were other passages and ways to escape the main building. Part of him wanted to protect the women, but part of Locke wanted to go after those fuckers.

All those girls lined up? Yeah. Big problem.

The footsteps and the light were back. Three people, from what Locke could tell. He had to assume they were armed.

The flashlight beam grew stronger as it swept side to side. One of the men repeatedly tapped the wall every few strides, as though they were looking for a door like the one Taisia's house had.

Five minutes earlier, their voices had been booming, and now they were just searching. Were they more desperate than before? Locke couldn't just shoot them, much as he wanted to—wait. The flashlight beam flashed across the hallway, and he squinted. That wasn't three guards. It was… two guards and a man in a suit. Ivan Mikhailov?

Holy shit. Delta didn't have Ivan, and he was trying to escape.

With twenty yards between him and what were probably the two strongest guards Mikhailov had, Locke readied for war, because the bastard was vengeful. If he saw his women lined up on the ground, it'd be a complete bloodbath. He'd slaughter them all. Ivan Mikhailov had a reputation for vengeance.

Locke pressed up against the wall at the corner. Ivan was in the middle, and the hallway was so narrow his bodyguards staggered in front and behind as they walked. Locke could take both—he could shoot the first one and then, assuming Ivan jumped back, go after the other. And then he'd capture the FSB jerkoff responsible for all of this.

In theory, that sounded possible. In reality… Adrenaline pumped in Locke's veins.

Their footsteps were upon him. No other options.

A bodyguard casually rounded the corner, having no idea what was around the bend, and Locke's best hit landed dead center on his face. The goal was to crack his nose so hard that it would take him out, knocking him into Ivan like a domino.

The flashlight dropped, rolling. Their only light source was pointing in the wrong direction. He couldn't see shit. But he surged forward. Locke stepped on the knocked-out bodyguard as he punched the other. The man on the ground didn't grab him. No arms reached up, and no legs kicked out. The man was out cold. Sweat poured down Locke's back, and he sucked down a deep breath, high on the satisfaction.

Ivan was a high-value target, but the other man was more dangerous. They both needed his focus. Locke's mind raced as adrenaline pumped. The two men yelled in Russian, and he had no idea what they said. But he triangulated their locations in the dark. Locke took a swing and hit the guard's neck. Growling and biting, the man warred back.

It was too dark for the guard to use a weapon with Ivan nearby. But Ivan might be armed, and he wouldn't care if he killed either of them. They had to keep moving. Locke swung his leg down and dropped the guard. They rolled on top of Ivan, who groaned as two men weighing easily two hundred pounds of muscle apiece slammed on top of him.

Locke reached for the gun at his waist as the other man reached for his. Eyes adjusted to the dark, it was a move they both knew, and they rolled back and then surged forward like battering rams, out of breath, knocking the other's shooting hand.

The man wrapped his fist around Locke's neck, choking off his air supply, tearing his fingers into his throat as though he were going to rip his esophagus out. *Motherfuck.* He couldn't breathe. Stars popped behind his eyelids. Locke drilled his knee into the man's groin—oxygen.

He gasped, falling over to catch his breath.

Ivan rolled, scurrying on his knees, and Locke launched, hooking his ankle and pulling him back. "Not going away."

They rolled to the side. Locke crawled on top of Ivan, wrapping a chokehold around his neck as they rolled over—

The cold barrel of a gun froze Locke. The guard had it pressed to his temple, and Locke's free arm dropped as though loosening.

"Let him go."

He bucked, twisting with Ivan, grabbing the blade from his boot and slamming his fist back. The gun went off. The knife lodged in the guard—his ribs, judging by the sound and feel—and a hot burn from the discharged weapon seared across Locke's forehead into his hairline. His ears rang. The shot still screamed in his ear.

He had no hearing other than the resounding, aching boom that echoed in his head, and still, he fought to find the fallen weapon. He swung his free hand onto the floor, no idea if the guard was dead or alive.

"Stay still!" a woman yelled.

Locke couldn't make heads or tails of what was happening in the dark. He couldn't let go of Ivan, and he didn't know where the other gun was, but he wrenched his grip on Ivan even tighter. The bastard still fought as Locke yanked again.

The abandoned flashlight moved and was directed his way, then the stabbed and knocked-out men on the floor, and went back up to the woman's face—Victoria—and returned to him as Ivan thrashed again.

"Stay still, you fuck. You horrible, horrible, awful fuck," she cried. "You fucking ruined my life."

Locke's ears rang and hurt, but he heard every word of that. She knew exactly who Ivan was, and she had a gun trained on him—while Locke held him. Not ideal.

"Victoria, I've got him." Locke sat up. "It's okay."

It was then that Locke noticed she held the flashlight and the gun in a way that only a professional would know. The woman was trained as much as she was a victim. He had no idea about her past, no idea what she had been through or where she had come from. But she had the strength to put the gun down if she wanted to.

"Victoria, listen to me," Locke said. "You are better than this piece of trash."

With the flashlight off her face, she was just a beam of light and the barrel of a gun. She sniffled, and he heard the hiccup of a tear. The weapon did not waver.

"I'm going to stand up. I've got him. He's not going anywhere," Locke said.

"*Don't move.* Don't let him move. He can't move. He wouldn't let me move. He can't move."

Locke jerked the chokehold on the man, who suddenly seemed to realize that the woman in front of him was going to fucking kill him. "I should let her, you sick fuck. Whatever you did to her, you deserve it."

Noises shuffled behind Victoria, and beams of light came into view.

Delta. Somebody from his team was there to help defuse the situation. Thank God.

Locke barely saw the outline of another man move next to Victoria as she tilted to look from Ivan to the Delta man. Still, the gun didn't move from Locke's direction.

"Locke," Ryder's Aussie accent called. "Seems you have yourself a handful, yeah?"

"Nothing I couldn't handle," he grumbled. "But since you're here..."

"Sweetheart, my gun is pointed at them. Do you want to drop yours?" Ryder held out his hand to Victoria. "Put it in my hand, and everything will work out."

Victoria sniffled, and her teary voice said, "No."

Ryder hummed as though contemplating what she had said. "I promise you, mine works as good as yours."

"But he never hurt you," she said, her voice breaking.

Ryder shifted, engaging the safety on his weapon and dropping it to his side after a show of standing down. "Hell..." He turned to her. "You're right."

"I am?" she whispered.

Ryder rubbed a hand over his face, shaking his head and cursing. "Yeah, you are. And that makes this so much harder. I'm really sorry." In one fast move, he grabbed Victoria, disarming her and hugging her to his chest as he slipped the weapon away.

Locke could take a deep breath as somebody behind Ryder tossed him a set of plastic ties to cuff Ivan.

Once he had Ivan secured and on his feet, Locke looked over at Victoria, who quietly sobbed in Ryder's arms. He didn't blame her for one second. He'd probably need a gun physically pulled from him too in certain situations. There were some pains in life impossible to understand and accept unless another person walked you away.

A flashlight was handed to him, and finally, Locke had eyes on who was there—Ryder and Trace. He flashed it down the hall to see Luke. "Hello, Delta. Where's the rest of you? Upstairs?"

"Brock's upstairs running through all the intel we found with Jax," Trace said. "Colin has Mikhailov dudes tied up and ready to talk to. I don't know where anybody else is. But this place is huge."

Taisia then came forward in the hallway and walked up to her father, ignoring all the Delta guys and Locke. Once she'd stepped over two bodies and was practically nose to nose with him, she glowered. "I may never forgive you, and I may never forget, but I will survive."

Ivan muttered, "Stupid girl. All of this, and they can't keep me. You think anything will change? Never." He spat on the floor. "Run and hide, Taisia. Whatever you had to do with this, run and hide."

Locke knew they weren't making an arrest, that the Russian government would not do a thing about Ivan Mikhailov and didn't care that he ran a prostitution ring and even maybe a pedophilia ring. Ivan was an influential man in their government and would be a useful man if what Alex said panned out.

Delta-team guys were ghosts. There would be no record they set foot in Russia, and even if Ivan wanted to make accusations that Americans had come in, he wouldn't be able to prove it.

At the moment, Brock was upstairs, overseeing the destruction of anything that could prove that they were there, all while they were data mining and collecting intel on anything that would help them find other traffickers. All Delta wanted to do was dismantle and disrupt the system.

Maybe Locke should just kill Ivan. They'd killed his bodyguards, but they did so while attacked. Victoria would never be able to charge Ivan with rape or whatever it was that he'd done, but maybe these other girls would.

Their purpose was to bring girls home, to save them from a life of hell. And bonus, they could keep Alex Gaev from selling intelligence to the Russian government or having Ivan Mikhailov use it as an insurance policy to protect his new trafficking business out of the US. Locke hadn't quite figured which thing Ivan intended to do—likely both. Either way, the information wouldn't be sold.

"I'm out," Locke said to Trace.

"Where you going?"

He flashed the beam up and down the hall, but the women were mostly gone, as was Taisia. "To find Cassidy."

"Brock says team meeting when we're done rounding up the pieces of shit."

"I'll be there."

Locke handed Ivan to Trace as though the man were a sack of garbage and went in search of his woman. He owed her a shower, normal clothes, and apparently, a pizza.

CHAPTER FORTY-THREE

CASSIDY'S FIRST UNDERCOVER assignment with Titan was done. She'd washed away all signs of the makeup from earlier and spent far too little time in the shower. With a towel knotted at her chest, Cassidy padded out of the bathroom in Taisia's palatial mansion and watched as Locke jumped off the bed. He'd promised he would be there when she got out, but the idea that he waited for her, eyeing her as hungrily as she felt in the shower, made her bold, even if they had places to go in short order.

"Would it be totally inappropriate to say—"

"That thank fuck, we are finally alone." Locke grabbed her like a starving man and ravenously pulled her close, his hungry mouth sinking over hers before she could utter a word of agreement.

Near-violent arousal overtook Cassidy, flooding her bloodstream with a lustful appreciation for his thick arms and talented tongue. But more than that, the familiar hold was like coming home. He'd hugged her half a dozen times since the ruse was up, but this was carnal and predatory. He wasn't holding back now but giving them both what they needed: each other.

"Do you know what you do to me, Mister?"

He tugged on her lip. "What do I do to you, Beauty?"

A blush hit her cheeks. Of course, she'd have to answer the rhetorical question. "Turn me on."

"And?"

"Mmmm." She grew wet as he dropped his mouth to her neck, letting his teeth rasp and his hands travel to her bare bottom under the towel. "You give me very good dreams."

"I like that."

"When I'm awake too," she said.

"I like that better." He moved to her ear, and he whispered, "Have you touched yourself and thought of me?"

"Yes." Her quiet voice didn't matter for the loud quake of excitement rushing across her nerves at the admission.

Locke groaned. "Mmm. Good, baby."

Her nipples ached, needing him against her ultra-sensitized skin, and her pussy lips clenched in anticipation of what she knew would come. The memory of his wet tongue sliding across her slick folds had her hips squirming as if they had a mind of their own. He brought his mouth back to hers, delving his tongue deep.

"If we talk like that, then you kiss me like that"—she pulled back, knowing they had places to be—"I can't promise that I'm good for getting to meet your team on time."

He tore off his shirt, putting rippled muscles and broad shoulders on display. "What makes you think I care?"

Cassidy bit her lip, flushed with desire that bloomed deep in her stomach. She stared at Locke, whose tattoos, scars, hard abs, and serious, come-to-me smile made her pleasure all the more vibrant. "I assumed you had manners."

He laughed, and his corded muscles danced under her palms. "Not at a time like this."

"Good to know where our priorities lie." She scraped her fingers down his abdomen to the top of his pants, mischievously dancing her fingers over the button fastener.

"We'll be on time." He ran his hands through her damp hair as she unbuckled his pants. "We'll be quick. C'mere."

"In a minute. Something I need to do first." She just wanted enough time to wrap her lips around him as she stroked, to feel the hot-steel length and the silkiness of his heated flesh.

"I promise." Locke tugged at her hair, urging her off her knees. "I'll take my time with you later. Nice and slow, for days, Cassidy."

"I believe you, baby." She slid her hand over his heavy erection. "But I need something from you too."

With a push, she urged his powerful thighs apart and settled to her knees, feeling her arousal slickening her sex as she readied to taste his precum, lick the thick shaft, and fill her mouth with the man who adored her.

He was perfect. Just the visual made her dizzy with want. When this hard-on pushed inside her…? Mmmm. Cassidy gripped him at the base and sucked the bulbous head into her mouth, running her tongue along the underside of his crown.

"*Damn.*" Locke sucked air. His thighs flexed, and his groan tore through the air, vibrating all the way to her clit.

His heavy breaths made her want to take more of him, and his near-failing restraint made her mouth water. "Mmmm."

"That. Mouth." Locke's hips lifted. "Beauty."

He ran his hands over her shoulders as she let him fill her mouth, slipping back into her throat.

"Good girl. Take my cock"—he groaned, leaning back to watch—"deep. Fuck. Suck it. Goddamn."

With every dirty word, she grew wetter. This was just like she dreamed. Just what she touched herself to—Cassidy kept a fist wrapped around the base of his dick and closed her eyes, relishing his heated, smooth skin working against her lips. She massaged his sac and then slipped her hand between her legs as she kept bobbing her head. His hips started to flex with her rhythm, and her fingers fluttered. Cassidy moaned at it all. His fingers kneaded her shoulders, her lips swelled around his pumping erection, and oh, now the bud of her clitoris—

Locke's hands went under her arms, pulling her off his hard-on. "Up and on the bed, babe."

Whoa. They rolled onto the bed, stripping away her towel. "Cold! I need my towel."

"You're fine."

He spun her around and upside down before she could grab the just-out-of-reach towel. "*Oh. God.*"

His hands grabbed her ass as she realized he'd spread her bare over his face. Locke licked her again. "Suck my cock, Beauty." His tongue delved into her entrance as his fingers stroked, curling, deeper and deeper.

Pleasure surprised her with each touch—one right after the other after the other. "God!"

"Don't care about the towel now?" He kissed, laughing against her sensitive folds, and she shook her head, getting her bearings. Every word he said made her body rejoice. Goosebumps spiraled across every inch of her skin. He worked her from the inside out, teased her open as she tensed, and made love to her body with his tongue again.

"Locke!" She whimpered and shook, grabbing his cock in her hands and stroking, hands stacked on top one another. "Don't stop!"

His hands on her held her down, and she moaned—*God*, he did too, lapping slow strokes as she melted for him and shuddering as she opened her mouth to him, letting him pass her lips at the same pace and insane voltage that Locke made her build.

She channeled every never-ending reaction, determined to suck him as well as he kissed her, and wrapped her hands around his cock, pumping while she sucked.

"Mmm," she moaned, needing to climax. Cassidy pulled back, moving her hands and gasping. "If I die, lie about how I went."

She was flying high. Her canal began to tighten, and her muscles began to quiver. Cassidy took him into her mouth, tightening and wriggling as his fingers dug to keep her lower half still.

Just like him, she took as good as she gave. Impaled with pleasure, dying to come, he gave incoherent groans and moans, and his hip thrusts into her mouth were harsher. They both toed the edge of orgasm.

"Cassidy, love, *do not stop*," he demanded.

Every single word pushed her toward an erotic explosion. His tongue thrust in and out, and his fingers held her still as she began to pull away from the near painful-pleasure the man was putting her through.

Cassidy dipped her head to take more of him. It wasn't fair. She couldn't think. Couldn't breathe. Maybe couldn't come. But goddamn, she wouldn't let him get away from a climax.

On the precipice of the orgasm, her thighs clenched, and she moaned. A hand shifted, and Locke slid two fingers inside of her, curling them just enough, sucking and teasing her clit until she could explode, driving her higher.

And higher.

And even higher.

"Locke," she begged with him in her mouth. "Please..."

His hand clamped onto her ass, holding her to him, and his tongue ran through her folds until he swirled into her, kissing her, pulsing and pressing, gliding in and out, and she couldn't stop the wave of orgasm that slammed.

Drunk on him, she sucked wildly on his shaft as she came, bucking; his hands held her to his mouth as she spasmed, shaking until she cursed, and Locke rolled away from her, abandoning her on the bed. Her arm reached for him, but limply. She could barely move a muscle. She was too weak to open her eyes, too lazy to drag more of a gasp into her lungs than she had managed.

Then he was by her side, tucking an arm under her head and putting a hand on her thigh.

"Where'd you go," she murmured as he kissed her.

"Condom."

"Oh, you're a good man."

Once they were on their sides, Locke hooked her knee over his. She draped over him and finally opened her eyes, taking in his erection, sheathed and bobbing heavily between them. "A very good, very thoughtful man."

"It's the manners." He palmed his shaft, rubbing it against her sensitive flesh.

She was wet with arousal, lubricated by his tongue, and as he teased her, she couldn't help but squirm. The thick, blunt head of his dick was so damn close to her entrance. "It's not polite to tease."

"My bad, baby." Locke eased deep inside her, and Cassidy's head dropped back as he held her tight.

The sensation nearly overwhelmed her, bringing her to dizzying heights. But there was more—his arms, his blue eyes. She trusted him. There was a depth to his gaze that was stronger than every inch that slid inside her.

"Locke." She needed him as much as she wanted him. The feeling had clawed its way inside her heart. She couldn't be without him. "When we get home, promise me you aren't going anywhere."

He rolled on top of her, caging the sides of her face with his forearms, and his lips danced with hers, easing her mouth open so their tongues could touch. "Not going anywhere."

Those three words were the best. "Good."

Locke lazily moved in and out of her, their effort to keep it quick long since given up. He was making love to her, and she'd never experienced a connection like that before. It was as though he could feel her thoughts, as though she could read his mind.

"I'm sorry I ever did anything to hurt you," she whispered, butterfly kissing him from his cheek to his ear.

"You didn't."

"But you were in a dark place. I was to blame." Emotion caught in her throat. It was almost as thick as arousal. How could she have ever caused someone like him to hurt?

"No, you were the key to letting all of that go." His throaty promise ran the course of her body as he gathered her tighter. Seated deep inside her, Locke held her eyes. "Beauty, I love you."

She clung to him, crying. She couldn't help it. He withdrew his cock and then slowly pumped deep into her body, giving her a reprieve long enough to gasp, "I love you too."

"God, baby," he growled. "That's what I needed to hear."

He pushed up on his fists, sliding his length, driving it, in and out, harder and faster, building until she lost her breath. Each thrust scored her longer, stronger, deeper than the last until she needed to scream.

Locke cursed and growled. "You're my woman."

"Yours." It was all she could manage. Him owning her was what she needed to hear. Cassidy went over the edge. She came hard, and he dropped against her, gathering her body into his arms as he strained, climaxing with her.

Their rollercoaster had started years before, and gathered tightly in his arms, Cassidy felt like it was still just starting. She needed this man, needed how he needed her too. That was something for the future. He was the one she never knew she was waiting for.

CHAPTER FORTY-FOUR

THE LAST TIME Cassidy had walked into Titan Group's war room was just a few short days earlier. Wait, that wasn't right. She counted back. Just over a week. Wow. So much had happened.

"Ready?" Locke took her hand.

That was one thing that was different. They were officially out of the closet, not that they'd been hiding before. But whatever happened overseas had transformed them from the brewing-relationship stage to most definitely in love.

Because this man was her world. And it wasn't puppy love or white-knight syndrome. She'd had boyfriends and substantial relationships before, and nothing compared to the depth of her connection with Locke.

Truthfully, Cassidy hadn't known that a single person could cause such a paradigm shift. But he had straggly hair, sexy blue eyes, and a secret hidden talent for saying dirty things when he wanted to set her on fire—which was always.

"Sure, I'm ready. Why wouldn't I be?" Locke had said something about people saying thanks, but that was ridiculous. They'd thanked her before she signed up, and she appreciated it. But that was said and done.

"All right, then." Locke let go of her hand and placed his palm on her back as she walked into the room.

Everyone had already gathered around the table, and Jared Westin stood. Then everyone else did too.

The room began to... *clap*.

Cassidy froze, and a blush hit in her cheeks. It overtook her entire body. Yes, she was a journalist and liked the spotlight, but oh, the accolades? This was too much. Locke put his hands on her shoulders as though she were some MVP of a championship game, and she tried to sidestep the attention. He gave her a quick squeeze, leaning to her ear. "You earned it, Beauty."

Her eyes bugged, and she tipped her head back to him. "You knew about this?"

"Ha." Locke winked. "Some things are best to never admit to."

"Come on in, Cassidy," Jared said, waving her in farther.

Oh, gee. If she didn't fall over from the attention, maybe she could walk in. "I get it. Thanks. Okay."

"Woot, woot," a guy in a cowboy hat said and rapped the table twice before he took a seat.

The whole room had the same type of response until they settled and sat down. Jared and Locke were the only ones who remained standing. Jared walked over to Cassidy, and Locke gave her one more shoulder squeeze and left her with his boss.

"If I *thought* that I would have all this attention"—Cassidy shrugged sarcastically, making Jared laugh—"I might not have agreed to do all of that."

"Well, Cassidy, we like to keep our people on their toes." He stuck his hand out. "Thank you for everything you did."

Oh, good gracious. Jared Westin was shaking her hand. It should have been the other way around. Still, Cassidy shook his hand, and the entire room erupted in hoots and hollers, table raps and whistles.

"I've heard that things mentioned in here are never to be mentioned again." Cassidy gave Jared a side-eye then playfully pointed at everybody. "All of this attention will never be mentioned *again*."

Jax protested loudly, and the rest agreed with good humor and smiles.

"I actually have something to share with you." Cassidy pivoted to Jared and then back to the table. "I wanted to let you know I plan on being in *here* all the time." She pointed to the ground. "In the war room, or at the very least, Titan. Let the gossipy guys chew on that for a minute." She bounced her eyebrows at Parker. "You will see me a lot."

Parker shifted and gave Locke a funny look. "Oh yeah? What's going on there?"

Locke leaned back in his chair, chuckling. "Don't look at me, though you'll probably see plenty of Cassidy Noble where I'm involved."

Parker looked back at Cassidy. "What gives?"

She drew in a breath, and it felt so good, getting ready to say this. Everything had come full circle. This was why she'd first started down the road with the job at St. Andrew's. "ZNN just offered me a primetime gig."

"Oh, hell yeah." Parker laughed. "You're going to be on all our TVs."

"You got it, buddy." Her on-air report on trafficking the night before had done so well and had gone so viral with people asking where she had been that the major news network made the offer that morning, and she'd gladly accepted while curled in Locke's arms.

What had started out as a goal to rise from the ashes as a fallen reporter had become so much more. Yes, she created a whole new career for herself, but then, there was everything else that she did.

She fell in love.

She helped her country.

She saved women from being trafficked.

And she watched a father meet his daughter.

It had been one hell of a week.

CHAPTER FORTY-FIVE

Two Months Later

EVEN THE COOL air conditioning pumped into the congressional hearing hall was stagnating with the hot air of the politicians. Cassidy had been in the hot seat for hours and said one-tenth the number of words said by the people questioning her. Maybe they just wanted to hear themselves speak and not ask a single question. Maybe they didn't actually care what she had to say and only wanted sound bites for their commercials. Or perhaps she had just grown cynical.

"*Again*, you used anonymous sources regarding government intelligence. Is that twice? Once years before, and now, a few months ago?"

And Cassidy would do it all over again if it meant saving people's lives. She gave zero fucks about furthering any politician's career. "That's what my calendar says also. *Sir*."

"Miss Noble," Senator Brown said with far too much spit coming out of his mouth. "I don't think we're going let you leave until we have a proper answer this time. The American public deserves it."

The chairman banged his gavel. "Be that as it may, you are out of time."

"I would request the chairman reconsider. She knows. The Russians know. Everyone in DC seems to know who her sources are—"

"We are out of time and adjourning. Even the Russians want to eat dinner."

Cassidy agreed. Not that the hearing chairman, Senator Land, was a fan of hers, but he was probably hungry, because she was. They had gone through lunch without adjournment and were pressing close to dinnertime.

She had given nothing up regarding her sources. They knew this wasn't her first congressional hearing or her first deposition with members of Congress yelling at her. They should realize that she wasn't going to give up her sources, and Senator Brown wouldn't get anywhere with her. All he could do was punish her.

Cassidy knew what was right, and she knew her rights. In the two months since they had returned from Russia, and she had been assured that Alex, Taisia, and Alyona had been safely stowed somewhere in the United States to start their lives under new names as Americans, Cassidy had gone about doing several things.

One: she finished that article for St. Andrew's.

Two: she worked with both the CIA and the Department of Homeland Security to map out the FSB network in Maryland and DC. Alex had explained that it existed just outside of the reach of the Russian embassy and tinkered in everything from low-level Russian crime families to attempted high-level espionage. It was quite the network—the FSB likely hated her for that. But what was a girl to do—hide?

And three: she worked with Brock Gamble and Titan's Delta team, which apparently had a niche focus on human trafficking, particularly sex trafficking. That was a global issue that Cassidy had learned more about and was taking as a career cause.

But she wasn't going to give up Delta team. Nope. She wouldn't even breathe their existence. A term she had heard regarding them was *ghost team*. They didn't exist. You never saw them. That was Delta… though she wondered if any of Delta ever stayed in touch with people they worked with.

Her mind wandered to Victoria. If Cassidy was to ever follow up with a rescued victim, she thought Victoria would be the one. There was something in her eyes, a bravery that spoke when her lips didn't.

And Cassidy wouldn't give up any information about Alex and his family to any politician who wanted to use love and a family to grandstand. They were aware he was in witness protection. End of story. Some members of Congress had received intelligence briefings; others had not. The choice of who to tell and to what degree wasn't her call. Cassidy would play no part in hanging others out to dry. Simply, all she would do was share the truth.

"She's in contempt of Congress," Senator Brown snarled with his spittle flying. His red cheeks grew ruddier, and his brow furrowed deeper. "*Again!*"

Cassidy tried her hardest not to roll her eyes. She was positive that Senator Brown had been briefed as to what actually happened. She had no fucks left to give about that either, so instead, she just smiled.

"This hearing is adjourned." Senator Land banged the gavel.

Ten seconds later, everyone was out of their seats, probably headed to find some food. She sure was, as soon as she could find Locke, who was probably asleep somewhere in the back row. She would've gone to sleep hours earlier, too, if she could have gotten away with it.

She turned around, and there her man was, gorgeous and sexy as ever, and wearing a suit. Couldn't beat that.

"I would've thought you were asleep." She laughed but still raked her eyes over him.

He winked. "My girlfriend's the devil, and I didn't know."

Cassidy gave him a push, and Locke threw his arm over her shoulder. "Hungry?" He held out a granola bar.

"You're an angel." She snatched it out of his hand and peeled it open.

"One of us has to be." They joined the crowd and proceeded into the hallway, making their way toward the exit.

She took a bite of the bar. "I'm not sure I'm going to make it to my place." And she certainly wouldn't make it to his. "There have to be more options for food. Did you see vending machines around here? We could do granola bars, fruit snacks, and juice. Make a meal out of it."

Locke chuckled and pulled her through the crowd. "As appetizing as that sounds—hang on—"

His eyes darkened, and the arm around her shoulder yanked her close. Confused, Cassidy tugged back. Staffers surrounded them, but he acted as though a threat suddenly loomed.

"Locke?" The crowd surged, and Cassidy peered over her shoulder. Her warning bells screamed at a man with dead eyes. He wore a suit, but his gait was mechanical. "Locke!"

Locke spun them into the thick throng of people. "Head down. We have to go."

"What's going on?"

"Don't know. Head against me." He wrapped an arm around her waist, lifting her off her feet, and pushed like a linebacker as people yelled at him for causing the disturbance. "Goddamn it."

"What—"

"Damn it. Head against me, Cassidy." He turned toward the wall as she saw another man like the first, but closer.

Two men. Both sides. Locke covered her head, curling her to his chest, trying to ram them through the crowd.

A gunshot popped. Pain exploded. Cassidy screamed until the strength to call for the pain to end left her.

COVERED IN CASSIDY'S blood, Locke watched the crowd run from around him as her body went limp. He had to lay her down because the bastard with the gun was disappearing into the panicked crowd.

Locke dove, catching the shooter from behind, and twisted him as they crashed to the ground. He smashed his forehead against the man's and drew strength from the satisfying crunch of a broken nose.

The man swung up, his undercut landing on Locke's stomach. Locke bore down, pounding fists into the other's face. Fuck, the dude was trained. Locke swerved and missed a punch, and the other man cursed—in Russian.

They'd come for her? No, no, Cassie wasn't going to go out at the hands of the Mikhailovs. Capitol Hill police crawled all over the place. Surely, someone had locked down the building and was hunting for the other man.

But this one was Locke's. They rolled apart and jumped to their feet. The silver glint of a makeshift knife flashed as the man freed a shiv from his jacket. Locke evaded a stab as the man swung, then he grabbed the man's wrist and wrenched it until it broke, slamming his other fist into his unprotected jaw.

It didn't stop the guy. Broken nose, broken wrist—he had to be former

KGB, one of those elite-trained fucking assholes.

Damn. Where were medical personnel for Cassidy?

Locke took a shot to his face that sent his dome ringing—and shit, a boot landed in his stomach. He staggered back, tripping over Cassidy. *Fuck.*

The makeshift knife fell, and they both rushed to it. The Russian had it, slicing across Locke's thigh as he felt his flesh tear and blood as it flowed down his leg.

"Locke," Cassidy hoarsely whispered.

Both men froze as if realizing that she was there, *alive*. It gave him new life to fight harder—and maybe the Russian too because he hadn't done his job.

The man growled and jerked toward Cassidy with the makeshift blade. Locke grabbed his elbow and cranked back, wrenching himself toward the man.

The blade stuck the man in his own chest. The deafening sound was just loud enough that Locke could take a breath as he let go and let him gurgle in his own blood. He let him fall and crawled over to his woman as Capitol Hill police in helmets and with AKs barreled down the hall.

"I'm not armed. She needs to go to the hospital." He tossed his hands in the air to show that he was weapon-free. "I'm going to check her pulse. I need to see where she's been shot."

They yelled at him to stay still, but fuck it; he didn't care. They could see what he was doing. Locke searched for a pulse. A faint one. *Thank you, God.* Where had she been shot? He carefully twisted her shoulder up and saw that it was… near her stomach? Side? Not good.

Capitol Hill police had them surrounded and were dealing with the dead Russian and rushing in the medical team. Seconds later, the med techs were by Cassidy's side and pulling Locke away.

Questions came at him. They knew who she was. But who was he? What did he know?

The woman who seemed in charge of the medical team grabbed his shoulder. "Who is she to you?"

"She's mine." And if Locke lost her, he would die too.

CHAPTER FORTY-SIX

LOCKE HAD HIS hands buried into the hollows of his eyes when he heard the shuffle of footsteps coming to the hospital's waiting room. Titan had special privileges that put him in a quiet place as Cassidy was operated on, but Locke wasn't sure if it was better to be alone or surrounded in a public area by people he didn't know. Didn't matter. He couldn't breathe, couldn't feel, couldn't see. No one could give him reliable information, and her prognosis scared him.

Whoever walked in waited. Locke didn't want to look up, because what the hell would happen if they told him bad news? He'd barely survived Sadr City and couldn't survive losing her.

"Locke." Jared's voice caught him off guard. "You need anything?"

Hesitantly, he tilted his head up, rolling his bottom lip into his mouth. He couldn't talk, not trusting his voice for the simple word no, and instead shook his head.

Jared walked across the small waiting area and chose a seat diagonal to him, leaning over and resting his forearms on his knees. "I can't tell you that it will be okay. I didn't even ask for an update before I came in."

Locke bit down on his bottom lip and held on to the hurt and the fear of losing Cassidy. He pinched the bridge of his nose and rubbed his fingers into his eyes.

"Sugar sat in a room very much like that, and it kills me that she was ever in your position. Every now and then, I think back to what wouldn't have happened if we didn't find each other. Asal and Violet..." Jared looked away. "Asal and Violet wouldn't be here."

Jared's kids were his world. Locke hadn't thought about children before, but damn, he had in the last hour.

"The point of entry, the angle," Locke mumbled. "It may have done some damage to her… there's a lot of things they're working on. Saving her fucking life. But—" His voice cracked. "Cassidy might not be able to have kids."

Did she want kids? Their relationship was so new—it wasn't a topic that had come up—and someone had already stolen that from them. They would never have the chance—or might not—because the FSB were retaliating. Because Ivan Mikhailov was a vengeful fuck.

They wanted to take her life. No. No… she wouldn't die.

Locke dropped his head and struggled for breath.

"Locke, man." Jared moved to a closer chair and tossed a hand over his back, clapping him twice, and then just let it hang. "I don't pretend to know your situation with her. But I do know that it doesn't matter how you end up with your children, because they're your kids." He gave him one more slap on the back.

Boss Man stood and walked toward the door, but as he pulled it open, he turned. "Cassidy Noble is strong as hell. Feisty as fuck. I don't know what the doctors told you, but what I say? Brother, you have to believe. Take a breath. Take one minute, one second, any increment of time you need to figure how to survive. Get through it. Because she's gonna need you."

With a nod, he left, and when the door closed and no one else was around, Locke fell apart, sobbing into his hands. He'd done everything he could to protect her. It wasn't enough.

He'd known her for so long and never given it a chance. If only they'd talked sooner. If only she'd never worked that job. If only, if only, if only! He slammed his fists on the arms of the chairs. *Damn it.* Locke wanted to spend the rest of his life with her and hadn't told her!

Fucking hell.

Locke dragged his shirt over his face, wiping his tears away. Five-second increments. Ten minutes. He couldn't handle the concept of surviving an hour. He didn't know what to do. But what he wouldn't do was sit here and fucking cry.

She wasn't dead. She wouldn't die. He sucked in a breath and wiped his face again with his hands, drying them off on his jeans-covered thighs.

If there was anyone who would kick ass enough, would be pissed enough that she had been shot, it would be Cassidy.

Locke grabbed a glass of water a nurse had brought him and guzzled it, then he slouched in the chair and waited. With every ticking minute, he decided that it was a good thing it was taking so long. She was fighting, and they were saving her.

Finally, the door cracked open. A clean-scrubbed surgeon walked in, and paralysis overtook Locke. The breathless, hefty weight held him until the man in scrubs smiled. *Thank fuck.*

"She's going to be fine," the surgeon said. "Cassidy is in recovery. Her vitals are where we like to see them, and I expect her to wake up soon."

Locke's jumbled words of thanks mixed with an elation he couldn't comprehend. He had to wait until a nurse walked in. The moment she arrived, Locke jumped to his feet, ready to roll.

They wound through the halls until he was brought to Cassidy's side, and as scary as it looked to see his already pale beauty lying in bed with monitors, Locke rejoiced.

"Cassidy," he whispered.

Her eyelashes fluttered as he took her hand, brought it to his lips, and simply held it there. Her drugged gaze and lazy grin slowly appeared. He would stand there, leaning against her bed, for however long it took until she sobered up enough to know that it was him.

"Hi, handsome," she whispered. "That didn't end like I thought it would."

Always with the sass, his feisty redhead. "No, it didn't."

She drifted back to sleep as nurses and techs came and went. Locke didn't leave her side.

Cassidy awoke again, and this time, Locke knew she was more with it. She was still under the hazy gauze of painkillers but not in a stupor anymore.

"I'm glad you're still here," she said.

His thumb ran over her knuckles. "I'm not going anywhere."

"I know. I dreamt that we were married."

"Good, baby. That's good. We are. We will."

She nodded.

"Soon," he said. Hell, what was he waiting for? He'd get the ring later and make it proper. They'd both seen enough horrors not to tempt fate anymore. "Cass, babe. You awake?"

"Mm-hmm."

"Can you open your eyes, Beauty?"

She gave him the blue-green eyes he needed.

"I'm asking right now: will you marry me?"

Her fingers gave a quick squeeze to his. "Find the chaplain."

"Oh, man." He laughed. "Good answer."

She tugged on his hand, and he leaned close, worried that touching her might hurt but not wanting to say no. "I'm yours."

"Mine." He kissed her forehead. "Forever and ever."

"We're getting married…"

Crazy how her whispering made his body light, as though an unknown burden had lifted. A gunshot wound and a hospital bed shouldn't seem like the fresh start to the life he'd always wanted, but he wasn't judging what fate doled out anymore.

Locke kissed her again. "Love you. Whatever the future holds, I'm going to make you happy."

EPILOGUE

Five Years Later

"HEY, LOCKE, CAN you come into the guest bedroom for me?" Cassidy shouted down the hall. She was trying to keep her redecorating plans a big secret, but big secrets weren't her forte, and Locke could read her like a book. She could walk into a room and blink funny, and he would know exactly what was going on. So… the best plan was to bury her face in the curtains. Perfect for redecorating.

"What?" Did the man have an entire bag of pretzels in his mouth? "You say something?"

Okay, her big plan was off to a rocky start. She tried a lot louder. "I said, can you please come to the guest bedroom. Guest. Bedroom."

"Give me two minutes."

Dang it to hell. This wasn't working the way she thought it would. "Okay, no problem. I'm on a ladder, but I'll be here."

About fifteen seconds later, Locke walked in. Not that he was that predictable, but she loved his protective tendencies. What did he think she was doing on a ladder? She had no idea. But nevertheless, it worked.

"I'm here." He rolled the top of the pretzel bag closed.

"I see. Thanks." Cassidy played with a measuring tape and motioned for him to grab the other side.

"There's no laddering going on, though, Beauty."

"But there is measuring. Grab this end, and tell me what it says."

She held out the end of the tape, and he collected it. As he read, Cassidy typed it into her phone. Then they did the same thing on an area rug on the floor.

"Why are we measuring the rug?" he asked.

This was almost too easy, almost like she'd written his lines. Cassidy beamed. "Because I want a new rug, babe."

"And you want new drapes. Got it. Since this room is never used, sounds like a good plan. I'm gonna go back to my pretzels. Unless you really want to use the ladder."

"What exactly do you think will happen if I stand on a ladder and measure things?" Her eyebrow went up.

"Don't know, babe. Consider it an excuse to look at my wife's butt." He offered her the bag. "Pretzel?"

"Ah, I guess that makes sense." She took one and pointed it at him before crunching down. "Because I don't see you holding the ladder for Winters when he comes over."

Locke pulled her in for a hug. "Whatever. I like holding your damn ladder. You like it too."

Mmmm. His arms were forever a safe place. "I do." She leaned back. "How do you envision this room?"

He loosened his hold but glanced at the floor and then the drapes. "Exactly as it is. I envision like this."

She rolled her eyes, tugging him closer to the window. "Pity."

"Yeah, no. There's no pity to not redecorating."

She picked up the drape that had come with the house when they bought it. "I could see fuchsias and pinks. Maybe something rosier."

He squished the side of his face as though trying to picture it—and failing. Cassidy chuckled and walked to the other window. She fingered the boring fabric. "Or maybe something totally different. Aquas? Blues? Light, dark, I don't know."

"Nope, I don't see any of that. But if you do, have at it, Beauty." Locke dug into the pretzels, and Cassidy scowled.

She didn't think that her grand-announcement plan was *that* subtle. "Come on, Locke. Stick with me for a minute."

He tossed a handful of pretzels into his mouth, mumbling, "Okay."

"Try this…" Cassidy came beside him and stole away the bag, earning a solid dose of side-eye. "Close your eyes."

He grumbled. "Really, whatever you want is good. This isn't my thing."

"It *so* is your thing. You have no idea." Maybe not the decorating, but… she bumped her hip into his and interlocked their fingers. "Just try it."

"All right, eyes closed."

She leaned forward to check. Yup. He'd closed his eyes. She wanted to watch him realize what she was talking about. "Think if we decorated this room with pretty pink drapes and little pink rugs and blankets. Or…"

His brow furrowed, but he didn't open his eyes.

"Maybe just little blue blankets. Either way, I think all white furniture and blue—"

Locke's lips parted before his eyes opened, rounding—then narrowed as if he didn't believe his thoughts.

Welcome to her world.

Her husband tilted his head downward, almost as though he were assessing what she'd said. "What are you talking about, Cassidy?"

She beamed, unable to contain her excitement anymore. She licked her lips, suddenly on the verge of crying in the mix of everything. "Decorating in pinks or blues."

"*Why* are you talking about decorating in pinks or blues?" Cautiously, Locke turned, inching toward her slowly.

"Because we're going have a baby." All the tears came. They fell. She couldn't stop them as she smiled, and his arms wrapped around her, hugging tight.

Locke had a hand threaded in her hair, the other arm plastering her close to his body. He spent forever promising her the world until he dropped to his knees, still wrapped around her, his cheek pressed to her abdomen, and repeated the same thing again.

What could she say to the man who never knew if he could be a dad? There were no other words than the same ones he said: "I love you, baby."

ABOUT THE AUTHOR

CRISTIN HARBER is a *New York Times* and *USA Today* bestselling romance author. She writes sexy romantic suspense, military romance, new adult, and contemporary romance. Readers voted her onto Amazon's Top Picks for Debut Romance Authors 2013, and her debut Titan series was both a #1 romantic suspense and #1 military romance bestseller.

Connect with Cristin: Text TITAN to 66866 to sign up for exclusive emails.

The Titan Series:

Book 1: Winters Heat
Book 1.5: Sweet Girl
Book 2: Garrison's Creed
Book 3: Westin's Chase
Book 4: Gambled
Book 5: Chased
Book 6: Savage Secrets
Book 7: Hart Attack
Book 7.5: Sweet One
Book 8: Black Dawn
Book 8.5: Live Wire
Book 9: Bishop's Queen
Book 10: Locke and Key

The Delta Series:

Book 1: Delta: Retribution
Book 2: Delta: Revenge
Book 3: Delta: Redemption

The Delta Novella in Liliana Hart's MacKenzie Family Collection:

Delta: Rescue

The Only Series:

Book 1: Only for Him

Book 2: Only for Her

Book 3: Only for Us

Book 4: Only Forever

Each Titan and Delta book can be read as a standalone (except for Sweet Girl), but readers will likely best enjoy the series in order. The Only series must be read in order.

Made in the USA
Middletown, DE
24 August 2019